# FIRELIGHT *at* MUSTANG RIDGE

## JESSE HAYWORTH

A SIGNET ECLIPSE BOOK

SIGNET ECLIPSE
Published by the Penguin Group
Penguin Group (USA) LLC, 375 Hudson Street,
New York, New York 10014

USA | Canada | UK | Ireland | Australia | New Zealand | India | South Africa | China
penguin.com
A Penguin Random House Company

First published by Signet Eclipse, an imprint of New American Library,
a division of Penguin Group (USA) LLC

First Printing, February 2015

ISBN 978-0-451-47081-2

Printed in the United States of America
10  9  8  7  6  5  4  3  2  1

*If you've ever felt like you've lost your way . . . this book is for you. May you find a new and unexpected path full of love and laughter. And pie, because you just can't go wrong with pie.*

# AUTHOR'S NOTE

*Dear Reader-Friend,*

*We all know what they say—things change; people change; live in the moment because you never know what tomorrow might bring. But even if we keep up with our fortune-cookie fortunes and do our best with our deep breathing, we're never quite ready for that moment where life goes* BOOM *and everything takes a left-hand turn, are we? I sure wasn't five or so years ago when I woke up one morning (or so it seemed at the time) to find myself with no partner, a house I couldn't afford, and no idea what came next.*

*Well, what came next was more life—those cookies tell us that life is what happens while we're making plans, right? Tomorrow comes whether we're ready for it or not. For me, a bunch of doors closed but a whole lot of windows opened, and suddenly that too-big house was humming with activity as my mom (who rocks) and a dear friend (shout out, Liana!) helped me paint and pack and get the heck out of Dodge.*

*Maybe I didn't go as far as Danny Traveler does—all the way to Mustang Ridge, Wyoming—and maybe the healing I needed to do was very different from hers. But, like her, I made a new home someplace I never expected to be. And, like her, one day I met a big, broad-shouldered man from out West—one who knows how to ride and shoot and fend for himself, and who I absolutely wouldn't have been ready for had I met him any sooner in my journey.*

*So welcome back to Mustang Ridge, dear Reader-Friend. Please join me in a story that is near and dear to my heart, about left-hand turns, moments that go BOOM, and how a former adrenaline junkie–turned–nervous Nellie puts the pieces back together with the help of a slow-talking cowboy who is far more than he seems. And if you're in the process of putting a few pieces back together yourself, please know that you're not alone.*

*Love,*
*Jesse*

# 1

Danny Traveler didn't put much stock in luck or fortune-cookie sayings, but as the shuttle bus rolled beneath an archway that spelled out WELCOME TO MUSTANG RIDGE in horseshoes, she was starting to think that the whole "if you're going through hell, keep on going" thing might have some merit. The last year or so had sucked eggs, but now, finally, she thought she might be seeing the light at the end of the tunnel.

Or, rather, the rainbow at the end of the tunnel. Because as the luxury bus glided between two pale, grassy fields—horses on one side, cattle on the other—it was headed straight for a perfect rainbow that arched over the pretty valley at the end of the driveway.

"Would you look at that?" Danny's seatmate had her face plastered to the window. "It's a sign!"

Danny made a polite murmur of agreement. Kiki-from-Cambridge had been talking in exclamation points for the entire three-hour ride, to the point that the heavily made-up—and generously endowed—brunette had seemed to be in danger of popping the snaps of her fringed Western shirt as she babbled on about everything from the gum-smacking guy who had sat next to her on the plane to the fact that she hadn't been on a horse since she got bucked off a lead-line pony at the age of six. That made Danny wonder why she had decided on a dude ranch for her summer vacation, but she kept the question to herself and gave Kiki props for facing her fears.

Too bad she was doing it in close proximity at top volume.

Most of the others on the bus—twenty-some dudes and dudettes of various ages—had tuned Kiki out by the thirty-minute mark, leaving Danny wishing she had taken the singleton seat in the far back.

"Can you believe we're finally here?" Kiki gave a happy sigh. "It feels like I've been waiting for this forever. What color horse do you hope you get? I want a yellow one! Pimento, they call it."

Danny couldn't help herself. "I think it's palomino."

"No, I'm pretty sure it's pimento. And did you see the cowboys on the Web site?" Kiki made a *yum-yum* noise. "I'd like to take a ride on one of them!"

Trying not to picture a horse made of pimento loaf, a deli product called palomino loaf, or Kiki riding anything two-legged, Danny pointed out the window. "Oh, look! There's the ranch! Isn't it pretty?" Kiki made a happy noise and flattened her nose against the glass once more. The move made Danny wonder what she looked like from the other side, then give herself a mental kick for being bitchy. It wasn't the other woman's fault that she was winding down just when everyone else on the bus was gearing up. Hoping her internal eye rolls hadn't been obvious, Danny asked, "Do you see any of those cowboys?"

"Not yet." Kiki stared raptly as the valley unfolded in front of them. "But I see more horses, and you're right. It's *sooo* beautiful down there!"

And, yeah, if Danny hadn't given up the window seat the second time Kiki leaned across her to *ooh* and *aah* before they even left the airport loop road, she would have been making a face print of her own on the glass. Because if the rapidly fading rainbow was a sign, Mustang Ridge itself was a vision.

The ranch was a mix of old and new, from the log-style main house and matching guest cabins scattered near an almost perfectly circular lake to the big steel-span barn that bumped up against an older wooden structure. Fence lines spidered out from the barns, enclosing horses, cattle, and riding areas, and bordering a dirt track that led through a perimeter fence and up a shallow slope to a ridge. Beyond that somewhere was Blessing Valley. Her valley.

Danny let out a soft sigh. It looked peaceful. Wonderful. And like it was exactly what the doctors had ordered.

"*Wow* is right!" Kiki said, which might or might not mean that Danny had said the word aloud. "Aren't those just the cutest cabins you've ever seen?"

The noise level increased as the other passengers roused from their travel fugue with exclamations of "There's the pavilion where they have dancing!" and "Do you think we can fish in the lake?" along with lots of "Ohh, look at the horses!"

The rising chatter bounced around Danny as the young cowboy in the driver's seat pulled the shuttle around in front of the barn and killed the engine. Getting on the intercom to project over the chatter of two dozen vacationers readying to make a break for it, he said, "Welcome to Mustang Ridge, folks! I'd like to invite you to hop on down, fill your lungs with some fresh Wyoming air, and connect with Krista, Rose, or Gran—they're the ones wearing the green polo shirts and carrying clipboards. They'll get you set up with your cabins and tell you all the cool stuff that comes next." He gave a dramatic pause, then deepened his voice. "So . . . are you ready to take your first step onto the soil that's been walked by cowboys of the Skye family for more than ten generations?"

As the group gave a ragged chorus of agreement, made up of lots of "Yeah" and "Woo" exclamations, Kiki scrambled over Danny and leaped into the aisle, where she did a shimmy-shake that set a whole lot of stuff shimmying and shaking, and hollered, "Let's ride 'em, cowboys!"

The driver's eyes went deer-in-headlights wide in the rearview mirror, and instead of doing the "I can't hear you" thing that was probably next in the script, he popped the doors open and called, "Watch your step, folks! And welcome to Rustlers' Week!"

Danny stayed put while the first wave of guests stampeded off. Then she and the stragglers filed out into a whole lot of sunshine. The minute her hiking boots touched down, she got a quiver of excitement in her belly. *You're here. You made it. Welcome to the next chapter of your life.* Which was totally the power of suggestion, thanks to the bus driver's rah-rah routine, but still . . . Moving away from the bus, she filled her lungs with dry, sweet-smelling air that carried the scents of horses, sunbaked grasslands, and a tangy kitchen-type aroma that made her stomach grumble and suggested that the claim on the ranch's Web site about offering the best ranch food around wasn't an empty boast.

"You must be Danielle," a voice said from behind her.

She turned, doing a double take at the sight of a pretty, perky blonde who wore a green polo and a baby sling, and was entirely familiar yet not. "Krista. Hi! Yes, it's me. But, please, call me Danny." She peeked inside the sling and saw an infant's head topped with blond baby-fine hair and a fat pink bow. "And this must be Abigail Rose."

Krista's lips curved. "Abby to her friends, which includes you. Any friend of Jenny's is a friend of ours."

"Jenny and I really only worked together for a month or so." In a faraway rain forest, where Krista's twin had been filming a reality dating show and Danny had been in charge of the zip-lining, bungee-jumping, and canyoneering dates.

It felt like another lifetime.

"If she says you're cool, then you're cool," Krista said firmly. Then, to the baby, she cooed, "Isn't that right, Abby-gabby? Your Aunt Jenny knows her stuff. And thanks to her, Danny here is going to hang out with the horses up in Blessing Valley for a while. Won't that be fun?"

With her throat tightening, Danny managed, "I'm grateful. Really. I don't know how to tell you what this means to me."

Krista patted her shoulder. "Don't stress about it—we're happy to help. Jenny wanted to be here to greet you, but she took on a filming gig down in Belize for a friend of a friend. She and Nick will be back in a couple of weeks."

"Seriously, you don't know me from the next gal. You're amazing to do this for me."

"You're welcome here at Mustang Ridge. And I mean it—we're happy to help, honest." Krista sent her a sidelong look. "I get that it feels weird, though. You're way more used to doing favors than needing them."

Danny eyed her. "Jenny told you that?"

"Nope, but like recognizes like." Krista adjusted the sling as the baby shifted, curving into her mother's body like a small, sleepy shrimp. "Up until a year ago, I had to be in charge of things no matter what. The ranch, the business, life in general . . . I might have asked for help now and then, but always on my terms."

"And then she came along?" Danny nodded to the baby.

"Well, first her father came along." Krista's brilliant blue eyes gained a glint. "Wyatt. We were college sweethearts who crossed paths again at a time when I needed a cowboy, he needed some saddle time, and neither of us was thinking about romance. At least that was what we kept telling ourselves."

"And you're getting married soon." Jenny had passed along that detail while Danny had still been trying to catch up to the idea that her freewheeling, country-hopping photographer friend was married to a veterinarian and living in Wyoming when she used to swear she would never return home for more than a quick visit.

A pleased flush touched Krista's cheeks. "We've got

a couple of months still until the wedding. Long enough to feel like I should change everything but not long enough that it's an option, so we're going with the plan we've got—family and friends under the pavilion as the sun sets behind the mountains." Her expression brightened. "You're invited, of course. Please say you'll come!"

Danny had to stop herself from backpedaling, which was silly. Maybe at one point she had hoped the next wedding she went to would be her own, but it was past time for her to stop flinching over that. "I'd be honored," she said. "Thanks for inviting me."

"Brilliant! Don't worry about dressing up, but if you want to shop, Jenny and I are always up for a girls' night, or afternoon or whatever. And our friend Shelby—she always manages to make the stuff she finds in town look like it came out of a fashion magazine."

"That sounds fun." She couldn't spend the whole summer alone, after all. Besides, she wanted to thank Jenny in person for e-mailing out of the blue to catch up, and then, when Danny gave her the short version of the past couple of years, responding with: *Come to Mustang Ridge. It's the perfect place to get your head screwed back on straight.*

"Sweetie?" a voice called from the other side of the bus. Moments later, a petite white-haired woman came around the front of the shuttle, eyes lighting when she caught sight of Krista. "There you are! I'm going to fix a few folk up with snacks while your mom and Junior show the others to their cabins. Do you need anything?"

"Nope, I'm good for right now, and Miss Abby is conked out." Krista patted the snoozing bundle within the sling. "Bless her for being a good sleeper, and pretty much the best baby ever—not that I'm biased or anything. But before you go, Gran, I want to introduce you to Danny Traveler."

The older woman's face brightened. "Hello, dear! It's so lovely that you're here. How was your trip?"

"It was fine." She had splurged on a direct flight and strapped herself in, chased an Ambien with a screw-top micro-bottle of white wine, and practiced her deep-breathing exercises. It hadn't been fun, but she had made it through.

Gran's eyes went sympathetic, as if she had said the rest of it out loud. "I stocked your camp with supplies, but come see me before you and Krista head out there. I have a little basket put together for you."

"And by *little*, she means approximately the size and mass of the average blanket chest," Krista put in.

Danny cleared her throat, suddenly overwhelmed—by the warm welcome, the chaos, all the people around her. To Krista, she said, "Do you need to help show people to their cabins? I don't want to keep you from your guests."

"You're a guest, too."

"I'm not paying nearly what they are." Which was yet another reason to be grateful.

"No, but you're staying far longer, and you're not going to require as much hands-on time. Though, for the record, you're welcome to participate in any activities you'd like. We've always got a spare horse or three, and there's something magical about a long ride in the great big wide-open."

"We'll see. I'm planning on spending most of my time in the valley. You know, reading, walking, chilling out." Working her way through the daunting collection of aptitude exams that had been a parting gift from Farah, her physical-therapist-turned-friend.

"Of course. But please consider it an open invitation." Krista touched her arm—like she wanted to do more but could tell Danny wasn't a hugger. "Come on. Let me hand Abby off to her nana, and then I'll show you to your valley." She laughed. "Now *that's* not something I get to say every day! See? I knew I was going to like having you around." She danced away, humming a happy tune and exchanging a few words with each of the guests she passed, introducing herself and the baby, and welcoming the newcomers to her family's world.

Danny watched her, thinking, *That*. That was what she wanted—not all the people and the hustle-bustle of running a dude ranch, but that sense of loving life and doing exactly what she wanted to do. Too bad she didn't know what that was.

Yet.

An hour later, Danny was gunning along behind Krista on a borrowed ATV, anticipation growing as they steered their four-wheelers toward a narrow cut-through between two rock walls. They rode through a gap nestled beside a sluggish river lying low on its banks—Jenny had mentioned that the region was in the grip of a drought, with water at a premium and the fire danger high. Then, when the rocks opened up, Krista slowed and stopped, waving for Danny to come up beside her.

As she did, her mouth fell open and she had to remember to hit the brakes, because otherwise she might've rolled right into the lush valley ahead of them. "Holy . . . Wow," she said reverently. "This is gorgeous!"

She had thought she was getting used to the dramatic beauty of the Wyoming backcountry they'd been bouncing through—all rolling hills and tree-shrouded rivers, with the mountains rising fat and purple in the distance. But this was something else entirely. Although the hills were dry and brown, the river valley was lush and green. Sloping banks ran up to the trees, and matching arms of stone wrapped around the green space, enclosing it in a geological hug that undoubtedly spanned hundreds of acres, yet felt safe and intimate. Especially when she saw a group of horses drift down to the water, almost lost in the distance as they stretched their necks to drink from the river.

"Welcome to Blessing Valley," Krista said, grinning as several of the horses lifted their heads and pricked their ears toward the ATVs. "And there are your roommates— those are the mustangs of Blessing's Herd, all forty of them, with Jupiter leading the way." She pointed to a dark gray horse that stepped in front of the others as if to say, *If you want to bother them, you'll have to go through me to do it.*

Danny didn't want to bother anybody, but her lips curved at the thought that she would be sharing her home with the beautiful creatures. She'd never been particularly horse crazy, but the gray mare had a wise, knowing air about her. "She's beautiful."

"It's thanks to her that we have the herd—Wyatt won a 'train your mustang from scratch in six weeks' competition with her last year, and the prize money went to buying an entire herd and setting up a sanctuary in this valley and the adjoining acreage."

"Why not call it Jupiter's Herd, then?"

"We thought about it, but we want the sanctuary to outlive a single horse or herd . . . so we named it after a foundling who was adopted by one of the earliest settlers in this area. Blessing. She married an early homesteader here at Mustang Ridge, making her my however-many-great-grandmother." Krista grinned. "She's a favorite of mine in the family tree, and the name seemed to fit."

"Blessing Valley." Danny drew in a breath of air that felt even cleaner and fresher than it had down by the ranch, though an hour ago she would have said that was impossible. She wasn't sharing this air, though—it was all hers. A blessing indeed.

"Come on." Krista restarted her ATV. "The campsite is about a mile in."

A short drive brought them to where a bend in the river formed a spit of smooth ground. There, a firepit was lined with flat river rocks and surrounded by a cut-log seating area. As they rolled closer, Danny scanned the campsite, looking for the equipment she had sent on ahead.

Instead, her eyes landed on a hotel on wheels.

A big silver and purple RV was parked under the

trees, with its awning extended to shade a small table, a couple of chairs, and an outdoor rug. The name RAMBLING ROSE was painted on the side of the RV in glittering script, and the tinted windows gave glimpses of pretty rose-patterned curtains and leather chairs.

And Danny was gaping again.

"I hope it's okay," Krista said, but she was grinning, like she could already see that it was far more than her guest had hoped for.

"Okay? Are you serious? I was expecting a pop-up camper and a six-pack tethered in the river. This is . . ." Too much, overwhelming. "Is the RV yours?"

"My parents'. He's Ed and she's Rose, and when the snow starts flying up here, they head south and go looking for stuff they haven't already seen. Thus, the *Rambling Rose*."

"They don't mind my using it?" *Please say they don't mind.* Danny had told herself that camping out in the middle of nowhere would be a good way to figure out what came next in life. But the posh bus tucked into the private valley suddenly seemed like her own personal slice of solo heaven.

"That depends. Are you planning on throwing any wild parties?"

"I'm not, but I can't speak for Jupiter and her buddies."

Krista gave her a shoulder bump. "I can pretty much guarantee she'll stay out of your way. She enjoys people well enough—I think we amuse her—but she takes her duties very seriously when it comes to keeping the herd out of trouble."

"Then we should be okay on the no-parties thing."

"Excellent. Let me show you around the RV. It's not big, but there's a whole lot of features packed into the square footage."

The whole *it's not big* comment didn't fully sink in until Danny put her foot on the steps going up and found herself facing a dark, narrow opening. And stalled as the oxygen suddenly vacated her lungs.

*Oh, crap. Not now. Please not now.*

Stomach knotting, she muttered under her breath, "Don't be a wuss. It's bigger than the airport shuttle." Except the shuttle had been all windows and open space, with a wide aisle and lots of room for people and luggage. What little she could see of the RV was packed to the gills, with drawers and cabinets tucked into every available square inch. And it was dark.

"So you probably saw outside that you've got solar and wind power." Krista flipped on the lights, brightening the gloom to unnatural fluorescence. "The keys are in the visor in case you need to move it." She wiggled into the narrow aisle that ran between the popped-out kitchen and the matching breakfast nook on the other side. "You can fold the table away to make this a sitting area."

As Krista demonstrated, Danny hovered just inside, keeping one foot hanging out the door.

"Then down this hall—it gets a little narrow here—you've got your three-quarter bath. There are a couple of tricks I need to show you, so you're going to want to crowd on in here with me." Krista said it like it was no big deal.

Then again, to normal people it wasn't.

Taking a deep breath, Danny forged down the tunnel, not letting herself see how it stretched out longer and longer, like a horror-movie hallway. Hoping Krista couldn't smell the fear oozing from her pores, she dug her fingertips into the doorway molding and managed to give a nod that she hoped related *Go ahead* instead of *I'm gonna puke.*

She could deal with this. She *would* deal with it, damn it. The last thing she wanted to do was seem ungrateful when Jenny's family was offering her the perfect getaway.

Krista gestured, lips moving as she went over a process that only half stuck—something about a cross of toilet paper in the bowl and keeping the gray water to a minimum. All Danny really heard, though, was a Charlie Brown–like *wah-wah-wah-whahhh* and a whole lot of blood rushing in her ears. *Breathe in, breathe out.* That was basic. It was mandatory. *In. Out. In. Out.*

Finished with the bathroom, Krista squeezed back through the narrow opening and forged even deeper. "This is the bedroom. We put the stuff you shipped in here, figuring you'd want to organize it yourself."

To a normal person, it probably looked like a king mattress flanked by a wardrobe and a drop-down desk, with two big duffels on the floor. To Danny, it was a cluttered dead end with a tiny window that let in the light but wouldn't let her out no matter how hard she screamed.

*For the love of God, don't scream.* Jamming her fingernails into her palms hard enough to draw blood, she sucked a thin trickle of oxygen through her nostrils.

"It's all pretty self-explanatory." Krista reversed

course and headed back up the tunnel, talking all the way as she pointed out a fire extinguisher and a stack of manuals sealed in a Tupperware box under the sink.

Danny's feet stayed glued at the bedroom threshold. *Breathe in. Breathe out. You're not stuck. You can leave anytime you want. See? You're moving now. One foot, then the other. Turn. Walk, don't run. You don't want her to know you're a head case. A weenie. Broken.*

One torturous step at a time, she trudged back up the tunnel, sweating like it was a hundred and ten degrees rather than a shady eighty or so. Until, finally, she made it down the steps, through a walled-in opening so narrow that her shoulders brushed against either side, and out into the bright yellow sunshine of the green, green valley, with its bubbling water and open sky.

Where she could breathe again. Sort of.

"Anyway, I think that takes care of the basics," Krista said, seeming unaware that Danny's brain had gone all Blue Screen of Death there for a few minutes, leaving her stomach knotted and her lungs struggling for air. "There's a satellite phone in the glove compartment for emergencies, and you've got the ATV for when you're ready to come back to the ranch for Gran's cooking, a real shower, and some company. You can explore with it, too, but watch your terrain and your fuel, and leave enough breadcrumbs so you can always find your way home."

She paused, as if it was Danny's turn to say something. Which it totally was, but she didn't know what to say or whether she could get it out even if she knew.

*Say something! Don't be a wuss.* Fixing her eyes on the

river—watching the water keep moving, never stuck in one place—she swallowed hard and managed, "I don't know how to thank you. I . . ." Horrifyingly, her eyes threatened to fill and she choked. "I'm sorry."

Expression shifting to one of utter sympathy—but not pity—Krista touched her hand. "No, I'm sorry. You came here to get away from people, and here I am nattering away at you."

"It's not that. You're lovely. It's me. I'm just—"

"Seriously. Don't stress." She squeezed Danny's arm. "I glommed onto you the second you stepped off the bus. I'd blame it on hormones or being a new mom stuck in babyland twenty-four-seven, but I'm surrounded by adults on a daily basis." One corner of her mouth kicked upward. "Confession time: I'm a little jealous of your getaway, and kind of wishing Wyatt, Abby, and I could set up camp farther upstream and hide out until the wedding." She sighed. "Which we totally can't do. But it sure sounds nice."

Okay. Danny could breathe again. She could think. Sort of. As her pulse started to slow, she made herself focus on the conversation, grateful to Krista for smoothing things over and giving her time to pull herself back together. "I guess you could camp out for your honeymoon," she suggested, her voice only a little wobbly. "Or, I don't know, a bachelorette party?"

"Ooh!" Krista straightened, eyes lighting. "I like that!" Then she laughed at herself. "And here I am, nattering again while my mom is undoubtedly spoiling the bejeebers out of Abby." She didn't sound at all put out by the prospect. "I'm going to go, and leave you to your valley. But if I could make one suggestion?"

Torn between wanting the other woman to stay and wishing she were already gone, Danny said, "What's that?"

"Don't wait too long to dig into that basket of Gran's. You look like you could use a cookie or three."

# 2

The black and green helicopter came over the trees and hovered above the clearing, looking like a giant dragonfly checking out some prehistoric field. Really, though, the rent-a-chopper pilot was probably just making sure his client hadn't been overly optimistic when he promised a safe landing spot. And, well, said client had admittedly been watching too many monster movies of late.

Sam Babcock grinned up at the flying machine. "What do you think, Yoshi? Should we buy a chopper and have it pimped out to look like Mothra?"

The brown-and-white-splotched paint gelding swiveled his ears back at the sound of his rider's voice, then forward again as the helicopter eased down, bobbling some in the crosswind.

"Yeah, yeah. You're right—waste of money, bad for the environment, think of the bunnies, yadda, yadda. Still, it'd almost be worth it to see the look on Axyl's face, don't you think?" The crusty old rockhound—a longtime family friend and Sam's right-hand man when it came to work stuff—was worth his carat weight in blue diamonds, but he didn't have much of a sense of humor.

Yoshi snorted as the chopper finally settled in for a landing and the rent-a-pilot killed the engine. Moments later, the doors popped open and Axyl emerged, wearing fatigues and his trademark bushy beard, followed by Sam's engineers, Murphy and Midas. With a stubby blond ponytail, battered sandals, and the sort of cargo-pants-plus-button-down getup that cool kids paid a ton for in Boulder, Murph looked more like an off-season ski bum than a whiz-kid mechanical engineer. In contrast, Midas was taller and bulkier, with cropped hair, dark clothes, and tattooed knuckles. But while Midas might look like a bouncer from the sort of club that wouldn't let Murph in the door, he was a top-notch geologist and mining engineer.

As they climbed down from the chopper and headed for Sam, Axyl was scowling, and Murph and Midas were arguing, with lots of hand waving and disgusted looks. In other words, business as usual.

Sam guided Yoshi out of the trees. "So, what do you guys think? Heck of a view, right?"

"View, shmew," Axyl grumbled. "I know you like to buy up open space, and that you wanted to field-test the prototypes out in the backcountry, but why here? It's in the middle of farking nowhere, and there are too damn many trees. Why not buy something closer to Windfall?"

Flipping open one of the bulging bags strapped behind his saddle, Sam said, "Because of this."

The wind died suddenly and he could've sworn the

sun brightened a notch as it hit on the six-sided rod of deep red gemstone he had dug out of the side of a rocky hill less than a half mile from where they were standing.

"No way!" said Murph, his eyes going round.

"Hot damn!" Midas said in a moment of rare agreement with his nemesis.

Axyl just looked at the stone for a minute, then sniffed. "Not bad."

"What do you mean, *not bad*?" Sam said. "That's a hell of a find and you know it!" Okay, maybe not five-figures good, but still. The deep ruby-red crystal pulsed with an inner glow that said jewelry-quality carats, and lots of them. It had been his first find on the new piece of land, confirmation of the quiver he'd gotten in his gut when he first rode up the shallow hill a few weeks ago.

"You didn't find that in the middle of all these trees," Axyl said, still looking unconvinced. He hated horses and helicopters, and only barely tolerated four-wheelers. As far as he was concerned, if he couldn't get to his destination on a Harley, then it wasn't much of a destination. Unfortunately for him, most of the remaining pockets of decent gemstone in the state—at least the ones that could be gotten at without stripping the land to the bone—were in the back of beyond.

"There's a gully on the other side of the trees." Sam pointed. "Past that is as gemmy-looking a hill as I've seen in a while. Come on, I'll show you." Seeing Axyl hesitate, he prodded, "Aw, come on, old man. What's the worst that could happen?"

"I could wind up living out here for the rest of the summer in some cobbled-together shack with solar panels on the roof, a cistern on one side, and a composting toilet on the other."

Midas elbowed Murphy. "Did you get all that?"

"Shut it," Axyl grumbled. But his eyes stayed locked on the crystals. "Any more like that?"

Sam patted his saddlebag. "I got lucky. Started poking around this morning and hit on a good-size pocket."

"Lucky is right. Let me guess. You had a feeling about this place."

"Something like that." And that was all he was going to say on the matter. All he needed to say.

The grizzled prospector glanced around, studying the trees now rather than scowling at them. "You name it yet?"

"I was thinking of calling it Misty Hill."

The crow's-feet around Axyl's eyes eased up. "After your ma. That's nice."

Actually, Sam had decided on the name that morning, when he'd woken up wrapped in his bedroll and found himself surrounded by a dense, low-lying fog despite the drought. But, yeah, maybe there had been something subconscious at work there, too. His ma's name had been Mary, but everybody had called her Misty—except his father, who had called her "My Mary" or, more often, "your Ma, bless her soul."

"Misty Hill it is," Sam said, his voice going thick. Clearing his throat, he added, "What do you think, Murph? You going to have enough sky to work with, or are we going to need to cut some trees?"

"Hm." Murph, who was the overlord of all things solar-powered at Babcock Gems, studied the clearing, squinted along his outstretched arm to make some thumb-level measurements, and got a look on his face that Sam recognized as meaning, *Stand back, folks, I'm doing calculus in my head.* After a moment, he nodded. "I can make it work."

"Good. Get going on plans and a supply list. You know the routine. Take Axyl's cobbled-together-shack idea, make sure there's room to sleep, cook, hang out, and sort rocks, and keep it as eco-friendly as you can get it."

"I want a separate building to house the proto-types," Midas put in. "We'll want as many as we can airlift or motor out here. It's time to do some serious field-testing."

Murph's mouth flattened. "Not if by *field-testing* you mean treating the equipment like a bunch of crash-test dummies. This is precision machinery we're talking about here."

Midas held up both hands. "Hey, it's not my fault that your inventions don't always stand up to the real world."

"There's a difference between regular use and 'Whoops, I just dropped a fiber-optic probe four stories into a cal-dera.'"

"The grip was like a wet banana."

Murph's face went a dull, infuriated red. "Only for someone who forgets he has opposable thumbs."

"So," Axyl said to Sam, his voice carrying over Midas's squawk, "you want to show me that crystal pocket?"

"Sure. Back here, through the trees." While the other two escalated from "Damn thing should've been shock-proof anyway" to "Oh, yeah? Says the guy who totaled his new mountain bike because he was watching a hawk," Sam patted Yoshi's rump. "You want a ride?"

Axyl snorted. "Not on your life, boyo."

They headed off as the engineers went straight past "your momma" territory into geological insults. It was background noise to Sam, though, like the crunch of a shovel or the ring of a hammer on stone, and it faded quickly once they got into the trees, with Yoshi picking his way and Axyl grumbling about the smell of sweaty horse.

When they reached the other side of the narrow forest band, the grumbles cut off as Axyl got his first look at the slope where Sam had found the gemstone pocket. The old rockhound came up beside Yoshi and scanned the huge, rocky expanse, which rose a couple hundred feet in almost no time, with streaks in the blocky stone chunks suggesting that most of it was metamorphic rock with some amphibole. The high temperature, high pressure, and slow cooling processes that went into forming the stones were also the forces that generated species of corundum—like rubies and sapphires—and other valuable deposits. Better yet, there were glittering inclusions of vermiculite schist, which was another marker that valuable stones could be nearby. And the rocky slope stretched on for miles.

Axyl whistled, his beard a-quiver.

"Admit it," Sam said, prodding. "It's a good piece of land, and not just for field-testing the new gadgets."

"It's okay." Then, with his expression flattening to something that was almost a smile, Axyl allowed, "It's better than okay. Even if you hadn't found that crystal pocket, I'd have to say it's got a damn good look to it. Gemmy as hell." He studied the glitters, which tempted a rockhound to imagine riches beneath. "Your old man would've liked this place."

"I thought so. It's got a great view, a good place to stick a campsite, and a whole lot of potential for surface mining, but no guarantees." Trooper Babcock hadn't been the best prospector out there, certainly hadn't been the luckiest, but he had loved the land and the thrill of the hunt.

Digging into his saddlebag, Sam came up with his custom-molded, reverb-dampening rock hammer—one of Murph's earliest contributions to the team—and held it up in challenge. "One hour, best specimen wins, Midas judges?"

Axyl unslung his pack and pulled out a scuffed rock hammer that probably had a cousin in a museum somewhere. Lifting it and getting a gleam in his eye, he added, "Loser buys the beer."

Danny's early days in Blessing Valley had passed in an odd slow-motion blur, where each hour seemed to stretch endlessly, yet somehow she was already into her second week and running low on food. She wasn't ready to return to the ranch, though—wasn't ready for chaos and human noise—so she had taken to supplementing her stores with the edible berries, greens, and flowers she found on long walks that took her along the river and up gentle slopes. She was usually dragging by the time she returned to camp, ready to wolf down a quick meal, fire up her solar-powered electric fence, and crawl into the tent she had set up beside the dark, narrow RV. She rarely made it through a night without the dreams finding her, though, and she never slept in.

On day nine—or was it ten?—she emerged from the

tent not long past dawn, to discover a beautiful morning of pale blues and pinks in the sky, with birds singing up in the trees, the river bubbling in its banks . . . and a pair of squirrels sitting on the table, surrounded by a mound of white paper confetti and in the process of tearing more shreds from a gutted paperback.

"Hey!" she said, stomping a foot. "Stop that!"

The bushy-tailed thieves levitated off the table, up onto the RV's awning, and from there to an overhanging branch, where they clung, chittering down at her like she was the one who was trespassing. Reddish brown, with tufted ears and puffed-up cheeks, they would've been cute if they'd been minding their own business.

"That's my book!" she exclaimed, recognizing one of the self-help, find-your-path-in-life guides she had packed in the bottom of her duffel. "Where did you get—" She broke off at the sight of a narrow gap where the RV's door should have been tightly closed. "Ohhh, no. I didn't!"

It was entirely possible, though. She had forced herself to go into the camper last night to snag the last of the canned soup, and although she had mostly gotten over feeling like the walls were going to snap in on her at any second, she still got shaky being inside the tight quarters, and she always rushed to get back outside.

Yeah, she might have left the door open. And a couple of squirrels might have gotten into the beautiful RV, with all its gadgets, custom touches, and shiny things.

"Please. Don't tell me." The chitters increased overhead when she opened the door the rest of the way and stuck her head into the dim interior, blinking to focus her eyes as she scanned the driver's seat, with its lush leather covering and the embroidery running down the side, spelling out RAMBLING ROSE. She didn't see any scratches or holes, though, and there didn't seem to be anything out of place farther down the narrow tunnel, in either the sitting area or the kitchenette.

The creatures had been in there, though. They had gotten into her duffel. Who knew what else they had done?

Forcing herself up the RV steps, she ignored the fear-prickles. *Knock it off. You've been in here a bunch of times. Nothing bad has ever happened, and nothing bad is going to happen this time, either.* Holding tight to that logic, she edged into the darker, narrower hallway beyond the kitchen, past the bathroom-coffin and finally to the bed-room. Where, darn it, she saw that her duffel was open, the contents torn and strewn across the bedspread, with shreds of bright yellow packaging—all that was left of a forgotten bag of Peanut M&M's—dotted over the things that had decorated her room at the hospital, then rehab: two gift-shop teddy bears, a mug that read CLIMB FASTER: GRAVITY IS ONLY A THEORY, and a dozen paperbacks—stories about climbers, castaways, and explorers, all with get-well notes on their inside covers that were signed "Love, B." And, front and center, a framed, zoomed-in snapshot of her standing alone at the tippy-top of a high, rocky precipice, wearing climbing gear and a bright, eager smile.

Hissing out a breath, she stumbled back a step, her vision graying around the edges. She remembered the cloudless sky and the perfect sunny day spent with her parents and sister, remembered her mother caroling

"Cheese!" as she snapped the picture, even remembered having a blister on the back of her left heel, where her sock had worn through on the long hike to reach the out-of-the-way Grade IV climb. But as she backed up another step and banged into the too-close bedroom wall, things shifted, turning the sunny day dark and dismal, and pulling the invisible ropes that suddenly wrapped around her so tightly that she couldn't breathe.

*High walls on either side of her, pressing in on her, folding her into an impossible pretzel and kinking her diaphragm, making it hard to breathe. Rocks beneath her, above her. On her. Trapping her.*

She clawed at her throat, part of her knowing that meant her hands were free, but unable to make it matter as her vision tunneled narrower and narrower until all she could see was the yellow confetti and the stranger in the picture, who looked like her, except that she was ready to take on the world, ready to—

Darkness.

# 3

The noon sun beat down on the horse and rider as Yoshi descended into a dry wash, his movements swinging the saddle back and forth while Sam whistled "Home on the Range" to the beat, thinking there was something seriously cool about playing cowboy, riding out under the big Wyoming sky with a scraggly scruff on his face and nobody else for miles.

Granted, the average old-timey cowboy wouldn't have had his saddlebags loaded with uncut gems—that would've been more the bailiwick of a pick-wielding miner with a couple of pack mules. Or maybe a bandit, riding a fast horse and looking over his shoulder to see if there was dust on the horizon. "Bandit, definitely," he decided. "Don't you think, Yosh?"

The gelding shook his head, making the bit jingle.

"I've got a month's pay in stones," Sam drawled, getting into character as the sure-footed horse started up the other side of the gulch, "a six-shooter, and a disguise. So, stick 'em up, pardner!"

Sure, the red bandanna that made up his disguise had started out wrapped around some muffins four days ago, courtesy of a stopover at Mustang Ridge on his ride out to Misty Hill. But he had tied it around his neck after breaking camp that morning, and now pulled it up to cover the lower half of his face, settling his Stetson on his brow and pretending it was bad-guy black felt rather than summer straw.

Dropping his reins as they hit the flatlands once more, he drew from his hip, cocked his thumb as if his index finger were the barrel of a pistol, and fired at a nearby rocky outcropping, imagining the posse that'd been sent from the nearby—in backcountry terms, at least—town of Three Ridges to take him down and recover the stolen gems. "Pew, pew, pew!" Okay, maybe the noises were more sci-fi blaster than Wild West six-shooter, but whatever. "Pew, pew!" The last imaginary shot took out the imaginary marshal who'd been right on his tail, and Sam blew across the tip of his index finger. "There you go, Yosh. That's the way it's done!"

The paint gelding snorted and broke into a jog, headed for the distinctively stacked landmark stones that were becoming clearer with each mile, letting him know that Mustang Ridge was just a few valleys away now, maybe a couple of hours at an easy pace.

"You want to bum some dinner?" Sam asked his horse, even though his stomach was already grumbling with a *hells to the yes* on that one. "Wyatt did say we should swing back by on the way home."

Granted, Sam's college buddy would no doubt get in some more digs about it being time for him to grow up and settle down—Wyatt was full steam ahead when it came to his new baby and upcoming wedding, and seemed to think Sam should be revving up to take the same fall. But he figured he could handle another dose of "You need to quit with the flings and find yourself a real relationship" if it came with chicken-fried steak, mashed potatoes, and gravy thick enough to walk on.

"Off we go, then," he said, nudging Yosh into a lope that rolled down one hill and up the next. The horse's hooves beat a syncopated tattoo on the sunbaked earth, kicking up dust that coated the back of Sam's throat, tasting like—

Smoke!

The flames roared up toward Danny, heating her skin and making her hair crackle around her face as she tossed in another paperback and watched the pages curl and blacken in the firepit. "Good-bye—"

A sudden clatter of galloping hooves brought her whirling around, her heart leaping into her throat as she pictured Jupiter and the herd stampeding through camp. Then a loaded-down brown-and-white-spotted horse burst through the trees, carrying a big cowboy wearing a mask on the lower half of his face.

At the sight of her and the fire, the man hauled back on the reins and flung himself out of the saddle, hitting the ground even before his horse had come to a skidding stop. He advanced on her. "What in the blazes—"

Survival instincts taking over, Danny threw the last paperback at him as hard as she could, nailing him in the face.

"Ow!" He reeled back as she fled past him to the four-wheeler.

Flinging herself aboard, she twisted the key and hit the button to start the engine, but nothing happened. Her breath hitched in her lungs as the stranger reoriented himself and started toward her. She scrambled off the ATV, grabbed her pack from the tent, yanked out her anti-critter revolver, and cocked the hammer. "Freeze!" she shouted, even though he'd already done exactly that, making like a statue when he saw that she was armed.

"Whoa, lady, hang on." His voice was low and resonant, his granite-gray eyes more focused than scared as he added, "Finger off the trigger. I'm not going to hurt you."

She kept her finger right where it was. "Then why are you wearing a mask?"

Sudden understanding dawned. "Oh, for— Hang on. Don't shoot. I'm just going to pull down the bandanna." He did just that. "Sorry. Forgot I was wearing it. Is that better?"

Not really. Because *dang*. Without the bandanna, his face was a whole lot of stubble, dark skin, and angles put together in exactly the right combination.

Which didn't mean he wasn't dangerous. Hot guys could be dangerous.

"Who are you?" she demanded, her heart drumming against her ribs. "What do you want?"

"I'm a friend of the people who own that RV," he said with a nod toward the *Rambling Rose*. "And what I want is for you to point that gun someplace else."

She kept it on him, but took her finger off the trigger. "Who?" she pressed. "I want names."

"Rose and Ed Skye own the bus," he said without hesitation. "Their daughter, Krista, is a month or two away from marrying my college roommate, Wyatt Webb. They've got a daughter, Abby, and—"

"Okay." Pulse slowing, she lowered the hammer. "I believe you."

"Good." His eyes sharpened on hers, putting a quiver in the pit of her stomach. "Then do me a favor and kill that fire before you torch the whole damn valley."

She glanced past him, to where it was starting to burn down, now that she wasn't lobbing pictures, books, and men's XL T-shirts into it anymore. "It's fine." And she didn't want to talk about the fire. The cathartic burn had seemed like a really good idea when she found herself sitting outside the RV with the contents of the duffel strewn around her. Now, though, it seemed silly and overdramatic, like skywriting TODAY IS THE FIRST DAY OF THE REST OF MY LIFE from one horizon to the other rather than just saying it out loud.

"Maybe. You've got it in the pit and the river is right there. But just last week an ember from a near-dead wildfire caught on a current of air, carried a mile, and torched Gabe and Winnie Sears's place. House, barns, and all. They got their five kids and some personal stuff out, and let the livestock run loose, but the rest is gone, just like that." He snapped his fingers. "Didn't take more than an hour. It's that dry right now. Anyway." He shrugged. "I was on my way to Mustang Ridge, smelled the smoke, and figured on the worst case. I'd apologize for overreacting—"

"Don't," she said. "I get it. I'll douse it, and keep the cook fire small from now on." She stuck her hands in her pockets, suddenly off-balance and feeling like she had already forgotten how to talk to another human being. Especially one that looked like him. "Sorry I clobbered you."

He touched his cheek. "Good aim you've got there. Between that and the gun, I guess I don't have to worry about you taking care of yourself."

"No. I like being alone."

"Well, then." He gave a low whistle, and the paint horse ambled over from where it had been standing hipshot near the RV. Mounting up, he gathered his reins, then leaned down and stretched out a hand. "I'm Sam Babcock, by the way."

That surprised a laugh out of her. "Danielle Traveler. Danny." His grip was firm, his hands broad across the palms, with strong, capable fingers, long thumbs, and big, sturdy joints. They weren't calloused right to be climber's hands, but he definitely worked with them. Was he one of those hunky cowboys that Kiki-from-Cambridge had been chirping about?

Drawing away, he touched the brim of his hat. "Maybe I'll see you around, Miz Traveler."

"Maybe." *Probably not*, she thought, and was surprised to feel a small pinch of regret. "And Sam?"

"Yeah?"

"Do me a favor and don't mention the tent, okay?" She figured that a guy like him, with eyes like that, wouldn't miss that she was living in a two-man tent rather than the camper. "Krista's been so sweet about the campsite, the supplies, the RV . . . I don't want to hurt her feelings."

"But you'd rather feel the breeze." Her surprise must have shown on her face, because he patted the bedroll strapped to the back of his saddle. "Your secret is safe with me."

Touching his gelding to a jog, he headed out along

the riverbank, man and horse making a heck of a picture riding beside the water with the trees closing in and the canyon walls rising up to the blue, blue sky. When he reached the cut-through where the river emptied through the rock wall surround, he turned back and lifted a hand in farewell.

Caught watching him, she returned the gesture. And darned if she didn't keep watching as he disappeared through the gap in the canyon wall.

"Tell me again how she clocked you with a copy of *Moby-Dick* and then held you at gunpoint?" Wyatt poked Sam below the swollen cut on his cheek. "Does that hurt?"

"Ow!" Sam socked him in the shoulder. "Yes. And it wasn't *Moby-Dick*, it was *Adrift*. Or maybe *Perfect Storm*. One of the Bad Things Happening at Sea books that got turned into a movie but didn't have a whale in it."

They were sprawled at one of the picnic tables out by the barbecue pit, where the first-aid kit had wound up after one of the assistant wranglers had split his thumb open with a hammer, working on a construction project that was new since Sam's last visit.

"Still, she really nailed you," Wyatt said with poorly faked concern. "That's going to bruise like a mother."

"I've had worse." Tipping his head toward where Ed Skye and several of the barn staffers were going to town with two-by-fours and a framing nail gun, Sam said, "What's going on over there? You having problems with the pavilion?"

Wyatt didn't quite roll his eyes. "Rose decided it wasn't big enough for the wedding."

Sam frowned down at the round structure, which was the epicenter of the Friday-night outdoor barbecues that Krista, Gran, and the others threw as a farewell for the guests of each themed week. Some fifty feet away, Ed and Junior were leveling off a new support beam. "How big does it need to be to hold you and Krista, the JP, and a couple of groomsmen and bridesmaids?" A daunting thought occurred. "Did you guys decide to expand things into one of those three-ring-circus deals?"

That got an emphatic "Hell, no."

"Phew. For a second there, I was picturing a dozen bridesmaids in sparkly pink dresses, and me, Nick, and Foster standing up there with all seven of the Lemp brothers and whoever else you could round up, the whole lot of us wearing glittery bow ties and suspenders to match the bridesmaids' outfits. Not that I wouldn't man up, mind you. For you and Krista, whatever it takes. But I'm really not a sparkly-pink-cummerbund kind of guy."

"Tempting, but no. It's just you, Nick, and Foster on the guy's side, and Jenny and Shelby on the girl's side, pick your own clothes. Lucky for you, Krista stood up to her mom on that one, or you might've been in a cummerbund, or worse."

Not wanting to know what counted as worse than a *My Pretty Pony*–pink cummerbund, Sam said, "Then what's with the pavilion?"

"Rose is afraid that it'll rain during the ceremony, so she wants to extend the roof to cover the guests." Wyatt shot him a *don't say it* look.

Unable not to, Sam said, "She knows we're in the

middle of the worst drought in twenty-some years, right? And that it hasn't rained more than a dribble since May?"

"When you're living on the same property as your in-laws, you learn to pick your battles," Wyatt said drily. "Especially when your mother-in-law-to-be is the resident events coordinator, interior decorator, and unofficial wedding planner."

"A deadly trifecta."

"Only if a guy is inclined to argue." Wyatt stretched his arms behind him and leaned back on the picnic table. "Which I'm not. You said it yourself—whatever Krista wants, she gets. I'm getting what I want, which is her and Abby Rose. Why shouldn't Krissy get everything she wants, too?"

Sam would've ribbed him about turning into a giant sap, except it was actually kind of nice to see the big guy go down so hard. "Well, hell. Looks like you've got yourself a pavilion-on-steroids, then. Maybe next season you could turn it into a covered horseshoe pit."

"I was thinking of a bowling alley. Great minds."

"I'm starving. Is my face patched up enough to brave the dining hall?"

"Let me throw on a couple of Band-Aids first. And if I could make a suggestion? You should come up with a better story than the attack of the killer paperback. Tell people you got caught in an avalanche, maybe, or a stampede."

Sam glared at Mr. Enjoying-This-Way-Too-Much. "I don't need a story—I got the cut galloping through the trees to save Mustang Ridge from looking like the Sears place."

Wyatt sobered. "Thanks for that, by the way. Seriously. This is . . ." He looked around, from the guest cabins near the lake, up to the barns and the main house. "It matters. It's home. I could live without it—we all could if we had to. But I'd hate to have to." And coming from a guy who hadn't stayed in the same place for more than a few months at a time before he arrived in Three Ridges, that was saying something.

Rather than think too hard about his own big empty house on the other side of town, Sam punched his buddy in the arm. "Don't worry, Webb. I've got your back, especially when it comes to the cute brunette staying out in Blessing Valley."

Wyatt zeroed in. "Jenny's friend is cute?"

"Yeah, she's cute." Hot, even, with long, dark, flowing curls, big blue-green eyes, and a killer set of curves that he had noticed even with her finger on that trigger. "You haven't met her?" he asked Wyatt.

"Nope. I missed her when she arrived, and she hasn't been back since. Krista and I figured we'd give her a few more days to come in for supplies. If she doesn't, we'll load up and head out for a visit."

"Sounds like a plan." It also sounded to Sam as though he should keep track of whether she showed up at the ranch, and if not, ride out and warn her to hide the tent. He didn't know exactly what was going on there, but he had to respect her for not wanting to hurt Krista's feelings—not to mention that he wouldn't mind seeing his assailant again. Lady like that, packing a fastball, a pistol, and a secret or two, made a man wonder what else was hiding beneath the surface.

# 4

The morning after the Bonfire Incident—that was how Danny had decided to think about it, focusing on her *aha* moment rather than on the man—she awoke just past dawn, tired and achy and feeling like she'd climbed a thousand feet straight up while she slept.

The squirrels were waiting for her, sitting on the cleared-off table and looking at her as if to say, *Well? What's for breakfast?*

"Shoo! Scat!" She waved them off.

Tails flicking, they boogied up the awning. Instead of dashing up the tree, though, they stayed on top of the RV, stomping their feet and chittering at her. One was fatter and more sandy gray, the other leaner and reddish, and neither looked particularly scared of her.

Narrowing her eyes, she said, "I've got a gun, you know."

They didn't look impressed by the threat. Probably knew she didn't mean it—the revolver was for predators and signaling for help.

"Okay, fine. You can stay. But I'm not feeding you!" Word of a sucker traveled fast, and the last thing she needed was two squirrels to turn into a dozen, then four dozen. Or, worse, a bear. She slept inside an electrified fence that was rated for the area's biggest predators, and made a point of keeping her food sealed and her compost far away from camp. The M&M's had been a rare misstep; she had no intention of letting the RV become a feeding station.

Turning her back on the squirrels, she went through her morning routine with more speed than usual, veins thrumming with an anticipation she couldn't quite pin down. Maybe it was leftover excitement from the previous day's break in the routine, or the buzz of knowing that if yesterday had been the first day of the rest of her life, today was the next first day.

Even her surroundings were a little different now. Whereas she had burned the bad memories that had come out of her duffel, she had spread the good ones around her camp. She was drinking her tea out of the cartoon mug her sister, Charlie, had given her while she was in the hospital; there was a picture of her, Charlie, and their parents visible through the RV's window, a rare indoor shot of them plopped together on a couch; and a brightly painted pottery bowl sat on the ground nearby, ready and waiting should she decide to transplant an herb or two.

And hanging from one of the awning supports, dangling like a fluorescent yellow chandelier, was the little stuffed toy butterfly that Farah had given her before she left rehab, the one that wore hiking boots, suspenders, and a tag that said its name was BUTTERS THE BUTTERFLY. But though Butters had looked cheerful and benign yesterday, now he watched Danny with big plastic eyes that seemed to say, *Aren't you forgetting something?*

And, yeah, maybe she was. Or not forgetting so much as avoiding.

"I know, I know. I'm sorry. I've been . . ." She couldn't bring herself to say "too busy," even when her audience consisted of a couple of squirrels and a stuffed butterfly, because it wasn't like taking walks and picking salad greens needed to be a full-time occupàtion, even on vacation. And this wasn't entirely a vacation, either. She was supposed to be making some decisions.

Sighing, she said, "Okay, fine. I've been avoiding the tests. The whole idea makes me feel silly." Which was ironic, considering that she was talking to rodents and a toy. But there was something inherently goofy about using a bunch of online personality tests—*What's Your Spirit Animal? What's Your Superpower? What Martini Are You?*—to decide what she wanted to do with her life, or even just the next couple of years.

Then again, it wasn't like she had made any real progress on her own. It was one thing to announce that she didn't want to work in the family business anymore, that she needed to branch out, find herself. It was another thing to figure out what, exactly, that meant.

Thus, the tests, courtesy of her physical-therapist-turned-friend, whose whole therapeutic approach involved taking grueling, painful exercises—whether physical or mental—and turning them into games.

"The goofier the better," Farah had said firmly when she gave Danny a list of the Web sites she wanted her to use. "Download the quizzes and answers onto your computer and do one a day. And promise me you won't just laugh at the answers but really think about them, too!" Fiftysomething and borderline frumpy, Farah was a whiz with everything from homeopathy to the newest gadgets, and had serious mother hen tendencies. She had appointed herself Danny's new best friend for the duration of her rehab, and they had kept in touch after, with Farah dispensing liberal doses of "Live your own life" and "Go someplace new and maybe you'll find yourself." And, when Danny had settled on Wyoming, Farah had added the silly quizzes to the mix.

So Danny had promised. She had downloaded. But until yesterday, she hadn't actually unpacked her laptop. Now it sat on the front seat of the RV, sucking up its solar charge and waiting for her to get to work.

"Fine." She squared her shoulders. "I'll do it. Happy?"

The squirrels had gotten bored and wandered off. The butterfly looked unimpressed. But a minute later, with the laptop open on the table in front of her and a whole lot of files to choose from, Danny closed her eyes, twirled her finger, and pointed to a random spot on the screen. She opened her eyes and said, "Hm."

*What Kind of Sandwich Are You?*

Deciding that finding her inner sandwich definitely counted as goofy, she opened the multiple-choice questionnaire.

The first question was "Who do you admire most?" which wouldn't have been bad, except that the answers consisted of "Mother Teresa," "the president," and three entertainers she couldn't have picked out of a lineup if her life depended on it. *Okay, Mother Teresa it is.*

The next couple were easy—favorite animal, eagle; favorite color, green—but then she got to "What's your favorite day-off activity?" and found herself wrestling with the choices. She could cross "getting a manicure" and "getting wasted" off the list, but that left her with "spending time with family," "being alone," and "doing something I've never done before." All of which fit, depending on whether she was answering as her old self, her current self, or the cooler, less neurotic person she wanted to be.

Deciding to go with what fit the now-her, she clicked on "being alone" and reminded herself she wasn't being graded. The test was just a tool.

Which was lucky for her, because after that the questions got harder, the answers weirder.

"What lifetime supply do you want?" She negged "Cheez Whiz," "reality TV," and "bagpipe music," and went with "books."

"What's your favorite condiment?" She skipped "hair gel," "motor oil," and "shampoo" on the theory that whoever wrote the quiz was messing with her, and picked "Cool Whip."

"Pick your transportation" offered up "mine cart," "magic carpet," "submarine," and "giant bat" as the choices. Magic carpet, definitely.

Doing her best, she filled out the computerized form, pretty sure she was headed for something bland and forgettable in the sandwich department, like bread and butter. When she reached the end, answering "dandelion" for her favorite flower, because she loved the tart greens, she hit the ENTER AND CALCULATE button, and steeled herself for bread and butter.

A picture of a fat, tightly wrapped burrito popped onto the screen.

Danny blinked at it. "Since when is a burrito considered a sandwich?" Since never, as far as she was concerned. But she paged down to the accompanying description:

"You are spicy chicken and jalapeno hot sauce hidden inside a layer of lettuce and tightly wound within a constricting tortilla. Your outer wrapping has been strengthened by your experiences, making it difficult for you to break free. But break free you must, because you have so much more to offer than you realize. So step outside your comfort zone, do something unexpected, and let yourself take a bite out of life today!"

Which resonated, darn it.

"So . . ." She leaned back in her chair, looking up to find a pair of beady eyes watching her from the branches overhead. "You got any suggestions?"

The eyes disappeared and leaves bobbed back into place.

"You're no help." But she pushed to her feet, snagged the picnic basket Gran had given her, and strapped it to the back of the ATV.

She didn't need a computer to tell her that it was past time for her to head for Mustang Ridge.

"Danny! You're here!" Beaming, Gran whisked down the kitchen steps and along the gravel path to where Danny had parked the four-wheeler. "We were starting to worry!" She was wearing a ruffled blue-and-white-polka-dot apron over jeans and a yellow shirt, and enfolded Danny in a no-nonsense hug that carried the scents of cinnamon and vanilla.

"I'm sorry," Danny said automatically.

"Oh, poosh, not your fault. We're programmed to fuss over our guests here. You've got every right to come and go as you please." Gran eased back and twinkled up at her. "And besides, Sam mentioned running into you."

She mostly smothered the wince. "I'm afraid to ask what he said."

"That he rode up on you and your fire, thinking you were a trespasser, and you set him straight." Her smile widened. "With a revolver."

"About the fire—"

"Don't fret. You had everything under control. Including him, from the sound of it!" She patted Danny's cheek, then stepped away and started untying the picnic basket from the back of the ATV. As her fingers worked, she said conversationally, "Good for you. Man like him needs to stay on his toes. Otherwise, he'll hide out in that big old house of his and play with his rocks."

Danny did a double take. "Is that a euphemism?"

Gran threw her head back and hooted. "No, dear. Although I guess we *are* talking about the family jewels here, aren't we?" Seeing Danny's confusion, she added, "He didn't let on that he's our local-boy-made-good?"

"We didn't exactly exchange life stories." And he had a workingman's hands. Aware that Gran was waiting for the go-ahead, Danny hesitated, then nodded. It wasn't gossip, so much as getting the lay of the land. He *had* ridden up on her like a stagecoach robber.

"His father, Trooper, was a mechanic, and a good one, but his true love was gem hunting. Sam's, too. They spent all their time and money on it, and never really saw much of anything back until Sam stumbled on a huge pocket of blue diamonds seven, maybe eight years ago. High quality, very rare. The stones sold for a ton of money, and *poof*!" She snapped her fingers. "Millionaires. Like winning the lottery."

Danny gaped. "I thought he was . . . I don't know. A local ranch hand or something." Though he had the eyes of a man who was used to being in charge.

"Well, Windfall used to be the family ranch. Now it's the center of operations for Babcock Gems. Sam built himself a big house up on Wolf Rock Hill. A mansion, really, though he only lives in a few rooms."

"With his parents?"

Gran's expression clouded. "No. Sam's mom passed when he was a baby—cancer, I believe—and Troop died not long after they broke ground up at Windfall. It was a terrible motorcycle accident."

"Oh." Danny's hand lifted to her throat. "That's awful." Her parents might not understand her now, or why she had needed to get away, but she couldn't imagine the hole it would put in her life if one of them suddenly wasn't there anymore. Both? Forget it. She didn't even want to imagine.

And she really needed to give them a call.

Gran nodded. "It was, though Lord knows folks around here—especially his dad's biker friends—did their best to step in and help. It took a while for Sam to come back out of his shell, but he came around eventually. Business is good these days, and I know he likes having Wyatt nearby. He's out here every week or so for a hot meal and some company, so we keep an eye on him, make sure he's not spending too much time up there alone on the hill."

"Playing with his rocks," Danny said with a small smile, as Gran's earlier reference cut through the ache.

"Exactly. Any-hoo . . ." Gran hefted the basket off the ATV. "Let's get you loaded back up. I know Krista will want to see you—she's out in the barn, helping the guests settle their horses before dinner."

"Actually, I need to make a call first, check my e-mail, that sort of thing. Is there someplace I can go that's out of the way?"

"Of course, dear. You can use Krista's office. Come on. I'll show you."

Ten minutes later, with her laptop open on the huge wooden desk that dominated Krista's small, crowded office and the window cracked to reassure the squirrelly part of her, Danny listened to the digital ring as the computer did it's *E.T.* thing and phoned home.

The image on the screen was a snapshot of the cabin where she grew up and where her parents still lived, deep in the Maine woods, all rough logs and a huge chimney, with pine trees crowded around it, blocking out the light. It struck her as odd how it seemed suddenly very crowded compared to Wyoming.

The computer gave a triumphant *badda-beep* as the video call connected, and her parents' faces blinked onto the screen. "Danny!" her mom said. "*There* you are." Rumor had it that she had said the same thing when Danny was born. A true Yankee, Bea Traveler had underreaction down to an art, though Danny could see the relief in her mother's sun-lined face. She could also see from her parents' dark green shirts and ID tags, and the office backdrop, that she had caught them both at work.

"Hi, Mom. Hi, Dad. Sorry it's been so long. I got settled in at my campsite, and time got away from me. You know how that goes."

"Of course we do!" Her father leaned in, making his nose look huge for a second. A grizzled gray contrast to her mother's bottle brunette, he was more laid-back, except when it came to racing. Now, looking happy to see her, even if only on-screen, he said, "Tell us everything."

Skipping over the nightmares and claustrophobia—it was fifty-fifty between them worrying and shrugging it off, neither of which would help her one bit—Danny told them about the valley and the mustangs, and made them laugh with a quick description of the sandwich test. Then she asked, "So, how are you? How's Charlie? The dogs?"

They chatted for a few minutes, with Danny paying more attention than usual, acutely aware of the way her parents overlapped each other on the screen and alternated finishing each other's sentences. Little things that seemed suddenly so important after what Gran had told her about Sam's parents.

"But enough about us," her father said. "We're more interested in you. How about it? Are you ready to come home yet and get back to work?"

And there it was. Not subtle, either. Then again, Mainers weren't big on beating around the bush. Or maybe it was just her parents.

"We miss you, sweetie," her mom put in. "Not to mention that if you were here to help out, Charlie would have more time to race."

It was the Traveler family motto: *If you're not competing, then why bother?* Except she didn't want to compete anymore, and she wasn't sure she wanted to be the flag bearer while the rest of them competed, either. Especially knowing that she would keep getting those sidelong looks, the ones that said, *You're all healed up, so why aren't you getting back out there?*

Doing her best not to bristle—it wasn't their fault that their lives were built around mountain sports when she was the one who'd lost interest—she said, "I'm sure you can hire someone to fill in."

"It's not about the shop." Her dad gave her mom a pointed look. "We want our girl back home."

"I miss you, too." She blew them both a kiss, but said firmly, "I just got here, though, so if I were you, I'd post a Help Wanted ad over at the mountain. There's got to be a few ski bums left looking for work, even this late in the summer." Her attempt at a smile went crooked. "Heck, call Brandon. Last I checked, he was saving up to climb K2."

There was a startled pause, followed by a parent-to-parent look that set off warning bells.

"Ohhh-kay." She drew it out. "What am I missing? Did something happen to Bran? Is he okay?"

"He's fine." Her mom visibly squared her shoulders. "Better than fine, I suppose. He's engaged."

"He's *what*?" The sudden buzzing in her ears must have made her hear that wrong. Because there was no way. Tall, dark, and handsome, with the swagger that came with being able to master just about any sport he set his sights on, Danny's ski instructor ex lived by the motto he'd had tattooed on his chest: NO BOUNDARIES.

Her father's face settled into deeper-than-usual creases. "It's true, baby. He and Allison got engaged last week."

"He and—" The name turned into a wheeze as the air vacated her lungs.

"Charlie said Allie was going to e-mail you," her mom added. "I guess not, huh?"

A shake of her head was all Danny could manage while her brain spun like someone had dumped it in a blender and hit the ON button. Allison and Brandon, engaged. Brandon engaged to anyone. It didn't compute, like trying to picture a flying shark or a mountain suddenly rising up on reptilian legs and stomping off in search of a beer. "I'm . . . I don't know what to say." Was she going to be sick? She didn't think so, but her stomach had turned to a queasy knot.

Her dad reached out, as if he had forgotten she was thousands of miles away. "I'm sorry, sweetie."

"It's not your fault." Her lips felt numb, as if the words were coming from someone else. "It's not anybody's fault. He's free to . . ." She couldn't get the word *marry* out of her mouth. Not in a million years. "He can do whatever he wants."

Apparently, he just hadn't wanted to do it with her.

"If it helps any," her father said gently, "Charlie said that Allie feels weird about it, seeing as how you got her the job over at the mountain."

"It really doesn't help," Danny said. "But thanks for trying. I've gotta go." She was suddenly dying to hit the disconnect button, and escape back outside, where she could breathe. "I'll call you guys next weekend, okay? Maybe the weekend after." Or the one after that.

"How about you buy a plane ticket instead?" her mom said, not unkindly. "You should be here, with us, at the shop."

Down the road from the mountain, where her ex and her second cousin—who could barely ski an intermediate slope and thought that an indoor wall counted as climbing—were planning the wedding she had once envisioned.

"Bye, Dad. Bye, Mom. Tell Charlie I said 'hey.' I love you all." She ended the call before her parents could respond, and the video feed went dark.

Then, even though the walls were closing in, the oxygen too thin, she sat staring at the home screen of her laptop, where the little red number in the upper left corner was in the double digits. *You've got mail.*

She should just empty her whole darned in-box. One click, and *poof*. All gone. Except that deleting the notes wouldn't change the reality, would it?

Hand shaking, she hit the icon and then looked down the list, seeing Charlie's e-mail address, and Allison's. And then, at the bottom, Brandon's. The subject line said *GOOD NEWS*, all douche-y and capitalized, like he somehow expected her to be happy for him.

*Don't open it,* she told herself. *It's just going to make things worse.* But if she didn't, she would only drive herself nuts trying to guess what it said. "Oh, what the hell?" she said out loud. "Rip the Band-Aid off and get it over with." And she clicked on the message.

Dear Danny,

I know that Allison already e-mailed you the good news, but I wanted to follow up personally.

"If that was true," she grumbled, "I'd have a voice mail. And what sort of dork uses letter formatting in an e-mail?" Which was bitchy, but she didn't care. Not when her pulse thrummed in her throat and the words blurred on the screen.

> I know our engagement will probably come as a shock to you. I hope you can see past that, though, and be happy for us as we embark on this new adventure, freeing yourself for whatever comes next. I treasure the memories of our time together, and wish you the absolute best.
>
> Your friend,
> Brandon

"Why, that arrogant, overhyped, ham-handed . . . *aah!*" Danny had always thought that the idea of steam coming out of someone's ears was a metaphor reserved for bad prose and kids' cartoons, but now she knew different. Her face burned and when she breathed, the overheated air scalded her nasal passages.

Shoving away from the desk, she slapped the laptop shut, jammed it back into its carrying case, and slung the strap over her shoulder while she fought the adrenaline buzz of a major fight-or-flight response.

She had to get out of there—not back to her parents and Maverick Mountain, where "don't wimp out" was a battle cry, but to Blessing Valley, where she could be alone. But as she rounded the huge desk, boot steps sounded out in the main room, and Krista's voice called, "Danny? Are you still in there?"

With her pulse thudding and her stomach tied in knots, she was seriously tempted to go out the window.

Knowing she owed Krista better than that, though, she concentrated on her breathing and forced her voice to stay steady when she called, "Yep. I just finished up."

Krista came through the doorway with Abby on her shoulder and her face alight with welcome. "I'm so happy you're here! I was just saying to Wyatt . . ." She trailed off, her expression shifting. "Are you okay?"

"I'm . . ." Danny dug her fingernails into her palms. "I'll be fine. Just some family stuff."

Krista hitched a hip on the desk. "Abby and I are good listeners, if you'd like to talk. Or I could hand her off and we could go someplace."

Normally, Danny preferred to keep private stuff private. This was far from normal, though, and she was supposed to be working on breaking free from her tortilla. She exhaled, and her shoulders came down a notch. "In a nutshell, I just found out that my ex-boyfriend of five years, who was all *I shouldn't have to give you a ring to prove that I'm committed to you* and *Marriage is a fascist institution*, is now engaged to my much younger, prettier second cousin. Who, by the way, only met him because I helped her get a job waiting tables at the ski resort where he works." Indignation sharpened her voice. "She doesn't even like being outdoors!"

"That wench!" Krista said in immediate solidarity. "Not for the outdoors thing, but for going there. As for your ex, he sounds like a royal"—she covered the baby's ears and, in a whisper, spelled out—"*a-s-s*. You ask me, you're far better off without him."

"I am. I know I am. And I shouldn't be upset, really. We broke up more than a year ago, and there's no reason he shouldn't move on. It's just the marriage thing. It makes me feel like—"

"Don't." Krista held up a hand. "Tomorrow you can be all logical and rational. Today, I'm giving you permission to be completely illogical and upset. In fact . . ." Her expression shifted to an *aha*. "I'm not just giving you permission, I'm going to give you a weapon. How does a sledgehammer sound?"

"Better than it probably should. Why?"

"Have you heard about the Sears place?"

"It burned down, right? An ember from a wildfire started it?"

"Exactly. It's a total loss, most of it torched to the ground. But there's lots of cleanup left to do before they can rebuild, so the mayor organized today as a demo day, and a bunch of us are taking the shuttle over there to help. It's strictly volunteer, a community-service sort of thing. You're welcome to join us."

Suddenly, Danny couldn't think of anything better than an excuse to smash stuff while helping out a family whose problems were way bigger than her own. "I'd love to," she said. "When do we leave?"

# 5

Sam left for the Sears place later than he'd meant to, but he made up for it by talking Murphy, Midas, and Axyl into ditching their evening plans and coming along for the ride. The parking lot was jammed; Mayor Tepitt's campaign truck, parked in the baked-dry front yard, had classic rock belting from the roof-mounted speakers; and a dozen empty picnic tables were set in rows near a bunch of coolers and a table stacked high with food. "See?" Sam said. "I told you there'd be snacks."

"We're going to need 'em," Midas said. "Get a load of this place. It's a disaster area."

"So the mayor tells us." Axyl frowned at the barn, where streaks of gray paint and white trim were interspersed with blackened char and blasted-out windows. "But the plan is to have the riding school back up and running by winter."

"The sooner the better," Sam agreed, struck once more by the randomness of the destruction. The fields on one side of the drive were untouched, with even the fine layer of ash mostly blown away and horses and cattle grazing like nothing had happened. On the other side, though, the earth was black and barren, the fencing turned skeletal. "Come on." He climbed out and snagged a tool belt and a sledge from the back of the truck. "I'm betting there are some smashables with our names on them."

Sure enough, after a quick check at the food tent, where the mayor and her terrifyingly efficient assistant were keeping things on track and handing out safety gear and lectures on using it, they split up to the spots that needed extra hands.

Boots thumping on the platform that had been cobbled together to span the burned-out wreck of the front porch, Sam stepped through an empty doorframe into the main house. He found himself in what used to be a sitting room, with a mangled flat screen on the wall over a stone fireplace, and rectangles of less-burned hardwood where couches and chairs used to be. The bulk of the debris had been cleared, but a few odds and ends remained. A soggy stuffed dog with only one eye. A half-melted toy car. A single pink bunny slipper, small enough to fit in the palm of his hand.

"Damn," he muttered behind his respirator. "Eerie." So was being alone in there. Most everybody else was working on tearing down the charred remains of the outbuildings, clearing the way for the big barn raising that was being planned, which left the main house feeling empty and strange.

As he moved deeper into the house, past a cordoned-off bathroom where nothing was left except a whole lot of porcelain shrapnel, a *thud-crash* echoed from a back room, followed by a few unintelligible words in a woman's voice. Following the sounds down a hallway that was mostly intact, save for a thick layer of soot on the walls, he stepped through a wide archway into a big, bright kitchen, where sunlight poured through to illuminate broken tiles, burned-out cabinets, a snakelike mess of dead wiring. There, a dark-haired woman swung a wood-handled sledgehammer like it was the bottom of the ninth and she was aiming for the walk-off homer as she nailed a caved-in section of the scorched Formica countertop. *Wha-bam!*

And darned if he didn't recognize her right off the bat. The book-wielding, revolver-toting beauty had her back to him, and should have been unrecognizable in a yellow hard hat, clear safety glasses, earmuffs, and alien-looking respirator, but he recognized her just the same. Mostly because he'd thought about her off and on, wondering how she was doing, and whether he should ride over and see for himself. Turned out luck was with him, though, because here she was.

Before he could step through the door and say hi, she lifted the sledge over her head and hollered, "Jerk!" *Wha-bam* went the sledge against the countertop. "Idiot!" *Rattle-slam*, and a cabinet door went flying. "Stupid to care." *Crash-bang!*

"Uh-oh," Sam said under his breath, realizing that he had walked into something more than community service.

But then she made a muffled noise and rubbed one wrist with the opposite hand. "Ow. Damn it."

*Just go,* he told himself. *She wants to be alone.* Heck, she thought she *was* alone. But she was hurting, too, and he couldn't just walk away from that. So, summoning a look that he hoped said *I just got here, didn't see a thing,* he stepped through the door. "Howdy, Miz Traveler. Fancy meeting up with you here. And look. This time, we're both wearing masks!"

Danny whirled and gasped, surprise banging up against the *oh, hell, no* of realizing that she had an audience. And then, a nanosecond later, a flush seared her skin as she recognized the figure in the doorway. "Sam!"

It was a very different version of the man she had met the other day, though, and not just because of what she knew about him now. Clean-shaven, with a high-tech-looking sledgehammer over his shoulder and the burned-out archway framing his body, he looked taller than she remembered, his T-shirt stretching across his chest to hint at rangy muscles. But while he might be trying to pull off the *hey, howdy, glad to see you again*, she could see the sympathy in those intelligent gray eyes.

She didn't remember what she had said just now—she'd been so caught up in the violent satisfaction of battering at the kitchen cabinets until her bad wrist was damn near on fire. Whatever she'd said, though, he had definitely heard. And between the way their first encounter had played out and now this, he probably thought she was completely mental.

Flushing harder beneath the mask and goggles, she said, "I didn't realize you were there." Which scored about a million on the one-to-obvious scale. "I don't know what you heard, but . . ." She shrugged. "I'm not as nuts as I look. I swear."

He studied her for a moment with those granite-gray eyes that seemed to go right through her. Then, instead of saying anything, he lowered the futuristic-looking tool from his shoulder and held it out to her, handle first.

The gleaming metal had a foam-wrapped grip, thin shaft, and complicated articulation where the head attached.

She frowned at it. "I've got a hammer."

"This one's better." He closed the distance between them, snagged her sledgehammer easily from where it was wedged into the side of a cabinet, and pressed the pimped-out replacement into her hand. "You can leave it in the back of my truck when you're done. Green Ford with 'Babcock Gems' on the door." With that, he sauntered out, carrying her sledgehammer by two fingers, like it weighed little more than a stick of gum.

Danny blinked after him, thinking she should go after him and make him trade back—she had been doing fine on her own, and she didn't need him coming in and trying to fix things for her. But even through the heavy work gloves, the spongy grip felt good against her palms and her wrist suddenly didn't hurt so much. So instead of chasing him down she adjusted her respirator and looked for a target.

The cabinet in the corner was about ready to fall. Growling, she lined up and swung. The lighter, faster sledgehammer blurred through the air, shattered the door, carved through the bottom shelf, and buried itself in the Formica with a shuddering impact that sent her reeling, not because of bad reverb, but because she couldn't believe she had just done all *that*. She gaped—first at the cabinet that looked like someone had wrapped it around a tree at high speed, and then at the caved-in counter and the robot-leg sledgehammer that should've come with a warning label, like LAST USED BY THOR. "Wow!"

A strange sort of fight-or-flight buzz kicked in—battle

lust, maybe, or hysteria—and she wrestled the sledge-hammer free. Not thinking of Brandon now, she lined up again on the mangled cabinet and swung again. And again. Three blows and it was off the wall, a fourth and it was squashed roadkill-flat and her pulse was pounding, her blood singing through her veins like she had just made an impossible summit. Jumping up on top of the pile, she did a little boogie-woogie dance. Then, hefting the SuperSledge, she headed for what was left of the kitchen's center island, which she had avoided so far because it was sturdily built and not that badly burned.

"Out with the old and in with the new!" she announced. And swung with all her might.

By the time the volunteers called it quits and straggled over to the picnic tables, the snacks had been demolished except for a couple of bruised apples and a radioactive-green, fruit-laden Jell-O mold that had survived the midsummer heat with terrifying tenacity. There was plenty of soda and beer, though, and pizza on the way, so the workers who didn't need to be anywhere grabbed cold ones and found places to sit, most of them covering up groans and muttering about how ranching was damn hard work, but demolition and cleanup used a different set of muscles.

Feeling just fine—prospecting and demo weren't that far apart in the swing-and-smash department—Sam spooned some of the Jell-O thing into a bowl and went in search of Axyl and the others. He found them leaning against a plastic-wrapped pallet of construction material and dropped down, discovering that the shingles made a far more comfortable backrest than he would've expected. "You guys have fun Dumpster diving?" he said to Midas and Murphy, who had been going through the demolition mess, separating the recyclables and hazardous materials from the stuff that would have to go to the landfill.

"Loads and loads," said Midas. "Literally."

Murph eyed Sam's Jell-O. "My great-aunt used to make that stuff. In fact, she might have made that batch. You never know—it's like the Christmas Fruitcake Phenomenon. There's really only six of them, and they rotate throughout the world forever in a cosmic cycle of regifting."

At Axyl's guffaw, Sam shrugged. "I figure someone brought it. I didn't want it to just sit there and make her feel bad." He felt pretty safe assuming it was a *her*—no guy in his right mind was floating fruit in Jell-O unless there was alcohol involved. "Besides, me striking the first blow might encourage the others to dig in."

"It might also encourage the Jell-O-and-fruit pusher to bring another one tomorrow," Murph said darkly. "Or maybe drop it off at your place."

"If that happens, I'll be sure to leave it in the break room so we can share."

"Only if you want to find it in your bed. Or worse."

"I'd better not see green Jell-O on the next supply list," Sam warned.

"You'd prefer orange? Maybe cherry?"

"I'd prefer a long-legged blonde who's looking for a good time, but she's not going on the list, either."

"Baloney," Axyl said to his beer. "I saw you with the brunette. Krista's friend. What's her name—Annie?"

"Danny. And it's not like that." Or maybe it was.

Sam hadn't entirely figured it out. He didn't usually go for women with loner tendencies or a ton of baggage— mostly because he had plenty of his own—but there was something about her that had stuck in his head, under his skin.

"Uh-huh. So how did she get hold of your sledge?"

Murph's head came up. "You let her use the Terminator?"

"Folks," Gabe Sears called, saving Sam from having to explain why he'd handed over one of his favorite prototypes without a second thought. The rail-thin farmer, wearing denim and a Rockies cap over hair that seemed shot through with new streaks of gray, climbed up on one of the picnic tables. He offered a helping hand as Winny—plump and pretty, with her face scrubbed free of the soot the rest of her was wearing—came up beside him. Then, as the crowd quieted, he said, "I'm, um . . . I'm not much for public speaking. But Winny and the kids and I want you to know how much it means to us that you all came out here today. It . . . ah . . . ." He cleared his throat. "It's a hard thing for a man not to be able to do for his own."

Squeezing his hand, Winny said to the crowd, "A week ago, we didn't think we were going to be able to rebuild, at least not right away. In fact, we didn't know what we were going to do. Now, though . . ." She looked around at the blasted landscape, but the way her shoulders squared and her chin came up made it seem like she wasn't seeing the devastation so much as the progress. "Now we've got hope. And hope is a powerful thing. So thank you for that. Thanks to each and every one of you, from the bottoms of our hearts."

A sudden fanfare blared from a car horn, an engine revved, and, as if ushered in by some cosmic director— *cue the mayor!*—the loudspeaker-topped truck flew up the driveway, bounced across the burned-out lawn, and skidded to a stop near the picnic tables. The driver's window buzzed down, and Mayor Teppitt leaned across her assistant to holler, "Hey, there! Who wants pizza?"

That got some whoops and laughter, and Gabe slung his arm around Winny and shouted, "Thanks again, everyone. Now, let's eat!"

As the hungry workers thronged around the truck like something out of a zombie movie playing on fast-forward, Sam couldn't help noticing one figure going the other way with her hands in her pockets—pretty and brunette, with the kind of curves and curls that stuck in a man's mind.

*Let it go*, he told himself. *Give her room.* But he couldn't very well let her starve, could he? Ignoring the logic that said there was zero chance of a guest—even one living out in the boonies—going hungry on Gran's watch, he worked his way through the crowd, snagged pizza and sodas for two, and dug through a first-aid kit for one of those smash-to-activate ice packs and a foil packet of painkillers. Then, ignoring Axyl's smirk, he followed her.

# 6

Tired of being around people and noise—even the happy kind—Danny slipped away from the party and down to the little pond she had glimpsed from the driveway. Tucked into a low-lying valley that had escaped the wildfire, it had a flat shore on one side that was liberally dotted with hoofprints, while the other side offered a rocky overhang that looked perfect for cannonballs.

Sitting at the edge of the overhang with her heels hooked on a narrow ledge and nothing but water below her, she gazed down at her own reflection, which blurred around the edges, like she was underwater. It was strangely hypnotic, oddly relaxing. Or maybe the relaxation came from the pull of overused muscles, the knowledge of a job well done, and the pleasant emptiness that had cloaked her mind.

"Hey," a voice said from behind her. "You up for some company?"

Oddly, the answer wasn't an immediate *hell, no,* and not just because she recognized Sam's voice. Twisting around, she found him standing some distance away, looking as sweaty and rumpled as she felt, but holding a couple of beers and a plate of pizza.

Her stomach growled, even though a minute ago she would've said she wasn't hungry. "Are you going to share?"

He settled in beside her and put the plate between them. Holding out one of the beers, he said, "To demolition."

She clinked her bottle to his. "To using the right tool for the job. And thank you."

"For the sledgehammer?"

"That, the privacy, the food." She shot him a sidelong look. "I got the *Hulk, smash* urges out of the way, so you don't need to worry I'm going to go psycho on you after dinner. I just had some things I needed to get out of my system." She stretched out her free hand and wiggled her fingers. "All gone."

He cocked an eyebrow. "You sure?"

"For now, yes. Beyond that, I'll take it day by day." Not so much when it came to Brandon—the shock had worn off and the sting had already started to fade. It would take longer to work through the dreams, though, and the fears.

"Yeah." He nodded. "I know how that goes."

"So I heard." At his sharp look, she said, "Gran told me a few things about you. I hope you don't mind."

"It's a small town. Gossip happens." He took a pull on his beer, then added, "I'm flattered my name came up."

Was he fishing to see if she was interested? She couldn't tell, not with him sitting close enough that she could feel an echo of his body heat on her skin and see that there was silver and blue mixed in with the gray of his eyes.

Leaning away, she said, "I figured I should apologize to her for letting the fire get out of hand. She kind of took it from there. Mostly, I think, because she wanted to tell me what a nice guy you are."

He rolled his shoulders, but said only, "Well, since you know my story, or at least some of it, it seems only fair for you to even things up by answering a question for me."

She hesitated, but then surprised herself. "Okay. Ask."

"What do you have against the *Rambling Rose*?"

"What . . . *That's* what you want to know about me?"

His teeth flashed. "Not necessarily. But it's a start."

A quiver of awareness went through her, a feminine *aha* that said he was interested, all right, or at least flirting a little. And the thing was, she was tempted to flirt a little right back. He had given her his sledgehammer, after all, and he had those big, wide hands. So she said, "I don't like small spaces, especially dead ends. The tent has zips in the front and back, and I sleep with a knife under my pillow in case I need to cut my way out."

"Always?"

"Do I always sleep with a knife under my pillow?"

Faint lines deepened at the corners of his eyes. "Have you always been claustrophobic?"

"It's only been the past eighteen months or so." Aware that she knew more about him than he probably wanted, and turnabout was only fair, she backed up some. "Before that, growing up in Maine, I was the one who was always poking in the smallest, darkest hidey-hole I could find, just to see what was inside." Which made it that much worse, having lost that, too. "It didn't even matter if I got stuck, because my parents were always there to pull me out. Or my sister, Charlie. Our parents never scolded us, never told us to be more careful. They just wanted to know what we had found. Bigger, better, faster, higher . . . that's the Traveler family motto. Or one of them, at any rate. We were all about the outdoors, all the time—skiing, climbing, obstacle races . . . If I could win it, I tried it, and usually did pretty well. I won a bunch, crashed some, healed up, and did it all over again. Until one day, my luck ran out." Her voice went hollow on the last word.

"You don't have to tell me if you don't want to." But his eyes were steady on hers and he seemed somehow very *solid* beside her.

"There's not much to tell, really." Not if she wanted to sleep tonight. "My ex-boyfriend and I were out climbing with a few friends—the route wasn't all that gnarly, and it had a great picnic spot at the top. There was this one section of chimney we wanted to try—that's a narrow gap where you put your back on one rock face, your hands and feet on the other, and work your way to the top." Swallowing to loosen the sudden tightness in her throat, she said, "It was a little sketchy because we had to drop in halfway and climb up from there, and things were real narrow, with jagged rocks at the bottom. But the upper part looked doable, so I volunteered to go first. I was the smallest and lightest . . . and, well, I liked being first. I roped up, set some safety lines, and started the climb." It had been wider than she had anticipated, slipperier. And she probably wasn't sleeping tonight after all. "I was about halfway to the top when it happened. There was this little ledge I had to get past. The rock looked solid, *felt* solid, but when I put my weight on it, the whole thing gave. And I went with it." She fought not to remember the noise, the moment of free fall. The impact. "I wound up lying at the bottom, pinned under the broken ledge. It was nearly eight hours before the rescue team could get me out."

"Damn." His voice was rough. "That's a hell of a thing."

Pain. Cold. Numbness creeping in. The terror of realizing she couldn't move her toes. Brandon and the others peering down at her, calling, "They're coming" and "It's going to be okay," but then disappearing to huddle together as they waited for the rescue team, leaving her staring up at the sky. Alone. Swallowing hard, she continued. "I broke my arm, and being pinned that long damaged the nerves in my spine. It was six months before I could walk across the room, a year before I was anywhere close to normal. Physically, at least."

Usually it bothered her when people stared at her like he was doing, but there was something about him that blunted the irritation. The lack of pity in his gray eyes, maybe, or knowing that life had knocked him around some, too. "And here you are," he said, "throwing books and swinging hammers."

A corner of her mouth kicked up at the reminder. Looking back at the burned-out farmstead, where the pizza party contrasted starkly with the ruined house, she said, "It's crazy, isn't it? How one split second can change everything? One ember from a wildfire, and a family loses everything. One cracked ledge, and I spend the rest of my life avoiding danger and counting exits."

"You flip over the right rock and you're rich," Sam said. "Then a couple of months later you take the scenic road rather than the bypass, and you wind up dead."

"I'm sorry," she said. "Really, truly sorry."

"Thanks." His eyes flicked to her. "Right back at you. And for the record, living out in the Wyoming backcountry with a bear fence and a six-shooter is hardly what I call avoiding danger."

She shrugged. "I don't want to climb anymore, don't want to race, don't want to do anything that involves faster, harder, or higher. My parents don't know what to do with me, or what we're supposed to talk about."

"I bet your dad wishes he'd been there that day, to pull you out."

He would see that, wouldn't he? She nodded. "He wants me to come home. I think he's afraid I don't trust them to have my back anymore, but that's not it. Or maybe it is, a little, because now I know it's up to me to have my own back. More, I need to figure out what *I* want to do next. Before, it made sense to stick near home and work in my family's pro shop, right at the bottom of Maverick Mountain. Skis and snowboards in the winter, mountain bikes in the summer, plenty of flexibility to compete at whatever, and it was all good advertising." She took a sip of her beer, was surprised to find it halfway gone, the alcohol giving her a low-grade buzz. "He wants me to take over the office work, build up the Internet sales, do some advertising. I've got a business degree, after all. But I don't know."

"It's not enough anymore?"

"The shop is huge. It's got tall ceilings, lofts, windows and doors everywhere. But when I'm in there, I can't breathe." She glanced sidelong at him. "And that's something I haven't told anyone else. Which I think makes us even."

His face was close, his eyes hard to read. But then the corners of his mouth tipped up in a sexy half smile and he angled the neck of his beer bottle toward her. "Then I'd like to propose a toast."

"Which is?" she asked, expecting something about life as a roller coaster, or how she should appreciate her family.

"To the strange and awesome powers of Mustang Ridge."

She blinked. "Excuse me?"

He nodded toward the party, where Wyatt and Krista sat at the edge of the crowd with a handful of the dude ranch's guests, all grubby and soot-streaked, but laughing like they were the best of friends, rather than just passing through for a week. "Wyatt has told me, over and over again, how people come off that bus enemies and leave friends, and how kids arrive not talking to anybody and wind up singing along at the bonfire. He'd be the first one to admit that he's a thousand times happier now than he was the first time he set foot on the ranch, and he's not the only one. So it seems to me that if you're ready to make some changes in your life, you came to the right place."

Grateful—that he understood, that he wasn't going to push—she tapped her bottle to his. "To Mustang Ridge."

Over the next couple of days, Danny attacked the personality quizzes with a vengeance, working her way through *What Kind of Donut Are You?*—a jelly-filled cruller covered in a hard chocolate shell, again with the barrier layer and the mushy insides—*What Is Your Myers-Briggs Animal?*—a cat, self-confident and a good listener, but overly private, needing her personal space, and not good with long-term commitment—and *What Is Your Superpower?*—time travel, which said she was a perfectionist, a planner, and a romantic.

She didn't know about that last one, but, hey, the goofier-the-better theory sort of implied the answers weren't all going to be spot-on. Besides, Farah hadn't promised lightning-bolt insights—she had thought Danny needed a new way of looking at things, something fun to push her outside her mental comfort zone. She also liked to say that when one rehab exercise got easy, it was time to switch it up to something else that wasn't nearly so comfortable, thus avoiding a plateau. Which was how Danny found herself setting aside *What Harry Potter Character Are You?* and *What's Your Favorite Medical Procedure?* and pulling out the tarot deck Farah had given her, instead. *Just go with the flow and relax,* Farah had instructed. *Shuffle until it feels right, then turn over the first card that calls to you.*

"Okay, okay. I'm shuffling." How would she know when it was right, though? It wasn't like there was an indicator light or a convenient *ding-ding-ding* sound to tell her when she was done.

A rustle brought her attention up just as two familiar bushy-tailed forms dropped from a tree onto the roof of the RV, and from there scampered down to the edge of the awning. Seeing that he had her attention, the bigger of the two flicked his tail and stomped his feet in the unintelligible—at least to her—squirrel dance that she had decided to consider a greeting.

"Howdy, Chuck. Hey, Popov." She had figured since they kept coming back, she might as well name them. "What do you think? Are my cards ready yet?"

Even as she asked the question, she fumbled the shuffle and a card fell out, tumbling to the table and skidding to a stop beside her laptop. Popov—smaller and reddish, and quicker to investigate than his companion—moved partway down the awning strut, attention fixed on the fallen card.

"Sorry," she said, snagging it. "And how many times do I have to tell you guys that I'm not going to feed you?" Though admittedly she couldn't police every crumb, which was probably why they stuck around. "Anyway. Let's see what the cards have in store for me today."

She flipped the card over, half expecting the Tower, which she was pretty sure symbolized change. Instead, she got a man and a woman in a full-body embrace and a title at the bottom: *The Lovers*.

"Whoa. That's . . . Hm." She wasn't sure how to feel about that one, especially when she'd caught herself thinking about Sam a few too many times since that night at the Sears place. Not that there was any reason *not* to think about him—he was as appealing in her mind's eye as he was in real life, with the bonus that she could stare without him knowing. She didn't want to lean, though, didn't want to get into anything serious when she needed to be working on herself. And she took her lovers seriously.

Grabbing her *Noobs Guide to Tarot*, she flipped through the table of contents, found the proper page, and read:

*Despite its name, the Lovers card isn't about romance, but rather relationships. In the positive, it speaks to intuitive choices and true connections. In the reverse, it refers to emotional conflict and contradictions. In a single-card spread, drawing the Lovers card suggests that it is time to make new connections.*

"Oh, okay. Phew." She leaned back in her chair and glanced over at Popov. "At least it's not trying to tell me that the next guy I see is going to be my soul mate."

Still, what it *was* saying bumped up against the low-grade urge she'd been fighting all day. She didn't need supplies, didn't have any real reason to head back over to Mustang Ridge, but she had a hankering to do exactly that. More, she had an open invitation, and Krista had offered her friendship. Which definitely counted as a new connection.

"Okay," she decided, gathering up the book and the deck of cards. "Sorry, guys, but you're on your own for the afternoon. Keep an eye on the place for me, will you? And don't even think of breaking into the RV and helping yourself to more candy!"

When Danny arrived at the ranch, the barn was abuzz with people and horses, and a group of guests were down in the arena, getting a roping lesson that seemed to involve lots of laughter and catcalls as they threw loops at wooden sawhorses decked out with plastic cow heads. Figuring that if Krista wasn't in her office, someone in the vicinity would know where she was, Danny headed for the main house, nodding to a mother and daughter pair in passing. Both fair-skinned, freckled redheads, they were wearing turquoise cowgirl shirts, sunburned noses, and matching vacation-happy expressions.

"Excuse me." The woman reached out and grazed her arm. "Do you work here?"

"Sorry, no." But Danny turned back. "Can I help you find someone?"

"Oh, no. It's not a crisis or anything. We were just wondering what kind of bird that is over there." She pointed to the far side of the lake, beyond the boathouse and floating duck to a cluster of trees.

It took Danny a second to pick out the big, hulking shadow perched near the trunk of a thick pine. "Wow, what is that, a pterodactyl?"

The woman laughed. "Okay, glad I'm not imagining things. When it flew over the boats, its shadow was huge!"

"I was afraid it was going to swoop down and eat me," the little girl announced.

Judging her to be a precocious six or seven, Danny said, "Actually, there wouldn't be much danger. It's a buzzard, and they're mostly scavengers."

"It eats dead things? *Ew!*"

"Not *ew*," Danny said. "Cool! Their stomach acid is so strong that they can eat stuff that's real old and rotten, which means they help stop other animals from getting sick. And they can glide for miles and miles without flapping their wings."

"Okay, that is cool," the mom agreed. "What do you say, Siobhan?"

"Thank you. What about that one?" The girl pointed to a soaring silhouette that was little more than a dot in the sky.

Danny squinted. "A hawk, probably. Maybe a red-tail? They're pretty common around here. You know how on TV and the movies, whenever you see an eagle, the sound track has that *scree-aaahh, scree-aaahh* noise? That's actually the sound of a red-tailed hawk, not an eagle."

"Wow, you know a lot about birds." Siobhan peered up at her. "Are you an orthodontist?"

"I think you mean ornithologist." Stifling a laugh, Danny gave her points for trying. "Nope, just someone who loves being outdoors, and enjoys knowing about the places I visit. Kind of like you, huh?"

They shared a grin.

"Okay," Siobhan's mom said. "Now that we've got that settled, what do you say we go get cleaned up for dinner, and let this nice lady get where she was going when we shanghaied her for the bird edition of twenty questions? Say thank you first, though."

"G'bye! Thanks!"

As they headed off, the mom waved and mouthed, *Thank you!*

Amused by the exchange, Danny continued on her way to the main house, only to catch sight of Krista emerging from the barn with a couple of coiled-up ropes in her hands, Abby in her baby sling, and a scruffy gray dog trotting at her heels. Changing her course, Danny headed over to intercept.

Krista's face lit up. "Look who's here, Abby! It's our resident hermit. Only she's not being so much of a hermit this week, is she?"

"I hope you don't mind," Danny said.

"Don't be silly! In fact, if you're sick of the RV, there's an apartment over the barn with your name on it. Just say the word."

"I couldn't."

"You could and should." Krista grinned. "But you're happy where you are, so you won't. The offer's open, though."

"Thank you. Seriously."

"I'm being selfish, of course. I'd like to see more of you, and Jenny's dying to get together as soon as she gets home. Which, for the record, is the day after tomorrow."

The gray dog bounced up on his hind legs and grabbed at one of the ropes.

"Klepto, don't you dare. Give that back." Lowering her voice to a *this means business* tone, she said, "Drop it, mister."

He released the rope instantly and plopped down on his shaggy butt to lift his paw endearingly.

"Ha!" Krista said. "Don't believe him for a second. He may look all cute and innocent, but this morning he ate my corn muffin and hid my keys." She ruffled the fur on his head, though, suggesting she wasn't holding much of a grudge.

"That's better than the other way around," Danny pointed out.

"I suppose." A calculating look crossed her face. "You could use a dog out there in the valley, right?"

"Oh, no you don't. I've already got a pair of squir-rels looking to rob me blind. I don't need a dog to help them do it."

"Worth a try." Krista shrugged. "Besides, Wyatt and Abby would miss Klepto. Wouldn't you, baby?" After giving the squirming sling a quick one-handed snuggle, she tipped her head. "Come on. Junior needs a couple more coils for roping practice."

As they headed toward the arena, a generously pad-ded fortysomething guy whooped and did a couple of celebratory booty pops at having gotten his lasso around one of the sawhorse cows.

There was a smattering of applause, and as she hung the spare ropes on the fence, Krista called, "Looks like the first round is on Rudy tonight!"

"You know it!" he agreed cheerfully, and the others laughed.

"The drinks are included in their stays, of course," Krista said as they moved off. "The ropers get special cupcakes tonight, though, complete with little lassos."

"You've got a great setup here," Danny said. "The guests always seem to be having such a good time."

"Thanks. We work at it, but we also seem to attract the right sort of people. Just lucky, I guess."

"My dad always says luck is ninety percent prepara-tion."

"Sounds like a smart guy." A burbling chirp rose up from the vicinity of Krista's hip. She held up a finger, patted the spot, and pulled out her phone. "Sorry. I'm waiting for a call. Give me a second?" At Danny's nod, she took the call. "Martin, hi. Did you hear back from your grandson?"

Danny wandered off a little way and watched as the roping practice shifted, with the guests now trying to lasso each other, with lots of ducking and laughter involved.

"Well, drat," Krista said, her disappointment clear. "No, that's okay. It's not the end of the world. I just wish . . . Well, anyway. Thanks for trying. If you think of anybody else, let me know, okay?"

A moment later, she came up beside Danny, smiling as Rudy made finger-horns on his head and pawed the ground, daring his partner to rope him. The stress crinkles remained at the corners of her eyes, though.

Danny hesitated, then said, "Something wrong?"

"Not wrong, exactly, it's just . . ." Krista sighed. "It's the Sears rebuild. They're working on the main house this week, skilled labor only, and my dad really wants to help with the wiring . . . but we need him here."

"For repairs?"

She shook her head. "No, we could work around that. It's the wilderness treks. He's in charge of entertaining the folks who don't want to ride on a given day, or at least offering them an alternative."

"Like bird-watching?" Danny asked, thinking of Siobhan and her mom.

Krista nodded. "Fishing, nature hikes, canoeing . . . Whatever he feels like offering, really. Unless we get a special request, I leave it up to him. A couple of years ago, I could have skipped the treks for a few weeks. But they're too popular now, and we've got repeat visitors who are coming with their families, expecting to have options." Her expression went rueful. "He's not pushing me, mind you—I'm the one who's pushing. I know he wants to go, and I know the rebuilding project could use him, but it's too late in the season to find a qualified guide and I can't hand the guests over to just anybody."

"What about me?"

Krista eyed her, but then shook her head. "You're a sweetheart to offer, but come on. You don't really want to hang out with the guests, do you? Five hours a day, five days a week for the next month, maybe longer? That's not what you signed on for."

No, it wasn't. But Danny didn't hate the idea as much as she would've expected—she was kind of intrigued, actually. Not to mention that it would be a way for her to balance the scales. "I can do the job. My family's shop offers hikes and guided bike rides during the summer for the tourists, and I did that stint with *Jungle Love*, helping keep the singles safe on their bungee-jumping and zip-lining dates."

"That's not the point. You're on *vacation*, girlfriend!"

"Which means I get to do what I want, right? And I want to help out." More than she would have expected, really. She was supposed to be stepping outside her comfort zone, after all, and trying something new, so this fit. "That is, if you'll have me? I know I'm not a local, but I've studied the flora and fauna, and gotten pretty familiar with the trails. I can do more reading, talk to your dad about fishing the river, and—"

"If I'll have you?" Krista's voice went up in a gratifying squeak.

"I know you don't know me very well—"

"Danny, seriously?" A broad grin split her face. "You'd do it?"

"I want to do it." Enough that a prickle of excitement

ran through her body and her head was suddenly full of ideas—plant hikes, bird-watching scavenger hunts, forays out to see the mustangs in Blessing Valley. "Come on. What do you say?"

With a whoop, Krista flung her arms around Danny's neck. "I say welcome to the team!"

# 7

On Wednesday, Sam gave Axyl, Midas, and Murph the day off, locked himself in the mansion, booted up Legend of Zelda in the game room, and let himself fall into the fantasy world that had been a long-ago birthday present, secondhand yet beloved.

The hours blurred as he worked his way up the levels, killing bad guys and gathering coins and spells. "Ha!" he said over the *bloop-dee-boop* music. "Gotcha!" Then, as a three-headed green alien-thing closed in on him, he worked the controller, ducking and weaving his body, even though the old-school tech didn't translate the movements on-screen. "Take that. And *that*!"

"Yo!" Wyatt's voice called from the kitchen. "Hey, Sam. You in here?" The game gave off a *bloop-diddly-beep*, and he chuckled. "Right." Boot steps moved from tile to hardwood, and he came through the door saying, "If he's in the house and not asleep, then he's in the game room."

Eyes glued to the screen, Sam said, "Everything okay at the ranch?"

Wyatt propped a hip on the battered couch that still

had the same duct tape patch it had worn back in college, when they had shared an apartment. "Yeah. Why?"

"I locked up. Figured you wouldn't have busted in unless there was a good reason."

"If you really wanted your space, you would've snagged the spare key out from under the mat."

On-screen, Sam splatted a couple of flying snakes, wishing he could make Wyatt disappear that easily. "I'm not really in the mood for company."

"Too bad, because you've got some." Wyatt was carrying a couple of beers he'd grabbed from the kitchen. Holding one out, he said, "To living on the edge."

A sword-wielding skeleton stabbed Sam's on-screen character in the gut, and damned if there wasn't something wonky going on, because the *doop-doop-diddly* became a death knell and the screen filled with two of his least favorite words: GAME OVER.

He glared at the screen. "What the hell was *that*?"

Wyatt took the controller out of Sam's hand and replaced it with the beer. "A hint that you're ready for a time-out."

"I was on Level Seven."

"Now you're back in the real world." Wyatt tapped his longneck against Sam's and took a swallow.

Sam exhaled. "If I drink my beer, will you go away?"

"Want to go for a ride?"

"What I *want* is to be left alone."

"Come on, slacker. Let's go pound some rocks out back. Unless you want to head out to the garage and finish up that project of yours?"

Sam glared. "I don't want to do a damn thing. I want

to be left alone." Then, because it was the sort of thing they never said to each other, he added, "Please."

Wyatt studied him for a minute, then said, "You're not going to do anything stupid, right?"

"I'm going to play Zelda for the next twelve hours straight." Until today became tomorrow.

His buddy set his beer on a precarious stack of magazines on a side table. "Are you sure?"

"It's tradition." The one day a year he let himself crawl back down into the hole.

"Doesn't mean it's a good one."

"It works for me." Sam set his mostly full beer aside. "Seriously. Thanks for checking on me, but I need space more than I need a babysitter."

He didn't know what part of that got through, but Wyatt finally gave a slow nod. "Call if you change your mind. Or just come on over. It's chili night."

"Will do," Sam said, though he wouldn't. He just wanted to get back to his game. Once Wyatt's footsteps faded away, though, and he heard the lock turn in the kitchen door—*very funny*—he had a hard time settling back into his groove. "Oh, come on!" he growled when he stumbled over a grave and lost points to a ghost. "He didn't even touch me!" But the damage was done, and the next hit finished him off.

GAME OVER.

Cursing, he shoved to his feet and used the remote to kill the screen. Suddenly needing to move, like his body had just figured out he'd been on his ass for way too long, he headed out through the kitchen to the side yard, where Yoshi stood by the barn with his head up and his ears pricked. "Hey, buddy. You want to cover some ground? I'm sick of sitting still."

"There's the ranch!" Christy Trimmer tugged on her father's arm. "See? And there's Gran out on the porch, waving. She must be waiting for us to make the salad!"

Sloan Trimmer patted his young daughter's head, meeting Danny's smile with one of his own. "I see her, pumpkin. Do you want to run ahead and tell her what we've got?"

"Do you remember all the names?" Danny put in.

The little girl—curly-haired and happy, with a seemingly limitless supply of energy—screwed up her face in concentration. "We've got dandelion leaves, wild onions, amaranth, and yellow sss . . ." She pursed her lips. "Yellow satisfy?"

"Close! It's salsify."

"Salsity."

"Sal-si-fy." When Christy repeated the syllables, Danny gave her a high five. "Okay, go on. We'll catch up in a minute. And no running near the horses!" She had to shout the last couple of words, because Christy was off like a shot, her gathering bag bouncing furiously with every pounding stride.

"Hope Gran doesn't mind bruised onions," Sloan drawled. Lean and Texan, the handsome businessman obviously adored his wife and two daughters—so much so that he was vacationing at a dude ranch, despite being violently allergic to horses. Which meant he and Danny had gotten to know each other pretty well over the past four days.

"They'll still taste good," she assured him. Besides, she had the bulk of their haul in her own pack.

"I've never done a hike-and-gather before." He shook his head in admiration. "It's amazing how many things out there actually have some nutritional value."

"Like those wild strawberries!" added Liza May—a bubbly salesclerk from Tucson who had opted to hike today so her rear end could have a break from the saddle. "They didn't taste anything like the ones at the stores near me."

Behind her, the other two members of their party— Liza May's equally bubbly friend Dee, and Stockbroker Simon from California—nodded in happy agreement. Despite having been out for a solid six hours, walking along the river almost all the way to Blessing Valley and back, the hikers were in high spirits, excited about the idea of consuming the edible plants Danny had helped them find along the trail.

"Just remember," she cautioned, "there are plenty of other things out there that'll make you seriously ill, or worse, and some of the good plants look an awful lot like the toxic ones, and vice versa. So no nibbling unless you're absolutely sure!"

"Only when you're there to tell us it's okay!" Dee promised. "Which means you're going to have to give us your phone number so we can send you pictures and stuff."

Danny pulled the main gathering bag from her knapsack, and held it out. "Who wants to bring the rest of our harvest in to Gran? She said she'd show folks how to prepare our greens, if you're interested."

"Ooh!" Liza May snagged the bag. "I'm in!" She

whirled away, with Dee bouncing beside her. After a moment, Stockbroker Simon followed.

Tipping a straw cowboy hat that would never get within twenty feet of a horse, Sloan drawled, "It's been a pleasure as always, Miz Traveler. See you tomorrow down by the boat shed at eleven?"

"I'll be there!"

As he headed after the others, she hung back, enjoying both the feeling of a job well done and a moment of quiet in the midst of the hustle-bustle of the ranch.

"Danny, hey!" Krista came out of the barn, cradling the baby's sling with one hand and waving with the other. "You're back! How did it go?"

"Good, I think." Danny offered Abby a finger. "Hey, kiddo. That's a good grip you've got there."

"All the better to hold the reins with, my dear." Krista grinned. "So . . . Hunt Your Own Salad Day? That was brilliant. Seriously genius. You should've heard the riders talking about it out on the trail, trying to figure out what your group was going to come up with for dinner."

"Onions, some wild berries, and lots of furry greens that I'm sure Gran will turn into something awesome."

"You're going to eat with us, right?" Seeing the answer in Danny's eyes, Krista urged, "Oh, come on. Stay. How can you bag out on your own salad? If you're worried about making the ride home after dark, you're welcome to crash in the apartment over the barn."

It wasn't the first night she had made the offer. But it was the first time Danny was tempted. Still, it had been a long day, and she had an hour or so commute on the ATV ahead of her. "Rain check?"

"Sure thing. How about Saturday? Jenny is dying to reconnect, Shelby wants to meet you, and I need to get into town to pick up a few things for the wedding. We'll make a day of it. I can get Mom and Gran to cover orientation for the new guests, and Abby can help Wyatt in the barn." She gave the cloth-covered lump a fond pat. "Us girls will grab lunch, hit a few stores, maybe find some trouble to get into. . . . How does that sound?"

"Is sounds good, actually. Fun."

"Perfect! We'll leave around ten, right after the airport shuttle rolls out."

"It's a date." Danny gave the baby a little finger wiggle. "And I'm out of here."

"You sure you don't want to stay for a Trailside Salad?"

"Is that what you're calling it?"

"Gran figured it sounded better than 'Stuff We're Pretty Sure Is Edible.'"

"Hey! I'm a hundred percent sure. But I'm still leaving." Danny headed for the ATV and fired up the engine, returning Krista's wave before she headed out along the two-lane dirt track that led up the ridgeline. And unlike the first few days of her stint as Ed Skye's replacement trekking boss, it didn't feel like a huge weight fell away when she passed the marker stones.

Instead, she felt . . . normal. And that had been a long time coming.

The slow summer evening stretched the shadows around her as she rolled back to Blessing Valley, her mind pleasantly empty. There was no sign of the mustangs near the canyon mouth, suggesting that they were watering down at the other end of the valley. Or so she thought, until she rolled into camp and saw a spotted horse grazing on the other side of the river. "Well," she said as she killed the engine. "What are you doing here?"

"He's with me," a voice said from the shadows beneath the awning. "Or maybe it's the other way around." Sam stood and came out into the light. He was wearing a T-shirt, worn jeans, and a stubble shadow, and there was a layer of strain evident beneath his greeting. "We were in the area. Hope you don't mind."

"No, of course not. It's good to see you." Which was the absolute truth. It suddenly didn't matter that she had been going hard since dawn, or that she had come back to the valley for some alone time. She had wanted him there, she realized, on some level had imagined him waiting for her like this, though without the sadness in the back of his eyes. "Are you hungry? I was going to put together some dinner and watch the sun go down."

"I'd rather walk a bit. Would you mind?"

She had spent most of the day hiking and had been looking forward to a glass of wine and a pretty sunset. The wine could wait, though, and the sunset would follow them. "Come on." She held out a hand. "We can visit Jupiter and the herd."

Sam hadn't planned on heading for Blessing Valley, and once he got there and found the campsite deserted, he hadn't really meant to wait for Danny. But the first sight of her coming up the trail toward him on her four-wheeler had loosened something inside him, and as they hiked along the riverbank, he was glad he'd stuck around. "Have a good run on the ATV?" he asked, breaking the companionable silence.

"I feel a little bad burning the gas, but it's a pretty commute."

He glanced over. "Come again?"

"I'm working over at Mustang Ridge now." She dimpled adorably. "Ed Skye wanted to help rebuild the Sears house, but Krista needed him to entertain the guests who opt out of riding. The next thing I knew, I was strapping on my hiking boots, updating my GPS, and speed-reading my copy of *Edible Plants of the Plains*."

"You sound happy about it."

"I'm enjoying it more than I expected." She turned away from the riverbank to follow a narrow game trail. "This way." There was a new lightness to her, a confident bounce in her step.

Intrigued by the changes, he followed her up a rocky incline to a flat ledge that hung suspended about halfway up the canyon wall. Blessing Valley spread out in front of them, rugged and green, and a handful of horses stood at the edge of the river.

As he moved up beside her, she whispered, "Aren't they beautiful?"

He stared at her profile. "Gorgeous."

Still watching the horses, she said, "So. Are you going to tell me what's wrong?"

"I'm fine."

"I'm sure you are. But that doesn't mean there isn't something wrong." She tapped her own forehead. "Takes a tough guy to know a tough guy. Tough guy."

Down below, horses milled and shifted by the river's edge, and several more drifted out of the trees. He recognized Jupiter by her dark gray dapples and the way she studied her surroundings before she moved to the water's edge and stretched her neck to drink, trusting the others to keep watch, if only briefly.

Attention caught by a pearlescent glint in his peripheral vision, Sam crouched, sifted his fingers through the chewed-up schist at the edge of the ledge they were standing on, and came up with a pinkie-size sliver of pink quartz. Thin and translucent, it had a thick white crack running through the middle, shaped like a lightning bolt.

Rising, he held it out. "It's not perfect. Still pretty, though."

Her fingers brushed his palm as she took it. She studied the flawed stone, then him. "You've got a good eye."

"That, and decent luck when it comes to finding gems. Not so much with other stuff." He stuck his hands in his pockets and looked out over the river, then surprised himself by asking, "How much did Gran tell you about my dad?"

If she was startled by the change of subject, she didn't show it. "She said he was a popular guy, and that the only thing he loved more than prospecting was you."

Ah, hell. Chest gone tight, he said, "And my mom. He loved her more than anything, I think. He never remarried, never even really dated. He used to talk to her all the time, too, like she was still there. On special days—my birthday, their anniversary—we'd go to the cemetery, leave a couple of our best stones, and tell her what we'd been up to. Just checking in, you know? Usually, it was all about how I was doing in school, or the jobs he'd been doing in the shop. Then we found the diamonds."

"And everything changed," she said. Because of course she knew firsthand how fast the world could shift on its axis, for better or worse.

He nodded. "Things sped up, got complicated. Dad and I started the business, got into the eco-friendly R and D side of things, broke ground at Windfall. . . . After a while, though, it started feeling like it was all complicated, all business, so we decided to buy ourselves a couple of presents to go along with the work. I designed a game room for the new house, with plenty of bells and whistles, and he decided to upgrade his motorcycle from an old beater to a new Harley."

Danny's quick indrawn breath said she'd made the connection.

"I was a stupid kid," he continued. "High on striking it rich. I told him he had to buy the biggest, baddest machine in the place, the new V-Rod, instead of the touring bike he had his eye on." One that would've ridden more like the bike he'd been tooling around on for years. "He'd only had it for a week when he missed the corner at Hangman's Curve and went over the guardrail." His voice was flat, his blood gone cold. "I don't even know why he was on that road. He always told me to stay off it, that it was a killer." He looked over at Danny, pretty sure he didn't deserve the sympathy he saw in her big brown eyes. "That was eight years ago today."

Suddenly, his watch gave the little double beep that said *Right this moment eight years ago, Officer Blundt called to say, "I'm sorry to tell you this, son, but there's been an accident."* Always before, the *beep-beep* had brought him back to that moment—the wrenching grief, the disbelief.

Not this year, though. This year, the *beep-beep* spurred him to action, telling him to get on with it and take what he wanted. What he thought they both wanted. So, as the noise faded, he leaned in and kissed Danny like it made all the sense in the world. Which it suddenly did.

Sam's lips were firm, his cheeks and chin stubbled, and those big, beautiful hands came up to frame Danny's face as his lips claimed hers and his tongue slid in to touch, taste. Take. He tasted of grief and a sharp edge of loneliness that reached inside her and made her yearn. But at the same time the kiss lit her system, hammering heat into her veins.

Maybe she should have been surprised by the kiss, definitely by the timing, but they had been headed this way since he first yelled at her and she beaned him with that paperback. And death had a way of stripping away pretenses.

He had come to her, needed her.

Tenderness swept through her even as her neurons hummed as if she were climbing and had her belay ropes strung too tight. Not just because he was a heck of a kisser, but because it was *Sam*.

He shifted against her, slanted his mouth across hers and kissed her again, then again, their bodies straining together at the edge of a long, hard fall. Her pulse hammered in her ears; his thrummed beneath her fingertips when she touched his temple, his throat, the hollow of his collarbone.

"Danny," he said as he broke the kiss, his voice a

harsh rasp that sent new vibrations down her nerve endings. "I'm—"

"Don't you dare apologize." She didn't want to hear that he hadn't meant to kiss her, that it had been just a meaningless impulse.

"Trust me, that's the last thing on my mind." He cupped her face in those big, rough-palmed hands. "But I really hadn't planned on making a move today. I didn't even mean to come here. It all just sort of happened. I don't want to rush things."

She wrapped her fingers around his wrists and felt his solid strength. "I'm glad you did. And I'm good at catching up." Even better at deciding how far she was willing to go, how deep she wanted to get.

He pressed his forehead to hers. "When can I see you again? Officially this time. Drinks, dinner, the works."

Pleasure spun through her, but she said, "Honestly? I'd rather play with your rocks."

His laughter echoed off the surrounding stones. "You've definitely been talking to Gran."

"I have, and she's got me intrigued." Plus, she was more interested in Sam the prospector than Sam the rich guy. "Take me rock hunting. Pretty please. I want to see what it's all about."

# 8

On Saturday, Danny got to Mustang Ridge early enough to get a farewell strangle-hug from Christy and turn down a too-big tip from Sloan while Krista, Gran, and Rose led a conga line onto the shuttle bus, keeping the guests laughing and clowning around like they were just arriving for their vacations rather than leaving. Danny's ears were ringing by the time the shuttle doors closed, and part of her said, *Phew, peace and quiet.* But when she stood with the others, waving as the bus headed up the driveway, she felt a definite pang.

"Well?" Krista said. "What do you think after week one? Are you ready to head for the hills?"

Making a show of clearing out one ear, Danny said, "Well, they were a little loud there toward the end . . ."

*"Danny!"* The whoop came from the other side of the parking lot, where a brunette flung herself out of a barely stopped Jeep. "You're here! I can't believe you're actually here!"

"Speaking of loud," Gran drawled good-naturedly.

"Jenny!" Danny laughed as Krista's twin, who was identical except for having short, dyed-dark hair and a sharper edge to her jeans-and-boots outfit, bulleted toward her. They met in a quick, excited hug.

"And here's Shelby!" Krista said as a sleek black sedan pulled in. Moments later, a woman emerged and headed their way.

With scarlet lipstick and painted nails, the newcomer might've been intimidating if it weren't for her wide, friendly smile and the way she reached out as she approached. "Danny! I can't believe we haven't met yet. Foster says the guests adored you. You're so wonderful to help out!"

Not sure which of those statements to focus on first, Danny returned the other woman's hand-clasp-cheek-kiss. "It's lovely to meet you!" She had been looking forward to this, too, after hearing Krista's stories about Shelby giving up a lucrative advertising career in Boston to marry Mustang Ridge's head wrangler and stay in Wyoming with her young daughter.

Shelby spun away to do quick hugs-and-kisses with Krista and Jenny, then announced dramatically, "You wouldn't *believe* the week I've had!"

"Let's hit the road," Jenny urged. "You can tell us on the way into town."

They piled into her Jeep, with Danny riding shotgun. She didn't know if Krista had done that on purpose—she'd had to 'fess up about the claustrophobia when it came to getting the canoe paddles out from their small, dark storage space beneath the boathouse—or if it had just worked out that way, but she was grateful to be able to crack the window and stretch out her legs.

"Let me guess, Shelby," Krista said. "Your week from hell involved the Burpee Baby account."

The other woman gave a dramatic shudder. "I knew I was in trouble the minute the client, Amanda, said she had lined up a dozen of her best customers and their little ones for the shoot, and that her husband would be taking the photos. That should've been my cue to exit stage left, let them flail, and then, after the fact, hire professionals to do it right. But—silly me—I sympathize that she's on a budget, and the setup sounded like it had the potential to be cute. So I caved when she asked me to direct the shoot."

"And wound up covered in drool while juggling screaming human larvae?" suggested Jenny, earning a whack from her sister, who had texted Wyatt twice in the past half hour to check on Abby.

"The babies weren't the problem," Shelby said. "It was the *mothers*. Every one of them wanted her special darling front and center of the shot, and a few of them didn't care what it took." She rolled her eyes. "I even caught one of them making scary faces at the baby sitting next to hers, trying to make it cry. And Amanda's husband was no help. He just sat in a corner, surfing the Web on his phone and waiting for us to get the shot set up the way we wanted."

"Sounds to me like the photog was the sanest one in the group," Jenny put in. "As usual."

"Anyway," Shelby said, "some of the moms got pretty annoyed when I started saying stuff like, 'What in God's name did you feed that kid this morning?' and 'No, we're not changing little Suzie's outfit six more times and doing some solo shots for her portfolio, but I'm happy to give you Jenny Skye's contact info if you want to do a studio session.'"

"Gee, thanks," Jenny drawled.

"What are friends for? In the end, though, we got the shots we needed for the print ads and online push we're planning for good old Burpee's Babies. Best of all, nobody looking at those angelic little faces will ever know that the photo was snapped in the single split second between little Billy picking his nose and baby Aimee projectile-vomiting on that cute little stuffed dog she's holding."

Krista nodded. "Kind of like how, when you look at a horse-for-sale ad, you have to assume that the picture shows the horse on his best day ever, and might or might not be from this decade."

"Or online dating," Jenny put in, "where it's fifty-fifty whether a guy's profile picture bears any resemblance to the person who knocks on your door. Or so Ruth tells me."

Remembering what Jenny had told her about her veterinarian husband's admin assistant—purple-haired, sixtysomething, and in love with life—Danny said, "I thought she was dating Nick's father."

Jenny nodded. "True, but she's taken up mate-shopping for her friends."

"The Bingo ladies?" Krista asked, amused.

"You betcha. A few of the guys, too. She loves browsing, and they're grateful that they don't have to wade through all the ads and figure out the hidden red flags. She'll even help with the first couple of e-mails, though they're on their own for the actual dating stuff."

Shelby leaned back in her seat. "I am profoundly grateful that I don't have to worry about that anymore."

"Hear, hear," Krista seconded, and Jenny gave a fervent nod.

Then they all looked at Danny. Even Jenny, who was driving.

She put up both hands. "Don't look at me. Online dating is the last thing on my wish list."

"So what *is* on your wish list?" Shelby asked with a wicked glitter.

"A perfect dress for me to wear to Krista's wedding. So give me some hints here. Are we talking evening-wear, ruffled calico, or what?"

"Ha!" Jenny hooted. "Subject change on Aisle Five!"

"And quite neatly done, too," Shelby said. "Especially when it brings up something we really do need to discuss." Fixing Krista with a look, she lowered her voice to intone, "Because *someone* doesn't have her wedding dress yet, which makes it awfully difficult to nail down the theme."

"She . . . Really?" Danny gawked at Krista.

"Yes, really," Shelby confirmed.

"It'll be fine," Krista said firmly. "I'll find something, but I'm going to do it on my terms. I've let Mom have her way with the decorations, but there's no way I'm letting her pick out my dress. You should see some of the things she's bookmarked on my computer." She shuddered. "They're like bad cake toppers come to life." But there was a lick of panic in her eyes.

"I hate to be the one to point it out," Jenny said, "since I'm usually the one who gets Mom going, but you may be cutting off your nose to spite your face on this one. It's one thing to prove that you can have an awesome wedding without custom making everything and spending a gazillion dollars—especially, hello, when you own the perfect venue. But if you don't find a dress soon, you're going to be getting married in jeans and a Mustang Ridge polo shirt."

"This is Krista and Wyatt we're talking about," Shelby pointed out. "I could totally see them getting married in their riding clothes. Though I reserve the right to bling the heck out of mine."

"No bling on the pockets or inseam," Jenny cautioned. "It scratches the hell out of the saddle."

Shelby nodded solemnly. "So noted."

"What I don't get," Jenny said, "is why you didn't drag us all into Laramie for the full-on *Say Yes to the Dress* experience five seconds after Wyatt proposed. I mean, you always wanted to play wedding when we were kids, right down to sneaking Great-Gramma Abby's lace tablecloth out of the sideboard to use as a veil. I would've thought you'd be rabid for a full-on princess dress."

"I was four months pregnant when Wyatt proposed," Krista said drily. "That's not exactly the right time to be trying on form-fitting dresses if you don't enjoy looking like a satin-covered sausage link."

"You weren't that huge, and corset backs are pretty forgiving."

"It's not that I'm *not* going to get a dress." Krista scowled at the road ahead. "I just haven't found one yet. I'm looking, though, and I'll know it when I see it."

"Have you asked Bootsy?" Shelby asked. "I know she runs the tack store, but she sells plenty of clothes, too, and she's got some serious style. She might have catalogs you could look through."

"Been there, done that, too many doilies and ruffles. It's like the Western wear designers hear 'bridal' and head straight for the 1800s, and not in a good way." Krista shook her head. "Nope. I want something casual and comfortable, but that still says I'm the bride. Bonus points for pockets."

Jenny snorted. "For what, your keys? Maybe a couple of sugar cubes?"

"Oh, shut up. It's the principle." To Danny, she said, "As far as what you should wear, that's up to you. You're feeling floor-length sequins? Go for it. You'd rather rock a sundress? That works, too. Heck, jeans and hiking boots are fine by me. I just want you to be there and enjoy yourself."

"Which is why we're here," Jenny said cheerfully to Danny. "Along with wanting to hang out with you, that is. Because the way we see it, a wedding is a wedding, and that involves getting dolled up. So you're getting a dress whether you like it or not."

"But that doesn't have to mean lace. For a little Western town, Three Ridges has some decent shopping options." Shelby pointed to a storefront as Jenny pulled into a parking spot right by the front door. "Welcome to Another Fyne Thing!"

The wide main street had lines of cars parked on both sides and some bustling sidewalk foot traffic. Most of the storefronts were squat and square, with facades that seemed to be channeling an old gold-rush town, or maybe the set of a spaghetti Western. There was a saloon called Spurr's Bar and Grill, a bookstore-slash-teashop called Read Me/Eat Me, and a whole lot of tourists in brand-new boots and Stetsons, mixed in with locals in their battered counterparts. The scene reminded Danny of Mustang Ridge, really, with tourist amenities layered on top of sturdy old structures that had seen the heyday of the cattle boom. Like the Disney version of the Wild West.

Seeing the magic words painted on the wide glass windows of Another Fyne Thing—UNIQUE VINTAGE AND REPURPOSED ITEMS—Danny grinned, relieved that they weren't headed for froufrou bridal land. "Rock on with the recycling!"

"I told you Danny is our kind of girl." Jenny hooked an arm through hers. "Come on! Let's see what Della's got on the racks today." She shot a glittering look back at Krista. "Who knows? Maybe you'll find a nice shiny polyester wedding dress with poufy shoulders, lots of sequins, and hoops you could fit a pony under. Mom would have a cow."

"I'm not doing this to torture her," Krista practically wailed. "I swear!"

A small brass bell gave a cheerful *ding-a-ling* when they opened the door and piled through, with Shelby calling, "Yoo-hoo, Della. Trouble's here!"

The store was bigger than it looked from the outside, with high, airy ceilings and thick beams that made Danny think it might have been a warehouse or factory at some point in the past. Now, though, the beams were wrapped with shirts and capris tacked up in disembodied hugs and high kicks, and mismatched sneakers hung from cables high above, dangling from their tied-together laces. One wall held a rack of hats and boots, another a long line of full-length dresses topped with signs like CATTLEMAN'S BALL, FLOWING AND FLIRTY, and

DATE NIGHT. The center of the space overflowed with circular racks of hanging clothes, bookcases filled with folded jeans and paired-up shoes, and a glass-topped counter that held jewelry and a register.

The bell was still doing its *ding-a-ling* thing when a perky brunette in her late teens bounced through a doorway on the hat wall, wearing a screaming purple tank top, a ruffled skirt, and a pair of old-school leather hiking boots. "Mom's on the phone," she announced at top volume, like she was shouting over music that the others couldn't hear. "She said she'll be out in a minute, and you guys should make yourselves at home."

Shelby inflated her lungs as if to holler back, then grinned and exhaled before saying in a normal voice, "Thanks, Tiffany. We're looking for stuff to wear to a wedding. Any suggestions?"

"A dress, maybe? They're over here." She led them to the wall, stopping between SASSY SUNDRESSES and DATE NIGHT. "Would you like to try some on?"

"I think we'll look through them first," Jenny said solemnly. "But then, yeah. Try-ons would be good."

The teen waved vaguely to a curtained-off area in the corner, near where long mirrors were hung intentionally crooked and a row of secondhand boots sat beneath a long wooden bench. "Yell if I can help you with anything else."

"Will do," Krista said, giving a good-humored eye roll as the girl drifted off to the front of the store, where she stood staring out at the foot traffic like a kid who'd been grounded and couldn't go out and play.

Shelby dove into the racks, going straight for RED CARPET and hooting when she pulled out a sequined gold dress that was backless and most of the way front-less, with little more than two narrow strips covering the non-PG territory. "Take a look at this one! It looks like all its fabric slid south."

"Don't even think about wearing it to the wedding," Jenny advised. "Mom would make you put an apron on over it."

Shelby pretended to consider it. "The cute one Gran's got with the dancing peppers on it would make a statement, don't you think?"

"If the statement you're going for is 'I cook naked,' maybe."

"Hm."

Deciding she wasn't getting into that debate, Danny went for the sundresses, but found them more tie-dyed than sassy, at least for her taste. "Okay, Date Night it is," she announced, and moved down a rack.

"What about Fun and Flirty?" Krista asked from a little farther down, where she was holding up a suede-fringed denim jacket in a full-length mirror.

"We'll see. I'm not sure I'm that kind of girl."

"Hey, you're on vacation. You can be whatever kind of girl you want to be."

"You should use that in your advertising."

"We do, sort of," Shelby said. Holding up a ball gown that had peacock feathers sewn onto it, fanning from a narrow point at her crotch to a full spray across the bodice and shoulders, she added, "What do you think?"

"That you look like the NBC logo," Jenny said with a mock scowl. "And that you're not taking this seriously. What gives? When Nick and I got married, you took one look at my dress, gave me three options for your and Krista's maid-of-honor dresses, and told me to pick one."

"Yeah, but you had a dress I could use as a starting point." Shelby made an evil face. "I'll buckle down when Krista does."

"Hey! No fair." Krista hung the fringed jacket on a nearby coat hook that bore a sign reading COOL THINGS I'M GOING TO TRY ON. "I've got everything under control. The menu is set, the cake is ordered, and the gazebo is finished. I've even got my vows written!"

"But no dress."

"Oh, shut up." Looking a little frantic, she turned to Danny as if to enlist support. But then she did a double take at the dress she was holding up. "Ooh, pretty!"

"You think?" Danny stroked the vivid blue-green fabric, enjoying the subtle diamond pattern and the way the Grecian-style top had a strap over one shoulder, but left the other bare.

"Absolutely." Jenny held up her hands and formed a square shape with her thumbs and index fingers, as if framing her for a photo shoot. "Look how it picks up the lights of your skin and the darks of your hair and eyes."

"Thus speaks the photog," Shelby intoned. Then she grinned. "But she's totally right. Here." She nudged Danny toward the mirror Krista had been using. "Check it out."

Danny obligingly put herself in front of the mirror. And stared.

The rehab hospital had been plastered with shiny, reflective surfaces, like it would've been counterproductive for the patients to forget that they were pale, pasty versions of themselves. Even back home, she had felt wan and drained. But now . . . "Wow." It was a whisper, little more than a breath.

Krista came up beside her in the mirror, her eyes kind, as if she got that this wasn't just about the dress. "You'll look amazing in it."

Danny didn't know about that, but all of a sudden she was herself again. She recognized the gypsy-dark ringlets that had driven her crazy until they went flat and lifeless, the familiar lines of muscle in shoulders that had been thin and wasted. And, most of all, she saw the spark that had been missing, the healthy tan and the restrained energy that said she was poised to move at a moment's notice, ready to try anything.

Maybe it was a different "anything" now. But at least it was something.

"You have *got* to try that on." Shelby propelled her toward the curtained-off corner. "And it's a Girl Zone rule that you have to come out and show us, even if it looks completely whack."

"*Especially* if it looks whack," Jenny clarified, pretending to get her phone ready to take a picture. Or, quite possibly, not pretending at all.

"Okay, okay." Danny threw up her hands. "But the first person to shove a pair of nosebleed heels under the door is going to be eating them."

Krista made a cross-my-heart gesture. Jenny, on the other hand, perked up and said, "So the second person is safe?"

"Oh, go shop. Unless you're thinking it would be good to take the Naked Chef idea to the next level and declare it a Naked Wedding?"

Shelby whooped as Danny swept through into the changing room. Through the curtains, she heard the others move off with comments like "Mom would have a cow if she thought we were serious about having a naked wedding" from Krista and "What if we just pretended for a couple of days to freak her out?" from Jenny.

Meanwhile, Danny stood for a second with the pretty dress clutched in her arms, and counted to ten while the dressing room tried to close in around her and the air went thin. Which was just stupid. The walls were curtains, not solid rock, and the cubicle was open above her head, all the way up to the ceiling. This wasn't a chimney, and the ceiling wasn't a slice of sky sandwiched between two cliff walls, getting darker and darker as the cold seeped in. *Breathe, darn it!* She was stronger than this.

"Here." A hand appeared under the curtain to place a pair of heels inside the dressing room, and Krista added, "Jenny said we're all the same size, and you won't break your neck walking on the grass. Besides, what's the fun of modeling a dress in hiking boots?"

And *poof!* The panic disappeared.

Danny was in a store, not a crisis, and her friends were right outside. Able to breathe again, able to speak again, she said, "That depends on your definition of 'fun,' I guess." It came out only a little wobbly.

"You ready to come out and do a twirl?" Shelby demanded.

"Did you guys find your dresses yet?"

"Ha!"

With her balance more or less restored, Danny shucked off her clothes, surprised anew at the image in the mirror—not just the reappearance of the subtle curves and muscles she had been missing without really realizing it, but the way her skin had taken on an all-over rosy tan. Thinking, *You've come a long way, baby*, she drew the dress on over her head and tugged it down to demurely brush her ankles while rising high on the sides, with slits that darn near showed the goods.

"I don't know," she began, then turned to the side and looked in the mirror. And stared. "Okay, I totally take that back."

The dress was a knockout. It clung to her breasts, accentuated her waist, and made her look like a better version of herself. She had a feeling it would've looked awesome on just about anybody it came close to fitting, but filed that under gift horses and mouths as she stuck her feet in the shoes Krista had brought her. High but not ridiculous, the black heels had diamond patterns of turquoise beads on each toe, and did good things to the glimpses of thigh and calf that showed through the side slits.

"Okay, fine," she called. "You guys win." Flinging aside the curtain, she swept out, did a few steps of wiggle-wiggle runway walk, and struck a pose. "Whaddya think?"

The others produced a satisfying chorus of whistles, and Jenny said, "Woo-hoo! The single guys of Three Ridges are going to swallow their tongues when they get a load of you."

"I think I know one a little closer to home who's already taking a second look." Krista wiggled her eyebrows. "Or was that someone else who had her head together with Sam the other day at the Sears place?"

Danny fought a blush as the others did a "wooooo" in harmony. She had known it would probably come up, figuring guy talk was a requirement during girl time. "That was me," she confirmed with a little kick of pride. "We're going out tomorrow."

"Ha! I knew it!" Krista danced in, gave her a little twirl that nearly put her on her ass in the pretty shoes. "Sam is the best. We've been dying for him to get with somebody who likes him for himself, and doesn't care about the money."

"Didn't even know about it when we met," Danny said, holding up a hand like she was swearing it.

"You both love being outdoors," Jenny added, getting a considering look in her eyes. "You're smart, tough, and don't waste time worrying about what other people think. Yeah. I can totally see it. Who knows? You might be just what he needs to knock him out of his rut."

*Don't ask, don't ask, don't ask.* "What rut?"

"Jen-ny," Krista said warningly. "You're going to scare her off."

"Danny doesn't believe in being scared," Jenny said staunchly. "Which could make her perfect for a guy who makes the ideal boyfriend until things get too serious. At which point, he bails."

"Or, more accurately, withdraws until the woman dumps him," Shelby added.

"You guys!" Krista practically wailed.

"It's okay," Danny said, though she wasn't sure if it really was or not. The air had gotten suddenly thinner, the floor less solid beneath her strappy shoes. "I'm only going to be here for a few months, tops."

"That's what I said when I first got here," Shelby pointed out, and Jenny nodded solemnly and said, "Me, too."

Krista glared at them, then said to Danny, "They're just trying to get you going. We love you and we love Sam, and we'll stay out of it. Right, ladies?"

"Sure thing," Jenny said, then winked. "Though we'll want to know how your date goes. The more details, the better."

"I can pretty much guarantee what will happen if she wears that." Shelby nodded at the green dress. "Since she's going to be saving that for the wedding, though, we need to find her some date clothes. Something for the Searses' square dance, too."

"Wait!" Danny protested, refusing to dwell on the whole commitment-phobe thing—she would file that under *Things that don't matter because we're not getting serious, period.* "Nobody said anything about a whole wardrobe. And isn't it you guys' turn to try stuff on?"

Krista headed for the racks. "We'll pull some shirts while you change back, Danny. Or if you want to stay in there, we can throw things over the top."

"I'll be right out." Not because she didn't trust the others to pick cool stuff, but because she didn't want to miss out on the fun.

As Danny rejoined the group, Jenny held up a shiny flamingo-pink blouse with linebacker shoulder pads and a big fat bow fastening it at the front. "How about this?"

"Not nearly loud enough," Danny claimed. "I was more thinking along these lines." She went for the nearest rack and whipped out a snap-studded rodeo-style shirt made of bright red stretch polyester striped with zigzag lightning bolts done in reflective tape.

"Green, people," Shelby said like a drill sergeant. "Think green!"

"You want green?" Tiffany stalled in the doorway to the back room, with a plastic-covered garment draped over her shoulder. "I thought you wanted stuff for a wedding?"

"We do, but—" Jenny cut herself off. "Never mind. What have you got there?"

"Something Mom got in the other week. I remembered it because I thought it was pretty." She crossed to them as she pulled the plastic up and off a floaty froth of white. While hanging it on a coat hook labeled LOOK WHAT I FOUND!, she said, "See? And P.S.? Mom let me try it, and it looks even better on."

Danny wasn't a super wedding-y person, but even she had to "ooh" along with the chorus that rose up at the sight of the wedding dress. The demure halter-top bodice was inset with Wedgwood blue fabric that was worked with white lace and a vee of embroidered wildflowers. A lace-edged blue ribbon embellished the bottom of the vee, and below that, layers of white satin underskirts and a white lace overskirt fell to midcalf, or maybe a little lower, coming to points like wildflower petals and stirring in the air currents of the shop.

The whole effect was light, airy, and casual, yet clearly bridal. Danny didn't know Krista all that well, but she could picture her in it. And when she glanced over, she found Krista staring at the dress the way a newbie skydiver would look back up at the plane during free fall—with equal parts wonder and terror.

"I think she likes it," Shelby said in a stage whisper. "What do you guys think?"

"But it's lace," Jenny said with feigned innocence. "I thought she was allergic to lace."

"Not this lace." Krista snagged the dress off the hook. "It's at least worth trying on, don't you think?" Her movements were jerky, her hands shaking as she fumbled to keep the dress from dragging on the floor.

"Hells, yes." Shelby gave her a little push. "That blue is going to do crazy things with your eyes. Go on. We'll find shoes." She herded the others away.

"She's freaking out," Jenny whispered. "Why is she freaking out?"

"Because she knows this could be it," Shelby whispered back.

"I didn't freak out when I got married. I just bought a dress."

"You two might have the same faces, but you definitely don't have the same brain." Shelby lifted the boots. "Come on, let's make it a dress-shoe exacta."

After a brief, giggling search during which they vetoed vinyl go-go boots and six-inch white patent leather stilettos, Shelby held up a pair of calf-high lace-up boots in white satin with a lace overlay. "Ladies, I think we have a winner."

The three of them trooped over to the changing area, where Krista's sock-clad feet were doing a little shimmying-into-the-dress dance. When Shelby tucked the boots under, Krista gave a happy little "Ooh!"

"How's it going in there?"

"Good, I think. Just give me a minute with these boots." They watched the bottom eight inches of her as she stood on one foot, then the other to put on the boots, giving her audience glimpses of the trailing lace petals as they moved around her. "Do you think the boots are too . . . you know?"

"Slutty?" Jenny grinned. "That's part of the fun, don't you think? They'll be mostly hidden anyway, unless you're planning on making us carry you around on a chair at the head of a conga line."

"Yeesh, no."

"Then you'll be fine. Just think of Wyatt's face when he gets that dress off you and the boots are still in the picture."

Krista made an intrigued *hmmm* sound.

"The shoes are negotiable," Shelby said, making an excited little *hurry up, hurry up* gesture. "We want to see the dress!"

"Okay." The boots moved to face the curtain. "Here goes." Sweeping the curtain aside, Krista stepped out. She had her hands nervously clasped in front of her, and twin color spots rode high on her cheeks. "Well?" For some reason she was looking right at Danny when she said it.

*Don't ask me. What do I know about fashion? Ask Jenny and Shelby; they know you best.* The logical answers spun through her head, telling her she didn't belong here, shouldn't be in the spotlight at this moment. But what came out was, "It's perfect."

Because, really, it was. Exactly perfect.

The lacy straps curved gently on Krista's ranch-muscled yet feminine shoulders, the bodice hugged her slim torso like it had been made for her, and the skirt moved with her, alternately cupping her hips and legs to hint at the shape of her body, then floating away to tease with hints of the lacy boots.

"Oh, Krista." Jenny clasped her hands in front of her just like her sister was doing, but from excitement rather than nerves. "It's beautiful!"

"Look at yourself." Shelby nudged her to the array of crooked mirrors. "Sweetie, look!"

Krista's eyes filled and she covered her mouth. After a moment, she said, in an awed whisper, "I'm getting married."

Jenny wrapped an arm around her waist and rocked her side to side. "Yes, you are."

"To Wyatt."

"Yep. Kinda funny how life works, isn't it? You thought when you were twenty that he would be your one and only, and it turned out you were right. It just took a while."

Sniffling, Krista turned in her sister's arms. "It's perfect," she said, her voice breaking with happy tears. "It's my wedding dress. Can you believe we finally found my wedding dress?"

As they hugged, Danny swallowed past a sudden lump in her throat.

"Come on." Shelby caught her arm, dragging her toward the twins. "Group hug. But don't wrinkle the dress!" She looped her arms around Krista and Jenny and, as Danny gingerly added herself to the mix, said, "Happy wedding dress on three. One, two, three, *Happy wedding dress*!" They shouted it together and then broke apart, laughing like fools.

"Hang on," a voice broke in. "Hey. Shoot. This isn't good."

Turning to the source of the voice, they saw Tiffany standing with the dress's protective plastic wadded up, staring at an attached tag.

"Let me guess," Krista said. "It's hideously expensive."

"We'll make it happen," Jenny said staunchly, earning an elbow jab and a mutter of "Way to negotiate" from Shelby.

"No, it's not that. This dress is on a five-day hold. Somebody's already got dibs on it." The teen went crestfallen. "That must be why it was hanging in the back."

"It's . . ." The color drained from Krista's face. "You're kidding."

"I'm sorry. I'm so sorry. I didn't know." She held out the hanger. "You're going to have to give it back."

Danny put herself between Krista and Tiffany. "Wait. There's got to be some way to work this out."

The teen looked at her like she had just sprouted a second head. "But there's a hold on it. With a deposit and everything."

"Maybe one of us could talk to the buyer. Explain the situation." *Make her an offer she can't refuse.*

"But—"

"It's okay, you guys." Krista tugged free from Jenny. "I'll take it off." Her eyes were sad, though, and her hands clutched at her waist like they wanted to keep the fabric right where it was. "Maybe whoever it was will decide not to buy it after all, and then I can have it. If not, at least we've found a style that works. I can find something else just like it."

"It's custom," Jenny said quietly. "There isn't even a maker's name inside."

"If it's meant to be, it will be," Krista countered. "Just like me and Wyatt."

"Oh, it's going to be all right. I'm going to make sure of that." Shelby moved up beside Danny and fixed Tiffany with a look. "How about you go see if your mom is off the phone yet." It wasn't a question.

Swallowing, the teen spun and hurried toward the back, trailing the plastic behind her like a comet's tail. "*Maaaaa!*"

As she disappeared through the door, Krista said, "Really, it'll be okay. It's just a dress." But her eyes were huge in her pale face and her hands worked on smoothing down the lacy skirt petals with a jerky, repetitive motion.

"We have to at least try," Shelby insisted. "You never know with stuff like this until you ask."

From the back room, a new and exasperation-edged voice said, "Tiffany! Why on *earth* did you show that dress to a customer when you knew it had a hold on it?"

"I didn't know." The kid's voice headed to whine territory.

"Of course you did. I told you yesterday that—" The owner of the exasperated voice came through the doorway, revealing herself as a late-thirties version of her daughter—in looks, anyway. Brunette, with long curls, a pixieish face, and the curves of a fifties pinup, she looked like she was on her last straw with the teen who tagged at her heels.

Her expression smoothed to professional regret, though, as she scanned the store and locked on Danny. "I'm so sorry, ma'am," she said, heading toward the changing area. "Tiffany never should have—" She broke off as she looked past her and saw Krista standing near the mirrors, wearing the dress and trying to look brave rather than forlorn. Eyebrows shooting up, the woman said, *"Krista?"*

"Hey, Della." Krista spread her hands. "Look, I don't want to make things weird. I'll understand if there's nothing you can do."

"But it's perfect for her," Jenny pointed out. "Look. I mean, really perfect. Like it was made for her."

"The wedding is super soon," Danny added. "And she's been holding out for exactly the right dress. What was it you told us earlier, Krista? That you'd know it when you see it?"

"This is it," Shelby confirmed. "That is, if you can help us out, Del. Maybe you could call whoever put it on hold and see if they'd be willing to let Krista have it instead?"

"I don't know . . ."

"Please." Danny urged. "I realize that you don't know me from the next tourist, but I owe Krista huge. Thanks to her and Jenny, I have a new job, new friends, and even a date tomorrow. Do you know how long it's been since the last time I woke up in the morning and got excited about the day ahead? Too darn long, but that's exactly what I did this morning. Because I was going shopping with Krista for a dress I could wear when she and Wyatt get married in the most beautiful place on earth, under a gazebo her dad helped build for her. Don't you want her wearing one of your dresses when that happens?"

The shop owner blinked at her. Then, lips curving, she stuck out her hand. "Hi, I'm Della. It's nice to meet you."

Danny paused, hoping that didn't mean she had gone too far. But the genuine pleasure in the other woman's eyes suggested that she meant exactly what she had said. So she shook. "Um. I'm Danny Traveler. An old friend of Jenny's from abroad."

"And a new friend of mine," said Shelby, crossing her arms like she was daring Della to go through her and Danny to get at Krista.

"Thanks, guys," Krista said, choking up. "No matter what happens, thanks. And, Della, if you would make the call—whichever way it goes—I'll be eternally grateful. I'll marry Wyatt wearing a trash bag with holes cut in it for my arms and head if it comes down to it, but I'd really rather be wearing this dress."

Della lips curved at the corners, and she nodded slowly. "Okay, I'll do it."

Shelby's head came up. "You will?"

"I will, but no promises. All I can do is ask." Della did an about-face and bumped into her daughter. Scowling, she added, "And don't think for a second that this gets you off the hook, young lady. We're going to have another talk about not yessing me to death while your mind wanders."

Tiffany hung her head. "Yes, Mom."

"You can start working off my annoyance by straightening up the stockroom. Now march!"

They went through the rear door single file. When the door thumped shut, Jenny let out a steaming-teapot noise. "Ohmigosh. Can you believe this?"

"It's just a dress," Krista insisted, still patting at the skirts. Then, forcing a bright smile, she looked at Danny.

"Weren't we trying to find you an outfit for the square dance?"

Sensing her need to put things back in their earlier groove, Danny made a face. "Gee, and here I was enjoying not being the center of attention."

"Suck it up," Jenny advised. "Because now you're the distraction."

They dove back into the racks, with Krista still wearing the dress and the calf-high boots as if she might be thinking of tossing down some cash and making a break for it. Instead, she pulled a red shirt from the rack, looked from it to Danny and back, and nodded. "This could work."

"You know what happens in *Star Trek* when you wear a red shirt, right?"

"Lucky for us, this is Wyoming." Krista looped it over Danny's arm. "Try it. I think you'll like it."

"And this one." Jenny added a shirt and a short sundress.

"Here are some jeans," Shelby said, though apparently *some* translated to about forty pounds of rhinestone-blinged denim.

"Eep!" Danny sagged under the sudden pile of fabric. "How many square dances are we talking about here?"

"Humor us. Who knows? You might find a few things in there you didn't know you couldn't live without." Shelby pointed to the dressing cube. "March, girlfriend! Unless you want us to keep going?"

"I'm marching, I'm marching!" Laughing, she entered the curtained space, dumped the clothes on the

remaining empty chair—the other held a haphazard
scatter of Krista's clothes—and refused to let any of the
hemmed-in feelings gain traction. But as she started to
shuck off her jeans and tee, Shelby's head popped
through the curtains.

"Della's back!" she blurted, then disappeared again.

Danny shoved her shirt back into her waistband and
bolted out of the dressing cube in her socks, leaving her
hiking boots behind as she joined the others, where
Jenny and Shelby stood on either side of Krista, forming a united front against Della, who had some stapled-
together papers in one hand and an expression that
wasn't giving away anything.

When Danny added herself to the end of the line,
Krista said, "Well? Were you able to get the other buyer
on the phone?"

"I was, and I explained the situation." A wide smile
spread across her face. "And she said I should go ahead
and sell it to you."

"She . . ." Krista's jaw dropped as the others went,
"Woo-hoo!" and "Yee-haw!"

Danny's "Yayyy!" got drowned out, but that didn't
matter one bit as she found herself swept up in an impromptu hug-and-dance celebration that involved lots
of whooping and twirls.

Krista whirled to face Della, glowing. "So I can have
it? Really?"

"Really." Della's smile gained an evil glint. "It actually wasn't that hard to convince the other buyer to let
you have it . . . seeing as you've got a long-standing
relationship with her." She held up the deposit paperwork. "See?"

At the top, in big Sharpie letters, it said: HOLD FOR ROSE SKYE.

Jenny groaned, Shelby whooped, and Danny swallowed a snort. She had met Krista's mom a few times, and could totally see it.

"She said to tell you that the moment she saw it, she knew it was the one." Della glanced down at Krista's feet. "She had a pair of kitten heels in mind to go with it, though. Do you want me to bring them out?"

"NO!" Jenny shouted, laughing. "Please, no. You can't let her win on everything. She'll be incorrigible."

"She'll be incorrigible anyway," Krista said fondly. "Especially because she was right. And, yes, I'd like to see the shoes."

"But the boots are awesome!" Shelby protested. "So-o-o sexy."

"So I'll buy both and decide later."

Looking very pleased with herself for having helped pull off the surprise, Della said, "Do you want to hop out of the dress and let me take care of getting it pressed for the big day, or are you planning on wearing it home?"

"Ha!" Jenny hooted. "Don't tempt her."

"You can keep it for pressing," Krista said, "but let me try on those shoes first. In the meantime . . ." She nudged Danny with an elbow and shot her a wink. "Go try on those clothes. You've got a date tomorrow!"

# 9

On Sunday, Danny borrowed a car from Mustang Ridge and drove to Sam's place, following Krista's directions, which had a whole lot of "Take a right at the mailbox made out of a tractor tire" and "Go straight past the milking parlor that's painted like a Holstein" localisms. The instructions had sounded like they would get her dead lost, but they soon brought her to a huge gray boulder that had been cut on an angle, polished to a gleam, and etched with foot-high letters that spelled out WINDFALL.

Turning in, she rolled past the marker stone and up to the crest of a shallow hill, where she got her first look at Sam's home, the place he had jokingly called a mansion.

Only it turned out that was no joke.

Ahead of her the driveway forked, with one lane going down to a large compound of steel buildings and machines, and the other going up to a high hill that was crowned by a conical boulder that rose four-plus stories into the sky, and was partially encircled by a big, sprawling house. Made of wood and stone, with solar panels galore, the mansion was modern yet somehow looked like it had grown out of the hill, or been left there by the same long-ago glacier that had deposited the huge rock. Flashes of color—warm reds, blues, and greens—reflected from the solar panels and windows, the wooden beams crisscrossed to make diamond patterns, and on a flagpole set at the summit of the boulder, a huge Stars and Stripes snapped in the breeze.

Easing her foot off the gas, Danny let the car roll to a stop at the fork in the road. "Wow."

She had steeled herself for something big and impressive, had decided to drive herself so she'd have time to take it all in. It would take longer than a minute's pause to wrap her head around the scope of Windfall, though. Not so much because she was intimidated, but because she wasn't sure how to make it fit with the Sam she knew—the one who would rather ride the countryside on horseback than in a helicopter, who had brought her pizza and beer because he figured she could use it, and who had kissed her like she could somehow give him the peace he was looking for, even though she was in search of it herself.

And, suddenly, there he was.

As if conjured by her thoughts, Sam appeared atop the boulder, fifty or so feet up, hooked an arm around the flagpole like he was riding the mast of a pirate ship, and waved down at her.

Danny's heart thudded and warmth flooded through her—excited prickles that said despite her intention to focus on herself while she was in Wyoming, there was a big part of her that would far rather focus on him. The realization brought a skim of warning, but instead of urging her to step back, the nerves only served to amp up the heat.

Was she in danger of getting in over her head? Maybe. Probably. But that had never stopped the old Danny, and she darn well wasn't going to let it stop her now. So, pressing down on the gas, she chucked caution out the window and sent the borrowed vehicle rocketing along the driveway.

As she got out of the car, he leaned back against a thick, knotted rope and walked himself down the side of the big boulder. When he hit the last ten feet or so, where the stone face curved back under, he kicked away, swung out, and dropped lightly to the ground below.

He met her halfway, his eyes gone pale silver in the bright midday sun as he caught her hands and held her at arm's length to give her a once-over. "You look incredible. Not that you don't usually. But, wow."

Her whole-body flush went up a couple of degrees, prickling her skin beneath the low-cut stretchy red shirt and butt-hugging jeans. "I went shopping with Krista, Jenny, and Shelby yesterday. I told them this was a grubbing-in-the-dirt date, but they insisted."

"Remind me to kiss all three of them the next time I see them. In the meantime—" He tugged her closer and bent his head to hers. And her nerves turned to liquid fire as she met him in a kiss that said *hello*. It said *I missed you*. And maybe it said more, but his mouth slanting across hers swept away any chance of thought and left her awash in the heat and pleasure of kissing him back.

As their tongues touched and slid, his hands stroked straight down to her hips, then went to the small of her back. He gathered her close, making her feel delicate yet somehow unbreakable as the kiss went deeper and a greedy heat flared in her belly, reminding her that it had been too long for her. And it hadn't ever been quite like this before.

Brandon hadn't been her first, but he was the type she had gravitated toward—the skiers and mountain bikers who came to Maverick, worked as instructors or did odd jobs for mountain time, and never turned down a dare. Back then, she had thought they were the coolest of the cool. After her accident, though, from the outside looking in, so much of it had seemed brittle and fake—a world where character didn't matter so much as who could throw the biggest trick.

But out here, everything was different. *Sam* was different. Whereas Brandon had been slick, Sam was rugged. Whereas Brandon had bragged, Sam stayed silent. And whereas Brandon had prided himself on living at the edge, Sam kept his boots on solid ground. Yet she didn't have a shred of doubt that if danger reared its head, Sam would beat the crap out of it with a souped-up sledgehammer.

She wasn't looking for a man to rescue her, but being with one who could was proving to be a definite turn-on.

Her pulse hammered in her ears as he eased away, and she could see the throb at the base of his throat, hear the quick in-and-out of his breathing. There was a faint rasp in his voice when he said, "Welcome to Windfall. I'm glad you're here."

She grinned up at him. "Me, too." The house was bigger and grander than she had expected, but she had known almost from the first moment that there was more to him than met the eye. "It's beautiful," she said, her eyes going from the boulder to the house and back again. "I never thought about putting my own mini-mountain in the front yard, but now I can see that it's a landscaping must."

"Actually, the boulder came first." He kept a loose hold on her, their bodies still touching, as he looked up at the huge stone face. "It's called Wolf Rock, because from a distance, especially under moonlight, it looks like a wolf sitting on its haunches and howling up at the sky. There's been a climbing rope for as long as I can remember, and Dad and I added the flag when I was ten or so."

"You grew up here?"

"Yep." His teeth flashed. "In a much smaller house. But you're not here for my life story, are you? I promised you a treasure hunt." He released her, keeping their fingers twined together. "Come on. Your chariot awaits."

Both intrigued and aware of the change in subject, she followed him around the base of Wolf Rock, into the shadowy courtyard where the U-shaped mansion bracketed the huge stone. "What kind of chariot are we talking about here? A burro team? Stagecoach? Oh!" She laughed at the sight of an ATV almost identical to the one she used back at Mustang Ridge, but with a small trailer hitched to the back, loaded with gear. "That looks familiar."

"Thought it might." He patted the tied-down bundles. "We've got everything we need for an afternoon out on the mountain, if you're ready to go." One corner of his mouth kicked up. "Hope you don't mind riding double."

Excitement skimmed through her—at the thought of

linking her hands across his six-pack abs and fitting her body tight to his, at the promise of a new adventure. "I wouldn't have it any other way. Let's get this show on the road!"

The hour-long ride was bumpy, the engine too loud for any real conversation, and Danny's helmet kept sliding down over her eyes, but she didn't care. She snuggled up against Sam's broad back and peered around, fascinated by the changing landscape. She didn't need the occasional pop of her ears to know they were climbing—she could see it in the trees turning from leafy to pine, and then thinning to sparse clumps scattered across the increasingly rocky slopes, where stones piled up against one another, looking very ready to fall.

She kept a close eye as they passed a big stack, hoping the vibrations wouldn't jar them loose. *We're not in Maine anymore, Toto.* Not that she had thought she was. But while Blessing Valley was a lush oasis and Mustang Ridge was a vacation playland, Sam's property was rugged and forbidding.

The ATV's engine changed pitch, and his body shifted against hers as he turned the machine off the trail and up onto a flat, rocky ledge. Killing the engine, he shucked off his helmet and twisted back to give her a grin. "I believe you said you wanted rocks?"

She laughed as she fumbled with the chin strap of her helmet. "I'd say you delivered."

He swung off the saddle and offered a hand. "Welcome to Hyrule."

"Is that the name of the mountain?" She took in the jagged, rocky slopes rising on one side of them and falling away on the other.

"This part of it, anyway. Most prospectors name their sites, or at least give them numbers. Makes it easier to keep things straight."

And he wouldn't use numbers, she knew. The land was too important to him. "Isn't Hyrule part of the Legend of Zelda?"

His teeth flashed. "It was my favorite when I was a kid. Hyrule is the Overworld, where you can find some of the stuff you're going to need to get you started. Money. Potions. A sword. That's sort of what this area is like. Dad and I found aquamarine from a few pockets right here, some blue beryl. A little gem-grade quartz and iodolite. Enough to pay some bills, keep us going when things were tight back in the day. So we named it Hyrule."

He spoke of his father easily enough, with none of the shadows he'd been carrying the other day. "Hyrule." She nodded. "I like it."

"The last time Axyl, Murph, Midas, and I were out here, we were testing a new scanner, a portable unit that looks for areas of very low density and flags them as possible vugs."

"Vugs?"

"Pockets that form from cooling lava. Add the right combination of minerals, pressure, and heat, and you've got a perfect setup to grow gemstone crystals, sometimes big ones." He described the different kinds of stones and some of the ways to get at them, his voice deepening and his gestures broadening. "We marked some likely spots that the scanner found, but haven't gotten back yet to check them out. I thought we could take a crack at one or two of them today."

Pulse bumping at the thought that she might be standing right on top of a fortune, she teased, "In other words, we're going to cheat."

His teeth flashed. "I prefer to call it using technology to increase our odds. Or would you rather poke around on your own? Either way is fine by me."

She held out a hand. "Hand me one of those shovels and point me to a flag, big guy. This girl is ready to dig some rocks."

By the time the sun had centered itself in the cloudless sky and the temperature notched into the upper digits, they had checked out two of the anomalies the scanner had picked up—one turned out to be a stress crack, the other a dud pocket empty of crystals—and were working on a third. But although they didn't have much to show for the digging time, Sam sure wouldn't call it a bust. Because, dang, he was having fun.

"I've got more sparkles!" Danny announced, looking up at him from the hollowed-out spot where they had cleared the overburden. "I think the seam of quartz is getting wider. It's even sounding a little hollow when I dig, though that might be wishful thinking." She was sweaty, dirt-streaked, and radiant beneath her safety goggles, and he didn't remember the last time he'd seen something so fine.

"Want me to take a couple of whacks at it with the pick?"

"Not on your life! Just pass me a hammer."

"Spoken like a true rockhound." He handed over the spring-loaded hammer, and leaned in, not wanting to miss when she broke through. He'd never brought a date out to the hills before. But then again, he'd never dated a woman like Danny before, one who didn't even bother to roll up her sleeves before she plunged head-long into life.

"I don't know that I qualify as a rockhound yet—I haven't actually found anything. Is there a level below rockhound? Rock noob?"

"Pebble pup."

Her eyes lit. "Perfect! Does it come on a T-shirt?"

"I'm sure we can find you one."

"Or maybe a baseball cap." She hunkered down, concentrating as she gave a couple of experimental taps here and there, listening to the reverb.

"That one." He got in close, their bodies bumping as he pointed to a spot. "Sounded hollow to me." He had gadgets galore to tell him exactly that, but he'd left them all behind, figuring going it old school would be more fun for her. "I'd give it a couple of good whacks and see what happens."

"Okay, here goes. Fingers crossed." She gave the thin-sounding spot a tentative tap, then used both hands and brought the hammer down with a resound-ing clang that turned into a rattling noise as the stone crumbled inward and the pieces fell into a sudden slice of darkness. "Oh!" Her hands flew to her mouth. "Look!"

The jagged edge where the pocket had broken through was encrusted with fat crystalline shapes. He didn't know what they were looking at yet, but he knew she would remember this for a long time. You never really forgot your first, after all. "See if you can find a loose crystal," he said, straightening away from her and reaching for his water bottle. "And let's take a look at what you've got here."

"What *we've* got," she corrected, coming up with a squat chunk of stone about the size of her thumb. "Hyrule is yours."

"But you're the first human to ever lay eyes on what's inside this pocket." He dribbled water over the gem. "How does that feel?"

Her eyes came up to meet his, full of wonder. "Like I just came over a hill and found an ocean I wasn't expecting." And, just like that unexpected ocean, the crystal brightened blue-green in the sunlight. "Look at that!" She clutched the shard close, then held it up to the light. "It's beautiful! It's . . . What is it?"

"Aquamarine, I think. We can do all the proper tests to confirm, but I'd bet on it. It may not look all bright and gemmy right now, but give it a couple of facets and a bit of a polish, and you'll have yourself a nice stone. Your first find."

"Oh!" She closed her fingers around it and surged up toward him. *"Thank you."* Her open, joyous kiss punched heat into his gut and put a spin in his head, leaving him on the edge of reeling as she broke away to dive back into the pocket. Then she stopped herself and turned back, rueful. "A little help here, oh experienced rockhound? What do I do next? How do I keep from messing things up?"

He could have talked her through harvesting the crystals, but they had been going for almost three hours straight, and he knew how easy it was to let the gemstone high take over. "How about you let me open things up in there? Maybe you could grab the cooler and pull out some snacks."

He had brought the makings of a romantic picnic, but could see from the flush riding high on her cheeks that she wouldn't want to stop now. Heck, *he* didn't want to stop—the crystals looked good from where he was standing, and there was no telling how far back the pocket went, or how deep. Aqua wasn't crazy valuable, but it held its own. Not to mention that pulling aqua out of Hyrule took him back a ways, to when a pocket like this would've been the find of the year, celebrated by a rare dinner out.

Happy to see that she was digging into the cooler and nibbling as she went, he dropped into the shallow depression, where he had levered several flat rocks away already. Crouching down and clicking on a high-powered flashlight, he shone the beam through the jagged opening.

Adrenaline kicked in at the sight of a whole lot of crystal structure and a big pocket that stretched way back and then dropped out of sight. Seeing a couple of big clusters near the opening, he chose a likely fracture plane and got to work with a four-pound hammer, loosening up the substrate. Rock dust coated his face, turned the back of his throat dry and acrid, and put a huge grin on his face.

Damn, he loved this part.

After setting the blocky crystals aside to be taken back to the tumbling shed to get cleaned up and polished, he used a smaller hammer to carefully loosen another layer, opening up the hole. The stones weren't all amazing—some were rotten, turning to greasy blue-green mush in his hands. There was enough good stuff to keep the grin on his face, though. More than enough. And it just kept going, with that drop-off in the back suggesting there was a second pocket beyond.

"How's she looking?"

He pulled his upper body out of the hole and twisted around to blink up at Danny. She was balanced at the edge of the cut, with her face alight and her hair damp where she had washed away the dust. Her jeans were muddy at the knees and she was wearing one of the spare work shirts he had brought along for the purpose, with the sleeves blousing down around her wrists and the tails tied at her waist.

"She looks amazing," he said, voice gone rough. "Exactly what I want to see."

Her excited flush deepened. "What's down there?"

"I haven't hit bottom yet." He flashed his light around. "There's another pocket in the back, looks like even better crystal formations, but I can't get my head that far back."

She hesitated, swallowing. "Can I try?"

Startled, he pulled his head out and looked up at her, squinting into the sun. "It's pretty tight quarters." And not just for someone who had been trapped in a rockfall eighteen months ago and still couldn't handle something as wide-open as the *Rambling Rose*. For most people, there was a very fine line between the awe of being surrounded by glitter, and that moment of realizing that the jagged ceiling had a lot of rock pressing down from above, poising the whole thing to snap shut like a bear trap. "Are you sure you want to try it? You don't have to impress me, you know. That ship sailed right about the time you let fly with that paperback."

"It's not for you. It's for me. I think I can do it. I *want* to do it." Her eyes were fixed on the hole, her expression tight. But not with fear, he thought. It was more like she was daring herself. "Is it safe?"

"The ground is solid enough." He banged the overhanging rock with the four-pound hammer. "But I'd be lying if I guaranteed anything." He wished he could, though. He wanted her to see the glitter, wanted her to be the first one around that corner. Wanted to be there when she beat the inner demons that made her think she was less than she really was.

She shifted her weight from one foot to the other, as if unsure which way to go. "Will I be able to breathe?"

"There's room enough. The rest will be up to you." Setting aside the hammer and shucking off his protective gear, he rose and crossed to her. With her standing on the grade, him in the cut, their faces were level. Her skin had gone pale, her eyes big, but there was excitement beneath the nerves. "The one thing I can promise you is that I'll be right here. I'll have your back. And if you need me to, I'll pull you out."

Her hands lifted to his shoulders, then slid down to his chest, fingers flexing. "Thanks," she said, voice gone husky. "That helps."

"You don't have to do this."

"I know." A sudden smile lit her face, banishing most of the nerves. "But the thing is, I actually *want* to do it. This wimp is having a brave moment."

"You're not a wimp."

"Not today." She pulled off her hat and safety goggles, and held out her hand for the flashlight. "Stand back. I'm going in."

*    *    *

The hole was smaller than it had looked from up above, but once Danny got her shoulders through, it wasn't so bad. Daylight shone in behind her and the pocket fell away in front of her like a crystal garden of muted blues and greens. *Beautiful.* The hot air was tangy with acrid dust and very still, but the urge to gulp it was all in her head. There was plenty of oxygen, plenty of room.

"How's it going in there?" Sam's shadow moved across the reflected sunlight, making strange patterns on the stone.

"I'm good," she said, feeling her pulse level off some at the reminder that he was right behind her.

"Crazy, isn't it, to think that the stones you're looking at haven't ever seen the light of day before?"

"I'm trying not to imagine them looking up at me right now and thinking, *What in the blazes is THAT?*"

He coughed to cover a laugh. "I can't say I've ever thought of it that way before."

"You're not wired to creep yourself out." She was doing okay, though. Her palms were slick, her hair sticking to her sweat-drenched forehead, but she could see, breathe, even talk. *You can do this.* A few more minutes and she could wiggle her way back out and celebrate the win. She panned the flashlight, catching flashes of another color mixed in with the blue-green. Excitement bumped alongside the nerves. "Is there something else in here along with the aquamarine? I'm seeing purple."

"You've got a good eye. There may be some tourmaline mixed in there. Should make some impressive clusters when they're all cleaned up."

She started to nod, felt her hair snag on the crystals

overhead, and ducked instead. "I'm going deeper. I want to see what's past this drop-off."

"Go easy," he cautioned.

Not letting herself think about how low the roof got toward the back, or that she'd be sticking her head inside a mountain that was no stranger to rockslides, she inched forward, pushing the flashlight in front of her. *Look forward, not back. It's an adventure.*

The walls closed in on either side, tugging at the too-big shirt Sam had loaned her. Before, she had caught herself tucking her nose into the collar and inhaling, as if she were back in high school and wearing her crush's ski jacket. Now she wished she had stripped down before starting her crawl, because the fabric wanted to twist and tighten around her.

Not letting herself think about that, either, or the view he was getting of her wiggling bum, she slithered a few more inches, to where the floor of the miniature cave disappeared into darkness.

"Do the crystals keep going?" he asked, suddenly sounding very far away.

Telling herself that he was still right there, that it was just a trick of the sound waves, she angled the light down and pushed forward another couple of inches, so she could look over the drop-off. "I think so," she called, her voice too loud in the tiny space. "There's an edge here, and another pocket beyond it. Very deep. I can't see the bottom." Heart hammering, she inched along even more, so her head and shoulders hung out over the emptiness. "It looks like—" The rock beneath her tipped suddenly, tilting her toward the darkness.

She gasped and slapped for a handhold, banged her

hands on the sharp crystals, and cried out as the flash-light went spinning. There was a disco-ball twirl of aquamarine and purple, and then a sharp crack of impact and the light went out.

"What is it?" His voice sharpened. "Danny, what's wrong? Do you want to come out?"

But she couldn't answer him, could hardly hear him over the roaring in her ears. She was in the dark, surrounded by rocks on all sides. And. She. Couldn't. Breathe. Someone was shouting, screaming, but she couldn't hear that either, couldn't see anything, couldn't—

Something clamped onto her ankle and pulled, and the too-big shirt snagged and tightened even further, compressing her chest and cutting across her throat. Trapping her.

"No!" She slapped around her in the darkness and found sharp points, struggled and heard cloth tear. "*No!*" The cry used up the last of her air and the world went spinning around her, drawing the shirt-noose tighter and tighter, until—

Nothing.

# 10

"Danny?" Sam shook her, but got no response. "*Danny!*"

Guilt hammered through him, thudding with the heartbeat rhythm that said *get her out, get her out, get her out.* But she was limp, unresponsive, and hung up somewhere in the pocket. He would hurt her if he pulled wrong, but he couldn't leave her like she was.

His hands shook as he lay flat and reached along her body, finding where the shirt had gotten hung up on crystal shards. He freed the snags and gave an experimental tug, and this time she slid back along the heavy canvas drop cloth he had used to pad the sharp rocks when they first started working. He pulled again, and she came the rest of the way free.

She was pale and terrifyingly still.

Heart hammering, he scooped her up, cradled her against his chest, and carried her up and out of the shallow cut they had been working. As he reached the ATV and lowered her to the cleared-off trailer, she stirred and made a soft sound. Her eyelids quivered, then opened to reveal blurry bewilderment as she looked up at him, then around at their surroundings.

"Hey," he rasped. "You're back."

"What . . ." she whispered, then gave a shuddery, "Ohhh." Comprehension flooded her face, followed by a blush. "Oh, no. Please, tell me I didn't just . . . Ohhh."

Relief trickled through him, followed by something darker and more complicated. In a voice that was still rough, he said, "Don't worry about it. You're not the first or last miner to panic underground, and you've got more of an excuse than most."

She pushed herself up, and he helped her sit with her legs hanging off the back of the trailer. Burying her face in her hands, she moaned. "I passed out on you."

"Yeah, you did. Scared the hell out of me, too."

"I'm sorry."

"Don't be. I'm just glad you're okay." He searched her face. "You *are* okay, right? There's a clinic in town if you want—"

"I'm fine."

"I dragged you out of there pretty fast." He reached for her hand, pushed up her sleeve. "Did you cut yourself on the rocks, or—"

She yanked her hand away and said sharply, "I said *I'm fine!*"

The ensuing silence was broken only by a rattle of rocks, as the cut shifted and settled.

She rose and paced to the edge of the hole. After looking down at it for a minute, she closed her eyes and tipped her face up to the sun. She stood like that for a long moment, and he got the feeling that she was proving to herself that she was out in the open. Then, exhaling, she opened her eyes and said, softer now, "Sorry. But I really hate this. I hate being afraid, hate not being able to control myself. Most of all, I hate that when I get in a situation when I need to be at my best—thinking, reacting—that's exactly when my brain shuts down and I go *poof*." She snapped her fingers. "Lights out."

He wanted to reach for her, to hold on to her and tell her that she wasn't a wimp, and that he knew what it was like to have a flashback reach up, grab on, and drag him someplace he didn't want to go.

He couldn't make himself reach for her, though, and the words stuck suddenly in his throat. Because now that she was sounding like herself again, a whole slew of what-ifs suddenly jammed his brain with worst-case scenarios. What if she hadn't made it out in one piece? What if he'd hurt her pulling her out? Hell, what if the cavern had collapsed on her? He'd taken out a whole lot of its support, busting through. It could happen.

One split-second disaster, and nothing was ever the same again.

Turning away, he cleared his throat. "You sit for a minute, have something to drink. I'll pack the tools and we'll head back to Windfall." Which wasn't what he wanted to say, but it would have to do for now, because he was too damn shaky to say anything else.

The return trip seemed longer than the ride out had been, but that was okay. It gave Danny time to level off and take a breath, time to feel the bumps and bruises she had given herself, appreciating them because they meant she was alive and not hurt worse. And it gave her an excuse to cling to Sam as the ATV bounced along the rocky trail, jolting the heavy leather bags that held the crystals they had collected. She burrowed into him, grateful for the solid warmth that made it easier to banish the memories of cold darkness and turn her face up into the sunlight instead.

Still, by the time Wolf Rock came into view, she knew what she had to do.

He pulled around by the front of the mansion, killed the engine, and swung off, then held out a hand for her. "Come on. I'll show you the house." A spark of humor lightened the pensive expression he'd been wearing since her panic attack. "I should warn you, though. I've only got four rooms' worth of furniture, and half of it came back with me from college."

If this had been a normal dinner-and-drinks sort of date, she might have asked why he didn't either downsize or hire a decorator. As it was, she let him help her off the ATV, but then reclaimed her hand. "You're ahead of me," she said as she got to work unbuttoning the borrowed—now ruined—shirt. "I've only got maybe two and a half rooms, most of it parental donations, and all of it in storage at the moment." She held out the garment. "Sorry about the shirt."

"Don't be." He took it, hooked it over his shoulder, and studied her. "Why do I get the feeling you're not coming in for the nickel tour?"

She wanted to, badly. It would be so easy to go inside with him and let him tell her stories about prospecting, video games, or what Wyatt had been like in college. She could picture herself sipping a glass of the wine she had seen in the cooler, relaxing with him, and watching the sun drop in the sky. Kissing him as it set. All very easy.

Too easy.

Tucking her hands in her pockets, she said, "Thanks for the offer, but I'm going to head back to Blessing Valley."

"Let me drive you back to the ranch and follow you out to the valley, make sure everything's okay."

"Everything will be fine," she said. "I can take care of myself." Swallowing the leaden ball that had formed in her throat, she added, "In fact, I think I need to focus on that for the time being."

He stilled. "Is this you giving me a brush-off?"

He sounded so incredulous that she would have laughed if she hadn't been afraid it would come out as a sob. "Maybe. Sort of. I don't want to, but . . ." She took a breath, tried to gather thoughts that wanted to scatter. "Look, you're good at fixing things. You see a problem, you invent a solution. I get that. I respect that. But the thing is, I need to do it myself. And if I'm around you, it would be way too easy to lean on you. So I'm not going to do this with you anymore. I'm sorry."

Regret pierced her at the knowledge that she wouldn't get to kiss him again, wouldn't ride into camp to find him waiting for her while his horse grazed on the other side of the river.

His lips flattened with the barest hint of a rueful smile. "This is a new one. Usually I'm the one who gets dumped because I don't want to get serious."

"I'm not dumping you, I'm—"

"I know. I'm sorry. That was my lame attempt at humor." He moved in, giving her time to step back. When she didn't, he slid his arms around her and drew her close, holding her lightly, as if she were something precious. "You're a very special woman, Danny Traveler.

You're bright, beautiful, clever, interesting, and one of the bravest people I know. You should give yourself more credit."

She sniffled, refusing to give in to tears because that would make both of them feel worse. "You saying stuff like that is exactly why I shouldn't be around you."

He brushed his lips across hers, then let her go and stepped back. "You know where to find me if you change your mind."

"Somewhere between a rock and a hard place?"

His expression lightened. "Exactly. Take care of yourself, Danny."

"You, too," she said, her voice going ragged. "And give Yoshi a carrot for me."

He just lifted a hand in answer, standing there in front of Wolf Rock as if to say, *I'm not going to leave. You're going to have to do it.*

So she did. She made herself walk away when she wanted to cling, made herself drive away when she wanted to kill the engine and tell him she'd made a mistake. And as she turned onto the main road and headed for Mustang Ridge, her surroundings blurred and a tear found its way down her cheek. Because, really, there was nothing she would have wanted to change about Sam— except for meeting him now, when she was in no place to get involved.

Sam stood there longer than he meant to, until there wasn't even a stir of dust anymore to say that she'd been there. Then he stood there a minute more, trying to shake the feeling that he should've done more to persuade her to stay. To convince her that she was okay, even if she didn't see it yet. To talk her into another date—one with wine, candles, and zero danger.

He didn't chase women, though, and he didn't make promises he couldn't keep.

"Like today, when you promised you'd have her back?" he asked himself, even though he already knew the answer. He hadn't broken his promise—he'd been right there, and he'd pulled her out as soon as he could. But that was the thing, wasn't it? There were times when you just couldn't stop bad stuff from happening.

Shoving his hands in his pockets—and finding them full of stones, which wasn't all that unusual—he looked up at Wolf Rock. "Guess it's just you and me tonight." Back when he was a little kid, his father had given the huge metamorphic stone a growly voice that told him to watch his mouth and do his chores. These days, it didn't have much to say.

Which was okay, because right now he didn't, either.

In his right-hand pocket, he felt the bulk of a single good-size stone. Recognizing the shape by touch, he pulled it out and studied the translucent blue-green of Danny's first find. He vaguely remembered her handing it to him before she dove into the hole, all full of nerves and excitement.

Should he have put the brakes on things right then? Maybe. But he had thought the cavern was solid, had wanted to watch her face down her fear monster and kick its tail.

He'd been wrong about that happening, though. Which was a damn shame.

Dropping the aqua in his pocket, he swung back aboard the ATV and headed for the sorting shack, figuring that if he wasn't going after her—which he wasn't—he might as well get to work cleaning up some of the new clusters. Because no matter what else was going on around him, there always was something very cool about taking a scuffed, dirty rock and making it shine.

When he got to the compound, though, he didn't go inside right away. Instead, he pulled out his phone, hit a number, and listened to the ring on the other end of the line. When it went live, he said, "Hey, Krista, It's Sam. I need a favor."

Which wasn't him fixing things for Danny. He just wanted to make sure she was okay.

When Danny reached Mustang Ridge, she hid the car behind the airport shuttle and made a beeline for her ATV, which was parked beside the barn.

"Danny, hey!" Krista appeared in the barn doorway, with Abby on her shoulder and a worried pinch to her features. "You're back!"

It was far too tempting to make a flying leap onto the ATV, gun it, and take off. Instead, Danny stopped and turned back to her friend. "Let me guess. Sam called."

"He was worried about you." Her *so am I* went unsaid.

"I'm fine," she said, fighting off the prickles of irritation. But, really, how many times would she have to say that before the people around her backed off?

Until she stopped going into a panic fugue when the lights went out, probably.

"Do you want to talk about it?"

The *no* was automatic, but Krista deserved better.

Tucking her hands in her pockets, Danny said, "There's nothing to post-mortem. I pushed it too far and panicked. It's not the first time, won't be the last." It was the first time in a long while that she had done it in front of someone else, though. "As for Sam . . . Well, he doesn't need to watch me look for all the pieces and glue myself together. That's not sexy. At all."

Krista made a humming noise. "I don't think he sees it that way."

*Don't ask, don't ask, don't ask.* "What did he say?" Her heart gave a little bump.

"Not much, really. He told me about what happened out on the claim and asked me to make sure you made it back safe and sound. But he cares. I can tell."

"I . . ." Danny blinked furiously, not sure if the heat-prickles behind her eyes were from tears or hope. And if they were hope, how to make it go away. "It's not a question of caring. It's that I need to do this on my own."

"I get that." Krista squeezed her arm. "I do, truly. But maybe there's room for him, too?"

It would be so easy to say yes. "I don't think that's a good idea. I need the time alone."

"Not tonight," Krista said firmly. "Tonight you're staying with us. In the bunkhouse with us, the barn apartment, or one of the guest rooms in the house—take your pick. But I want you someplace close by."

Telling herself it wasn't stubborn to insist on what she needed when it wasn't going to hurt anybody else, Danny said carefully, "I get what you're saying, really I do, and you're sweet to worry, but I need my own space." The nightmares were going to suck, and there was no way she wanted them going public. And, really, she just wanted to be alone, where there was no point in being embarrassed, and she was the only one who knew when she failed. "Besides," she said, trying to lighten things up, "I won't be totally alone. I've got Chuck and Popov to keep me company."

Krista's brows drew together. "Who?"

"My two squirrel buddies back at camp. I named them after the guys who brought those flying squirrel suits into the mainstream. We have a standing break-fast date."

Krista studied her, still looking worried. After a moment, she said, "If you insist on heading back to Bless-ing Valley, will you at least do me a favor?"

"What?"

She gave a little whistle, and a big black dog trotted out of the barn. Mostly Labrador, he was ribby and had a stray's rough fur, but sat squarely at Krista's heel like he'd been trained to the hilt.

Remembering what Krista had said about her need-ing a dog, Danny quickly shook her head. "Oh, no, you don't. No way."

"Yes, way. I want you to take this guy with you. His name is Wysiwyg—for 'what you see is what you get,' which sums him up perfectly. I call him Whiz for short."

"I'm not calling him anything," Danny protested, ignoring the twinge of guilt when the dog's ears flat-tened at her tone. "I don't need a guard dog."

"Well, that's lucky, because Whiz here is kind of a wimp about loud noises." Krista patted his upturned head. "We don't know his exact story, but I wouldn't be surprised if there was some abuse in there, definitely neglect. One of Nick's clients found him on the side of the road and brought him to the vet clinic. He and Jenny just need someone to foster him for a bit, give him some time to heal up and chill out."

"I don't . . ." Danny began, then trailed off, because the dog was looking at her with big, soulful brown eyes. "Knock it off," she told him. "I'm not taking you."

The end of his tail gave a hopeful thump.

"I'm not," she insisted, even though she was starting to feel like a jerk. First she turned Sam down, and now this. But was it her fault that all she wanted right now was to be left alone?

"If you're not going to stay here, then I want you to take the dog," Krista said softly. "Please. You'll be help-ing Jenny out, and I'll feel better knowing that you're not all alone. Whiz is good company, even if he's a bit of a wuss."

Battered and wimpy, and needing some time to heal. Invisible walls closed in, making Danny want to shove back, even if it was futile. "What if he gets eaten by a bear, or chases the horses? And what am I supposed to do with him during the day?"

The corners of Krista's mouth kicked up. "He'll stick right with you—I think he's afraid of being abandoned again. And there's no reason he can't come to work with you. The guests love him."

As if sensing that it was decision time and she was on the fence, Whiz gave her the full-on puppy-dog eyes, cocked his head endearingly, and lifted a paw for her to shake.

*Oh, come on.* Scowling—she'd had a heck of a day

and she just wanted to relax, darn it—Danny said, "He won't fit on the ATV."

"You can take the Gator. It's a two-seater with a dump back." Krista hooked a thumb over her shoulder. "It's parked next to your ATV."

In other words, this was a setup. Not sure if she should be amused or outraged—and mostly just tired and ready to head for the hills—Danny said accusingly, "You knew I wouldn't stay. You were planning on foisting the dog on me all along."

"I don't have any idea what you're talking about." Krista tossed her the keys. "There's a bag of kibble in the back. Have fun, you two. I think you'll be good for each other."

# 11

*C*rack-boom!

  The noise sounded like a bomb, or an avalanche, rocketing Danny awake to flickers of light and the earth shaking around her.

  Her arms were trapped, her legs were folded so tight to her chest that she could only suck air into the top few inches of her lungs. A heavy weight sat on her, pressing her into—

  The weight lurched up, stepped on her with big, pointy feet, and slurped her face. "Whuff!"

  "Gah!" She sat bolt upright, pawing at her face, then for her flashlight. "Whiz. What the—" Sheet lightning flashed outside, close enough to make the air crackle. The dog yelped and launched his whole weight onto her. "Off!" She shoved without strength or leverage as thunder roared. "For the love of—Get *off*!" When he finally moved, she dragged herself up, coughing and wheezing for air, for control. "Damn it."

  She couldn't stop shaking. *Slippery rock walls. Night closing in. A storm coming. Flinging her head back and screaming, "Get me out of here!" and having it come out as a whisper.* She doubled over her folded arms, her breath coming in rattling gasps as the lightning flickered again, charging the air with electricity but no hope of rain.

She fumbled for the flashlight, took three tries to turn it on. And realized she wasn't the only one struggling to hold it together.

Whiz was pancaked on his belly, shaking like he was caught in a one-man earthquake. His ears were flat against his head, his white-rimmed eyes big and apologetic, and his throat vibrating with a series of anxious whines that sounded like he was channeling a dental drill.

Guilt stinging, she scooted over to him. "I'm sorry, you startled me. It's okay, it's just heat lightning. Nothing to be afraid of." Her voice steadied as she tried to soothe the dog. "You're a good dog. Good man. Brave boy." She patted him. "Easy, buddy. I've got you. You're safe."

Lightning sheeted around them, so close that the air crackled along the tent walls and the hairs on her arms stood straight up, and a sudden gust of wind buffeted the tent around them, the sound and pressure making it feel like they were right next to a high-speed train.

Whiz lunged for the front of the tent and scratched at the zipper, then started pawing with both front feet, hunched over as though he was trying to tunnel out.

"Knock it off. You're going to rip it!"

But the dog dug like he was headed for the earth's core, panting and whining, and thoroughly unglued.

"Do you need to go out?" she asked, thinking the poor guy was probably fighting a stress piddle. "Okay. Hang on." Rattled and shaky, she stuffed her feet into her boots, got him into the harness and leash that Krista had sent with him, and unzipped the fly.

A gust of wind ripped the tent open and filled it in an instant. The material billowed around them, terrifying Whiz. Howling, "Yi-yi-yi," he bolted out of the tent, yanking the leash from Danny's grip.

"Whiz, wait! No!" Envisioning him disappearing into the darkness, she surged out of the tent. *"Whiz!"*

She got a flurry of barks in answer, turned her flashlight toward the sound, and found him reared up against the RV door, clawing at the screen.

"Whiz, no!" She grabbed his leash and pulled. "Down!"

*FLASH-BOOM!* Lightning and thunder cracked simultaneously and a huge wind gust hit the campsite, flipping the table and sending the chairs flying. The dog yanked on the leash, trying to get free. And if he did, she was pretty sure he'd be gone.

"Okay," she shouted over the storm. "Okay, you win!" She wrenched open the door to the RV. "Go on, get in!"

The dog flung himself up the steps and disappeared into the darkness. Danny, on the other hand, stalled just inside the door, her heart pounding. Because if for a minute there she had been able to level herself off and focus on Whiz, now it all came back full force as she stared into the long, narrow center aisle and felt the unnatural stillness of the air.

The wind slapped at the RV, making the broad walls shudder.

"Damn it," she muttered between her gritted teeth, "you're fine. This is no big deal."

That was what she had told herself about the crystal pocket, though, and look how that turned out. She should just go sleep in the tent. Whiz would be fine without her. Unless he wasn't. Krista had said he wanted to stick right with his person, so she wasn't sure she dared leave him alone in the RV. Two squirrels had done enough damage. What about an eighty-pound dog having an anxiety attack?

*Darn, darn, darn.* She couldn't do it. She took a step back, then another. Felt for the stairs with her toe.

"Whuff?" The sound came from the back room.

"You're okay," she called. "Don't worry. I'll see you in the morning." But every instinct she had—even the ones that were telling her to sleep in the tent—said that she didn't dare leave him in the *Rambling Rose* alone.

She hesitated as lightning flashed. Counted to three until thunder rumbled. Then, muttering under her breath, she cranked the cockpit windows open.

Air moved past her, telling her that there was a way out. Sure, it also meant the squirrels could get in, but she had to figure that the dog would be a good deterrent. Maybe. Hopefully.

*Okay. You can do this.*

Pulling the cushions and blanket off the mini-couch, she made herself a nest near the door, where everything smelled fresh and she could see out. Her pulse drummed as she settled down on the RV's carpeted floor. "Fine. You win. We'll sleep in here. Happy now?"

There was the sound of padding feet. Then the big dog sank down right beside her, tightening the blanket and sending little panic sparks through her system. Steeling herself, she patted his head. "Good dog."

She might as well suck it up and give him what he needed. It wasn't like she was going to get any more sleep tonight.

So she draped an arm over his ribs as the storm noises settled in around them—the whistle-moan of wind through the open windows and door, the rattle-flap of the awning, and the scratch-bang of the branches on the . . .

She slept.

"You got a dog?" Charlie's face got really big on the computer screen as she leaned in. Then she laughed at herself and said, "Tilt the camera so I can see him." When Danny obliged, she waved and chirped, "Hi, Whiz! I'm Auntie Charlie!"

A scant thirteen months younger than Danny, she was lighter-haired and finer-boned, with a scattering of freckles and an utter inability to sit still.

"You're his *temporary* aunt Charlie," Danny corrected, putting the laptop back up on Krista's desk. "I'm not keeping him."

"Why not? There's room at the house."

*Because I'm not sure I'm coming back.* She didn't say it out loud, though. She wasn't ready for it to hit the parental grapevine, especially when she wasn't yet positive she really meant it. "I'm sure Jenny and Krista are working on finding him a home around here." She patted Whiz's head. "Until then, he's helping me with the guests." And that wasn't the only thing he was helping with. Ever since the night of the storm, she'd been sleeping in the RV. In the back bedroom, even, albeit with the windows wide-open. And she hadn't had a nightmare in days. She didn't think it was the company, either. It was that she had someone to worry about other than herself. Someone who needed her to be brave and didn't judge.

Charlie made a face. "Nature hikes. Bleck. Bo-ring." Then she added quickly, "Don't get me wrong, though. They're fine for you."

"I'm having fun," Danny said, letting it roll off her back. They chatted a few minutes more—about Charlie's upcoming mud run, their parents' plan to do a half marathon in every New England state the following year, and how the store was doing.

It was a little odd to realize how superficial their conversation was, how polite they kept everything. Then again, she and Charlie had always hung out with different friends and competed against each other in just about every sport possible, so maybe it wasn't that odd. And maybe it was something they should think about changing.

"How's Jase?" Danny asked. "Is he still aiming for the big century race this fall?" Charlie's boyfriend was a serious road biker and all-around nice guy.

Charlie blinked in surprise, but answered, "He's good. Dad's going to sponsor him for the race. He said it would be good advertising."

And he probably missed having two kids to cheer for. Letting herself feel the pang—she was finally getting what Farah meant about it being impossible for a sane woman to make everybody happy and still take care of herself—Danny said, "Good for him. Just don't let Mom design his uniform. Remember the Halloween mountain bike race debacle." It had involved matching ballerina tutus, sparkly wings, and shirts plastered with the shop's name and logo. Mom had claimed they were fairies, but once they had their full-face helmets and body armor on, they had looked more like cross-dressing ballerina hockey players.

"No way. I already told her that Jase and I would handle his jersey. Better that than fairy wings." They shared a grin over the memory. It hadn't been funny at the time, but fifteen years later, the pictures were pure gold. Then, hesitating a little, Charlie said, "I, um, saw Allison the other day. She asked how you were."

It wasn't nearly the kick in the gut that Danny would've expected. More like a poke in the solar plexus. "Have they set a date yet?"

"They're doing a Christmas wedding."

Okay, a poke in the stomach with a couple of chopsticks. But she wasn't going to dwell on it. "Next time you see her, tell her I said congratulations. Actually, on second thought, don't."

"No?"

"I'll e-mail her myself. Brandon, too." If she held a grudge, she would be the only one who knew it, or really cared. So why bother? "Are you going to the wedding?"

Charlie ducked her head. "She, um, asked me to be a bridesmaid?"

"Are you asking me or telling me?"

"I said I'd have to talk to you."

Moved, Danny said, "Aw, Chuckie. That's so sweet."

That got a snort. "Don't call me that. I take it you're cool with me being in Allison and Bran's wedding?"

*Bran.* The nickname tugged, but that was life. "You don't need my permission, but thanks. And go ahead. Have a ball."

"You'll be back by then, right? You're not going to miss ski season." She made it sound inconceivable.

"We'll see."

Charlie cocked her head. "You're really okay with this, aren't you? What happened?" Her eyes sharpened. "Did you meet somebody?"

"No. I mean, yes, I'm really okay with Allison and Brandon getting married. And no, it's not because I met somebody new. Or maybe I did." Danny grinned. "Me."

Her sister's brows furrowed. "You met yourself?"

"Yep. And you know what? I think I like me."

"I don't get it."

"That's okay, because I do." At least she was starting to. Hearing Shelby's voice in the main room, she said, "I gotta go. We're heading over to the barn raising."

"The *whut*?"

"Barn raising. There's going to be a square dance after, which sounds fun."

Charlie was looking at her like she had just started spouting off about alien landing parties and nasal probes. "What are you, in another century out there? Sheesh. I thought Maine was bad."

Laughter bubbling up, Danny waved. "I'll talk to you later, Sis. Tell Mom and Dad I called, and that I'll try them again in a week or so." She aimed for the disconnect button.

"Wait!"

Danny froze, her finger hovering. "What?"

An impudent grin lit Charlie's face. "Whoever this guy is—the one you're trying to pretend you're not thinking about—I think you need to ask him to dance. What have you got to lose?"

*     *     *

Sam didn't claim to be an expert gem cutter by any stretch, but he enjoyed the process, and on a good day he could produce a decent cut and polished stone. So far, he was having a good day, at least when it came to the work. With classic rock pumping through the sorting shed and the gem wax-mounted on the drop stick to keep it immobilized, he was in the groove.

Earlier, he had cut a flawed section off the rough aquamarine and ground down the outer surfaces, shaping it toward the teardrop outline that would maximize the usable stone. Now, referring to the cutting chart at his elbow, he started on the facets of the pear cut—a flat oval table on the front surrounded by a precise set of angles, with a deeper starburst pattern on the back that would turn the blue-green bright and brilliant when the light hit it.

It required exact precision, especially for a stone this big, so as he started faceting the front, he ignored the movement in his peripheral vision. Until it started flapping at him.

He drew the stone away from the grinding face, killed the motor, and fixed Midas with a look. "This better be important."

The geo-engineer's facial hardware gleamed in the fluorescent overheads as he did a mime routine, complete with silent screams and invisible walls closing in on him.

Sam tapped his ear protectors. "They're digital, so I can hear you just fine, just like I can hear the music. Which you darn well know. And I repeat: this better be important."

The engineer's eyebrows rose. "Axyl's right. You're cranky." He held up both hands. "Hey, don't pound the messenger. He sent me in here to see if you want to ride over to the Sears place with us."

Right. The barn raising. "You guys go ahead."

"You're coming later?"

Sam shrugged. "I bought all the steel and hired the machines."

"So?"

"What do you mean, *so*?"

Midas studied his tattooed knuckles—*ROCK* on one hand and *STAR* on the other. "I've never heard you pull the rich-dick card before, and sure as hell not as an excuse for getting out of hard work. So I figure there's another reason you don't want to go to the barn raising. Like maybe that brunette who's been staying over at Mustang Ridge?"

Sam bristled. "What do you know about her?"

"I know she helped you find that aqua pocket over the weekend, and you've been in a mood ever since."

"I'm not in a mood."

"Whatever it is, I've never seen you like this over a woman before." A penlight came out of Midas's pocket, got clicked on. Leaning in, he studied the stone. "Nice aqua. Good color, really good structure. Not used to you cutting your own, though. This for her?"

"I'm just playing around. And you're breathing on me. Go away. Go build a barn."

"Come with us. Talk to her."

Sam fired up the grinder. Over the noise, he said, "She doesn't want to see me."

"She said that?"

"Not exactly." Not even close. "She doesn't think she's in a good place to start anything romantic."

"What do you think?"

*I think that she's stronger and braver than she realizes, and that I miss her a whole hell of a lot more than I should.* "I think you should go away, because I'm busy."

"Moping."

*"I am not—"* He bit off the muted roar and pointed to the door. "OUT!"

Midas wisely scrammed, letting the door bang behind him and giving Sam his peace and classic rock. The damage was done, though.

As Sam checked his chart to confirm the next cut, he pictured the look on Danny's face when he rinsed off the stone and she caught her first glimpse of aquamarine. As he started the next facet, his fingers remembered the softness of her skin. And as the acrid smell filtered through his mask, he tasted her kiss, amping up the churn in his gut . . . The one that said, *What the hell are you doing?*

He was being a stubborn idiot, that was what.

Cursing, he removed the stone from the grinder and killed the engine. He was out of his chair before the wheel stopped spinning, had his gear off before the next song started. He stiff-armed the door, saw that the others had already left, and made a beeline for his truck.

"The hell with it," he said as he fired up the engine. Maybe he'd made it a rule to never chase a woman. But he'd never before known a woman like her.

# 12

"Woo-hoo!" Danny cheered as she helped lift the heavy beam into place alongside Krista and two of the ranch's guests—Magnus and Cathy Kees, who ran a Christmas tree farm on the other side of town and had insisted on being part of the barn raising. "It's up!"

"Hold it right there," Wyatt ordered, then stood back and studied it. "What do you think?" he asked Magnus and Cathy's seven-year-old son, Ike, who he'd deputized to hand him lag bolts and washers. "Should we level it off again?"

Ike, all serious, nodded. "Looks crooked to me."

"Just bolt it, buster!" Krista shouted. "You know darn well it's level!"

Laughing, Wyatt clambered up the stepladder and drove the long bolts in deep, then added a couple of angled two-by-fours to finish the frame for this section of stalls. Then he scanned back down the row, nodding. "Looks good, team. And, hey, here come our walls!"

They cheered as a forklift came through the extra-tall door and scooted down the cement aisle toward them, carrying a pallet of precut, prestained panels that would fit right into the team's framing to create a row of stalls, including a foaling stall for Marigold—a beloved broodmare who had survived the fire and was getting close to her due date. The stalls faced a huge indoor riding arena, where several other teams were working on building a chin-high plywood kickboard around the perimeter. Other groups were busy installing the bus-size mirrors and enclosing a windowed viewing room that could be heated in the winter. Nearby, a short office-lined aisle connected the indoor arena to the main barn, where other crews were installing additional stalls and storage areas.

Paid crews had done the site prep and built the outer shells of the big steel structures over the previous week, which Danny figured was probably a good thing. The steel beams and panels called for heavy equipment rather than many hands, and the thirty or so teams scattered between the two buildings had made some serious progress over the past five hours, filling in the wooden guts that would put the riding school back in action.

Standing back and propping her gloved hands on her hips as she surveyed the busy scene, Danny said, "What do you think, Whiz? Should we take up building barns for a living?" There was something very satisfying about watching the place take shape.

The big black dog had started out the day frisking from one human to the next and gleefully chasing whatever got thrown, but he had soon downgraded to sticking close to Danny, watching the action as Wyatt's team worked on the stall blocks they had been assigned. Now, as they got close to quitting time and a couple of the teams switched over to setting up a stage in the big open space of the riding arena, all the dog managed was a couple of tail thumps.

"I vote yes," Krista said, "but only if we're working with nice stall kits like these." She hefted one of the prefinished pieces. "Heck of a nice donation."

The offhand mention shouldn't have kicked Danny's senses into high gear, just as she shouldn't keep darting looks over at one particular kickboard crew to see if it had gained another member. But it wasn't much of a secret that Babcock Gems had sponsored most of the rebuild, and Sam's guys kept looking around like they were waiting for someone.

"Hey," a woman hollered over from the stage-building team. "Can we borrow your extension ladder for a minute?"

"Sure thing!" Krista called back. Then, to Danny, she said, "Want to grab an end? Even folded up, it's a beast."

When they got to the stage, they found two crews conferring at the bottom of a tall support column. Located at the edge of the arena, the column stretched up thirty feet or so and was topped by a pair of loudspeakers on one side and a row of floodlights on the other.

"Problem?" Krista asked.

"A wire came loose." An older farmer-type with a hitch in his getalong peered up, brows furrowed. "Which wouldn't be a big deal, except that we don't have the keys for the bucket truck, and we'll need the speakers for the square dance. I'd climb up there, but . . ." He slapped his bum leg. "No can do."

"And the rest of us plain don't like heights," said the woman who had called Krista over, giving a little shudder.

"I'll do it." Danny said it without thinking, without hesitating, the way she would have before. *Cliff diving? I'll do it. Hang gliding? Sign me up.*

Krista's head snapped around. "Are you sure?"

"Thirty feet up a steel girder? No problem." She wouldn't let it be a problem. The fear could have its dark little cave. She was taking back the heights. "What do I do once I'm up there?"

Five minutes later, armed with instructions, a rudimentary safety rope, and shouts of "Go, Danny!" she scaled the ladder seven feet up, to where the beam offered a series of hand- and footholds running the rest of the way to the top. Nerves skimmed as she started up and her center of balance shifted, making her acutely aware of the downward tug of gravity and the empty air beneath her. Focusing on her goal—*look up, not down*—she climbed, running through the repair in her head.

She saw the problem before she was even all the way there—the main connection hung loose, the wires separated.

"Do you swear you killed the right breakers?" she called down.

"Pinkie swear," Krista hollered back. "My dad triple-checked it."

Taking Ed Skye at his word, Danny climbed the last couple of rungs, used the safety rope to give her a little extra leverage, and got to work on the connection, screwing it together and adding a layer of electrical tape for good measure. Then, backing off a couple of rungs, she waved. "Okay. Fire it up!"

There were a couple of relayed shouts, and then a

*click-hum* as the loudspeakers came online and the lights flared to life.

"Woo-hoo!" Krista led the cheer. "Way to go! Come on down, girlfriend!"

Instead, Danny stayed where she was and gazed around from three stories up, surprised anew at how a little altitude could change her perspective on things. From there, the alternating opaque and see-through roof panels seemed to go on forever, and she could see over the kick panels to the crews finishing up their stalls on the other side. More, she could gaze through the nearest skylight panel, over the new barn and scorched fields to the mountains in the distance. And darned if she didn't feel a tug, the kind that said, *I bet there's good climbing up there*.

She had roped up twice since the accident—once at an easy traverse she could do in her sleep, and once at a stupid-simple indoor wall—and she had panicked both times, winding up scared and sad, convinced she would never climb again. Now, leaning back against her rope and feeling that much closer to the sunlight coming down through the clear panel, she felt joyous warmth spread through her. Relief. Excitement. She could do this. She really could.

Maybe—probably—she wouldn't ever again spider her way up a chimney or crawl down to explore a crevice that barely left her room to breathe, but that was okay if she could still go up.

"Seriously," Krista called, teasing now. "You can come down any time. I'm not leaving without you, and Wyatt is itching to get back to work."

"Coming." Danny waved acknowledgment, then

tightened her grip to release the safety rope and get it set for a rappel. Checking below to make sure she was clear to land, she saw that the crowd had grown and shifted, thronging now around an open cooler of sodas and a platter of cookies; those gathered looked like Jupiter and her mustangs jostling for position down by the river.

Except for one outlier. Because there, at the edge of the crowd, Sam stood with his work boots planted shoulder-wide and his thumbs hooked in his tool belt, looking up at her. When their eyes met, he lifted a hand in greeting, then gave her a thumbs-up.

And not because he was propping her up, but because she darn well deserved it.

"Hey!" She waved back and held up an index finger for him to wait. Suddenly in a mad rush to get back down, she shifted her weight and kicked away from the beam, letting the rope play through her fingers as she swung out and then back, rappelling down. And, for a few brief seconds, she was flying like she used to do.

Sam wanted to catch her on the way down, wanted to sweep her up and carry her off somewhere alone, where he would do his damnedest to convince her that she should take a chance on the two of them. But as she came smoothly down the last few feet of rope and her feet touched the ground as gentle as a kiss, all of his arguments backed up in his throat at the sight of her face, alight with triumph and the thrill of adventure.

"Sam!" she said. "I didn't think you were coming."

"Were you looking for me?"

Her lips curved in a smile that lit a fire in his gut.

"Maybe I was. Maybe I've been thinking that I was wrong the other day, and that you were right—I've got more guts than I think. And maybe I was hoping that you'd show up and ask me to dance."

Blood firing in his veins, he closed the distance between them and lowered his voice so it was just the two of them in the middle of the crowd. "Well, now, that's a shame."

Her eyes widened. "Excuse me?"

"I had it all planned out, how I was going to throw you over my shoulder and whisk you out of here. Maybe even tie you to the back of my horse and ride off with you into the sunset."

"Oh?" Interest lit her expression. "Where were you going to take me?"

"Keyhole Canyon, maybe. Someplace where we could hide out for as long as it took me to convince you that I'll give you whatever room you need, whenever you need it, and that I won't try to fix you." A corner of his mouth kicked up. "That last part is going to be a cinch, by the way. Because I think you're just about perfect the way you are."

"Let's not go overboard." But she leaned into him. "So what exactly are we talking about here? What do you want from me?"

"Everything." He didn't have to think it through—it was right there, caught between the burn of desire and the tight spot beneath his ribs that said his feelings for her ran deeper than they should. Keeping his voice low, so she was the only one who heard, he said, "I want to go out with you, stay in with you, hunt rocks with you, climb mountains with you, kiss you, go to bed with you, wake up with you . . ." He closed the last little bit of distance between them, and said against her lips, "For starters, though, I want my first dance with you. Tonight. And then I want to be part of whatever happens next."

For Danny, the rest of the workday passed in a blur of prefinished wood, stainless-steel hardware, little Ike always being cheerfully underfoot despite his parents' best efforts, and her shooting a whole lot of looks over to the kickboard crew, where Sam was helping cover the last of the outward-angled half wall with heavy plywood panels.

"It's not too soon," she said as she wrestled a stall panel into place, banging it tight against its neighbors. "Is it?"

Whiz, who was sitting nearby, having roused when the cooking crew fired up the barbecue, tipped his head and gave a "whuff."

"Too soon for what?" Krista said, coming around the corner with the hardware they would need to hang the sliding stall door.

Too soon to sleep with someone after only one official date, Danny thought. Too soon to be thinking that she was getting her brain back under control. Way too soon to think she could handle getting involved with someone who made her feel the way Sam did.

Aloud, though, she said, "I was just wondering if it was too soon to stress about the fact that I don't know the first thing about square dancing."

"Sure, you were." Krista shot a pointed look over at Sam's crew, but she just grinned. "As for the dancing?

Don't worry. Fiddler will explain all the terms and how to do the steps, and he's good about helping everybody keep up. And if you mess up, you just laugh and move on."

Danny blew out a breath, relieved when Krista got to work on the door and didn't press her further. She liked her new friends, maybe even loved them. But this wasn't a committee decision. It was hers.

She still hadn't decided by the time the volunteers wrapped up their work for the day and the Mustang Ridge crew went back to the shuttle bus to change into their party clothes. She decided to let it go, though, and—like Sam had said—see what happened next. It wasn't an entirely comfortable sensation, rather like making a one-handed grab on a free climb . . . But it darn sure wasn't the sort of thing a burrito would do.

"Ha," she said to Whiz, "I'm finally unwrapping my inner tortilla."

Jenny paused in the middle of pulling on a fresh shirt and screwed up her face. "Huh?"

"It's the squirrels," Krista confided to Abby, who had spent most of the afternoon with her grandma in the snack tent, and now lay in a frilly little carrier, making cute baby noises. "Talking to them every day has made her nutty."

"Very funny." Danny stripped off her grubby work shirt. "I was just saying that I feel good. Like I'm finally making some progress."

"I'll drink to that." Shelby held up an imaginary glass.

"Hear, hear!" Jenny said, and they mime-clinked. But then she made a rueful face. "Though I'd rather be toasting a shower right about now, instead of changing straight into party clothes."

"On the bright side," Krista put in, "the grunge is going to be a badge of honor. The only people who are going to be clean are the ones who skipped out on working and just showed up for the fun." Her eyes lit up as Danny wiggled into a tight, lacy green shirt to go with the silver-studded black pants the others had talked her into on their shopping trip. "Wowza. Shower or no shower, you look hot."

"Hey, I come from the land of ski bums, where turning your shirt inside out is considered getting dressed up for a date." Not all the time, granted, and certainly not among the rich-and-famous set, but often enough that she wasn't bothered to be pulling her hair back in a ponytail, tamping her feet into a pair of pointy-toed boots, slapping on a little makeup, and calling herself ready for a party.

"No wonder you fit right in here." Shelby faketoasted her again. "You look amazing. And I'm not just saying that because I picked out the shirt. In fact, I predict that Sam is going to swallow his tongue when he gets a load of you."

Danny didn't know about that, but when they made their appearance at the picnic area a few minutes later, to scattered applause and a few good-natured wolf whistles, she felt like she had regained the swagger she hadn't even realized she'd been missing.

Sam stood as she approached, his eyes locking on her with a hunger that rippled through her body. She was aware of Wyatt, Nick, and Foster nearby, along with others from the Mustang Ridge crew. But her attention was wholly focused on Sam as he caught her hands and held her away for a long up-and-down and a rumble of masculine approval. "You look incredible."

"Thanks. And for the record, that was going to be my line." He had lost the tool belt and changed his shirt, and had a dead-sexy stubble shadow on his jaw.

He grazed his lips across hers. "I said it first."

"Come on, you two," Shelby urged, being tugged along by her tween-age daughter, Lizzie, who was wearing a sparkly purple cowgirl hat and smudges of work-dirt. "We've got to get in line before the good stuff's all gone and we're stuck with lima bean casserole and fruity Jell-O."

"Sam has dibs on the Jell-O," called Midas, earning a guffaw from Axyl.

Danny had met the other members of Babcock Gems earlier. Now, easing out of Sam's embrace but keeping hold of his hand, she raised an eyebrow in their direction. "Do I want to know the story there?"

"It's nothing bad." Sam folded his fingers through hers. "But I'm with Shelby. I'm jonesing for Gran's pulled pork, and it'll go fast."

Their bodies bumped as they went through the line, where he hit the meat and potatoes and she snagged a chicken breast and a rainbow of local veggies.

"Watch out, boy." Axyl nodded to her plate. "Next thing you know, she'll have you eating rabbit food."

Liking the bearded prospector already—and aware that he was the closest thing Sam had left to family—she said, "No way. We have a deal—if he doesn't try to fix me, then I won't try to fix him."

"Smart girl." He winked at Sam. "Like I said, you'd better watch out."

It wasn't exactly a meet-the-parents moment, but it was pretty close. Grinning, she plopped a walnut-studded brownie on her plate, then defiantly added a second. "See? I'm not a health nut. I'm just saving up my calories for the good stuff."

"Smart girl, indeed."

Laughing, Sam whisked her back to their table, where they were soon sandwiched in by the others, with lots of shifting around and queries of "Is this my beer or yours?" And to Danny's surprise, she didn't even mind the close quarters. The jostling didn't feel scary or suffocating. It felt . . . normal. Fun, even. And not just because she was so totally aware of the feel of Sam's body very close to hers.

The conversation was lively, bouncing from the food, to the day's work, to the plans for next week's guests at Mustang Ridge. And from there to Wyatt and Krista's wedding.

"Centerpieces," Krista said, darting a quick look to make sure that Rose wasn't within earshot. "Seriously, who cares what's in the middle of the table?"

"So tell her you're not doing them," Jenny said.

"I tried. It didn't work."

"Admit it—you're a wimp when it comes to Mom."

"I'm not!" Krista nudged Wyatt. "Tell her."

He lifted his dessert. "Good brownies, don't you think, Sam?"

"An excellent vintage." He studied what was left of his own. "Rich and chocolaty, with just the right bite to them. And do I detect a hint of spice in the top note?"

Krista narrowed her eyes dangerously. "Laugh it up, you two. But I've got three words for you: *sparkly pink cummerbund.*"

Sam winced. "You told her? Dude, that was classified."

"The baby got it out of me." Wyatt lifted Abby from her carrier and draped her over his shoulder for a little pat.

Enjoying them—all of them—Danny nudged Sam. "I think you'd look cute in sparkly pink. I've got matching fairy wings you can borrow."

"Hey, you're supposed to be on my side!"

"Sorry." She smiled sweetly. "Girl power."

"Howdy, folks!" a cheery amplified voice hailed from the indoor arena. A lively fiddle tune struck up as the man said over the loudspeaker, "My name is Fiddler, and I'm going to be your caller tonight. This is your ten-minute warning, so finish up your food and get your fine selves on in here." His voice dropped an octave. "For those of you ladies who are virgins to the square, you've got nothing to fear. I'll talk you through your first time. And don't worry. I'll be gentle."

"Well." Danny fanned herself with her napkin. "Sexy square dancing. I had no idea."

A corner of Sam's mouth kicked up. "Fiddler's got a way about him."

*And so do you.* Her whole body was aware of him. Not because she was leaning on him, but because she wanted him with a deep, insistent throb that was getting stronger by the minute.

"You want to get in there, let him talk us through some patterns?"

"Lead the way!"

The next two hours were pure, unadulterated fun. Fiddler proved to be short and bowlegged, with merry eyes almost lost beneath layers of wrinkles, and feet that never seemed to stop moving as he sawed away on his fiddle and called the square dances. He coached the dancers through pattern after pattern—bowing to their corners and their partners, doing do-si-dos, swings, and promenades—starting slow and picking things up so gradually that Danny didn't really notice until suddenly she realized her hair had fallen out of its ponytail to whip around, flung by the force of Sam's spinning her at arm's length, then snapping her in close to his side to parade around the square.

He grinned down at her. "You've got this."

"I really do!"

"Okay, ladies and gentlemen," Fiddler shouted into the microphone. "Enough with the warm-up. Are you guys ready to *square dance*?"

There was a cheer from the crowd, and two new musicians appeared suddenly and stepped onto the stage—a bass guitarist and a jug blower. They joined in, adding a deeper note to the music.

"*Annnd first you whistle, then you sing . . .*" Fiddler called, his voice taking on a new twang that went straight through Danny and made her bounce to the beat. "*All join hands and make a ring.*" She followed directions, hanging on to Sam's hand and grinning up at him. "*Into the center with a whinny and a neigh . . .*" Into the center they went, then out again on his call of, "*Feed 'em oats and a bale of hay.*" Then, grinning like a madman, Fiddler hollered, "And a one, two, one, two, three, FOUR!"

The musicians kicked it into high gear, zooming from an easy jog to a flat-out gallop in no time at all, and Fiddler started calling hard and fast, blurring his words together like an auctioneer. And Danny and Sam swung their partners, do-si-doed, centered, and cornered like crazy people, while the world spun and the dance floor got crowded.

Eventually, winded, laughing, and practically holding each other up, they stumbled back outside to grab drinks, split another brownie, and sneak several kisses in the moonlight. The music drew them back in, though, and they soon plunged into the heated, whirling crowd again. They found a square and fell into the call, trading partners around and around in a daisy chain. But no matter how far they went or how many partners they traded, they always came back to each other as if magnetized.

That was how it felt. Like Danny was elementally drawn to him—the press of his body against hers, the taste of his kiss. She couldn't get enough, didn't want it to end.

Finally, though, when she was dizzy and couldn't really feel her feet hit the ground anymore, the music softened and Fiddler leaned into the mic to rumble, "And now we're going to shift gears, folks. Gentlemen's choice, so grab your favorite lady and let's slow it down."

Sam hooked an arm around her waist and drew her close, and even though she hadn't doubted she would be his pick, the smooth move sent a drugging warmth through her body, making her sigh as she melted against him.

"I'm guessing I don't need to ask if you're having a good time." Sam said, his voice a sexy rumble against her temple as they swayed together.

"I can't remember the last time I enjoyed a party this much." Maybe never. "But . . . I'm about ready to call it a night." She turned her lips against his throat, tasted him. "How about you?"

He stiffened, his hands drifting an inch or so down from her waist. "Can I drive you home?"

"You can," she said. Breath thinning in her lungs, she added, "Or you could take me to Windfall."

He drew away just far enough to search her face with eyes gone suddenly hot and urgent. "Tell me you're sure."

Her lips curved. "I'm sure. This is what I want. *You* are what I want. Not because I'm expecting you to make things better for me, but because things already *are* better. And I want to celebrate that. With you." The decision was made, and it was delicious. "What do you say?"

He swept her into his arms, into a kiss, and said against her lips, "I say let's round up your dog and get the heck out of here."

# 13

It wasn't until he led Danny past Wolf Rock, with
Whiz zigzagging around with his nose down and his
tail whipping, that it hit Sam just how few women he'd
brought home. Two, maybe three, and he'd known
them pretty well by the time he invited them to Windfall. It wasn't a rule, hadn't even really been intentional.
B and Bs were simply easier, more romantic. He wanted
Danny here, though, wanted her in his bed.

He paused with his hand on the kitchen door. "I
warned you that it's really a bachelor pad hiding inside
a much bigger house, right?"

Her lips curved. "Does your bedroom have a window?"

"Lots of 'em. Even sliders to a deck."

"Then we're good."

It really was that simple with her, he realized. She
didn't care about the big house or the money. She'd
rather help rebuild a stranger's barn than go out to a
fancy dinner, liked treasure hunting more than she did
the actual gems. And how cool was that?

Moved, he turned and kissed her, feasting on her
mouth as they stood there together at his kitchen door,

like a couple of teens who weren't ready to say good night. The embers that had sparked again and again on the dance floor fanned suddenly to flames, along with the triumph of knowing he didn't have to hold himself back now, didn't have to stop. They were alone.

Blood pounding in his veins, he cupped her breasts, shaping their soft, feminine weight and swallowing her moan. "Inside," he said. "Bedroom." That was as far as he could think.

She twined her fingers through his. "Lead the way."

Sam's kitchen said *non-slob bachelor* with its stack of local menus, two mismatched towels and a lack of decorations to offset the austere angles of granite and steel. The sitting room had been turned into a home gym, with a flat screen over the carved fireplace mantel and exercise equipment instead of furniture. Stairs curved around an atrium with expensive-looking woodwork and bare walls. A long hallway opened to many doors—a bathroom, several closed panels, a game room that looked like something out of a sci-fi movie. And then the bedroom.

Finally, the bedroom. Where it felt like they had been headed all night. Or longer, because even when she had thought they were done with each other, she had still wanted him, still wondered what it would be like—the sizzle of his kiss when he turned to her in the doorway and pressed her against the frame like he couldn't wait any longer; the glide of her palms beneath his shirt; the way his voice rasped when he broke the kiss to say, "My beautiful, brave Danny."

Then he swept her in his arms, and carried her to the

bed, and need coiled inside her. She wanted to know, wanted to feel. Wanted *him*.

She was peripherally aware of a plush rug, a framed mountain landscape, a few photographs on the bureau, and the big glass doors looking out on the night sky. But rather than focusing on their surroundings, she wrapped her arms around his neck and kissed him as he lowered her to the bed. Then, as he came down beside her, she drew him in closer, above her. There was no fear, no suffocation. There was only Sam's good, solid weight and the sparks of color that reflected from his eyes, gone silver with desire as they kissed and kissed again.

She popped the snap studs on his shirt and curled around to kiss his throat, his collarbone, and lower. A groan rattled in his chest as he tugged on her shirt, slipping it up and over her head, then tossed it aside. He cupped her breasts, captured her lips in a deep, dark kiss, and moved against her with inciting friction. He skimmed his lips over her belly, the point of her hip, and slid the clingy black pants down and off, along with her boots, then dealt with his own.

Desire flared, restless and urgent, as she watched him strip, uncovering the rugged, no-nonsense musculature of a guy who worked with his hands and his back, and spent more time with a pick and shovel than with the weight bench in the front room. His broad shoulders angled to narrow hips, and the lean muscles of his thighs made her want to cruise her lips along the path of those indentations, then up to the hard flesh they framed.

He caught her look, and his eyes darkened with lust.

A quick trip to the bedside table—then a low curse and a longer trip across the hall to the bathroom—yielded a box of condoms. It warmed her that he hadn't known quite where they were, and the flames fanned higher when the mattress dipped beneath his weight and he kissed his way back up her body.

She welcomed him, curled her arms around him, and kissed him as he settled between her legs, the blunt head of him nudging her slick opening. She stretched against him, inviting him in. He joined them together with a powerful surge that stole her breath with pleasure. She gasped and clutched at him, arching her body to take more of the delicious fullness.

"Danny," he rasped, his breath hot on her cheek. "My brave, brave Danny."

Then he paused, waiting until she opened her eyes.

Their gazes locked, his lips curved, and he began to move—slowly at first, but quickly picking up speed as she moved against him, meeting his thrusts and urging him on. Her fingers dug into the bunch and flow of the muscles on either side of his spine and she bowed against him, glorying in the slide of his flesh within her.

The end, when it came for her, was hard and sudden, almost brutal in its intensity, yet at the same time gentle and joyous. She coiled and whispered his name as her inner muscles contracted around his hard length, and a moment later he shuddered and followed her over.

She stretched out around him, feeling like she was free-falling without a chute, cartwheeling through the air without wings, flying free.

Then, slowly, coming back down to earth.

The room took shape around her—the big bed, with its no-nonsense blue sheets and striped down comforter; the painting, which reminded her of Blessing Valley; the big doors looking out on the night; the dog curled up on a fallen blanket, carefully not looking at them.

And the wonderful press of Sam's body on hers.

He propped up on his elbows to ease some of his weight, his beard stubble grazing her temple as his breathing slowly came back to normal. "Sweet Danny," he said, voice low and husky. His lips touched where his jaw had rested, then her cheek, her nose. Her lips.

She savored the kiss, and the pleasure pang that shuddered through her body when he disengaged from her, then rolled onto his back and gathered her against him. Splaying a hand over his heart, she pillowed her cheek on his chest and let herself drift while he stroked her back, his hand cruising from her shoulder to her buttocks and up again.

After a long, delicious while, he stirred. "Can I get you anything? Snack? Drink? Whole-body massage?"

That last one sounded good, but his voice was sleep-slurred.

"I'm good," she said with a sleepy smile. "Wouldn't change a thing." And it was wonderfully true. In the heavy lassitude of the aftermath, her brain was quiet and the chatter stilled. "It's been a heck of a day, hasn't it? When I woke up this morning, I never in a million years would've guessed I'd be spending the night in your bed."

He tightened his arm around her. "The first of many, if I have anything to say about it. Because I wouldn't change a thing, either." He kissed the top of her head and fell silent, his chest rising and falling beneath her, hypnotic in its rhythm. Rising and falling. Rising and falling. Rising and . . .

Danny slept. And the dreams stayed far away.

The next morning Danny awakened, momentarily disoriented by the bright light and cloud-soft mattress. But a gentle snore coming from beside her and the heavy weight of a man's arm across her hip quickly oriented her.

She was in Sam's house, Sam's bed. And she had zero regrets.

Exactly the opposite, in fact. Her skin carried their mingled scents, and her body tugged with lovely aches from taking him inside her twice more during the night, making them well and truly lovers. She should have been exhausted, worn out, but instead she was suddenly wide-awake and ready to face a new day. A new reality, even, because becoming Sam's lover might not have changed her, but it definitely changed things.

Stretching, she eased out from under his arm and to the side of the bed, not wanting to wake him. It didn't seem like she needed to worry, though—he stayed deeply asleep, moving only to breathe and looking ever so slightly stern, even while conked out. She smiled at him, feeling tender, grateful, and darn pleased with herself as she found the thick rug with her feet and stood.

In the light of day, the room turned out to be a big square space with white walls and elegantly carved wood trim. With a bureau and a clothing-loaded book-case taking the place of a closet, and the bathroom across the hall, it likely hadn't been intended as a bed-room. They were probably upstairs. But the space suited Sam—there was a heck of a mountain view through the glass doors, and the rest was bare-bones and practical. The only exception to that was one level of the shelving unit, which held a jumble of stones and fossils, and three pictures.

Pulling on her clothes, Danny studied the collection. There was a snapshot of a pretty blonde wearing dated clothes and kneeling in a freshly turned garden with her arms around a tousle-haired toddler, the both of them mugging for the camera. The other two pictures showed an older version of that same kid with a dark-haired man who had his smile. In one, they held up arrowheads and wore nearly identical expressions of *Look what I found!* In the other, they stood on the pinna-cle of Wolf Rock, running an American flag up the pole. The sight tugged at Danny, reminded her of seeing him standing up there alone, waiting for her.

Her vision blurring, she turned her attention to the other items on the curio shelf. The stones were an odd mix of beautifully prepared crystal clusters, perfectly preserved fossils, and a jumble of knapped arrowheads, rough gemstones, and plain rocks of unclear signifi-cance. She smiled as she drew her fingers along one of the arrowheads, imagining him as a boy, discovering the cache. And smiling wider when she saw the small piece of flawed pink quartz he had found at Blessing Valley.

A soft "whuff" drew her attention to the corner, where Whiz had spent the night. He cocked his head, as if to say, *Well?*

"Okay, come on. I'll let you out." She hadn't needed to think about that too much in camp, but Krista had been right about his training. She let the dog out, gave him a few minutes, and then called him in, still leery of leaving him alone for too long. Then, hoping for a spare toothbrush, she headed back up the hallway and pushed through the door to the bathroom.

Only it wasn't the bathroom.

Danny froze as motion-activated lights flipped on, illuminating a huge, echoing garage that was big enough to hold a couple of school buses but housed only a single motorcycle. "Whoops. Wrong door." She started to pull the panel shut, but then paused, her blood chilling as she realized what she was looking at.

Not just a motorcycle. A wrecked Harley.

Black and mean-looking, it might have just rolled off the showroom floor if it hadn't been for the mangled front wheel and fork, the deep furrows and staved-in pannier, and the replacement parts that had been stacked nearby, as if the repairs were a work in progress. Except that it all wore a thick layer of dust, and the calendar hanging on the wall nearby was seven years out-of-date.

"Oh," she said, connecting the dots. Flushing at the knowledge that this was private and she was accidentally snooping, she backed up—

Right into a warm, solid body.

"*Oh!*" She jumped and spun. "I'm sorry. I . . ."

Sam stood behind her. And he didn't look happy.

\*      \*      \*

*Damn it*, Sam thought hollowly. *Just damn it*. But seeing her dismay, he said, "It's okay. Not your fault." And it wasn't her fault, of course. But it also wasn't okay.

Not when seeing the V-Rod's black-and-chrome gleam reminded him of going into the bike store that day with money to burn, talking his dad into the bigger, faster bike . . . and, a few days later, the officer's voice on the phone, saying, "I'm sorry, son . . ."

He swallowed hard. *Should have locked the damn door*. Waking up, slow and satisfied, he had thought only of finding breakfast and talking Danny back into bed, and not necessarily in that order. Now his appetite was gone and the bedroom seemed miles away compared to the crumpled mess of metal in the garage and the hash he had made of fixing it up.

Well, not a hash, exactly. The work he had done was good and the parts were all there. He just hadn't seen the point in finishing. He wasn't going to sell it, and he sure as hell wasn't going to ride it. And after the first couple of weeks, he'd stopped seeing his father's silhouette in the doorway and hearing the echoes of his voice . . . until one day he had just put down the socket wrench he'd been using, wiped his hands on a rag, and walked out.

"Truly." She crossed to him and gripped his arm. "I'm sorry. Let's just close the door and forget about it."

And she would, too, or at least put it out of her mind, because she understood privacy and wasn't looking to fix him. "Yeah, that'd probably be best." He reached past her and pulled the panel shut, knowing it would take longer to erase the afterburn on his retinas. "Thank you."

"Hey." She went up on her toes and brushed her lips across his. "Being lovers doesn't mean we stop being ourselves."

"That's . . ."

"Too cheesy?" She grinned up at him, trying to get him to play along, lighten the mood, as if she knew that sometimes when the big stuff was bothering you, the best thing to do was pretend everything was okay. Until, eventually, you weren't pretending anymore.

Then again, she did know that. Heck, she was living it. And, looking down at her and seeing everything that was in her eyes—the shadows, the softness, and a sadness that was more fellowship than pity—something shifted in his chest, telling him that this moment was important. She was important. And he'd better not screw this up.

"Not cheesy," he said, voice going low and husky as he slid his arms around her. "In fact, I'd say it's pretty darn perfect. Just like you."

"Ha!" She flattened her palms on his chest, but nestled close rather than pushing away. "Flattery will get you nowhere, buster."

"Then how about we take a trip out to Hyrule to open up that vein of aqua—all aboveground, I promise—and go out to dinner later? You're off today, right? Are you free?"

Excitement sparked in her eyes, reminding him that he'd gotten damn lucky finding a woman who liked him just the way he was. "I am, and definitely yes to Hyrule. As for dinner, yes there, too, but if we're going to do this," she pointed from him to her and back, "then we alternate who pays."

How was it that she could fascinate him, frustrate him, and level him off all at once? "I believe I've mentioned that I'm rich. And as you can see"—he gestured around them—"I'm not blowing my budget on décor. So how about you let me spend some of it on a night out? I promise I'll still be able to make payroll."

She nodded like they were in perfect agreement. "Fine, then I get our next dinner out." He groaned, and she shot him a sidelong grin. "And speaking of playing with rocks, I wanted to talk to you about that. I had this idea for a guest field trip I'd like to offer at the ranch—"

"Sold," he said, pushing aside the ghosts and swinging her back toward the bedroom.

"You haven't even heard my idea yet!" she protested.

"So? I trust you." And he didn't say that lightly. At all. "So why don't we fool around for a bit, then we can throw together some breakfast and you can tell me what I just got myself into?"

"Rockhound Week!" Krista did a little jiggle-the-baby happy dance. "Danny, I love it. It's brilliant!"

"Well, maybe not a whole week," Danny said, not wanting to go overboard with it, even though she and Sam had brainstormed plenty of gem-focused guest activities over the past week, refining the concept before she brought it to Krista. "I know you've got your themes all planned out for the summer, so we were thinking just a day or two at first, as a side offering for the dudes. Sam could give a talk about geology and show them some of the inventions he and his guys are working on, and we could take whoever wants to go up to the claim for a day or two of rock hunting. So far up there, they've found turquoise, topaz, and tourmaline. There's even a fossil bed!"

"Listen to you, turning into a rock expert." Krista winked. "Sam must be a good teacher."

"He's . . ." Danny hesitated, not sure where the line fell between friendship and privacy, between girl talk and gossip. Finally, she said, "He's smart, funny, and loyal. He loves the outdoors as much as I do, loves the land more than me." Her pulse picked up a notch at what she was saying, and the tone she heard in her own voice. "He's a special guy. I'm glad we decided to take a chance on each other."

He had left for Misty Hill a few hours ago, and she already missed him.

Krista's eyes went soft. "You really get him, don't you?"

"I'd say we get each other." And if there were some doors she was better off not opening—literally and figuratively—she was okay with that. Losing his father had taken a toll. "As far as rock hunting goes," she added, "I'm no expert." Though she *had* found a fingertip-size, top-quality topaz the other evening, earning her Queen of the Claim status for the day. "But I sure am having fun, and I think the guests would, too. So if you're into it—"

"Oh, I'm into it." Krista tapped her lower lip, considering. "Next week is Singles Week, which might not be the best fit—the singles tend to be more interested in each other than the activities. The week after, though . . . Yes, that would work. It might actually be perfect. It's a Reunion Week, heavy on the families. I'm betting some of them would jump at the chance to ride out for an overnight."

"Ride? We were thinking of ATVs, or maybe chartering a helicopter."

"But wouldn't it be way cooler to ride? Dude ranch, after all. And the guest horses are good about picket lines and portable electric fencing. Foster and Junior can go with you to manage the herd." Her expression brightened. "Strike that. Wyatt and I will! We haven't camped out since before Abby was born. She's about ready to stay the night with her grandma, and I'm past ready to have a night away."

Remembering how many times the new mom had texted Wyatt the afternoon of their shopping trip, Danny wasn't so sure about that. Drily, she said, "And that week being the one right before the wedding has nothing to do with it, I'm sure."

"Hush!" Krista flapped a hand at her. "I wouldn't be ducking out of anything important. And this sounds really fun. We'll get Gran in on it, have her come up with some gem-related meals, like Emerald Salad and Ruby Red Potatoes."

"Nice," Danny said approvingly. "And something with blue diamonds, in honor of Babcock Gems— maybe blueberry pie with diamond-shaped cutouts? Or—" A digital bleat cut her off. "Is that your phone?"

"I think it's yours," Krista said, amused.

"Well, would you look at that?" Danny dug it out. "It doesn't usually get bars out here." She checked the ID, expecting to see Sam's name. Instead, she got an unfamiliar number with a Wyoming exchange. "Hello?"

"Danny, it's Shelby. Whatever you do, don't say my

name! And act casual! You can't let on like you're talking to me."

It took a major effort not to screw up her face and say "What the hell?" Instead, scrambling, she came up with, "Oh, hey, Mom."

"Good! Now I need you to ditch Krista and meet me and Jenny on the other side of the barn. But you can't let her know what you're doing. Got it?"

"Er . . . What's up with Dad?"

"We'll tell you what's going on when you get here. Hurry!" There was a dual giggle, and the line went dead.

Putting her hand over the bottom of her phone, like she didn't want the person on the other end to overhear, Danny said, "Do you mind if I take this where I get better reception? She and I keep missing each other."

"Of course! Please." Krista waved her off. "Though don't even think you're getting out of here without giving me the four-one-one on how things are going with you and—" She gave the phone a wary look and mouthed, S-A-M.

"I will, I promise. But until then, I've got one word for you." Still pretending her mom was on the phone, she mimicked Krista, mouthing, W-O-W. Then, as Krista's laugher pealed out behind her, she scampered to the barn, pretending to be doing a "Can you hear me now?" with her mom.

Jenny's Jeep was waiting on the other side, out of view from the main house. When Danny came around the corner, the passenger door flung open and Shelby stuck her head out, waving madly. "Hurry! Come on!"

The vehicle was already rolling when Danny got there, and it accelerated as she jumped in and slammed the door. Jenny was behind the wheel, Shelby in the back, and the air crackled with excitement.

Heart pounding—from the run, the ruse—Danny buckled in, cracked the window, and demanded, "Okay, you two, what gives?"

"We're kidnapping you," Shelby announced. "You're in our power for the next couple of hours."

"That sounds good to me. What are we doing?"

"Planning Krista's bachelorette party, of course!"

# 14

The first stop on Operation Bachelorette Plan was a honky-tonk bar called the Rope Burn—a low, sprawling wooden building with a big neon sign and a dirt parking area, where a couple of motorcycles were pulled up to an old-timey hitching rail.

The door was heavy, the interior dim after the bright afternoon sunlight, and it took a moment for Danny's eyes to adjust. When they did, she found herself standing just inside what could've been a Hollywood set labeled COWBOY BAR. It was that kitschy, that wonderful, from the boots and coiled ropes hung over the bar to the mechanical bull in a fenced-off section at the center of the dance floor. The place was midmorning-deserted and looked to be closed, but a cook popped his head out of the kitchen, caught sight of Shelby, and waved. "Hey. You guys want anything?"

"We're good. We're just going to put our heads together, make sure we've got all the plans nailed down."

"Cool. You need anything, just give us a shout." He disappeared back through the swinging doors, cutting off the kitchen noises.

*Small towns*, Danny thought. *Gotta love them.* Especially when you were hanging with a couple of very well-liked locals.

"So?" Jenny gave her a hip bump. "What do you think?"

She held up her hands. "This is your show. I'm just along for the ride."

"Speaking of riding." Shelby patted the mechanical bull with obvious affection. "How about taking a spin on Old Snortypants here?"

The usual plain, leather-covered slab of a mechanical bull had been taken up a few notches by the addition of a realistic-looking bull's head, complete with fiery red eyes and a pair of wickedly pointed horns that flexed easily when she touched them, proving to be made of foam rubber, the head of stuffed plush. The upgrades didn't stop there, either, with a tail at the back, foam-rubber legs hanging from each corner, tipped with fat cloven hooves that looked like they had been lovingly hand-stitched . . . and a pair of blue jeans hitched over its back legs for comic relief.

*Tempting*, Danny thought, lips curving, but figured she should really wait a couple of weeks—not because she needed the audience, alcohol, or music, but because Jenny and Shelby had assured her that dancing and riding the mechanical bull were the name of the game when it came to a cowgirl's bachelorette party in Three Ridges. "Snortypants, huh?"

"He's had a bunch of names through the years," a new voice said from the other side of the room. "Snortypants is the latest, thanks to Dingle Reedy losing his jeans in a bet last summer." A woman came through from a back room. Short and curvy, with bottle-red hair, high-heeled boots, and a pair of jeans that had probably taken a while to get into but sure made a statement, she was a sexy fortysomething with a wide smile. Making a beeline, she held out a hand. "You must be Danny! I've heard so much about you."

"This is Bootsy," Jenny put in as Danny found the handshake turning into a happy hug. "Owner of Bootsy's Saddlery, and our local queen of style. Well, outside of Della, that is."

Bootsy gave a breezy wave. "Dell is a genius with the vintage stuff, no question about it. But when it comes to the latest and greatest rodeowear, I'm your girl."

"So . . ." Shelby let it draw out. "Did you get them?"

"Of course I did! I wouldn't let you down." Bootsy swept a hand to a nearby booth, where a couple of flat shipping boxes were stacked on the table. "Your wish is my command."

"Ooh!" Jenny headed for the boxes. "Show us, show us!"

Not really sure what, exactly, was going to come out of those boxes—the girls had been closemouthed aside from divulging that Krista's bachelorette party would kick off at the local steakhouse, where they would have dinner in a private room before heading for the Rope Burn—Danny followed the others and watched as Bootsy opened the first box and pulled out something white, fringed, and sparkly. "Voilà!"

Danny craned to see. "What is it?"

Jenny took the leather, snapped it open with a fringed flourish, and looped what proved to be a pair of snow-white chaps around her hips. She buckled the belt at her waist, zipped the wings, and announced,

"They're the tackiest rodeo princess chaps ever. And they're perfect."

The word BRIDE was painted along each leg in black-lined silver, and spelled out across the back of the belt in rhinestones.

Shelby whooped. "You can say that again! Krista is going to be horrified."

And, Danny knew, she would love it, too—because her sister and best friend had arranged it for her, wanting her to be the star of the show.

"Don't forget the hat." Bootsy went into the second, bigger box and came up with a snow-white cowboy hat that trailed a pouf of veil in all directions, making it look like a bridal jellyfish.

"Nobody could forget that hat." Shelby plopped it on Jenny's head. "Now *that's* making a statement!"

"Yeah," Jenny agreed, striking a pose near Snorty-pants's head. "Step back, cowboys. Here comes the bride!"

"Did you guys do stuff like this for your weddings?" Danny asked, laughing.

"No way." Jenny's headshake was emphatic. "Nick and I kept the whole deal pretty low-key. Me, Krista, and Shelby treated ourselves to a spa weekend instead of doing a bachelorette party, Nick had a few beers with his buddies, and we swapped vows up at Make-out Point and came back to the ranch for a barbecue."

"It was fabulous," Shelby put in. "Totally their style."

And more like Danny's. Not that she was looking at getting married anytime soon. "What about you and Foster?"

"We had our ceremony at his family's ranch, the Double-Bar H. He had just bought it back and the renovations hadn't gotten far, but it's hard to beat the view. It was the second time around for both of us, and we didn't want anything big and fancy." Her lips curved. "Lizzie was my maid of honor, and Foster had the JP add a little piece, asking her to be his daughter. So all three of us got married, really."

"That's lovely."

"I thought so. And very much our speed." Shelby flicked the veil as it floated near her. "But now we're changing gears and doing things a little differently, because our girl deserves to know she's the star!"

"Krista was always the one who wanted to play wedding," Jenny put in, handing the hat back to Bootsy. "Between Abby, the guests, and trying to keep things on an even keel with Mom, we're afraid she's not having much fun with the whole wedding thing at this point. So we want to make sure the bachelorette party is ridiculously entertaining."

"Which brings us to . . ." Bootsy pulled out a stack of screaming pink cowgirl hats with spring-loaded antennae topped with sparkly hearts that bobbed and swung as she held one out to Shelby. "For the rest of the party."

"Perfect!" She stuck one on her head and made a duck face. "How do I look?"

"Like a cross between a flamingo and a giant ant," Jenny said, and whipped out her phone to snap a picture.

Shelby swatted at her. "No paparazzi allowed." Turning to Danny, she tipped the silly hat at a rakish angle. "What do you think?"

"I think you look like you're gearing up to have a ton of fun."

"Then I'd say it's mission accomplished!" She stripped off the hat and tossed it back to Bootsy. "Perfect. Every bit of it. You've got twenty of the pink hats?"

"Plus a few extras. A good bachelorette party always seems to gain a couple of people at the last minute. And this is going to be a good one." She put the hat on, tipped it and posed, somehow managing to turn the antennae into a fashion statement rather than a joke. "I'll bring these with me when I come out to the ranch, and we can load them in the shuttle. You still looking at five o'clock for the kidnapping?"

Danny raised a brow. "Kidnapping?"

Jenny's grin turned wicked. "Did we forget to mention this is going to be a surprise party? We're going to dress up like bandits, hit the trail ride on its way back to the ranch, grab Krista off her horse, and ride out to meet the shuttle, which'll be waiting on the main road. We've got a suite at the Card Sharps' Inn for the night, where we'll have a shower, clean clothes, and a bottle of champagne waiting to get the night started off right."

Shelby added, "We've got the guys in on it—they'll make sure she's out riding when and where we need her to be."

Did it make Danny a bad person to envy a good friend for her other friends? "It sounds awesome. She's going to love it."

Something must have come through in her voice, even though she hadn't meant it to, because Shelby bumped her with an elbow. "Hello? You're totally riding with us. It wouldn't be the Girl Zone without you!" And Jenny nodded emphatically.

Could it really be that simple? To Danny, coming

from a world where respect and friendship were earned by how fast you made the summit and how many bruises you could take before you complained, it seemed impossible. She was peripherally aware of Bootsy giving a little wave and heading for the kitchen. But mostly she was looking at her friends.

*Friends.* When had that become such a powerful word in her universe?

"Don't look so surprised," Jenny advised. "Like it or not, you're one of us now. And no matter where you go, you'll always have that to fall back on."

"I don't . . ." When her voice threatened to crack, she stopped and blew out a breath. Tried again. "Some days, when I'm sitting out at Blessing Valley or on Sam's back deck and watching the sun set, I think about that day you called me out of the blue . . ." She had been feeling particularly low, alone in the store while her family cheered Charlie on, and found herself blurting out the whole story—about the accident, breaking up with Brandon, losing her nerve. "We barely knew each other, but the next thing I knew, you called back and told me to pick a Saturday and buy a ticket to Wyoming." Her breath whistled out. "I can't thank you enough."

"Poosh!" Jenny said, borrowing her gran's favorite saying, which seemed to cover everything from *You're welcome for the biscuit* to *No biggie. All I did was throw you a lifeline.* "Besides," Jenny added, "we owe you for stepping up to work at the ranch. Did Krista tell you she's already filled Eat from Nature Week for next year? The word is spreading."

"And word of mouth is a wonderful thing," Shelby

added. Expression shifting, she glanced at Jenny and then back to Danny, and said, "Speaking of which . . . we had an ulterior motive for bringing you out here today."

She blinked. "Oh?"

"Sit down." Correctly reading Danny's sudden *uh-oh*, Shelby said, "Don't stress. It's good. At least we think it's good."

When the three of them were tucked into a booth, with Danny on one side, Jenny and Shelby on the other, looking serious and hopeful, Jenny slid a piece of paper across the table—lined notepaper, with a numbered list written in her neat block printing.

Danny stared at it, seeing that the first line read: *There are other dude ranches and B and Bs in the area looking to expand their offerings.* "What's this?" But a little shiver went through her, because she already knew.

Shelby folded her hands on the tabletop. "It's the top five reasons we think you should stay in Three Ridges and start your own business." She tapped the page.

Number four—they were counting backward—was *We love you and we don't want you to leave.*

Emotion lumped in Danny's throat. "You guys . . . I don't know what to . . . Wow." She blinked back the threat of tears, quick and unexpected. "Maybe. I don't know. I love it here, but there's my family to think about, and the store." In Maine, where the trees were very close together.

"That's your decision to make," Jenny said. "But take it from the rebel Skye—the family business isn't the right answer for everybody."

"But Krista . . ."

"Will understand if you decide to go off on your own," Shelby said firmly. "Sure, she'll be sad. She might even get cranky, especially if she finds out before the wedding." The corner of her mouth kicked up. "I'll bet you a hundred bucks and a ride on Snortypants that she's planning on asking you to stay on at the ranch. But . . ." She tapped the page. Number three was *You're going to outgrow Mustang Ridge.* "You may not see it now, but it'll happen sooner than you think, because . . ." *Tap, tap.* Number two was *You really want to be your own boss.*

Jenny leaned in. "Trust us on this one. If you've got a marketable skill set—which you do—and you've got the street smarts to run a business—check mark in that box, too—then you can make the life you want out here."

"I think . . ." Danny scrubbed both hands over her face. "I can't breathe." Because maybe she'd been having some of those same thoughts—she hadn't gone as far as a list, but she didn't have much in the way of arguments against the idea, either. As much as she loved Krista and Mustang Ridge, she wanted something that was hers. She hadn't fully admitted it, though, even to herself. Because that meant coming to grips with the fact that she was thinking about staying.

Oh, holy moly. She was really thinking about staying.

"That's only reasons two through five," she said, sounding about as shaky as she felt. "What's number one?"

Triumphant, Shelby flipped the page to reveal a pen-sketched logo—the silhouette of a curly-haired woman standing on the apex of a craggy climb, with a big dog at her heels and a hawk in the sky above, surrounded by an arc that suggested the setting sun. Below it was the company name: WYOMING WALKABOUTS. And below that was their number one reason why she should stay and start her own business: *Because we dare you.*

When Sam and Yoshi crested the last low hill and Windfall came into view, the paint gelding tossed his head and bunched beneath his rider, itching to race for home.

"Easy there," Sam chided, reining in the eager horse. "I know it's past your dinnertime." Then he saw a shadow move up on top of Wolf Rock, all curves and curls, and his body tightened. *"Danny."*

It had been almost three days since he kissed her good-bye and rode out to Misty Hills. Maybe he hadn't missed her every single one of those sixty-some hours, but he'd sure thought of her plenty. And seeing as how she was waiting for him up on Wolf Rock, he had a feeling that went both ways. He lifted his hat and gave it a wide sweep, and got a wave in return. And even though it was breaking the Cowboy Code not to walk his horse the last mile in, he clucked. "Come on, big guy. Let's go home."

A few minutes later, with Yoshi blowing lightly and tugging at the bridle, he reined up at the base of Wolf Rock, saddle aches falling away at the sight of Danny waving down at him. "Welcome home!" she called. "Hang on, I'll be right down!"

"No, stay there. I'm coming up." He hopped upright onto his saddle like Yoshi was a surfboard, caught the free end of the knotted rope, and used it to walk himself up the side of the big stone.

"You . . . Oh!" She clapped a hand over her mouth to hold in a happy laugh. "What about your horse?"

"He'll be okay for a minute. Long enough for me to do this." He reached the summit, tossed the rope, took her in his arms, and kissed her.

Lips. Curves. Sweet fire. He feasted on her, filled himself with her, feeling like he'd been away for weeks, not just a few days. His body heated and hardened, and it was all he could do not to take her there, on the top of Wolf Rock.

Instead, reining himself in the way he had tugged on Yoshi a mile ago, he eased the kiss and pressed his forehead to hers. "I'm glad you're here."

"Really? I couldn't tell." Her smile was impudent, her cheeks flushed.

"Were you waiting long?"

She shook her head. "Foster saw you on the high trail, and took a guess when you'd get here. I thought it would be fun to come up here and wave you in like Gran and the others do when the riders return to Mustang Ridge." She leaned against him and looked out over the undulating grasslands to the mountains he had come from. "I was right."

"It's a good tradition." One he wouldn't mind continuing. As soon as the thought surfaced, a big part of him went, *Whoa, wait, since when?* But it was more a reflex than anything, and quickly lost ground to the feel of her curves against his body, her hair tickling his jaw. "Stay," he said, "enjoy the view. Or go in and grab a drink, whatever you like. I'm going to get Yoshi settled for the night, jump in the shower, and then take you out to dinner. And"—he leaned in to give her a mock-stern look—"there's going to be a tablecloth involved, whether you like it or not."

She grinned. "Are you saying I'm lowbrow?"

He kissed her again, because he couldn't be in range of her and not want to have his lips on her, his hands on her. "Give me ten minutes?"

She nodded, but as he turned away and reached for the rope, she touched his arm. "Wait. Before you go, there's something I need to tell you."

"That sounds serious." He straightened, got a look at her expression, and felt his own face fall. "It looks serious, too." A big old *oh, hell* punched him in the gut. The summer was winding down and her confidence was ramping up. The next stop in the progression was for her to spread her wings and fly.

*Don't go,* he wanted to say, but he didn't have the right. Instead, he took her hands, twined their fingers together, and squeezed. "What is it?"

She centered her weight as if getting ready to run a hang glider off the edge of a cliff. "I'm thinking of staying in Three Ridges."

He was so prepared for *I'm leaving* that it took a three-count for that to sink in.

She rushed on. "I love it here. I love the mountains, the people, the work I've been doing . . . I'm thinking of starting my own business, in fact, expanding on it. Hiking, rafting, climbing, maybe even fossil hunting and prospecting. I've already got Krista, Jenny, and Shelby on board." Her eyes searched his face. "This isn't because of you and me, I swear . . . but I'd like you to be okay with the idea."

"You're not leaving." The words came out rough and ragged.

Nerves flashed in her eyes, but she held her ground.

"I haven't decided for sure, but I'm leaning that way. I know we got together thinking I was just passing through, but—"

"You're not leaving!" He shouted it from Wolf Rock, hearing the words echo from the upper levels of the house, as he swept her up in his arms and spun her like he had at the dance.

She laughed up at him. "So I guess you're okay with it."

He drew her close, kissed her. Said against her lips, "I'm not ready to say good-bye." It was as close as he'd ever gotten to declaring himself to a woman, as far as he intended to go. And maybe his luck had finally changed when it came to women, because it seemed like it was enough for her.

Face alight, she leaned into the kiss. "Then let's not say good-bye. Let's put Yoshi away and hop in the shower. That was the plan, right?"

"If it wasn't, it sure is now. Let's go." He took hold of the rope, but then turned back. "Oh, and by the way?"

"Mm?"

"When we get to that restaurant I was talking about? The one with the tablecloths? We're going to toast your new venture with a bottle of wine that's so ridiculously expensive that you won't insist on flipping a coin for the bill." He winked, then kicked away from the rock. And for a moment, he was weightless.

# 15

"Look!" Sara Fitch pointed to a wingspread shadow soaring beyond the main barn at Mustang Ridge. "It's an eagle! I'm sure of it this time!"

She had been sure the last four times, too, and those had turned out to be a pair of crows, a hawk, and a Boeing. It was the end of Raptor Day, though, so Danny obligingly squinted hard enough to blur the dark, gliding outline. "You know, you could be right!" Which wasn't entirely a fib.

"Woo!" The curvy blonde did a hip-hoppy victory dance and collected a high five from the guy behind her, which took her shimmy-shake up a notch. But then the guy—a handsome, perfectly muscled gym owner named J.D. whom Krista had dubbed the most likely to score and not follow up once the week was over—immediately turned back to Minn, the short, stacked brunette he'd been talking to for most of the hike.

The two of them had barely taken enough of a break in their full-court eye contact to "ooh" and "aah" over the up-close-and-personals the group had gotten with a juvenile red-tail and a couple of woodpeckers, never mind the awesome waterfall where they had stopped for lunch. And now, as the group of eight dusty hikers piled into the parking lot where they had met up this morning, J.D. and Minn gave a couple of distracted waves, chorused "Thanks for the hike," and made an unsubtle beeline for J.D.'s cabin.

*Ah, yes*, Danny thought. *Singles Week.* Krista had warned her it would be an interesting time, and she had been braced for something like the high-octane romance on the rain forest set of *Jungle Love.* It hadn't turned out to be quite that bad—probably because there weren't any cameras or wannabe starlets involved—but there had still been plenty of Stetson-wearing drama lovers. Like when East Coast Dana caught "her" man slipping out behind the barn with West Coast Dana on day two. Or the time J.D. named himself the prize of a friendly game of horseshoes, and the competition had spiraled out of control, fast. It hadn't quite come to hair pulling, but it had been close.

Come to think of it, Danny had probably gotten off easy. It had been a quiet week for hiking and fishing, and most of the people who had joined her excursions had been coupled off and enjoying each other. With a few notable exceptions, of course.

Now, Sara came up beside her and gave a big sigh. "Oh, well. I tried."

Danny nodded. "You did. And, bonus, you learned how to spot an eagle on the fly." Sort of.

The other woman brightened. "I did, didn't I?" She made a face in the direction of J.D.'s cabin. "Who needs perfect teeth and pecs you can bounce a quarter off of? I've got—" She broke off, suddenly riveted on something beyond Danny. "Whoa, hang on. Who is *that*?"

Danny turned, getting the distinct feeling she knew exactly who had caught Sara's attention. Sure enough, Sam stood near his pickup, having paused to exchange a few words with Foster and Wyatt. It made for a whole lot of good-looking cowboys, with Sam standing a couple of inches taller and looking like he was in charge of whatever they were discussing. The upcoming rock-hound trip, probably.

The sight sent heat skimming through Danny's veins—a mix of feminine pleasure and anticipation of the night to come. Any worries she might've had that he would pull back when she started thinking about staying in the area had been squashed over the past week, with the two of them spending most of their free time together at his place or hers, out with their friends, or hanging at Mustang Ridge. They had gone back out to Hyrule several times, digging out gorgeous, almost alien-looking crystal formations of aqua and iodolite. Tonight, several of them were going to be on display at a convention center in the city. And, girly though it might be, she was jazzed to be going to her first gem show with Sam.

Who looked over at her and shot a wink that had Sara sucking in a breath. "Did you see that?" she practically squeaked. "He's totally checking us out!"

"That's Sam Babcock. He's sort of a neighbor," Danny said, then couldn't help the goofy grin that spread over her face as she added, "And he's taken."

"Oh?" Sara glanced from him to her and back again, then said again, more knowingly, "Ohhh. Sorry. Then again, I guess you've got to be used to it. A guy like that is going to get his share of second looks."

Not sure what to say, Danny went with, "We're headed out for the evening. Have a nice night, and I'll catch you later. Oh, and Sara?"

The other woman's attention came back to her. "Yes?"

"If you don't mind a word of advice, maybe think of sitting next to Ben at dinner tonight and seeing if you can get him to talk to you. He's really smart and funny when you get past the quiet."

Sara looked dubious. "I don't know about that beard . . ."

"I think there's a really nice guy underneath it." One who lived in the same state as Sara, even, and whose eyes had followed her across the dining hall more than once. Danny nudged the other woman. "Give him a chance. What have you got to lose?"

"Some of the skin on my face?" But she didn't sound too put off by the prospect, and she nudged Danny in return. "Thanks. For everything."

"Anytime," Danny said, and meant it. "Catch you later." Then, warming with anticipation, she headed to meet Sam, who was coming her way. "Hey there, handsome," she said, taking his outstretched hand and spinning into him like they were back at the square dance. "Rumor has it you need some arm candy for some big shindig tonight."

He dipped her, then leaned in and brushed his lips across hers. "I thought it was the other way around."

"Mutual arm candy, then," she declared, straightening to give him a proper kiss. "Just let me grab my bag and round up Whiz, and we can get out of here." She hadn't moved anything to his place despite the invitation, but she didn't have any problem snagging his shower and parking her dog at Windfall, knowing they'd be coming back there for the night.

"You look pleased with yourself." He glanced at Sara's retreating back. "Playing matchmaker?"

"Maybe a little. It's Singles Week, after all."

"Any love connections so far?"

"We'll see. Krista said they've had a bunch of Singles Week success stories come back for their honeymoons, and I guess a few of the couples that've made it have surprised her. Some folks just get lucky, I guess." Not wanting him to think she was fishing, she added, "How about you whistle up Whiz and I'll grab my stuff? I don't want to be late for my first gem show!" They didn't need to analyze what was going on between them, after all. They were just in it to have a good time.

Make that a *very* good time.

Sam had never brought a date to a gem show before— that was too much mixing business with pleasure for him. With Danny, though, he hadn't hesitated for a second—she had a real feel for gems, and his guys already treated her like she was part of the team. And, besides, he flat out *wanted* her there with him, wanted to see the show through her eyes.

"Well?" he said as they came through the main doors into the ballroom. "What do you think?"

The echoing space had been decked out with banners and trade show booths, with the Babcock Gems display taking up three stalls' worth of prime real estate opposite the main entrance. The huge wilderness-style tent was made of dark green fabric and had the front roped open to show display tables and cabinets of strategically lit gems. Dark green signs were labeled with the company name and Web address in flowing silver script, and the blue-diamond Babcock logo was big enough to be seen from the other side of the enormous space. Behind the showcase tent ran row after row of displays from other outfits, selling everything from rain gear to rock hammers. With bodies thronging the aisles, a snack bar in the back, and a hum of voices that drowned out the Muzak coming from the overhead speakers, the whole effect was one of activity, suppressed excitement, and glittering stones.

"Ohmigosh!" Danny bounced on the balls of her feet, putting a little swish in the floaty blue shirt she was wearing with painted-on black pants and low heels. "This is amazing!" As the crowd eddied around them, she tugged on Sam's arm. "Quick, show me everything!"

He had lost count of the number of these things he'd been to—heck, he'd probably attended his first with his father, strapped in a baby backpack or hooked to a toddler leash or something. Over the years, he'd hit everything from informal get-togethers consisting of a couple of folding tables in the back of a Grange hall, where he could sometimes find amazing gems for a song, all the way to black-tie affairs where he could make good money selling shiny clusters to well-heeled collectors. The Pioneer Trail Gem Show fell between the two extremes, mostly aimed at the more experienced prospectors. The organizers had taken the theme and run with it, marking the corners of each aisle with wooden barrels and bales of straw, dressing the event staffers like they were part of a wagon train, and decking out the snack bar like an old-timey chuck wagon.

And he had a feeling Danny was going to dig every kitschy second of it.

Slipping an arm around her waist, he said, "How about we start with the home team, so I can check in with the guys?"

"You're on. I want to get a look at the clusters we pulled out of Hyrule. I haven't seen them since you cleaned them up."

He didn't know which he liked better—how quickly she had taken to his world, or the sway of her backside as she led the way to the display tent. Good news was, he didn't have to choose. They came together in the same curly-haired package, along with a quick wit and an active mind that always seemed to be a couple of steps ahead of his.

"Boss." Murph nodded in their direction when they came through the flap into the well-lit space. Wearing all black, with discreet silver accenting his piercings and his hair slicked back, he looked ready to take on the world. Or at least sell some stones. His expression lighted at the sight of her, and he said, "Hiya, Danny. You want to see what we did with the aqua from Hyrule?"

"Absolutely!" She hunkered close to the display case he indicated, where three of the best clusters were spotlighted on the top shelf, the blue and purple crystals bursting from the rocky substrate like the spray from a gemstone breaker crashing into a rocky beach. The glass case reflected her eyes as they went wide and bright. "Oh!" she said, catching Sam's hand and squeezing tight. "They look amazing. What did you guys do to them?"

Before Sam could answer, Murph said, "First we touched up the facets on a few of the shafts and got rid of some small flaws. Then we polished the surfaces. Here, let me open this up, and you can feel how smooth they are now."

As the geologist popped open the display and handed over one of the clusters, going on about the different grits he had used to polish the two types of stone, Sam stepped back and took a look around the tent, pleased to see Midas going over the controls of one of the new scanners with Trudy Snow, whose family had a good-size claim north of Three Ridges and a wide network of contacts. Some good word of mouth from the Snow family could help them sell out the new production run in no time flat.

"Not worried about protecting your territory?" Axyl said, stepping up beside Sam as Murph puffed out his chest and did a charades version of the polishing process.

Sam snorted. "He'd better put in as much effort with the actual customers, or he's going to be in trouble." Murph and Midas had a standing bet over which one raked in the most sales at each event. "Any idea what the stakes are tonight?"

"Loser has to buy a round over at the Rope Burn on karaoke night."

"That's not bad."

"Then get up and sing 'The Lion Sleeps Tonight.'"

"Ha. Count me in."

"For the bet?"

"No, for karaoke night." Sam grinned as Trudy patted the scanner and Midas pulled up an order form on his computer tablet. "Looks like Murph has some ground to make up."

"So stop distracting him, and go buy your girlfriend

something sparkly." Axyl said it with a sidelong look that said he knew darn well Sam had never given a woman a cut gemstone, and didn't often use the g-word. *Girlfriend.*

"I doubt she'd let me," Sam said, refusing to take the bait with her standing a few feet away. "Darned woman insists on paying every other date."

The old prospector chuckled. "She knows you're rich, right?"

"I don't think she cares."

"Good for her. Now go on. Get out of here before she figures out that Midas is halfway in love with her. We'll hold the fort while you make the rounds of the booths. Keep a close eye on her, though. You know how some of these guys can get."

It took another couple of minutes—and a threat to make a video of karaoke night and post it on YouTube—for Sam to liberate Danny from the Babcock Gems tent. Finally, though, they made it back out into the flow of human traffic. "Let's take a look around," he suggested. "I'd like to get a sense of what some of the other crews have found so far this season."

Over the next hour or so, they cruised from booth to booth, checking out some nice clusters of beryl and yellow amethyst, chatting with fellow prospectors and trying a couple of hammers on for size. Over Danny's laughing protests, Sam bought her a T-shirt that read I DIG ROCKS, a baseball cap that proclaimed her an official pebble pup, and a soft pretzel slathered with spicy mustard. And darned if he didn't find himself looking at a hammered silver bracelet set with a good-size teardrop-shaped aquamarine.

Looking wasn't the same as buying, though, and he had plenty of gem-grade aqua at home.

"Who do you think is going to win the bet?" she asked as they circled back around to the Babcock Gems tent.

"Historically, Midas and Murph are about even," Sam said, "but when the wager involves public humiliation, Midas usually finds a way to come out on top. So I'm betting on him today."

"Maybe I should bet on Murph, then. How about a side bet, just between us? Loser has to sing backup on karaoke night."

"Sam!" A voice called from behind them, saving him from having to figure out how to get out of a bet that involved inflicting his so-called singing voice on the public.

Pivoting them both, Sam grinned with real pleasure at the sight of a wiry, hunched old guy with a walrus moustache and a thin fringe of white hair. "Chucky T. How the heck are you?"

"Still breathing, boy. Still breathing." The old rockhound's faded eyes shifted, brightened. "And now I'm breathing faster. Who is this pretty lady?"

Tightening his arm around her waist, Sam said, "This is Danny. Danny, this is Chuck. He's a buddy of my father's from way back."

"It's a pleasure to meet you, Chuck." Danny gave the older man's arthritis-gnarled hand a gentle shake.

"And you, my dear." He patted her hand, then shifted his attention back to Sam. "And Danny is . . ." He trailed off, turning it into a question.

Sam hesitated for a beat, flipping through and discarding the options. Then, knowing it was Axyl's fault for putting it in his head, but surprised how good it felt, he said, "She's my girlfriend."

Chucky T's face brightened. "Well, then, that's a fine thing, isn't it, boy?"

"I think so." Though Danny was looking up at him with an expression he couldn't quite read, making him wonder if he had overstepped. Before the other man could make things worse by asking if it was serious, Sam said, "So what have you been up to? You still working that Colorado claim?" They chatted for a minute about places and people they used to have in common. It brought a twinge, talking about the old days, but Sam was used to that by now. Whenever he went to a show, it seemed he was bound to run into someone who knew him before. Tonight, though, he was equally aware of the woman beside him, shooting him sidelong looks that said she was wondering what he was up to, what he had meant by the g-word.

Thing was, he wasn't even really sure himself. But he didn't wish it back, either.

"How is Axyl doing?" Chucky T asked. "Is he still riding around on that bike of his?"

"You know it. In fact, he's here tonight, over by the big green tent." Sam pointed to the back of the Babcock Gems setup. "I know he'd get a kick out of seeing you."

"I'll head over there right now so me and old Axyl can swap some lies about fast cars and pretty girls like the one you've got here." Chucky winked at Danny, then added, "Take care of her, boy. It's good to see you happy."

"Thanks, Chuck. It's good to be happy." Which

wasn't something he'd really thought much about before. He considered himself a pretty upbeat guy in general, but, yeah, he was a different sort of happy these days. He only hoped he hadn't made things weird just now or set himself up for a fall. Because history said that once he and a girlfriend got to the serious-discussion stage, it was the beginning of the end.

Danny was different, though. She understood him, wasn't looking to change him.

He hoped.

The walls weren't exactly closing in—the room was huge, after all, even with all the tables and people—but as the older man moved off, Danny couldn't quite catch her breath as the word *girlfriend* ricocheted around inside her head. Sam's expression was wary, but he had been the one to bring it up, and she had to say *something*, darn it. "*Sooo . . .*" she said, drawing it out and doing her best to keep things light. "Does that make you my boyfriend?"

"Seems only fair, doesn't it?" He said it easily enough, but his eyes measured her. "I mean, if I'm going to introduce you as my girlfriend, I guess that makes me your boyfriend. We're exclusive and we enjoy each other, right?"

With another guy, she might have thought he was angling to see how serious she thought they were, but with Sam, she was willing to bet that he didn't mean anything more or less than he was saying. Whiz wasn't the only one where what you saw was what you got, and she liked that she didn't have to guess when it came to Sam. More, she liked that he was happy taking things day by day, because that was all she was really up for right now. So she wrinkled her nose and nodded. "Okay, you can call me your girlfriend, but only on one condition."

"Which is?"

"I get a pet name."

His expression cleared and a smile touched his lips. "You want me to give you one?"

"Nope, I get to call you by one. I'm thinking of Snookums."

His eyebrows came down. "Not on your—"

"Pookie Bear? Snuggy Wumpkins?"

He closed the distance between them, so they were almost nose to nose, earning them a few curious looks. Lowering his voice, he said, "I prefer Stud Muffin. But whatever you do, don't call me Snookums."

"Okay. Stud Muffin it is."

"Good choice. That'll save me from having to call you—"

"Sam Babcock, is that you?" They broke apart as a bald guy about Sam's age came toward them, work-calloused hand outstretched. "How the heck are you? It's been forever!"

"M.J., hey!" Sam shook. "I'd like you to meet my girlfriend." And darned if Danny didn't get a kick out of hearing him say it, even if it didn't really mean anything new.

# 16

The next morning, Danny let Sam sleep while she puttered around his kitchen, starting a batch of pop-up biscuits while Whiz followed her every move with his big, serious eyes, as if to say, *An egg sandwich is the least you can do after you left me home by myself last night.*

"You wouldn't have enjoyed it," she told him as she laid bacon in a skillet that looked like it had seen its share of camping trips. "It was just a bunch of people standing around, looking at rocks."

At least from the doggy perspective. To her, it had been a fabulous adventure—learning about Wyoming's geology was like taking on a new language, and it had been a major turn-on for her to see yet another side of Sam, as he worked the booth for the final hour of the show and sold two of the bigger crystal clusters for enough that Midas and Murph were going to have to sing a duet.

"There were pretzels, though," she said to the hopeful-looking dog. "You probably would have liked them." Then, because she was a sucker, she broke off a piece of cheddar and tossed it to him. "That's all you're getting for now, though," she warned. "The good stuff is going to have to wait until Sam gets up."

She flipped the bacon, checked the timer on the biscuits, and debated between slipping back into bed to wake him with a kiss or letting him sleep a little longer. They had gotten in late, after all, and had finally dozed off even later, with his arm around her shoulders and her face pillowed against his neck.

She was glad she hadn't turned the girlfriend thing into a big deal. They were doing just fine the way they were.

"What do you say?" she asked Whiz. "Wake him up or let him sleep?"

As if in answer, her phone rang and Jenny's name popped on the screen.

"O-kay." Danny drew it out, grinning. "I guess that's a vote for let him sleep." Hitting the button to take the call, she said, "Hey, there! Did Krista and Shelby delegate you to find out how my first gem show went?"

"They did, but that's not why I called."

"Oh?"

"Nick has a client that's interested in adopting Whiz."

"He . . . Oh." Danny's legs went suddenly wobbly, forcing her to lean against the counter. "Wow." Alerted by her tone, Whiz crowded close. "It's okay," Danny told him, sinking down to the floor and wrapping an arm around him.

"It is?" Jenny said.

"Not you. I was talking to the dog."

"So it's not okay."

"No. Yes. Shoot." Danny pinched the bridge of her nose. "Give me a second here. This is good, right? It's what we agreed on, and he's certainly ready to go be somebody's pet." She tightened her grip on his warm, solid neck and pressed her forehead against his. "Who is it? Do you know them?" Even as she said it, everything inside her shouted, *No, no, no! Don't even think about it!*

"Do you remember Magnus and Cathy Kees from the barn raising? I guess little Ike hasn't stopped talking about Whiz since then. They've been talking about getting a dog for a while, and after seeing how good he was with Ike . . . Well, they called Nick last night to see if he was still available."

"Oh." That made it even worse, because he'd do just fine with them. Better than fine. He'd have his own little boy to play with. They were good people, with their own place in the foothills. He would probably love it there.

But she would hate not having him around. She had gotten used to his slurping tongue, his galumphing feet, and his big brown eyes. She liked the way he tried so hard to follow along when she talked to him, and how when they were leading a group out into the back-country, he scouted ahead and alerted her to tracks and spoor. And, darn it, she had even gotten used to him hiding behind her when he got scared, trusting her to take care of things.

"So . . . is he?" Jenny asked. "Available, I mean. Because as far as Nick and I are concerned, you've got first dibs. That is, if you want him."

"Yes," she blurted. "Yes, of course!" Because although she hadn't been planning on keeping him, she suddenly couldn't imagine not having him around.

"Yes, he's available, or yes, you want him?" But Jenny's tone said she knew exactly what Danny meant.

"I want him. Tell Ike and his parents that I'm sorry, I didn't mean . . ." She sucked in a breath, laughing as Whiz picked up on her change in mood and bounced up to lick her face. "Hang on. Knock it off. Gah!"

"Is that the whole message?"

"No!" As excitement bounced through her, Danny fended off her dog—Whiz was *hers*, how cool was that?—and struggled to her feet. After taking a couple of deep breaths, she said, "Nick can find them another dog, right?"

"Absolutely. Don't worry about it for another second. Whiz has been yours since just about day one."

"Maybe night one," Danny said, thinking of the thunderstorm. "But, yeah. We're a team now, and I want us to stay that way, no matter what happens next."

"What happens next is that I call Krista and Shelby, and the three of us hook up to celebrate your new family member."

As Sam stepped into the doorway, shirtless and bedheaded, wearing a pair of faded sweats low on his hips, Danny's pulse kicked up a notch. "Give me a few hours, and then I'm in."

"Oh? Do I want to know what's going to be keeping you busy in the interim?"

"Use your imagination. I intend to." Danny cut the connection, dropped the phone into her pocket, and crossed to her man while Whiz frisked between the two of them, tail wagging furiously. "How much of that did you hear?"

One corner of his mouth kicked up. "Enough to

know we've got something to celebrate." He caught Whiz's face between his palms. "Did you hear that, big guy? You've graduated to a permanent position with Danny here, you lucky dog!" He reached out and drew her against him, nuzzling her hair and surrounding her with his sleepy warmth. "Congratulations. It's a big step."

She started to nod, then laughed at herself. "You know what? It doesn't feel like a big step at all. It's more like I made the decision a long time ago, and am just now getting around to saying it out loud. Kind of like . . ." She trailed off as her stomach did a quick flip-flop.

His arm tightened around her. "Kind of like what?"

She sighed. "Kind of like knowing I need to call my parents and tell them that I'm probably not coming back to Maine. Which is *not* going to be fun."

Danny meant to phone home that day but got sidetracked by egg sandwiches followed by a return to the bedroom. After that, sated and loose-limbed, she met the girls for a celebratory lunch. And after *that*, she and Sam rode out to Misty Hills to help Axyl and the others finish getting the camp ready for Rockhound Week.

Finally, though, back at the ranch and out of excuses, she sat down in Krista's office with her laptop, to make the call to her parents. Which, it turned out, was a day too late—because when she opened up her e-mail, the first thing she saw was an e-ticket for a flight back home, leaving in less than forty-eight hours. Below it was a formal proposal for her to develop the shop's Internet business and handle the advertising, complete with a generous salary, a flexible schedule, and a new

FIRELIGHT AT MUSTANG RIDGE    221

bike. Apparently, her mother had decided she should get into road racing next.

Instead of irritating the heck out of her, the sight had her misting up. "Oh, boy. This is going to be even worse than I thought." Not because they had the right to order her back to Maverick Mountain, or because she was tempted, but because this was their version of love.

Whiz gave a low whine from the corner of the office, where he had curled up on Klepto's bed.

"Exactly," she said, feeling like giving a little whimper herself. Instead, she made the call.

It blinked live on the second ring, as if her father had been waiting for her—which maybe he had, given the plane ticket thing. He was at home, his face framed by the familiar cabin walls and a giant display case that overflowed with ribbons, medals, and trophies.

"There she is!" he exclaimed, as if he'd been searching for her. Then, turning away from the camera, he called, "Bea, Charlie, Jase, come in here. Danny's on the computer!"

*Oh, great,* Danny thought, heart sinking. It was going to be a family affair then, complete with her sister's boyfriend. Not that she had anything against him, but . . . But nothing, she decided, forcing her mood back where it had been—determined and affectionate. Because she was rapidly learning that being independent didn't just mean doing what she wanted. It also meant making hard decisions, and owning them.

"So? Did you get our e-mail?" her father said as the others gathered in behind him, their expectant faces making it seem like the stiff, stilted business proposal had been a happy surprise. Or at least her parents looked at it that way. When she met Charlie's eyes, though, she got a thumbs-up and a mouthed, *Stay strong, Sister!*

Which she was learning wasn't the same as going faster, higher, harder. Warmed by the unexpected support, Danny squared her shoulders and looked from her dad to her mom and back. "I love you guys. You know that, right?"

Whatever they had been expecting her to say, it hadn't been that. Her mother actually drew back, as if afraid that whatever had gotten into her older daughter might be catching. Her father, though, looked suddenly sad. Which was a hundred times worse. "We love you, too," he said, though it wasn't a word that was used often in the Traveler family. "Which is why we want you to come home and let us help you get back on your feet."

"My feet are fine right where they are. *I'm* fine here. Better than fine, even."

He studied her. "But . . . ?"

"No buts. I'm happy here. And I'm sorry, but I won't be using that ticket."

"What?" Her mother's face blanked, as if she hadn't even considered the possibility. "But it's nonstop. Do you know how much that costs?"

"I'm sorry," she said again—and she really was. She didn't *want* to make them unhappy . . . but Three Ridges already felt more like home than Maverick Mountain had in a long time. "You should have asked first. I hope you can get a refund."

"We can reschedule—"

"For a visit, sure," Danny said firmly, "but I'm not

moving back, and I'm not taking over anything at the store." The words threatened to stick in her throat, especially when her father's face fell into worry lines that made him look suddenly old. But she continued, saying firmly, "I'm staying here in Wyoming."

It was the first time she had said it straight up, without a *maybe* or an *I'm thinking about . . .* But just as the decision to keep Whiz had been an easy one when Jenny pushed her on it, saying the words felt right. She was happy here. She wanted to make a life here.

"Danny!" Her mom raised a hand to her mouth, honestly shocked. "You can't be serious. We *need* you!"

"I'll visit, I promise, and you're always welcome here." Her parents hadn't left the East Coast in twenty years, and didn't like to close the shop, but she thought Charlie and Jase would come. "It's beautiful here, in a different way than Maine."

"It's not about seeing each other. It's—"

"You're all alone out there," her father cut in. "You need to be back here, with your family."

Danny wasn't sure when she had gotten to be the square peg of the Traveler clan—maybe it had been the accident, or maybe she had been headed in that direction for a while. Heck, maybe that had been part of why she and Brandon hadn't clicked all the way. Perhaps even that far back there had been something about her that said she wasn't in the right place. She didn't want to hurt them by saying that, though, especially to her dad. "I've got friends here, and a good job."

"You've got friends and a job here, too," her mom insisted, her voice gaining the raspy edge that said she was losing patience with the conversation. "You're being ridiculous, Danielle. It doesn't make any sense for you to—"

"Whoops!" Danny said, catching sight of Krista in the doorway. "Listen, guys, I'm sorry, but I need to hang up now. We're doing a presentation in a few minutes. I'll call you in a few days and we can hash this out."

"Hang on a second!" her father said, looking incredulous. "What do you mean a few days? Call us after the presentation. This conversation isn't over."

The part of her that once upon a time would have done just about anything—climbed higher, pedaled faster, skied harder—to hear him shout, "That's my girl!" wanted to say of course she would call back. But if she had learned anything over the past two years, it was that she couldn't control what other people felt about her. So instead, she said, "Sorry, but I need to pack tonight. We leave for the backcountry first thing tomorrow, and won't be back until the end of the week. I'll call you then, okay?"

He blustered, "For God's sake, Danny—"

"That'll be fine," Charlie cut in, to everyone's surprise. Leaning over their father, she hovered her finger over the disconnect button. Shooting Danny a wink that was just between the two of them, she said, "Bye, Sis. Have fun camping."

Then the screen went dark.

Danny stared at it for a few seconds. "Okay," she said. "That wasn't so bad." And the bad parts weren't on her, really. She hadn't done anything wrong. Still, no matter how old you got, and how far you flew from the nest, it still sucked to butt heads with your parents.

Krista propped a shoulder in the doorframe, all sympathy. "Sorry to barge in. You didn't have to hang up on my account."

"Oh, you didn't, and I really did." Danny scrubbed both hands over her face, trying to erase the tension. "That's the best strategy when it comes to my parents—lob a grenade, watch it explode, and then retreat while the pieces are still falling. They'll stomp around and argue about whose fault it was for an hour or so. Eventually, one or both of them will go for a run or a bike ride or something, and when they come back, they'll be ready to talk about it." Maybe. Hopefully. At least it looked like she had Charlie on her side. She wasn't sure if her sister had an ulterior motive or if she was legit, but right now she would take all the help she could get.

Krista crossed the room, slung an arm across her shoulders, and said, "Look on the bright side —at least you can cut the connection. Up until a year ago, my parents' bedroom was right down the hall from mine."

"Me, too." Danny's throat tightened at the thought of her old bedroom upstairs in the cabin, where a big bookcase overflowed with trophies and prizes and there was a picture on the wall of her father parading her around on his shoulders while she held up a medal and grinned like it was the best day of her life. "But," she decided, closing the laptop and pushing away from the desk, "I'm not going to let it get me down. Are we all set for Gemstone Night?"

"We sure are! Thanks to Gran and her assistant, Dory, we've got stone-ground grits, Emerald City salad, orange-glazed Rock Cornish game hens, ruby-braised short ribs, rock shrimp quesadillas, gemstone kale, and stone fruit cobbler with chocolate diamonds for dessert." Krista linked an arm through Danny's, and steered them both out of the office, leaving the laptop behind. "Come on. It looks to me like you could use a drink. On the rocks, of course!"

Later that evening, stuffed to the gills with Gran's jewelry-themed food, Sam leaned in and brushed his lips across Danny's. "Wish me luck."

She gave him a smacking kiss. "Good luck." Though there had been shadows in her eyes earlier in the evening, put there by the call to her parents, she seemed better now. Wrinkling her nose, she added, "Though I don't think for a second that you need it. I bet you're a natural at this sort of thing."

He went in for another kiss—he couldn't help it, she was too cute with her nose wrinkled up like that—and then headed for the front of the room, where a low stage held a microphone and a table he had loaded with his show-and-tell rocks, with a big screen behind and off to one side.

As he stepped up, a whole lot of heads swiveled around and the conversation died off, then Krista took the stage and did a *tap-tap* on the microphone. "So?" she said with a big grin that had a bunch of the guests smiling back at her. "What did you guys think of our first ever Gemstone Gourmet Night?"

That got a round of applause and, from the back of the room, a shout of "It totally rocked!"

Krista joined in the ensuing laughter, then said into the mic, "Well, then, to continue the theme, I'd like to introduce a friend of mine. Back in college, he worked two jobs and lived on ramen. These days, thanks to his legendary luck and a huge find of blue diamonds, he lives in a mansion and is the brains and brawn behind Babcock Gems, which isn't just a prospecting outfit— it's also one of the top developers of cutting-edge, eco-friendly mining tech." As a murmur went through the room, she cranked the volume and said, "So please join me in welcoming Sam Babcock!"

There was a wave of applause and a whole lot of enthusiastic faces as Sam snagged the cordless mic off its stand and said, "Hit it, Danny!"

She moved over to his laptop and cued up the attached projector so the screen behind him went live with an image of six perfectly faceted, deep blue stones that were polished to the hilt and backlit to a gorgeous hue.

Ignoring the tug that came from seeing the blue diamonds blown up on the big screen, he said, "Howdy, folks, and thanks for sticking around tonight." He scanned the packed-full dining hall, which held most of the Mustang Ridge staffers and a smattering of neighbors in addition to the two dozen guests. "Before we ride out to the claim tomorrow, I wanted to go over some mining dos and don'ts, and let you get your hands on some of the stones we might be lucky enough to find."

In fact, he and the guys had made sure of it, salting a couple of played-out sites with some low-grade stones, in case they didn't have any luck elsewhere. Not to mention that he had something big up his sleeve in the form of a crystal-lined cave they had stumbled on earlier in the week.

"To get us started," he continued, "I'd like to run through a few definitions, so we're all on the same page. There are three basic types of rock." At his cue, Danny started forwarding through the slides, so the screen showed local scenes with good examples as he said, "Sedimentary rock is where you'll find most of your fossils. Igneous rock is basically cooled-down lava. When it solidifies around bubbles and empty spots, you get pockets where gemstone crystals can grow. Then there's metamorphic rock, which comes from deep in the planet's crust. Thanks to the pressure and heat down there, metamorphic rock can give you some big, valuable gems if you're having a lucky day."

Hefting a one-pound chunk of shale, he handed it to Mindy Bright—a bleached-blond mother of two from Pittsburgh who hovered over her kids and wouldn't meet her husband's eyes. Krista had given Sam and Danny the rundown on the Reunion Week guests who had signed up for the overnight trip. Jon, Maura, and Abel were half siblings in their twenties who had recently connected through adoption records. Chase and Doug—mid-forties with football physiques and an extra layer of padding—were college buddies who met up every now and then for a guys-only vacation. And Mindy and Declan Bright were trying to put their marriage back together for the sake of their two kids, nine-year-old Kevin and his little sister, Sonja.

Sam didn't know how much use he was going to be on the reunion end of things—he did beginning better than he did reconnecting—but he wished Mindy and her husband well, seeing how there were kids involved.

As the chunk started going around the room, Sam

picked up his lecture. "All the rocks I'm going to pass out have labels on them, showing the identification and sampling location of each specimen. If you're going to get at all serious about collecting, you'll find that keeping good records is key. This first one I'm sending around is a piece of shale. You'll see how it's made of lots of layers stuck together. That's where you'll find your fossils—in between those layers."

Kevin shot a hand up. All arms and legs, he was wearing a dinosaur T-shirt and an expression of barely suppressed excitement. "What's the biggest fossil you ever found?"

"Personally? A footprint this big." Sam spread his hands about eighteen inches. "It was when I was little, and as far as I know the folks at the university are still arguing over what kind of dinosaur might've made it. As for the biggest that's been found in the area . . . Danny, can you skip ahead a few slides for me?" Moments later, the screen filled with the image of a huge mounted skeleton with a tiny, triangular head, a long neck and tail, and a big, humping back. "I don't know if this guy is the biggest," Sam said, "but he's certainly up there. This is an Apatosaurus—what they used to call a Brontosaurus—on display at the university. It was found not that far from here." He could've talked dinosaurs for the rest of the hour, but they had a lot of ground to cover, so he handed Kevin a fist-size chunk of granite. "This is an example of an igneous rock. You're going to see plenty of granite out there tomorrow, but when you're prospecting for gemstones, there are certain signs you can look for that tell you you're getting warmer."

He spent the next twenty minutes passing around samples and talking about the differences between vugs and veins, semiprecious and precious gemstones, and going over safety procedures, interspersing the information with historical snippets and stories of hunting rocks alongside his dad. Eventually, he said, "Now it's time for some hands-on stuff. Who wants to take their first crack at prospecting?"

A big paw on a thin arm shot up immediately, then a bunch of others.

"I saw yours first." He pointed to Kevin. "Come on up here. First, help me haul this to the front of the stage."

"Woo-hoo!" The boy took the other end of the big, heavy Tupperware container and did his best with it, tugging like a puppy on the end of a rope toy as Sam pushed from the other side. The rocks inside rattled with the peculiar high pitch of shale.

"Okay," Sam said once they had the bucket out in front of the crowd. "What we've got here is a load of sedimentary rock from a washout near my house. I've gotten some little fossils out of the deposit over the years—leaves, coprolites, that sort of thing. I'm not making any promises, but in a minute I'm going to invite you all to come on up and pick a rock, and we'll see if there's anything interesting about it." He nodded down at his junior assistant. "Kevin here is going to show us how it's done."

The boy bounced in his sneakers, but kept his hands behind his back as he peered wide-eyed at the rocks. After a long moment, he looked up at Sam. "How do I know which one to pick?"

That brought a tug. He had asked his father the same thing back in the day, when they used to pack a lunch and head out with picks, shovels, and a whole lot of optimism. So, just like his dad used to do, he answered, "Sift through them—watching out that you don't get your fingers squashed—and pay attention to what your body is telling you. Does one feel warmer to you? Maybe give you a funny feeling? That's the one you should try first. It's not a guarantee, mind you. But it's a place to start."

Looking deadly serious, the kid shifted a couple of rocks, poked a couple of others. Then his expression cleared, and he grabbed a flat, plate-size chunk of shale from the edge of the collection, and held it up two-handed. "This one."

"You sure?"

That got him an emphatic nod. "Positive."

"Can I take a look?" Sam took the stone and held it up for the crowd to see. "You might not be able to see in the back, but this is a nice piece of shale with good seams along the sides. That means two things—one, you've got layers of fine silt that got added over the years, and two, you've got a chance to pop it open and see if there's anything inside." To Kevin, he said, "You ready?"

The kid gave a head-blurring nod.

"Okay, then." Sam held out one of the butter knives Gran had donated to the cause, deeming them ready for replacement. "Be careful with the blade. Find a good-size crack that looks like it runs most of the way along the long side, and work your knife in there. Careful, though—you don't want to chip it. You're trying to open up the whole thing, not bust off a corner. Yeah, that's it. Now give it a little wiggle."

"The rock or the knife?"

"Whichever one feels right."

The kid went with the knife, rocking it back and forth and then giving a sharp twist that had Sam wincing. But the rock gave a satisfying *click* and the crack widened.

"Would you look at that?" He grinned at the kid. "You've got the touch. Now go ahead and open it up, and see whether you picked a winner."

Kevin opened his rock like a comic book, and his face lit like a switch had flipped. Encased in the stone was a perfect relief image of a palm-size bony fish that seemed caught in midswim, with its fins extended and its tail curved off to one side. "It's a fish!" He held it up. "Mom, Dad, look. I found a fish!"

There was a round of applause, and his sister hopped up for a closer look.

When the buzz died down, Sam said, "It's called a Knightia, and believe it or not, it's the state fossil of Wyoming. And, congratulations, Kevin! It's yours!" To Sonja, he said, "Do you want to go next?"

She glanced over at her mom, got the parental okay, and nodded solemnly. "Yes, please." The words were super soft, more just a motion of her tiny lips.

Behind him, Danny started organizing a line.

Hunkering down to little Sonja's level, Sam said, "Pick a rock. Whichever one you like best." He coached her through the process and helped with the knife. And when the stone came up blank in the fossil department and her face fell, he showed her how a swirl of light and dark at the fracture plane sparkled ever so slightly when she turned it in the light. "And see how this dark part looks like a face? With the eyes here, and the nose. The ears."

Her expression lit. "It's a bunny! Look, look! Mommy, I found a bunny rabbit!"

"You did! Let me see." Mindy opened her arms to her daughter, and together they studied the plain gray rock.

From the safety of her mother's lap, Sonja stuck her tongue out at her brother. "Nyah, nyah, Kevin. I found a bunny, and you just found a stupid fish."

"Sonja," their mother chided, "that's not nice. Tell your brother that you're sorry."

The little girl pouted for a second, then said contritely, "I'm sorry you only found a stupid fish, Kevin."

Chuckling, Sam said, "Next!"

He went on down the line, answering a rash of questions ranging from "What kind of rock is Kryptonite?" to "So how much did you get for those diamonds, anyway? Are there any where we're going to be mining?"

Finally, when all of the guests were armed with their own shale samples and butter knives, he stood back, slipped his arm around Danny's waist, and nuzzled her hair, already thinking about the night ahead. They were staying in the apartment over the barn so they would be ready to ride out bright and early in the morning. It already felt like he was on a mini-vacation, and he was damn glad to be sharing it with her. "I think that went well, don't you?"

She went up on her toes to kiss his cheek. "You rocked it," she pronounced. "I wouldn't be surprised to hear that a few more people add themselves to the camping trip after tonight. In fact . . ." Her voice went teasing. "You'd better watch out, or Krista's going to try to hire you away from that tyrant boss of yours."

"Ha! I'll have you know, I give myself at least one vacation day a year, and a fruit basket at Christmas."

"Such perks! Though I'm not sure I see Axyl as a fruit basket kind of guy. He strikes me as more of the balloon-o-gram type."

"More like three weeks paid vacation he uses to bike over to the Sturgis rally, plus a hefty bonus at the end of the year," Sam said drily. "Welcome to the wonderful world of being your own boss. Next thing you know, you're going to be filing a buttload of paperwork, getting outrageous insurance quotes, and paying taxes you've never heard of."

"Not to mention finding someplace to live," she added. She ticked off the points on her fingers while Sam's chest went oddly tight. "With plenty of room for Whiz, an office, and a garage big enough to store all the equipment I'm going to need. Shelby put me in touch with a Realtor friend of hers this morning. It was a little out of the blue, but I liked her well enough, and Shelby says she's the best. We're going to look at a couple of places next week."

"I found one!" Abel shouted, throwing up his hands like he'd just scored a critical touchdown. "It's a . . . Well, I don't know, but it's something!" He twisted around and held out the flat, crumbly piece of shale, which bore a mishmash of brownish fossil marks. "What do you think?" he asked Sam. "Is it a bird? A plane? Slime mold?"

Sam hesitated for a minute, figuring he should say something about Danny looking at rentals. Like how his place was plenty big enough, and they already spent most nights there. But when he thought about saying the words, he got the warning dip in his stomach that came when he was standing on the edge of a rockslide zone, with his instincts telling him not to take that next step.

"Go on." She nudged him. "I'll see how the kids are doing." There was nothing in her expression suggesting that it had been a test, or a hint, and he was grateful as hell for that.

"Just don't get in the middle of the fish-versus-imaginary-bunny debate," he warned, figuring that if he could make her laugh, then they were okay. And when she chuckled and headed for the kids' table, he watched her go, thinking he was damn lucky to have found a woman who got him the way she did, one who didn't play games.

"Yo. Earth to Sam." Abel grinned when he said it, though. He held out the stone. "A little help here?"

Reorienting, Sam took the shale and made himself concentrate. What was he stressing about, anyway? What he and Danny had together was working exactly right, and if he had learned anything from rockhounding, it was that sometimes it was best to leave well enough alone rather than bring things crashing down around his ears.

# 17

The following day, the group set out on horseback for Misty Hills, riding into a darn near perfect summer morning. Danny—loose-limbed after a delicious round of morning lovemaking—rode on one side of the double column of horses. Sam rode on the other, with the two of them helping Krista and Wyatt keep the guests safe and happy. Or doing their best, anyway.

"Did not!" Kevin's indignant protest carried on the dry air.

"Did too!" Sonja had to shout the retort up at her brother, who was riding a placid full-size horse that towered over her purposeful brown pony.

Their father turned in his saddle and leveled a finger between the two of them. "Don't make me come back there."

"But he—"

"I don't care," Declan said. "Knock it off."

Danny started to head in their direction, but Sam was already on the move, riding in from the other side with a cheerful, "Hey, kids. Do you know why a whole lot of dinosaur fossils were discovered in these parts back in the 1870s?"

Two pint-size cowboy hats, one pink and one white, zeroed in on him. "No," Kevin said. "Why?"

"Because of the railroad." As he launched into the story of how employees of the Union Pacific saw a huge skeleton protruding from the side of an eroding bluff, and how it sparked a turf war between two rival paleontologists, the others rode in closer so they could hear. Most of them, anyway.

Seeing Mindy's horse drift to the back of the pack, Danny reined around beside her. "Hey there," she said. "Everything okay?"

The other woman sent her a shy, embarrassed smile. "I'm sorry. I didn't mean to fall behind. It's just . . . sometimes I just want a minute or two of peace and quiet."

"A woman after my own heart. I'll leave you to it."

"No, stay. Please." Mindy's expression clouded. "I guess I should say I wanted peace and quiet without my family in it. Some days I wonder . . ." She shook her head. "Never mind. I shouldn't even think it."

Krista had warned Danny that Reunion Week could get tricky, especially when there was a shaky marriage and kids involved. The hollow sadness in the back of Mindy's eyes tugged at Danny, but she didn't know what to say, how to help. Or even if she should try.

Mindy didn't seem to notice the silence as she watched Sam entertain her kids. "He's good with them," she said. "He talks to them rather than just barking orders like Declan does."

"Your kids are easy to like. They're smart as a pair of whips."

Mindy made a wry face. "That's one of those good

news, bad news things. Don't get me wrong. I love them, but—" She broke off and sucked in a breath. "Oh. I didn't just say that, did I?"

Completely out of her depth, Danny tried to think of what Farah would say in this situation, and came up blank.

The other woman shook her head, looking devastated. "I always swore I wouldn't be one of those mothers who said I love my kids, then followed it with something bad. Especially when none of this is their fault. It's me and Declan. We can't . . . We don't . . ." Her eyes filled, and she whispered. "We never talk anymore, unless it's about the kids, the cars, or the house. I thought that coming to Wyoming would make things better, but all this vacation has done is prove that we don't have anything to say to each other anymore."

"I'm sorry," Danny said, close to tears herself. "I don't . . . I think . . ." She slowed herself down, thought for a moment. "I wish I could think of something clever to say, something that might help."

Mindy gave a sad smile. "Me, too. But thanks for listening. I think I just needed to get that out there."

"Campfire, ho!" Wyatt's call rang out down the line. Standing in his stirrups, he waved toward a smoky column in the middle distance, where a clearing showed through the trees. "It's Misty Hill!"

And that was it for Danny and Mindy's quiet moment together. As Sam rode up to confer with Wyatt, Kevin twisted around, looking for his mother. "Mom? Hey, Mom. C'mere!"

The two women rode up, Mindy to her family and Danny to where Sam, Krista, and Wyatt had their heads together. The meeting broke up as Danny reached it, and Sam reined in beside her to say, "Right on schedule. We'll be in camp and have everyone settled by dinnertime, then get a bonfire going at sunset."

"That sounds perfect, especially the part about dinner. I'm starving."

Something must have shown in her face, because he glanced from her to Mindy and back again. "Everything okay?"

"I'm just tired from the long ride. Give me my hiking boots any day." And that was all it was, she told herself. That and knowing she couldn't do anything to help Mindy. There wasn't any other reason for her to be wistful, wasn't any reason for her to feel like there were clouds on the horizon when the sky was crystal clear. She had a whole new life unfolding in front of her, complete with wonderful friends, an amazing boyfriend, and a dog of her very own. It would be beyond greedy to wish for more.

As much as Sam loved riding onto an untouched claim alone, on a horse that was loaded down with bedrolls, food, and prospecting gear, there was something equally cool about leading a dozen or so riders into a fully functional base camp that was ready to rock and roll. Axyl, Midas, and Murphy had worked their butts off to finish the solar- and wind-powered bunkhouse, with its outdoor shower, detached latrine, and dedicated cookshack. They had even raked everything clean and used scrap wood to build a stacked set of street signs that pointed in different directions, letting them know that it was three miles to the Crystal Cave, twenty miles to

Mustang Ridge, thirty to Windfall, eight hundred and sixty to Disneyland, and three thousand to Alaska.

"Impressive place you've built here," Wyatt said, riding up beside him and clapping him on the shoulder. Then, nodding to the sign, he said, "What cave?"

"A formation that Midas and Murph found with one of the new gadgets—they scanned a pocket at the back of a rock niche, and when they broke through . . . Well, let's just say I heard them yelling all the way on the other side of the hill. You have to see it to believe it."

Wyatt's eyes lit with interest. "Can we check it out while we're here?"

"That's the plan. Danny and I figured we would tell the others about it tonight, then make it be an end-of-the-day treat tomorrow, after we dig."

"You guys really have this planned out. And get a load of this setup." Wyatt swept a hand around the camp. "I'll have to tell Krista to double what we're paying you for the overnight."

"What's twice nothing again?" Sam asked. "Oh, right. Still nothing."

"How about a round at the Rope Burn for you and your guys when we get back?"

"Plus a basket of fries," Sam said, upping the ante because it was Wyatt. He was happy to help out with the guests, and he was enjoying the teaching side of things more than he would have expected. Most of all, though, he wanted to help Danny find her footing with her new business plan, wanted her to know she could do anything she set her mind to, and that he'd be right there with her.

"She's over there." Wyatt hooked a thumb, letting

Sam know he hadn't been at all subtle scanning the clearing for her. "And I want it noted that I told you so."

"Told me what?" Sam was only half listening, watching Danny with little Sonja, who was still mounted on her fat, sassy pony.

"That one of these days you'd meet the right woman and change your mind about pairing off."

"Whoa." Zeroing back in on his friend, Sam held up his hands in a *time-out* gesture. "Hang on. Don't go hanging labels on me and Danny. We're doing our own thing."

"Yeah. It's called a relationship."

"Sure, we're"—lovers, sleeping together, just plain *together*—"involved. Boyfriend and girlfriend, even. But don't go painting me with your baby-and-wedding brush. That's your thing, not mine."

Wyatt just shrugged. "You keep telling yourself that, Babcock." He reined his horse around and rode off, headed for where Junior was working on the picket line and portable electric fence. Turning back, he called, "Oh, and when you change your mind? You can buy *me* a round down at the Burn."

Over the next few hours, everyone settled into the camp routine, helping tend to the horses and put together a dinner that might not have been up to Gran's standards, but was far better than the pick-a-can meals Danny had eaten over the campfire at Blessing Valley. It was strange to think back on those weeks with nostalgia when it really hadn't been that long ago, but she supposed it was a sign of how far she had come.

As night fell around them and the horses dozed on

their picket line, Sam and Wyatt built a bonfire, and the guests all gathered around. Jon—tall and quiet, and still seeming wary around the half siblings he was just getting to know—pulled out his harmonica and led the way through some campfire songs. The haunting notes floated up on the air, and in the firelit darkness with Sam's arms around her, it was easy for Danny to imagine they were back in time, driving a herd of cattle to the railhead. Or prospecting for gold.

When the last note trailed off, she joined in the applause that swelled up. Jon's half sister, Maura, gave an approving whistle. "That was amazing! I can't believe it. Mom always said she couldn't carry a tune in a bucket."

Abel poked her in the ribs. "Sst. He doesn't want to talk about her, remember?"

Jon ducked his head, scrubbed the back of his neck, and said, "It's okay, I guess. My real parents . . . I mean my other parents. Well, you know what I mean. Anyway, even though they told me that my meeting you guys wouldn't ever change things, I kept thinking that I didn't have room for another whole family. Now, though. Out here." He tipped his head back and looked up at the stars. "It feels like there's room for everything, doesn't it?"

Maura leaned forward. "Does that mean you've got room for us?"

Abel poked her again. "Mo!"

"It's okay." Jon cracked the first smile Danny had seen out of him. "I'm getting used to her. In fact, I'm getting used to both of you. And, yeah, I think I've got room for more family, if it includes you two."

Maura whooped and launched herself at Jon, who caught her reflexively and nearly went over backward. He held himself stiff for a second, then awkwardly hugged her back as a second round of applause broke out.

As Abel peeled his sister off, then gave his big brother a manly half-hug-half-backslap, Mindy drifted back into the circle and sat next to Declan, the two of them separated by several feet. It wasn't until she reappeared that Danny realized she had slipped away.

"Are the kids asleep?" Danny asked.

Mindy nodded. "They're down for the count. It's hard to tell if they're even breathing, they're that tired."

"They'll be up early," Declan predicted. "Kevin especially is dying to look for fossils."

"There's a likely spot near where we'll be," Sam said, his voice rumbling beneath Danny's cheek. "I'll show you where it is, what to look for."

"I'd appreciate it."

"Why don't you two take a walk, get some alone time?" Krista said. "Wyatt and I will keep an ear out for the kids."

"Oh!" Mindy glanced at her husband. "We couldn't impose."

"We insist." Krista shooed them away from the fire. "Go on, they'll be fine."

Unable to find a good reason not to—at least that was how Danny interpreted his expression—Declan stood and silently held out a hand for his wife. Moments later, they disappeared into the darkness.

Danny crossed her fingers for them.

The group around the fire stayed quiet for a minute,

save for the crackle of wood, making Danny think she wasn't the only one straining to hear the start of a healing conversation. After a moment, Krista stirred and stood. "We're going to hang out in the lodge for a bit, so we'll be in earshot if the kids wake up."

"I'm going to call it a night, too," Doug said. "My saddle sores have saddle sores."

By ones and twos, the others drifted to the main building, which had been set up with extra cots and bedding, until eventually it was just Sam and Danny, cuddled together and staring into the fire—warm, drowsy, and content.

"I've got a surprise for you," he said after a bit, his words echoing in her ear and through her body.

"Oh?"

"Let's douse the fire, and I'll show you."

They made short work of the burned-down bonfire, and as the darkness closed in, he clicked his high-powered flash on and took her hand. "This way."

It wasn't until the nighttime quiet closed around her that she realized how loud her day had been, how crowded. She let out a soft sigh. "Ah. Peace and quiet."

"That was what I was thinking." He brought her up beside him, slipped an arm around her waist, and shone his flashlight ahead of them, to where her tent was pitched between two trees and surrounded by her bear fence—a small oasis of privacy away from the others.

"Oh, Sam!" She put her hand to her mouth. "You did this for me?"

"Well, I got Murph to help me. He swung over to Blessing Valley and grabbed everything for us, and brought it all up here yesterday." He gathered her close and kissed the corner of her mouth. "Normally I don't mind bunking with the guys in the camp shack, but these days I'm not interested in sharing cot space with anyone but you."

"Thank you." She turned in his arms and kissed him, long, slow, and sweet, thanking him for his thoughtfulness, and for understanding her so thoroughly. And, really, that was all that mattered. She didn't need to know exactly what things were going to look like a year from now, or even a few months. Because now, right this minute, they were pretty darn perfect.

The next morning, with the breakfast dishes washed and the crowd starting to get restless, Danny finished lacing her hiking boots and announced, "Okay, now I'm officially in heaven."

Sam shot her an amused look over his second mug of coffee. "All it takes is a pair of hiking boots? I'll have to remember that."

"Hiking boots." She leaned in and laid a smacking kiss on him. "Bacon and eggs. A pretty morning. A tent away from the crowd. Sharing a sleeping bag with my sweetie. Take your pick."

"How about all of the above?"

"That'll do." Stepping up on one of the sawed-off logs that had been set near the firepit as makeshift seating, she waited until the buzz of conversation died down. Then, pitching her voice to carry, she said, "Okay, Mustang Ridgers. What do you guys say? Are you ready to hunt some gems?" That got her an excited cheer, with lots of clapping and happy noises. As it died down, she took a quick headcount, relief kicking in when she caught sight of Mindy and Declan at the edge of the crowd, each with a kid by the hand. She couldn't tell if they had worked things out, but at least they were standing within touching distance of each other. When things went quiet once more, she continued. "I know you're all itching to get on the trail just as much as I am, so I'm just going to say watch your step, keep an eye on each other and your surroundings, speak up if something starts hurting or you see something that doesn't look safe, ask as many questions as you like . . . and above all, have fun!"

Sam led the rousing cheer that followed, and the prospectors-to-be set off down the path. As they strung out along the trail, Jon lifted his voice, clear and cheerful, leading them in a cadence. "*I don't know, but I been told . . . Misty Hills are full of gold . . .*"

As the repeats echoed off the rocky hillsides that rose on either side of them, Danny looked back and saw Krista and Wyatt holding hands and marching along, with the Bright family behind them, linked together with the kids in the middle.

"Mus-tang Ridg-ers," the chorus rang out loud and clear. "Mus-tang Ridg-ers!"

There was no doubt about it—today was going to be a good day.

# *13*

"I think I found one!" Maura shouted from the shallow pocket she'd been working, where bluish streaks of crumbling stone hinted at gemstones beneath.

Feeling the familiar kick of interest, Sam headed to where the others were crowded around her, doing the ooh-and-aah thing. "Well, gang? What's the verdict?"

"Gemstone, definitely," pronounced Doug, squinting at the rock with all the expertise of a guy who had flipped through a couple of field guides. "I'm thinking topaz."

Maura squealed and held it out to Sam. "Topaz! Say it's topaz!"

"Geez, Mo." Abel pretended to clear out his ear. "Bordering on dog-whistle territory there."

But Sam grinned. "You know what? I think you may have something here."

Her brothers cheered, and Danny stepped up with the rinse bucket. "Here. Give it a swish." She was wearing a T-shirt that read WE WILL ROCK YOU across the front, her hair was pulled back in a ponytail, and dirt was smudged along one cheekbone. And as far as Sam was concerned, she was looking mighty fine.

Shooting her a wink of thanks, he swished the stone in the rinse water, then whistled as he caught a gleam of greenish blue. "Hello."

"Is it topaz?" Maura demanded.

"Looks more like aqua." He held it out to her. "And a nice one to boot."

"Boo-yah!" She did a happy dance, arms and legs flying. "Queen of the Claim! Oh, yeah. That's me!" Hooking arms with Danny, she did a do-si-do.

"Is there more?" Abel hunkered down where she had been digging.

"Maybe." Sam held out a rock hammer. "How about you have a go? You're going to want to look for—"

"*No!*" The sharp word cracked across the claim, whipping Sam's head around, to where Mindy, Declan, and the kids had been digging. Except now she was glaring at her husband with her fists balled at her sides like she wanted to take a swing at him.

Flushing, he snapped, "Calm down, Mindy. We can talk—"

"No, I won't calm down, and no, we can't talk about it later. We never do."

Kevin and Sonja had been picking through the shale at their parents' feet, looking for fossils. Now they were frozen in place, staring up at their mother's angry face as she drilled a finger into her husband's chest. "I've had it, Declan. I can't take it anymore. I want a di—"

"Time-out!" Wyatt stepped between them, making a T shape with his hands. Krista was right behind him.

As Sam started forward to help, Danny swooped in and crouched down between Kevin and Sonja. "Hey, you two. I think it's time for us to check out the Crystal Cave. Are you up for an adventure?"

"Great idea!" Sam dropped the rinse bucket so hard that it sloshed. "Everybody make sure you've got your flashlight, and a camera if you've got one. You're not going to believe your eyes." And if moving the cave up on the schedule meant that the kids didn't have to hear whatever was coming next, he was all for it. Especially when their mother—red-faced and miserable—shot them a grateful look.

Maybe it was losing his own mom early on, but Sam had never understood why someone would want to hold on to something after it had gotten so bad, so hurtful. More, he didn't get how parents could put their kids in the middle of something like this, or even on its edges. Sonja was pale and wide-eyed, her brother resolute, like he wasn't all that surprised by what was going down. And damn, that pissed him off. If a man couldn't commit a hundred percent to sticking by his wife and kids, then he shouldn't have signed on in the first place.

Wyatt caught his eye and jerked his head. "Go on. Get them out of here. Krista and I have got this."

Which was probably a good thing, because if Sam had to deal with Declan right now, it wouldn't be pretty. Gritting his teeth, he said, "Okay, gang. We're moving out. Next stop is the Crystal Cave!"

Grateful to Sam for taking the lead, Danny kept up a bright, brittle-feeling stream of chatter as the group walked the short distance to the cave. She pointed out a hawk soaring high overhead, a bush loaded with poisonous berries, and the tracks of a lone coyote. Kevin nodded now and then, but Sonja kept looking back over her shoulder with her lower lip aquiver.

Whiz, bless him, stuck close to the kids, sniffing from one to the other like he wanted to chase away their held-back tears as the group turned off the main trail and clambered up the rocky hill.

"This is it," Sam announced, stopping at a pounded-flat spot where there were numerous bootprints in the dusty soil. There, Midas and Murph had dug out a low triangular opening, worming between huge slabs of rock.

Keeping up the facade, Danny enthused, "I know it doesn't look like much from out here, but that's part of the fun." She hadn't been inside, but she had seen pictures. So she wasn't exactly fibbing when she went down on her knees in front of Kevin and Sonja and said brightly, "It's really pretty in there. Like a cave full of treasure!"

Abel, Jon, Maura, Chase, and Doug crowded close, peering at the opening with exclamations of "I don't know if I'm going to fit through there" and "What happens if we get stuck?"

The last one hit a little too close to home, but Danny kept her attention on Kevin as his eyes darted from her to the cave mouth and back. "Do you want to go first?" she asked. "Sam can take you, if you want."

"Me!" Sonja piped up suddenly, unexpectedly. "I'm first!" She grabbed Danny's hand and looked at her with utter trust. "Come with me?"

"I—" It came out as a wheeze. "Oh, no, honey. I can't

go in there. I'm . . ." She trailed off, not wanting to say she was scared of the cave when the little girl had every reason in the world to be afraid. But that same world pressed in on Danny and threatened to spin when she looked at the dark opening leading into the hillside.

She couldn't go in there. She just couldn't.

Right?

A reassuring hand gripped her shoulder, and Sam crouched down close enough that she felt his warmth on her too-cool skin. "I'll take you in," he said to Sonja. "I'm a cool dude, remember? We found the bunny in your rock the other night."

The little girl's lips curved slightly, and she echoed, "Bunny." But she didn't let go of Danny's hand. If anything, her grip tightened.

"Danny needs to stay out here," Sam said. "You can either stay with her or you can visit the cave with me."

Sonja's eyes filled, but she didn't argue. She probably didn't dare, after what had just happened. But, darn, she was tough. She was the one with the here-and-now reason to be afraid, and she was trusting herself to a bunch of adults she barely knew. A thin trickle of oxygen made its way back into Danny's lungs, and for a second, she felt the stomach-swooping terror-slash-excitement that used to grip her in the last few seconds before a race began, when the timer counted down and the barrier fell. Then, not sure she believed the words were coming from her mouth until she heard them out in the open, she said, "It's okay. I'll do it."

Sam's grip on her shoulder tightened and he leaned in to say in an undertone, "You don't have to prove anything. Not to me, and not to them."

No, but maybe she had to prove something to herself. "I can handle it," she said softly. Seeing the doubt shadows, she added, "Please."

She didn't need his permission, of course. But she could sure use his support.

He held her gaze for a long moment—long enough for her to wonder what he saw in her, whether it would be enough. Then he nodded and held out his flashlight. "Take this. It'll be pitch-dark in there without it."

The words brought a shiver, but his approval steadied her. She took the flashlight, gripping tight where it was warm from his body heat, and studied the opening. She had heard the others talking about the short tunnel and had seen pictures of the cave. And if Murph and Midas had fit, then she and Sonja would have room to spare.

If she kept telling herself that, she might not hurl.

"Okay, kiddo," she said to Sonja. "You ready?"

The little fingers—as hot and sticky as her own—tightened on her hand, and the child nodded, stern and serious. "Ready."

"I've got your back," Sam rasped. He pressed something into her hand. "And I won't leave you behind. I promise."

For a second, she flashed back. A little piece of sky visible overhead. Heads poking through and looking down at her, calling, "They're sending a helicopter with better equipment" and "Hang on, Danny! It won't be long now!" Most of the time, though, that piece of sky had been empty, the chimney silent as she lay there, looking up and fighting to breathe.

Brandon had left her alone, let her down. Sam

wouldn't, though. He would be there for her, no matter what.

Emotion lumped in her throat, and she nodded. Opening her hand, she found that he had given her another light, this one a compact lantern. Pocketing it, she got down on her hands and knees facing the cut-through. "I'm going to go in first with the light," she said to Sonja. "Then, when I say to, you crawl in after me. Keep your head way down. Okay?"

The little girl nodded solemnly, and mouthed, *O . . . kay*.

Danny stuck the flashlight in her mouth like she had done a thousand times before in her other life. And, moving fast so she wouldn't have time to think this through and back out, she went headfirst into the rabbit hole with no helmet, no gear, no nothing. Just her and the rocks.

Cool stone closed in on her, cutting out the light and sparking a wave of panic. But the fear couldn't close her throat when she had the flashlight in her teeth and a little girl counting on her. *Just keep going. It opens up soon*. She could see the inner chamber up ahead, glittering like a disco ball. The short passage narrowed, though, forcing her to crouch, almost belly-crawl. *Just keep going*.

Her head and shoulders made it through, and her body followed. And the first breath she took in there was a gasp of wonder. "Oh!"

The pictures didn't even come close. The beehive-shaped cave had a smooth stone floor and curved walls lined with pink quartz. The crystals glittered in the flashlight beam, creating shadows that moved and danced across her vision.

"How are you doing in there?" Sam called, his voice echoing strangely along the passage, which looked so much shorter from this side.

"I'm good. I'm fine. It's so pretty! Send Sonja in."

There was a pause, then a scuffling noise filled the chamber and a small body blocked the outside light. Danny didn't let herself think about the mountain surrounding her, or the fact that her only exit was blocked. Her only air supply. Instead, she closed her eyes and pictured herself out in the great wide-open, happy and free. She had meant to imagine herself at Blessing Valley, sitting at the table and looking out over the river with Whiz at her feet and the squirrels carrying on overhead. Instead, she found herself picturing the view from the top of Wolf Rock, from within the circle of Sam's arms. Startled by the image, by its clarity, she opened her eyes. And realized that her pulse was under control, her hand steady.

Training the flashlight on the passageway, she called, "You're doing great, Sonja. Just a little more."

Moments later, a blond head appeared in the opening, followed by a compact body, staying low and wiggling along like a little tadpole. Then, wide-eyed but unafraid, the little girl gathered herself, sat up, and looked around.

"See?" Danny panned the flashlight, making the crystals dance. "Isn't it beautiful? And just think, we're two of the first people in the world to see it, ever in all of history."

She wasn't sure how much of that registered, but the little girl's lips parted in wonder and she gazed, transfixed. "Woooow."

Remembering the lantern, Danny dug in her pocket. "Let's try this." She clicked it on, but instead of white light, it glowed purple. And where the flashlight beam wasn't touching, the pink rocks glowed. "They're fluorescent!"

Sam's chuckle reverberated along the tunnel. "It gets even better if you kill the flashlight. Just for a second, though. You don't want to give yourselves a tan in there."

Danny barely hesitated. She clicked the flashlight off, plunging them into purple-tinged darkness. And she marveled as pink and purple danced through the air, seemingly floating in midair. "Isn't it beautiful? Sonja, isn't it pretty?"

There was a shuffling noise, and a little body hit her, driving the breath out of her lungs. Thin arms went around her neck tightly enough to strangle her, and little feet stepped on her thighs hard enough to bruise.

Danny knew it wasn't an attack, that it was just Sonja, just a hug. Still, panic slapped and the lantern slipped from her fingers. Bounced away. Went dark.

Dark.

Panic slashed, locking her senses. She was blind. Deaf. Insensate. She couldn't move, couldn't breathe, couldn't—

*Don't you dare*, she shouted at herself. *You can do this. You can do anything*. She refused to panic—she couldn't do that to Sonja or Sam. Or, most of all, to herself. She would pull it together, darn it. She was stronger than this! *Breathe*, she told herself. *Just keep breathing*.

And pretty soon, the darkness within the darkness started to ebb and the panic subsided. Then, suddenly, like a switch had flipped in her head, she could hear

Sonja's quiet sobs and her own harsh breathing. And she could feel the little arms around her neck, hanging on like she was salvation.

She was okay. She could do this. Sonja needed her.

As her heart broke for the child, Danny wrapped her arms around the shaking little body and rocked them both. "Hush," she said. "Shh. It's okay. Everything's going to be okay."

"Are they going to get a d-divorce?"

Danny closed her eyes, wishing she had an answer. "I don't know, Sonja." When that didn't seem like nearly enough, she added, "But I do know one thing for sure. They both love you very much. And that's never going to change, no matter what happens."

She kept rocking, kept soothing, lost track of the time it took for Sonja's tears to fade to hiccups, and from there to steady breathing. "You're okay," she whispered into the child's sweaty, dusty hair. "It's going to be okay." One way or the other.

"Danny?" Sam called. "How's it going in there?"

"I'm fine. We're fine." *Getting there, anyway.*

"Can you come on out? There's someone out here who wants to talk to Sonja."

Figuring that Kevin was probably getting anxious—either to see his sister or take his turn in the cave, Danny groped around, found the flashlight, and clicked it back on. "What do you think?" she asked, her voice steady though her lungs ached like she had run a marathon in the space of ten minutes. "You ready to get out of here?"

Sonja eased back, blinking reddened eyes. "O-kay." Again, a whisper. "Kevin misses me."

Thinking it was good that the kids had each other, Danny said, "Let's go see him, and you can give him a good nyah-nyah because you were in here first."

That got a small, wobbly smile that made her feel like a million bucks.

The trip out was far easier than the way in, especially when Sonja went from a belly crawl to a sudden blur and shot out of the tunnel, hollering, "Mommy! Daddy!"

With her out of the way, Danny could see the kids' parents standing near the cave mouth, looking strained and awkward, but standing closer together than before.

"Sonja!" Mindy went down on her knees and caught her daughter in a fierce hug. Moments later, Declan crouched beside them and put his arms around his wife and daughter with Kevin sandwiched in the middle, in a whole-family hug that had Danny's heart swelling in her chest.

"I'm sorry." Declan's voice was rough with emotion. "I'm so sorry you guys saw that, and that it got to this point. I don't want to be like this with you and your mom. Not anymore."

Mindy nodded against his throat, eyes wet. "We're going to fix things," she told the kids, sniffling as she said it. "We promise. We love you and we love each other, and that's all that matters."

"Ohh," Danny breathed, her chest tightening with hope.

"Hey, you okay?" Sam's face appeared suddenly at the end of the tunnel, and his hands reached for her. "Come on. Let's get you out here." He pulled her the rest of the way out, and then into a hard hug that squeezed the air out of her lungs. "I can't believe you did that," he said into her hair. "You're incredible!"

It didn't matter that she couldn't breathe, couldn't even really move. She burrowed into him, her pulse throbbing as it hit her—not just that Mindy and Declan had had the breakthrough they so badly needed, but that she had just conquered the fear monster. "I did, didn't I?" She levered herself away to grin up at Sam. "I did it!"

He lowered his head and kissed her in celebration, his lips avid and ardent on hers, and blocking out all rational thought. It suddenly didn't matter that the others were right there, or that this was her job, as informal as it might be. What mattered was the way they fit together and the heady knowledge that he hadn't tried to fix things for her. He had stood back and let her fix them for herself.

She had come to Wyoming to find herself, and she had done that. But she had found something very special with him, too.

Friday afternoon, as the rockhounds crested Mustang Ridge and headed down into the valley, where the ranch spread out pretty as a picture and distant horses whinnied a welcome, the mood was high. Each saddlebag contained a stone or two; Jon was making plans to head home with Abel and Maura to meet his bio-mom; and Declan and Mindy rode close, with their heads tipped together as they talked and talked, as if a dam had broken between them.

As prospecting trips went, Sam figured they had

done just fine. And as Reunion Weeks went, they had struck gold.

"See down there by the lake?" Danny asked Sonja and Kevin. "Where all that wood is piled up? That's for the bonfire we're going to have tonight. And the smoke there is from the barbecue. Gran and Dory have probably been cooking all day, getting ready for the party. We're going to have pulled pork, chicken, burgers, the works . . . and then, once it's dark and the bonfire is going, we'll toast marshmallows and learn some line dances."

Face alight, Kevin reined his horse around. "Mom! Dad! Did you hear that?" When they didn't answer immediately, he sent his horse back toward them, with Sonja and her pony tagging doggedly behind, the little girl calling, "Ke-vin, wait for meeee!"

Sam chuckled and nudged Yoshi up beside Danny's docile bay gelding. "I used to think it must be a drag, having to get excited for the same big send-off barbecue-slash-bonfire each week and trying to act like it was new and different."

Her lips curved. "And now?"

"Now I figure the whole guest routine is far more like prospecting than I realized. You might find two pockets right next to each other, might even find the same kind of crystals inside. But everything else is going to be different—the clusters, the way they come out of the ground, the way they polish up . . . No two gem deposits are ever going to be identical, and I'm never going to get tired of mining them."

She knocked her boot against his, in the mounted

version of bumping him with her shoulder or squeezing his hand. "That's exactly the way I feel. Every tour group is different because the people are different. Sure, some are more fun than others, but that's life. If I hadn't been leading tours out of Mustang Ridge, I would have missed getting to know some really interesting people, and I wouldn't have gotten to see their faces when they saw their first eagle or ate their first wild berry."

"Or found their first piece of aquamarine."

"Exactly! And next year, I'll have even more variety. Six adventure treks with Mustang Ridge, six that I'll be leading for the Card Sharps' Inn, at least two for the tourism bureau." She ticked them off on her fingers, her face alight. "I've already started doing the research on old-timey gambling in the area, and brainstorming some new themes. How does Wagon Train Walk sound, or Railroader's Ramble?"

Her enthusiasm was infectious, beyond adorable. Giving her a boot knock in return, he said, "They sound spot-on. Mark my words, Wyoming Walkabouts is going to be a huge success."

She twinkled over at him. "That's nice to hear, especially since you're not the slightest bit biased."

"Maybe I am, but I'm also darn good at seeing a whole lot of stones and picking out the rough gems."

"Are you saying I need polishing?" she challenged.

He dropped his reins to hold up both hands, trusting Yoshi to follow the other horses through the big gate into the ranch proper. "Hey, we're talking about Wyoming Walkabouts here. As far as you're concerned, there isn't a thing I would change."

"Ha! Good save." But she was grinning at him as they came around the corner of the barn into the parking lot. There, barn staffers were helping the guests down from their horses, and several of the other guests—the ones who had opted for cattle roping rather than rock hunting—were waiting to see what the prospectors had found. Danny guided her mount to a clear spot and swung down, saying over her shoulder, "I think you're right, though. I've got a really good feeling about—" She broke off, her expression going slack as her boots hit the ground. "Oh. My. God."

Sam stiffened. "What?" Not seeing any reason for the sudden horror in her voice and on her face, he scanned the horizon. "Do you see smoke? A fire?"

But her attention was fixed on a man and a woman standing some distance away from the other guests, waving at her. "No," she said in a dire tone. "It's my parents."

# 19

"Danny!" Bea Traveler flapped her Red Sox cap, startling a snort out of the horse nearest her. "Over here!"

Danny almost couldn't process the sight of her parents standing there, so out of their normal context, but hard on the heels of shock came a rush of emotion. "Oh! What are you . . . How did you . . . I can't believe this!" She took a step toward them, then realized she was still holding her horse.

Out of nowhere, Wyatt stepped up. "How about I take the horses?"

She didn't ask whether he had known they were coming—was this a setup, or had her parents just crashed the Mustang Ridge party? She didn't dare ask, not right now. She just tossed her reins, grabbed Sam's hand, and said, "Come on!"

There was no point in asking if he wanted to meet her parents when they were standing thirty feet away.

"Mom!" she said as they drew near, "Dad! I can't believe you're here."

"They wouldn't refund the ticket," Bea Traveler said briskly, her eyes going to Sam. "Who is this?"

And that was it, Danny thought. Her own big re-union for the week. No giddy squeals, no happy tears, not even a *Hi, sweetie, you look great*. But that didn't mean she had to play the same game, so she stepped up and hugged her mom. "I missed you." She didn't get much of a return clasp before she moved on to her dad. "This is such a nice surprise!"

He hugged her back, and his eyes held a hint of amusement when he drew away. "Is it?"

"Of course." She stepped aside. "Mom, Dad, this is Sam Babcock. Sam, these are my parents, Bea and Harris Traveler."

Her father gave him an up-and-down. "And you are . . ."

"Very fond of your daughter," Sam said, settling an arm around her shoulder. "It's a pleasure to meet you both."

"Danny never mentioned she was seeing someone."

Flushing, she looked sidelong at Sam. "I didn't want it to sound like I was moving so I could stay with him."

"Are you?" her mother asked.

"No." Saying it put a twist in her belly, though. Not wanting to examine that too closely, she added, "Why don't we go for a walk? I'll show you around and we can talk."

"Do you want company?" Sam's quiet offer came in an undertone, and his eyes were steady on hers. His expression said *I'm here if you need me*, but he didn't push. Once again he was there to back her up, not fix things for her.

She went up on her toes and brushed her lips across

his. "Thanks, but I need to do this myself. See you later, at the barbecue?"

"I'll save you a seat."

"Save three." One corner of her mouth kicked up. "I'm going to do my best to get them on my side." Not because she was afraid they would try to force her onto a plane headed back east, but because she didn't want to fight. She might not totally get her parents, and vice versa, but life was too short, too fragile, for her to take her family for granted. "Come on," she said, turning back to them and gesturing toward the trail she and the others had just ridden down. "Let's take a walk. From up on top of the ridge, it's like you can see forever."

Of course, it was one thing for Danny to decide she was going to convince her parents that she was making the right decision, but quite another to actually *do* it. They had barely made it through the outer fence line before her father said, "So . . ." then let it trail off.

It was his favorite interrogation technique, and had long worked with her and Charlie, who invariably filled the silence.

"It's pretty up here, don't you think?" She looked west, to where the sun was just kissing the distant mountains. "Can you imagine the guts it must've taken to claim a homestead up here back in the eighteen hundreds? That's how Mustang Ridge got its start—Jenny and Krista's great-great-whatever grandparents built a little log cabin and bought some cattle. By the time the market started dying off, Mustang Ridge was one of the biggest cattle stations in the state. Now, thanks to Krista, it's one of the most successful dude ranches."

Turning to her father, appealing to his love of good business, she added, "The tourist industry is trending up, fast. There's room for an outfit like mine."

"You don't have a company yet," her mother pointed out. "Just some ideas."

"But they're good ideas." As they neared the top of the hill, she laid out her plan point by point, like she had done at the tourism council meeting last week. She finished by saying, "I already have a dozen trips booked for next summer, and that's not even scratching the surface." Reaching the marker stones, she stopped and looked out toward Blessing Valley. "And, really, you can't tell me this isn't heaven on earth."

Barely glancing at the rolling, sun-toasted fields, her father turned to face her. "We're not saying it's a bad idea, sweetie. But if you want to lead hikes, why not do it from the shop?"

*Because it's your shop. And it's in Maine.* But she didn't want to hurt them; she just wanted them to understand, or at least try to see her position.

Before she could think of another angle to try, though, her father said, "About this Sam . . ."

"He's a good man, Daddy. He makes me happy. But he's not the reason I'm staying."

"You're still shaky," her mom said, "still having nightmares. Of course you'd look for someone strong to—"

"*Don't,*" Danny said, the word coming out harder than she meant it to. Blowing out a breath, she said, "I'm sorry. I know this is probably hard for you to believe, but Sam really doesn't have much to do with my decision. I like it here. I like who I am here."

"You should talk to someone," her mother insisted. "A sports psychologist, maybe. Or, what was her name? Farah?"

"You're not listening," Danny said. "I don't need more therapy, physical or otherwise." She would tell Farah, of course—they were friends, and it was thanks to Farah's gentle nudging that she had wound up at Mustang Ridge. But she wanted to make all her decisions first, on her own. "This isn't a democracy, Mom. It's my life, and I'm calling the shots."

Bea sniffed. "It sounds like you're not open to discussing this. I don't know why we came all this way."

*Me, neither.* Jamming her hands in her pockets, Danny said, "Do you have someplace to stay?"

"We had a room at this little motel about a half hour away, but when the head chef—Gran, is it?—heard that we had come looking for you, she insisted on us staying in one of the guest rooms at the main house."

"That sounds like Gran." She had probably thought she was doing Danny a favor. And under other circumstances, she would have been. This wasn't working, though. It might never work—her parents were so convinced that they knew what was best for her, they couldn't see beyond what she had looked like right after the accident. Which came from love, she knew, and concern. But that didn't make it any easier to bear. Dashing away a tear prickle, she said, "We should head back down. You won't want to miss the barbecue."

The return trip passed in the silence of a whole lot of things left unsaid.

\*        \*        \*

By the time the barbecue was well under way at the pimped-out gazebo, with Dory and Gran manning the buffet and the guests sitting at scattered picnic tables to plow happily through their piled-high plates, Sam was getting edgy waiting for Danny.

"Go on." Wyatt elbowed him. "Go find her already."

"She doesn't want me butting in."

"So? That's what guys do." Wyatt grinned. "At least that's what Krista tells me when I get it wrong."

Movement near the barn drew Sam's attention, and he blew out a breath. "There they are." The sight wasn't entirely a relief, though, because Danny's jaw was set and she walked several steps ahead of her parents. He stood and crossed over to her, then gripped her shoulder, because he had a feeling that if he did more she might shatter in front of all the guests, and she would hate that. "Tell me what I can do."

"There's nothing. But thanks." He didn't like the hollow defeat in her voice, but her shoulders were square, and when she turned toward her parents, there was a smile on her face. "Come on in, you two. I'll introduce you to Krista and Wyatt, and we can grab some food."

Pride kicked deep in Sam's gut. She wasn't giving up, wasn't giving in. But standing her ground was taking its toll.

"Sit," he said, leading her to an empty picnic table. "Give yourself a minute. I'll get you a plate." To her parents, he said, "If you'll follow me, I'll do a couple of introductions, and we can load up on some of Gran's famous pulled pork and biscuits."

They hesitated, looking from him to her and back

again before nodding and following him. He hadn't gone more than a few steps before Danny's father said, "So, Sam. About you and my daughter . . ."

"Danny is a wonderful woman," he answered, turning to meet the other man's eyes. "She's smart, warm, caring, and funny, and she's one of the bravest people I know. Did she tell you about how she saved the day by climbing up into the rafters of a half-built barn and fixing the electrical connection? She had to be thirty feet in the air."

"That's nothing for my girls," Bea said. But then she added, more softly, "She didn't tell us."

Taking that as an invitation, Sam launched into the story, giving them the background on Gabe and Winny Sears, and how the community had come together to help get them on their feet. He didn't know if there was any hope of changing Bea's and Harry's minds about Mustang Ridge, but it looked as if it was going to be a long night.

Later on, with the bonfire lighting the darkness and music playing from the gazebo, Danny got a lesson in toasting the perfect marshmallow.

"Like this." Kevin concentrated on hovering his stick a consistent height above the flickering flames while rolling it between his palms. "You gotta keep it moving, or it'll burn."

She felt bad abandoning Sam with her too-quiet parents—they weren't far, only on the other side of the fire, but the distance felt greater. She had needed a minute of peace, though. And considering how the rest of her day had gone, a cooking lesson from a nine-year-old totally counted. "You don't like yours burnt?" she asked him.

He scrunched up his face. "Not for s'mores. The burnt part makes the chocolate taste funny."

"Gotcha." Withdrawing her stick from the fire, she held out her marshmallow. "How does this one look?"

He leaned in for a careful inspection, then nodded. "That's a good one. Now you take a graham cracker and a piece of chocolate . . ." He walked her through the procedure, which involved making sure the crackers and chocolate were perfectly parallel, then okayed her to take a bite.

It was too sweet and coated her mouth with sugar, but she grinned. "Best one I ever had."

"Me!" Sonja piped up, reaching for Kevin's stick. "I'm next."

"Yes, you are." Declan scooped her neatly into his lap and produced a marshmallow-loaded stick as if by magic. "Here, help me hold it just right. Kevin? Do you want to show me how you got it to twist like that, so it cooks all even?"

Smiling, Danny returned to the other side of the blaze and settled back into the chair between Sam and her parents. She bought herself a few extra seconds by finishing her s'more and then licking the stickiness off her fingers, just like she had back when she was a kid and she and Charlie had competed to see whose marshmallow burned the longest. "Well," she said, feeling the strain already creeping back. "I think I'm officially an expert marshmallow toaster."

Sam caught her hand and squeezed, warming her with his continued support.

"So you do this every week?" her mom asked.

"The ranch does," Danny answered, trying—and

failing—to interpret her mother's expression. "I try to make it as often as possible, especially when I've gotten close to some of the guests." She nodded over at Kevin and Sonja. "Like them. They're good kids."

"And they owe you more than they'll ever realize," Mindy said from behind her. Fabric rustled and she came around in front of Danny, her boots sinking into the soft lakeshore sand as she crouched down in front of Sam, Danny, and her parents. "I wanted to thank you for what you did for Sonja. And I wanted to say that if you ever need anything—and I mean anything—you call us."

"No, Mindy." Danny leaned forward and caught the other woman's hands. "There's no obligation, truly. Anybody else there would have done the same thing. She just picked me, that's all."

"Maybe that's true, but it wouldn't have been as hard for the others as it was for you, would it?"

Flushing, Danny said, "Krista told you."

"I saw your face when you came out of that tiny little cave. I knew there had to be a story."

"I'm sorry," Bea said, puzzled. "What are we talking about here? What cave?"

"Oh!" Mindy's face lit up. "You didn't hear how your daughter saved the day for my little Sonja?" She launched into the story, fumbling a bit when it came to describing the fight between her and Declan, then making Danny sound like she had kicked into superhero mode, swooping down and spiriting Kevin and Sonja away from the fight, and then lighting the crystal cave with her UV-laser eyes.

Okay, not really. But Mindy gave her way too much

credit. "Like I said," Danny protested, "I just did what any of the others would have, if Sonja had asked them to take her into the cave."

"But she asked you," Mindy insisted. "And you came through for her."

"She did," Sam agreed, pressing a kiss to her temple. "She did us all proud. Better yet, she did herself proud."

*Yeah,* Danny thought. *I did, didn't I?* Not that she expected it to matter to her parents—caves were nothing to them, her fears just a weakness. "I'm glad I could help," she told Mindy, appreciating the other woman's style and wishing she could find some of the same common ground with her own mom. Turning to her parents, she said, "You guys should see this cave. It's—" She broke off. "Mom?"

Bea Traveler's eyes were drenched with tears. "Oh, sweetie." She grabbed Danny's hands and gripped them tight, then let go to swipe at her tears. "I'm sorry. Just give me a minute."

Pulse thudding, Danny looked past her mom. "Daddy?"

He cleared his throat. "It's okay, peanut. It's that . . ." He exhaled and reached out to take his wife's hand, lacing their fingers together. "We don't like the idea of leaving here without you. But we're seeing that we're going to have to."

Suddenly, it wasn't such a bad thing feeling all the air leave her lungs. It left her giddy, even hopeful. "You mean it?" Not that they would be leaving without her, but that they were admitting it.

Her mom sniffed. "You love it here."

A lump gathered in Danny's throat. "Yeah. I really

do." She realized that Krista was standing nearby, with Abby cradled against her and Wyatt nuzzling her hair. Rose and Gran were there, too, and Declan and the kids, and the others were drawing in closer as word spread that something important was happening.

"You were so banged up after the accident," her father said, surprising her with the rasp of emotion in his voice. "The doctors were saying you might not ever walk again, and you were just lying there, pale in some places and so bruised in others . . ." He cleared his throat. "It's hard for your mom and me to get those pictures out of our heads when it comes to you. But I guess we're going to have to."

She went down on her knees in front of her parents, shattered by their admission. "I'm sorry. I didn't realize . . ." That they had been so worried. That they had been smothering her the only way they knew how. That it had been about more than them wanting to keep things at the shop in the family.

"We didn't want you to know." He brushed the hair back from her forehead, bringing the sudden memory of him doing the same thing in the hospital, back when her forehead had been one of the few spots on her that didn't hurt. "You had too much on your plate already. Rehab, the dreams, the panic attacks . . . We just wanted to give you a safe place to heal." His smile went crooked. "I guess we overdid it."

She caught his hand and pressed it to her cheek. "You did it exactly right. I'm fine now. Good as new."

"No, baby," her mom said, stroking her hair. "You're better than that."

The tears caught her by surprise, ripping out of her

throat in a sob as she hurled herself into her parents' arms, knowing they would catch her. And as they hugged like they hadn't done since long before the accident, someone hollered, "Three cheers for Reunion Week!" And darned if all the others didn't lift their drinks, marshmallows, and empty hands to chant, "Hip hip hooray! Hip hip hooray! Hip hip hooray!"

As the cheer faded, she pulled away to swipe at her face with a shaky laugh. "Well. I didn't expect that."

Her father wrapped his arm around her mother's shoulders and tipped their heads together. "We didn't expect any of this. But that's okay. We'll get used to it."

"You'll visit," she said, not letting it be a question.

"We will. And you'll come home now and then." Face softening, he said, "No matter where you are or what you're doing, you'll always be our little girl."

Bea dabbed at her eyes, which were looking raw from the tears. "I think I should maybe . . ." She made a vague gesture in the direction of the main house. "I'm sorry."

"Don't be." Danny rose and lifted her to her feet, then pulled her in for a hug. "Thank you," she said. "For everything. I love you."

That got her a watery smile and a one-armed hug from her dad. "We'll see you in the morning?" he asked. "We'll need to leave around ten to make our plane home."

The word *home* brought a twinge, because it wasn't hers anymore. But the little pinch was far outweighed by the happy ache of knowing that she and her parents were finally okay. Maybe more okay than they had ever been.

"Sam and I will meet you in the dining hall at eight

for breakfast," she promised, and then stood and watched as they walked up the pathway to the main house, with their hands clasped and their heads together.

They had been together almost thirty-five years, and they still held hands.

"Hey." Sam came up behind her, kissed her temple, and twined their fingers together. "You okay?"

"I am. Very okay." And maybe a little wistful all of a sudden, at realizing how much her parents cared.

"Do you want to get out of here?" he asked, cruising his lips around the outer edge of her ear.

Her lips curved as she thought of the comfortable bedroom in the cozy little apartment over the barn. "I thought you'd never ask."

The next morning, Danny had more than the usual number of good-byes to say—not just to Mindy, Declan, and the kids, and the other guests she had gotten to know over the course of the week, but to her mom and dad as well.

As the bus gave its trademark *beep-beep* and trundled up the driveway, she followed her parents to their rental car while Whiz ran zigzags around them, reading the ground with his nose. Danny hugged her mom and said, "I'm glad you came."

Bea gave her the same crooked smile she often saw in the mirror. "You weren't at first."

"No, but we worked it out."

The smile widened. "We did, didn't we?"

Laughing, Danny turned to her dad. "Bye, big guy. Be good to yourself."

"You, too." He enveloped her in the sort of bear hug

he used to give her when she crossed the finish line before everyone else. "It makes me feel better knowing you've got Sam," he said, surprising her. "You two seem like a good match."

She was tempted to let it go, but it would have felt dishonest. "It's not like that, Daddy. Sam and I are just . . ." *Friends, lovers, having a good time.* When none of those seemed to fit quite right, she went with, "I don't think we're headed in that direction."

"Oh?" His attention sharpened. "Was that your call or his?"

"It was mutual."

"Harris? Are you ready to go?" Danny's mom jingled the keys to their rental. "We have a plane to catch. Remember, Jase and Charlie are racing tomorrow."

"Go on." Danny hugged him. "Safe travels."

That was their usual good-bye, a family motto right up there with *higher, faster, farther*, but he didn't move. Instead, he hung on a moment longer, and said in her ear, "If you want something, ask for it. Better yet, fight for it. And don't be afraid to lose."

She drew away, surprised. "Daddy?"

"You know where to find us." He shook a scolding finger at her. "And no more lobbing grenades and then going camping, you hear?"

Laughter bubbled up. "Charlie told you."

"Maybe. I'll tell her you send your love."

"I do. And tell her to come visit! I think she'd like it out here. She might not ever want to go home."

"Don't tell your mother that." He lifted a hand. "Safe travels, peanut. And think about what I said."

"I will." How could she not? In fact, as her parents

drove off, waving out the car window, his words kept playing in her head, over and over again. *Don't be afraid to lose. Don't be afraid to lose. Don't be afraid to lose.* And along with the words came a little shiver as an awful possibility came to her.

Was that what she had been doing with Sam? Could that explain the wistful twinges that came when she thought about next year, two years from now, five years? Had she fallen so thoroughly for what they had that she was afraid to risk it by asking for more? The possibility resonated. And the more she thought about it, the angrier she got. Not at him, but at herself.

Hadn't she learned anything from Brandon? She knew better than to take less than she really wanted, even subconsciously.

"Drat." She scowled. "Drat, drat, drat."

Whiz bounded over. "Whuff?"

"I'm fine. I'm just . . ." Mad at herself. And suddenly nervous, because she had so very much to lose. But what if she won?

Making her decision, she headed for the kitchen.

Gran's face lit when Danny let herself into the long, narrow space, with its exposed beams, dried herbs, and stainless-steel worktable. "There you are! I was just wondering how you were doing after saying good-bye to your parents. Can I get you some coffee? A muffin? Some for Sam, too?"

"He's on his way home with Yoshi. I'm going to meet him for lunch, and I want to ask him something. And, well, I was thinking maybe you could help me put together a romantic picnic. Something that will get him in the mood."

"Oh!" Gran put a hand to her mouth as it widened to a brilliant, knowing smile. "If you want a romantic picnic, my dear, you've come to the right place!" She tapped her chin a couple of times, thinking, then said, "Strawberries, definitely, with dipping sauce. No champagne for Sam, though. He's too much of a beer man. We've got a small-batch ale that will do the trick. I've got leftovers of the chicken he likes so much, and biscuits, of course. Then something chocolate." Her smile went wicked. "By the time you get to dessert, he'll be well-fed putty in your hands, ready to give you your heart's desire."

# 20

When Sam came within sight of Windfall, the first thing he did was look at the top of Wolf Rock. And damned if she wasn't right there waiting for him, like he had wished her there.

"Hey!" He stood in his stirrups and waved his hat, grinning like a fool and thinking that there was something very special about riding up the slope toward home and knowing his woman was waiting for him. More, knowing they had something to celebrate after her parents' visit. As he rode in close, he called, "Give me five minutes to put Yosh away, and I'll be up!"

She shot him a cheeky finger wiggle, and caroled, "I'll be wait-ing."

It had been only a few hours since he rode out from Mustang Ridge, but it felt like too long. He was itching to touch her, hold her, see the glow that kindled in her eyes now when he mentioned her family.

He nudged his horse toward the barn. "Come on, Yosh. Let's get you some hay and check your water."

Five minutes later almost on the nose, he caught the free end of the knotted rope and used it to walk his way up the back of Wolf Rock, to the flat spot near the flagpole where she was waiting for him. He meant to say something—that he was happy to see her, or that he had seen a wildcat's tracks on the ridgeline—but the words got tangled up in the heat that blazed through him, and he swept her up against his chest and kissed her instead.

She didn't seem to mind. In fact, she kissed him back like they had been apart for weeks rather than hours. Which was about how he felt. Wanting to be with her, lose himself in her, he said, "What do you say we climb back down, go inside, and—"

"I have Gran's fried chicken with me."

His head came up. "Where?" Catching his first sight of the picnic spread out nearby—which just went to show that she did a good job of blinding him with lust—he grinned. "Okay, you got me. Chicken first, then bed."

"How about we start with strawberries?" She took his hand, led him to the corner of the red-and-white-checked blanket she had spread and loaded with goodies from one of Gran's jumbo picnic baskets.

"Are we celebrating a very successful Reunion Week?" he asked as she uncovered a container of fat strawberries and dipped one in creamy white yogurt.

"Among other things," she said, and held the fruit to his lips. "Open up."

*There's no doubt about it*, he thought as he bit in. *This is the life.*

They fed each other a lazy, leisurely lunch, pausing for kisses and soft words as they devoured the chicken and sides, and then the dark chocolate cake that they ate in small bites, savoring the dense richness.

"That's it," he announced, flopping back on the sun-warmed blanket. "You win. Whatever you want, it's yours."

"Actually . . . ," she said.

He laughed at the joke. "Your father does that, too, you know. Sort of trails off, hoping the other person will jump in."

She nodded. "He mostly does it when things get serious."

"Is that what we're doing here?" he asked with a chuckle. "Getting serious?" He expected her to laugh, too. When she didn't, the meal felt suddenly heavier than it had moments ago. "Danny?"

She hesitated, reminding him of the woman who had pulled a gun on him out at Blessing Valley. She looked that determined as she said, "Where do you see this"— she gestured from him to her and back—"going?"

His heart damn near stopped on a whole lot of *oh, hell*, because there it was. The Question. The one that spelled the beginning of the end, always.

Chest tightening, he fought to fill his lungs, fought not to let the pain show. He hadn't thought they would wind up here for a while yet, maybe not ever.

*Keep dreaming, buster*, said an inner voice. "Danny," he began, then shook his head. "I don't think you're going to like my answer."

"Why? Because you've got a habit of getting to a certain point with a woman and then pulling back?" At his narrow look, she said, "Yes, I heard about that."

*Then why are you asking?* But he knew. She was hoping for a different answer because what they had between them was different. It was special. It was something he probably wouldn't find again, certainly didn't deserve.

But where she was different, his answer wouldn't be. Not when the thought of her moving in tied him up in knots just as thoroughly as the thought of her going back to Maine had done. Seeing the hollow sadness start to gather in her, he wanted to go to her, to hold her and tell her they could get through this. But that wouldn't be fair, because he had tried to get through it before, and knew better than to try again.

So he stayed where he was, and said, "I care about you, Danny. More than I've ever cared about anybody. But I can't promise . . ." He hated the sudden darkness in her eyes, but he had to be honest with her and true to himself. "Can we just leave things the way they are? I can do that. I'm good at that." It was the other stuff he couldn't handle.

Her pause went on long enough that he thought she might not say anything at all before she stormed off. But then she gave a long, shuddering sigh, and the light came back into her eyes. "Okay." She nodded like she was trying to convince herself. "Right. Then that's what we'll do. We'll just leave things the way they are. Because I don't know about you, but I'm not ready to walk away from what we've got."

"God, no." He moved then, fast and sure, propelled by a hard, hot surge of relief. Catching her against him, he wrapped his arms around her and held her close, rocking them both. "No, I don't want to lose this. I don't want to lose you."

She looked up at him with drenched eyes, but she didn't point out the obvious. Instead, she managed a weak smile and said, "Well, nobody can accuse me of being a wimp now."

"No, they can't." He kissed her flushed cheeks, her pale forehead, her pert nose, her soft lips. "You're no wimp. You're so strong, so brave." For a moment he thought she was shaking. Then he realized it was him.

"It's okay." She stroked his back, pressed her lips to his throat. "We're okay. We'll just keep having fun."

"That's not so bad, is it?"

"No." Her laugh was watery, but it was real. And when she reached up and cupped his cheek, rubbing along his jaw with her thumb, the affection in her eyes was real. "There's nothing wrong with fun. Which, by the way, this has been, despite the detour into Seriousville."

It was an effort to match her smile. "You can pack me a picnic any day."

"Well, Gran did most of it."

"But you asked."

She smiled and brushed her lips across his. "Speaking of which, I need to get the basket back."

"Don't go." She was still pale and drawn, and his chest was still hollowed out from knowing that he had let her down. "Stay a while. Or if you have to go, I'll come with you."

He saw the answer in her eyes even before she shook her head. "I need a little space right now."

Always before, he had been the one saying that. Now he felt the sting. "You're coming back, though."

Her smile was real, though strained. "Of course. Nothing has changed, Sam. We're still the same people we were ten minutes ago. I just need to, I don't know. Take a drive. Clear my head. Talk to the dog. You know how it goes."

Yes, he did. He also knew that decisions got made during drives like that. Sometimes big ones. "Promise me you'll come back, or call me to meet you. Don't just start driving and wind up in Maine."

"It's Krista's car." But she leaned in and brushed her lips across his. "I promise." Then, looping the picnic basket over her arm, she dropped nimbly down the rope, disappearing from sight. Moments later, she reappeared and whistled for Whiz, who shot out from behind the barn with several sharp barks and hopped in the station wagon when she opened the door.

Always before, she had turned back and waved to him before she got in the car. But not today.

*Don't be an idiot*, he told himself as she drove away. *Go after her.* But his feet stayed planted and the larger part of him said, *Nope. Not happening.* He didn't chase women, and he didn't make plans for the future.

This wasn't just any woman, though. It was Danny, and she was upset. Hiding it well, maybe, but still . . . He should at least call Krista and give her a heads-up. But as he bent to grab the rope, he caught movement out of the corner of his eye as a car came down the drive. He turned, relief kicking through him at the idea that she had turned back.

It wasn't the station wagon, though. It was a ridiculous little red Volkswagen Beetle that didn't belong anywhere near the Wyoming mountains.

What the hell?

He lowered himself down the rope, so he was on solid ground by the time the foolish car stalled out on his lawn. Before he could react to that, the door flung open and a leggy twentysomething blonde swept out.

Catching sight of him, she rushed over in a billow of fabric and frantic energy. "Sam! Thank God you're home. I need your help!"

Danny made it a couple of miles from Windfall before she pulled over on the side of the road, shaking too hard to drive. Almost too hard to breathe. "God!" The breath burst from her, and her eyes blurred as she fumbled for her phone and took two tries to dial, whispering a broken "Please pick up, please pick up."

The line went live. "Danny!" Jenny said. "We were just talking about you. Did your parents get off okay?"

Her throat closed and her breath made a little whistling sound. "I . . ." *Can't think about them right now.* Her chest hurt. Her whole body hurt.

"Danny?" Jenny's voice went instantly concerned. There were exclamations in the background, Krista's and Shelby's voices doing a two-part harmony of, "What's wrong?"

"It's S-Sam."

"Is he hurt? Are *you* hurt?"

"No. Yes. I don't know."

"Where are you?"

"Driving. Well, pulled over."

"We're at the Sears place. Can you make it here, or should we come get you?"

Closing her eyes and pressing the phone firmly against her cheek, Danny let out a shuddering sigh. "I'll be there soon."

She didn't know exactly how she got to the horse farm. In fact, she almost drove past it, not recognizing the house, with its glossy white siding, blue shutters, and windows so new they still had stickers on them. The big, brightly painted sign read SEARS RIDING ACADEMY, though, and the big indoor arena and attached barn looked familiar. Turning in, she looked at the horses in the newly fenced paddocks on one side, the cows pastured on the other. It was easier to do that than think about the look that had crossed Sam's face when she asked him about their future.

Shock. Grief. Guilt. Accusation.

Whiz whined and licked her face, and she didn't have the heart to push him away. Instead, she parked, slung an arm around his neck, and pressed her face into his shoulder.

She wasn't going to cry. This wasn't the end of the world. It wasn't even the end of her and Sam. If anything, it was the end of a dream she hadn't even let herself acknowledge.

"There you are!" Jenny came out of the barn and made a beeline for the station wagon, with Krista and Shelby right on her heels. "What happened? Did he do something wrong?"

She climbed out of the station wagon, a little surprised to find that her legs would hold her up. "No. I did. Or maybe neither of us did anything wrong, except tell the truth."

Then the story came tumbling out of her, starting with her father's advice. Her voice broke when she got to the end, and how part of her had been so hoping that he would have a two-year plan for the two of them. Maybe even a tentative five-year theory. She had told herself she wouldn't cry, but the tears came anyway, warning her that Sam might have told the truth, but she hadn't. At least not all of it.

"I'm not okay with leaving things the way they are," she said, probably louder than she needed to. "I didn't tell him that, though." Her shoulders sagged. "I wimped out."

"Don't say that." Jenny looped an arm around her shoulders, eyes ablaze. "Stop beating yourself up. He's the jerk here."

"He's not a jerk," Danny protested. "He's just being honest."

"Or maybe he's the one being the wimp."

Krista caught her hand. "Come on. I want to show you something." She led the way into the barn. Unlike the day of the barn raising, the structures smelled of hay and shavings, and carried the *rustle-thump* sounds of horses. Stopping in the block of stalls that they had all built together, Jenny cracked the door of the big foaling stall and motioned her forward. "Come on. Take a look. Marigold had her baby."

Danny wasn't really in the mood, but it was easier to follow orders than argue, especially when her friends were trying to help, so she crouched down in the opening and gazed through, to where a tiny golden foal lay in a tangle of its too-long legs and a wispy white mane and tail. Marigold stood over her, watching the door. On guard.

"Oh," Danny breathed, and then, softer as she got Krista's point, "Ohhhh."

The foal was a new beginning for the Sears family, even more than rebuilding the barn had been. It said that life went on, that they could survive the worst that the universe could throw at them and come out the other side because they had each other.

"I want this," she said. "Not the horse part, but a baby. With Sam." It wasn't nearly the shock it should have been, as if the knowledge had been there for some time, waiting for her to be ready to see it. "And I want him to want them with me, and to want me enough to fight for it. Which isn't going to happen."

"It might," Shelby said.

But Danny shook her head, her chest going hollow with grief. Regret. "You guys warned me. You said he was the perfect boyfriend up to a certain point, but always bailed when it looked like things might be getting serious. But I thought . . ." Her lips twisted. "It sounds stupid, but I really thought that I was different."

"You are," Krista said firmly. "Trust me. I've known Sam a long time, and I've never seen him like this before. I think it was hard for him growing up without his mother, but I know his father's death really knocked the wind out of him. He withdrew, shut himself off. Beer, video games, frozen dinner wrappers piling up . . . He snapped out of it eventually, but he's stayed wary, tends to keep everyone at arm's length." She paused, then said softly, "I think he's lost the people closest to him too many times. Whether he realizes it or not, he's protecting himself from ever being hurt that way again."

A shiver of shock ran through Danny as the pieces lined up, but she shook her head. "I can't compete with that. Besides, he made his decision."

"So give him a reason to change it," Jenny said, her expression fierce. "I was damn sure that things were over between me and Nick when I headed for the airport to get the hell out of Wyoming, do not pass Go, do not collect two hundred dollars."

"Wyatt and I split twice before we finally worked it all out," Krista chimed in. "And Shelby was on her way back to Boston when Foster made his move. So I guess there's only really one question. Do you love him?"

"I . . ." Danny's throat tightened completely, cutting off the rest of her reply with a wheeze as the world closed in around her, sparking panic and making her want to hide or run and not look back. "He doesn't love me."

"Are you so sure of that?" Krista asked. "Because we've all seen the way he looks at you."

"I . . ." Her mind filled with the memory of his face when he had come up the side of Wolf Rock, rushing to hold her. Kiss her.

What if he did love her? What if?

She pushed to her feet. "I've got to go."

"Where to?" Shelby asked. "Not back to Maine, right?"

"No." Danny grinned, feeling suddenly reckless and wild. Brave. Like she was about to throw herself off a cliff and hope her ropes would catch her just right. "I'm going back to Windfall."

When she got there, though, she found a strange car parked with its nose up against Wolf Rock. "What the heck?" She took her foot off the gas and let the wagon roll to a stop in the drive.

The car wasn't just unfamiliar. It was completely out of place—a bright red VW Beetle convertible with black spots that made it look like a giant ladybug on wheels. It was very female, very much the antithesis of her own style, and it had her hackles up before she hit the gravel.

Sure, it could have been work-related, could be a friend. But he conducted his work meetings down at the sorting shack, and he'd said himself that Krista, Jenny, and Shelby were his only real female friends. And they wouldn't be caught dead driving a Disney-pimped Beetle.

*Don't jump to conclusions*, she warned herself, aware of a gut-deep urge to protect territory that might not even be hers anymore. But it shouldn't be anybody else's either, less than three hours after the fact.

With her body strung even tighter than it had been on the drive over, she stalked to the front door and knocked. Hard. "Sam? It's me."

He must have seen her coming up the drive, because he opened the door almost immediately. "Hey. It's . . . Hey." His eyes searched hers. "You came back. Is everything okay?"

It shouldn't have hurt so much to see him, shouldn't have made her want to simultaneously fling herself into his arms and shake him until the stubborn rattled loose. Locking her knees so she wouldn't give in and do either, she said, "We need to talk."

He glanced over his shoulder, past the weight machines to the hallway by the bedrooms. "This isn't a great time. I—"

"Have company," Danny said levelly as a woman stepped out into the hallway and studied her. Honey-haired and willowy, with a smooth, angular grace that said she spent far more time on ballroom dancing than shooting the rapids, she wore yoga pants and a cropped-off tank that showed the glint of a belly button ring.

"That's Ashley," Sam said. "She's—"

"I. Don't. Care." Maybe Danny would feel bad later for being rude. But probably not. Because as much as she was trying not to care, she most certainly did.

"But—"

"I lied to you."

That cut him off, fast. "Excuse me?"

"When I said I was okay with keeping things the way they are between us. That was a lie. Not because I don't like how things are now, but because I want more." Heat raced through her, feeling like panic, but not. Instead of pressing in on her, the world wanted to rush out away from her, explode out of her. "I want a real relationship, one that's heading somewhere. I want to know that you're open to the idea of us making a life together, with all the bells and whistles. Marriage, babies, joint tax returns. The works."

The Ashley person did an about-face and tiptoed back into the room she had come from. Sam didn't seem to notice, though. He just stared at Danny with an unreadable expression.

Her palms went sweaty as she said, "The only guarantee we've got in life is that we're all going to die eventually. Question is, what are you going to do with the time you've got? Jump from girlfriend to girlfriend, so you're always beginning something new rather than working on what you've got? Or is it time to try something different?"

He lifted a hand like he was going to touch her, hold her, tell her he wanted it, too. But then that hand fell and his eyes went hollow. "I'm sorry, Danny. I can't give you anything more than I already am. That's all that's inside me. I'd be lying if I said any different."

It turned out that heartbreak was more than just a word for the pain that came when the man you loved didn't love you enough. Because she could feel it happening as she stood there—feel her heart shattering into a dozen broken pieces that somehow still beat, still pushed blood through her body, but wasn't capable of anything else. "That's it, then," she said, her voice sounding strange in her own ears. "That's your final answer—I'm supposed to take it or leave it?"

He nodded. "I'm sorry."

"I'm leaving it."

"I figured."

She could see the resignation in him, the sense that he'd been there, done that, knew the routine. And it pissed her off. "Don't you *dare*," she hissed, closing on him and drilling a finger into his chest. "I'm not like the others. What we have isn't the same. You're just treating it that way."

He swallowed. Voice harsh, he said, "I wish—"

"Don't wish unless you're going to do something about it."

Eyes stark and hurting, he shook his head. "I can't."

"You mean you won't." She held up a hand, feeling the tears course down her cheeks and hating the pity she saw in those gorgeous gray eyes. "Now I'm the one who's sorry. Not because I tried, but because it wasn't e-enough." Her voice broke on the last word.

"Danny." He reached for her.

"Don't touch me." She jerked back, not sure she remembered how to breathe. "You don't get to touch me anymore."

Then, unable to hold it together any longer, she turned and fled, rocks kicking up beneath her hiking boots as tears scalded her with the realization that whatever Sam felt for her, it wasn't half of what she felt for him. And it sure as hell wasn't enough.

Sam stood watching Danny drive away for the second time that day. The brake lights flashed cherry red, the car whipped out onto the main road, and the engine went to a roar. And, just that quick, died off again as she sped off, fading into the distance.

Gone.

There was a raw emptiness in his gut, one that wasn't hunger, wasn't grief or rage, but something beyond all three. "Damn it." The words came out rough and hard, rasping at his throat like trail grit lashed by a hot wind.

He hated that he'd hurt her, hated that she had forced the issue.

There was movement behind him, a whisper of the clothes Ashley was barely wearing. Tensing, he said, "I don't want to talk about it." There was no point in asking if she had overheard.

"Well, that was interesting." She said it from right behind him, where she was no doubt looking out over his shoulder at the empty driveway. "And for the record, you're an ass."

He spun and glared at her. "What do you know about it?"

"I know that you could've introduced me."

"I don't think she cared. She was on a mission." A mission to dangle something he didn't want in front of him, something that made his lungs freeze up and triggered a saber-tooth-size fight-or-flight response.

Ashley rolled her eyes. "Urrgh. Men! Of *course* she cared. How would you feel if you drove out to talk to her and found her sharing air space with a total stud? You know"—she swept a hand down her body—"the male equivalent of me, maybe a few years older, and with a whole lot more muscle mass."

Anger gnawed at his gut. "I'd kill him. I wouldn't care who he was or why he was there; he'd be dead."

"Which I'll bet you a million dollars is how she felt just now." She moved in and patted his cheek. "And somewhere in there, you knew it. Which is why you didn't tell her. You wanted to push her away, and make it stick this time." Her eyes flicked to the door. "Congratulations. It worked. And you're a dick."

"Ashley," he growled.

"She was right, by the way. This is totally about your father. What do you think he would say about the way you treat women?"

He bit off the roar that rattled in his chest, knowing that if he let himself go now, it would get ugly. "Okay, that's it. We're done here. Help yourself to food, towels, whatever. But otherwise you're on your own."

"Are you going out?"

"No. I'm staying in." Turning on his heel, he headed for the game room. Where he could turn up the volume loud enough to drown out the world, and with one push of a button, start over fresh, again and again and again.

# 21

It shouldn't have seemed strange that the campsite looked the same as Danny had left it, shouldn't have annoyed her that the sky was streaked purple-pink with one of the most gorgeous sunsets she'd ever seen, silhouetting the black mountain shapes in the distance.

The world hadn't ended just because she and Sam were through. She had said it herself: nothing lasts forever.

"It just sucks when something really good ends too soon," she said, swiping at her face, which felt hot and raw, as if scoured by the same avalanche that had pummeled her body, leaving her battered, bruised, and aching from head to toe. Whiz, sitting beside her in the Gator, looked over at her and thumped his tail. Reaching across, she ruffled his fur. "Well, big guy, I guess we're home." For now, anyway.

He gave a low "whuff" and hopped off the Gator, tail sweeping as he did a nose-down circuit of the campsite. Slowly, stiffly—*Lord, what a day*—she shouldered her pack and headed for the RV.

The door was dark, though, and there wasn't anything for her inside, really. She wasn't hungry, wasn't thirsty, and sleep would be a long time coming tonight, if it came at all. So she sank down at the table beneath the outstretched awning, brushed off the leaves that had fallen on it, and stared out at the river, her mind going blank.

"What now?" She wasn't even aware of speaking until she heard the words, and then an answering chitter from above. Chuck and Popov didn't have an answer for her, though. Neither did Butters the Butterfly, who still hung above the table like nothing had changed. She didn't want to think about the bachelorette party tomorrow or the wedding the day after, and she definitely didn't want to think beyond that. Right now, all she wanted to do was get into the fetal position and cry.

"Damn it, Sam." It came out ragged and broken. He didn't want what she wanted, didn't want *her*—at least not enough to work for it. And, damn it, he had another woman in his house. She still wasn't sure of the deal there, was trying not to care, but it wasn't working.

"So, what now?" she asked the butterfly, which swayed in the slight breeze. The plush toy still didn't have an answer, but it made her think of Farah. She wished she could call her friend. Since that wasn't an option, she dug into a nearby storage bin and grabbed the tarot cards. Why not? It wasn't like she could feel any crappier, and maybe they would give her some reassurance—like telling her that she would soon meet a tall, dark, and handsome stranger who would be the perfect guy for her.

Except she didn't want some perfect guy. She wanted Sam, with his quick mind, insatiable curiosity, and bad furniture. But if part of her thought she had gone about it all wrong just now, another, larger part said the fight wasn't hers. If he had wanted to make room for her in his life, he would have found a way rather than breaking things off.

And, damn it, there went the tears again.

Whiz trotted over and plopped down at her feet, looking up at her with big, faintly worried doggy eyes that seemed to say, *Why are you sad? You're not leaving me behind, are you?*

And, yeah, she was totally projecting there. But it resonated.

"Don't worry, buddy. Whatever happens next, we're a team, and we're staying right where we are." But what if she didn't? What if she went somewhere else, close enough to stay in touch with Krista and the others, maybe even run some excursions out of the ranch, but far enough away that she wouldn't have to pass Windfall, wouldn't see his truck coming the other way and feel like she was feeling right now?

She wanted to think the pain would fade eventually if she stuck around, but the idea rang hollow.

Sniffing back tears that were proving as stubborn as the man himself, she shuffled the cards, feeling them warm in her hands. What was it Farah had said? Something about how, if she had a specific question, she should hold it in her mind as she shuffled, then say it out loud and cut the deck.

Trying to concentrate, she shuffled until the cards slid freely in her hands. Then she said, "Should I set up shop here in Three Ridges?" Except that as she cut out a card that seemed right, what she actually said was, "Does he love me?"

And there it was. The "L" word. Like the tarot was a flipping daisy, and she'd gotten down to the last two petals.

Her breath hissed out. "Wait. I didn't mean it."

There was the card, though, lying facedown on the table.

Whiz whined.

"I know, I know. I should put it away." But, of course, she flipped it over. And recoiled at the sight of the Death card staring up at her, reversed. "Oh," she breathed. "Oh, no." Not because it meant anybody was going to die, but because of what it *did* mean. She didn't need to check the *Noob's Guide*; she knew.

Death meant an ending and the impermanence of things. Reversed, it meant that she was resisting a necessary end.

Her throat closed on a wrenching sob. Not because she believed in magic, or tarot, or any of it, but because it was telling her what she already knew. What she had known since earlier, when Sam had looked her straight in the eye and let her know he had gone as far as he was willing to.

"Oh." She sucked in a shuddering breath. "Oh, Whiz." Her voice broke, the dam against the tears broke, and she slipped out of the chair, onto the ground beside the table. Rocks bit into her knees and Whiz crowded up against her, whining urgently and dancing on his goofy, too-big paws. She looped one arm around his neck, and then the other.

And, curling herself around her dog like she had fallen overboard and he was a life preserver, she buried her face in his ruff and wept like her world was ending. Because, damn it, it was.

Coins, ghosts, dragons, hidden chambers—Sam had blasted through the easiest levels, sending his animated character slashing and leaping from room to room and skyrocketing the score. Things got harder as he went, but that was a relief, as it distracted him from the oppressive ache that started behind his eyeballs and ran through his chest to the hard, hurting lump in his gut.

*Don't think. Just play.* He bore down, sending his avatar busting through a line of zombie-lizard things that turned to fireballs as they died, saying, "I'm out of here."

It took Sam a beat to realize that hadn't come from the zombie lizards.

"Did you hear me? I'm leaving."

Pulling himself out of the game, he paused the action on-screen and scowled at the door, where Ashley stood with her ridiculous pink overnight bag at her feet. "I thought you needed someplace to crash."

"Thanks to you, I've decided to face things head-on instead of hiding out."

"Has anybody ever told you that you're seriously annoying?"

"You don't have to be rude. You're getting what you wanted, aren't you?" She gave a breezy wave. "In a few minutes, you'll have this big place all to yourself, without anybody here to tell you that you're being a stubborn ass and you should go apologize and do whatever it takes to get her back."

"You know," he groused, "back when I was a kid, I used to wish sometimes that I had a little sister. Right now I don't envy Wyatt one bit."

She blew him a kiss. "See you at the wedding, Sam. And for the record, don't even think about skipping out on Krista and Wyatt. You try it, and I'll tie you up and drag you there myself. Don't think I won't."

"If I say I'll be there, will you go away?"

"Okay." She waited a beat. "So? Do you promise?"

To go to Mustang Ridge, where he knew he would see Danny again? "I promise," he said, because he just damn well wanted to be left alone to wallow for the next forty-eight hours, at a minimum.

"Cool. See you there. And, Sam? If I were you, I would think about some of the things she said. She seemed like a pretty smart lady to me." She sent him a finger wiggle, snagged her rolling bag, and finally disappeared from the doorway.

Which was a good thing, because he was about five seconds away from throwing something at her.

He waited until he heard the kitchen door open and close, half expecting her to pop back with an "and another thing . . ." She didn't, though, and after a moment he heard her silly car fire up and drive away, leaving him in peace.

Except she had messed with his peace, and once she was gone he couldn't get it back.

He couldn't settle into the game. Heck, he couldn't even make himself unfreeze the screen—he just kept staring at it, thinking about Krista and Wyatt getting married in a couple of days. And how, when the hubbub died down, everybody's lives would go back to normal, including his. And not in a good way.

There wouldn't be any more rock-paper-scissors over who was paying for dinner, no more big, wiggly dog galumphing around Wolf Rock, no more gem show dates. And there wouldn't be any more sweeping Danny up in his arms, no more kissing her until his head spun and his body burned for her. No more waking up when she did, and cuddling her close for a few minutes before they made sweet, urgent love.

"Damn it." He dumped his controller and pushed to his feet, suddenly restless. He didn't want to sit on his ass anymore, not when his brain wouldn't get quiet. He headed out of the game room, thinking he should take Yoshi for a gallop, or maybe just grab some hammers and a collecting bag and drive up into the hills.

But when he got out in the hallway, he stalled at the door leading to the garage. It loomed suddenly large and solid. Important. Which didn't make any sense, because whatever had gone on between him and Danny, it had nothing to do with his old man.

But as he twisted the knob and pushed the door open, and the garage lights came up to gleam off the busted-up bike, his gut fisted hard, and he had to force himself not to backpedal. Damn. He didn't want to be in here, didn't want to look at the bike. Didn't want to remember. But he made himself take the two steps down to the concrete floor, and let the door shut at his back.

As long as he was cleaning house, maybe it was time for him to face this particular ghost.

*    *    *

Some time later—it seemed like forever and yet no time at all—Sam was fighting with the front brakes when there was a noise at the main door, which he had opened to let the stale air out.

"Well, hell," a voice said. "What got into you?"

Sam looked up from the brake and blinked at the figure silhouetted against the bright sun, confused because the last time he looked it had been night, and because for a split second it looked like his father standing there. Then the figure shifted, the years came back, and it was just Wyatt. Who was about the last person he wanted to talk to right now. Returning his attention to the Harley, Sam said, "What are you doing here?"

Wyatt crossed the garage, studying the strewn bike parts. Nudging aside an exhaust manifold, he said, "I asked you first."

"I just figured it was time to deal with the crap in the garage. Can't leave it sitting here forever, can I?"

"You can if you put up a whole 'nother building for your cars."

Ignoring that, Sam tightened up the plate-size disc brake, giving each of the bolts a half turn in order, around and around, to keep things even. "What's up?"

"Just thought I would swing by, see how you're doing."

Translation: Ashley told on him. "I'm not really in the mood for company."

"So I heard." Wyatt wandered over to the workbench, which had been clear last night—Sam thought it had been last night, anyway—but was now heaped with a collection of tools, rags, packaging, and empty beer bottles. Propping a hip, he added, "I also heard you dumped Danny."

"We broke up. It was mutual." Sort of.

Wyatt studied a wrench like it had all the answers. "Why?"

"The usual." Shoving a length of pipe onto the end of the wrench to add leverage, Sam kept going at the bolts, around and around, making sure the disc was on there good, that there wouldn't be any chance that the brakes would fail going around a hairpin curve. "I can't give her what she wants."

Wyatt tossed the wrench. "And seeing as how you could buy most of the town a couple of times over, I'm guessing we're not talking about a pony or a Porsche here."

"You know what we're talking about."

"I do. What I don't know is why you're so dead set against it, and why you bail the second it starts looking like you'll have to do a little compromising to keep a relationship heading in the right direction. What gives? It's not like you're afraid of hard work." Wyatt's gesture encompassed all of Windfall. "You've built this place and made it into something important. Why aren't you willing to do the same with a woman?"

"That's not what this is about."

"Okay, then let's talk about your parents."

When had it gotten so cold in there? "Let's not."

"Why not? They're right here with us."

No, they weren't. And that was part of the problem. He had come out here hoping he would hear his old man's voice, the way he had right after the accident. Or his mother's wisdom, the way his father used to channel it, like he was talking for her, not just making stuff up.

Apparently taking his silence as a go-ahead, Wyatt

continued. "What would you give to have them back, even just for a day?"

"Anything!" Sam cranked on the wrench so hard that the head sheared straight off the bolt and went flying. Surging to his feet, he rounded on Wyatt. "Everything. This whole damn place. I'd give up the money, the business, all of it, if I thought it could bring them back."

"What about Danny?"

"What about her?"

Wyatt closed on him, still holding the wrench, like he wasn't so sure Sam had control of himself. "What if she were hurt? What would you give to save her?"

"Anything," he said, the anger draining away. "Everything. My life, if she needed it."

Wyatt didn't look the slightest bit surprised, the bastard. "So why are you pushing her away?"

Because the idea of moving her into Windfall made him want to drive off Hangman's Curve. Which had to be his instincts telling him something important.

"Don't you have wedding stuff to do?" Sam grated.

Seeming satisfied that he had made his point, Wyatt nodded. "Sure do. I'm helping the girls surprise Krista for her bachelorette party tonight. Limo, dinner, drinking, hotel suite, the works." He paused. "They'll all be at the Steak Shack for dinner, then the Rope Burn after. If I were you, I'd get over yourself, get down there, and do some serious groveling in public, with all the other ladies watching. Girl like that, been through what she's been through, she deserves a to-do."

Frustration tore at Sam, making him want to snarl. "I can't—"

"There's a big difference between *can't* and *won't*." Wyatt clapped him on the shoulder. "Take it from me. There was a time not long ago that I would've sworn long and hard that I'd never walk down any sort of aisle headed for a woman wearing white, never have a family of my own. Now I can't picture it any other way."

"I'm not like you," Sam grated, staring at the broken bolt. "That's not my life." If it were, the very thought of walking down an aisle wouldn't suck all the oxygen out of his lungs.

"If you say so." Wyatt headed for the doorway. "Me? I'd say that love can change a man in very good ways if he's smart enough to let it." Then, before Sam could muster a decent response to that—if there even was such a thing—Wyatt disappeared out into the bright day.

Sam glared at the empty doorway, tempted to go after his so-called friend and tell him that it wasn't about being stupid, stubborn, scared, or whatever else he thought was going on. It was about knowing his own damn limits and not setting him and Danny both up to fail. How was that wrong?

"It's not wrong," he muttered. "It's smart, and it's the right thing to do."

And if part of him wondered why it hurt so much if it was the right thing, there was a plenty easy answer to that: sometimes doing the right thing bloody well hurt.

# 22

When Danny rolled into the parking lot at Mustang Ridge in time to be part of the planned abduction, she was grimly determined to either enjoy herself at the bachelorette party or do a good job of faking it. But as she parked the Gator, Shelby and Jenny rushed out of the house to meet her, and their faces left zero doubt that the grapevine had been hard at work.

"Sweetie!" Jenny threw her arms around Danny. "Are you okay? Do you want to tell us about it?"

Danny fended her off, feeling her brittle shell of self-control crack around the edges. "I'm fine. And, no, I don't want to talk about it." Talk about it, think about it, even admit any of it had happened. The last thing she wanted to do was bring down the mood. Forcing a smile, she asked, "Is everything set for the kidnapping?"

"Yes and no," Shelby said. "Come inside. There's somebody we want you to meet first."

Danny hesitated. "It better not be a guy." She might kill somebody.

"It's not." Jenny tugged her along. "Come on."

Figuring it was one of the friends Krista had invited

from out of town, Danny let Jenny lead her up the hewn-log steps and through the main door into the ranch house, where the guest services desk sat in one corner of a family-style sitting room. There, a tall, willowy blonde stood up from one of the rustic, overstuffed sofas and gave her a little wave. "Hey again."

It was the woman who'd been cozying up with Sam.

Danny stopped dead as a hot flush suffused her. "What is *she* doing here?"

"Don't freak," Jenny said, grabbing her arm like she was afraid she might bolt. Or maybe attack. "Ashley is Wyatt's little sister."

"She's—" Danny snapped her mouth shut, suddenly seeing the resemblance. "What the hell? Why . . . ?"

"Why did I go to Sam's place rather than come straight here? Because I'm a wimp. I told myself it was because I didn't want to mess with Wyatt's mojo right before the wedding, but it was really because I didn't want to have to tell him I lost another job. I needed a place to stay, and I figured I could crash with Sam." Ashley made a pair of lost-puppy eyes. "I didn't mean to start trouble."

Danny wasn't a big fan of the *don't be mad, I'm so cute* routine under the best of circumstances, and this was a far cry from the best of anything. But she managed to say, "You didn't start the trouble. I guess you just walked into the middle of it."

"I told him he should have told you who I was right away. And I'm not staying there anymore, either." Ashley clasped her hands in front of her body, looking anxious and suddenly very young, and making Danny think that maybe it wasn't entirely an act. "After you left and Sam locked himself in with his video games, I came straight to Wyatt and told him everything. I think he went over there to see what he could do."

Danny didn't want to know any of it. Didn't want to envy Sam the ability to close the door, plug in, and tune out the rest of the world. In fact, what she really wanted to do was go outside and lock herself in a guest cabin and wait for the pain to stop. She couldn't, though—not with Jenny and Shelby standing there, looking expectant, their faces practically shouting, *Please hug and make up so we can get this show on the road!*

A week ago, she had been looking forward to the bachelorette party. Now, she wished she could bail.

*Suck it up,* she told herself, and pasted a smile on her face. "How about we give ourselves a do-over?" She stuck out her hand. "Hi, Ashley. My name is Danny, and I'm a friend of these guys." She nodded to Jenny and Shelby, who wore identical looks of relief. "I live in an RV, work as a wilderness tour guide, and I have a dog named Whiz. I just broke up with my boyfriend, which sucks, but I'm not going to mess with Krista's wedding mojo, either. So for the next six hours, I'm going to have fun or die trying."

Ashley's smile said she sympathized, maybe even that she had been there, done that. But as their handshake turned into a hug, she said, "Now you're talking. Let's go kidnap ourselves a bride-to-be!"

As the sun hung in the hot, dusty sky, Sam stood back and looked at the bike, which he had propped up in front of Wolf Rock. Long and low, with the V-shaped engine buried in its chest and the double-barreled exhaust stacked like rockets on the back, it looked like something out of *Aliens*, only faster and meaner. She wasn't good as new, of course—he'd left the more superficial scrapes and dings alone, and the replacement gas tank had been in the to-be-painted pile when he walked away from the project. She was badass, though. The kind of machine that made a man want to throw a leg over and fire up the engine for real—not just the test revs he'd been giving it along the way but a real blast of noise and speed.

He remembered the look on his dad's face when he'd brought her home, leaned her up on her stand, and swung off. The bones of the mansion had been up, the brick face had been getting mortared into place, and there had been a plywood walkway covering the granite steps. So Sam's boots had echoed as he jogged down. When he hit the bottom, he made a whole lot of "Whoa, dude, awesome!" noises, even though he had helped pick out the bike. Because it was just that kind of machine.

What was it his father had said right then? Something about dreaming big? No, it was the one about the only chances you would come to regret being the ones you didn't take. Which had sounded good at the time, but now put a fist in his gut as Sam jammed a helmet on his head, kicked the bike off its stand, and climbed aboard.

The engine growled to life right away, a deep-throated rumble that vibrated in his clenched-tight gut. Catching movement out of the corner of his eye, he glanced over to see Yoshi staring, ears pricked. "I'll be back in an hour or so," he called to his horse because there wasn't anybody else around to notice he was leaving. And damned if that wasn't what his dad had said to him that night. *I'll be back in an hour or so.* Only he hadn't been. He hadn't ever come back.

Sam knew he damn well should have gone with his old man that night. Shouldn't have pushed him on getting the V-Rod. Should have said he loved him, that he was the best dad ever, with or without the money. Instead, he had halfway waved and headed back inside to talk to the wiring guy about the surround-sound setup for the game room.

Forty minutes later, he'd gotten the call.

Four days later, the wrecker had dropped off what was left of the bike.

Four months later he had cleaned up his tools and locked the garage door behind him.

Now, eight-plus years after the V-Rod took his father off the edge of Hangman's Curve, Sam sent it back up the driveway and out onto the open road. As the too-dry air plastered his clothes to his body, he tried to imagine his father's ghost channeling through the roaring machine. What had he been thinking about when he hit the road that day? The mansion? The road trip they were planning? The way their lives had changed so much so fast?

Probably all of those things, and more, Sam decided as the road unrolled beneath the aggressive rubber tread. There was something elemental about being back on two wheels, without the big truck around him. The bike wanted to surge ahead, like a fresh horse pulling on the bit. And, as he leaned into curve after curve and felt the old rhythm come back, the anger and frustration started to bleed away, leaving him raw, sore, and tired, and not paying much attention to where he was going.

Until, that is, he reached a familiar turnoff, where the main drag went down and the scenic route headed up and a big, diamond-shaped yellow sign read DAN-GEROUS CURVE AHEAD.

Always before, he had followed the main drag, or avoided the intersection altogether. Now he headed up. Mouth gone sour, he steered along the winding road, not seeing the view so much as the narrow shoulders and knee-high railing on the drop-off side as he climbed. Coming around a sharper turn, he saw another yellow diamond, this one warning of falling rocks. Then, when he reached the top, where the world disappeared beyond the edge of the tarmac, with only open air all the way to the distant mountains, there was another damned yellow diamond. DANGEROUS CURVE—10 MPH.

Riding onto the hard, sunbaked shoulder, he killed the engine, propped the bike on its stand, and walked to the edge. When he reached the chain link–topped railing, he stared off over the edge to where a green-brown valley stretched from one set of mountain foot-hills all the way to the next. A silver-blue river zigzagged across the landscape, and scrubby trees were brushes of darker green against the putty-purple, sun-hazed scene.

It was the last thing his father had seen before the V-Rod had left the road. And then . . . He hooked his fingers through the chain link and looked down.

Way, way down.

Time and weather had shifted the terrain, but he could still pick out the flat spot where the bike had ended up. "Well?" he said. "Is this what you wanted me to do?"

He listened for an answer. Didn't get one.

"Stupid," he muttered. It was stupid to be disappointed. His father was dead and gone, and ghosts didn't really talk to the people they left behind. Even as a young kid he had known that his dad wasn't channeling messages from the other side—he was sharing what he thought his beloved wife would have said if she were still alive, just like when he pretended that Wolf Rock could talk, and that it cared whether Sam took out the garbage. But that was his dad—always imagining things, always dreaming. Which had been one of the best things about him.

*So why did you stop with your own dreams?*

The thought came out of nowhere, popping into his head full-blown. And damned if it didn't sound like something his father would've said, like his subconscious was suddenly playing his old man's part. It was the wrong question, though—he wasn't worried about the future right now. He was chewing on what Wyatt had gotten him to admit earlier, about how he would give anything to keep Danny safe, even his life. So why couldn't he wrap his head around taking a chance with her? Why did the very thought of it make him want to get back on the bike and ride hard and fast, until he was hundreds of miles away?

*How is your faith?*

It was something his father used to say when they were out hunting for stones, not so much asking where Sam stood with God, but more with himself. Was he in the zone? Was he trusting his instincts? And the answer was usually yes. Now, though, he wasn't so sure. Because if he trusted himself, he'd be able to imagine how he wanted things to look going forward. Faith. Dreams. Taking a leap over the edge. Those were all things his old man used to talk about. All things Sam had blocked out because the grief had been too raw, the guilt too huge. But his father had also talked about forgiveness, and about how that was part of what made a man.

*Forgive us.*

"There's nothing to forgive." He said it aloud without thinking, like it was an actual conversation. Like his father's ghost was really there.

*Forgive us.* It rang in his head, not letting go.

"What are you talking about? Who's us, you and Mom? Should I forgive you for dying? That's ridiculous. You didn't do it on purpose."

*Neither did you.*

"I . . ." Sam's breath whistled out and he found himself leaning up against all that chain link, looking down. "Oh, hell." And suddenly, like lightning striking up in the high country, he got it. Adrenaline seared through him as he damn well got it.

For a minute he just stood there while the world spun around him, coming back into focus in a way it hadn't ever before, as if he'd held a faceted gem up to the sunlight and turned it a few degrees to create a pattern that he'd never seen but had been there all along. Then, stirring, he pulled out his phone and punched in Axyl's number.

"Hey," the old prospector answered. "What's up?"

"I need a favor."

"Name it."

Grinning as his pulse picked up, sending the blood racing through his veins like a Harley hugging high-speed turns, Sam said, "Get a group of bikes and riders together, the louder the better. I need to make a grand gesture." And he hoped to hell he wasn't already too late.

# 23

"Is there a bride-to-be in the house?" The furry brown animatronic buffalo head on the wall of the small private dining room flapped its long eyelashes and scanned the table of laughing pink-hatted women. "Where are you, darlin'?"

"Here!" Krista waved a buttered roll. "I'm here!"

Tucked into a back room of the casual-fun restaurant—where the stuffed fish sang three-part harmony and the fake deer, elk, and bear heads hassled the diners in the main room—the bachelorette party was in full swing after a very successful kidnapping and a quick stop at the B and B suite for champagne and clean clothes.

Sitting halfway down the table, with Ashley on one side of her and Shelby across the way, Danny clapped along with the rest of them as the shaggy brown head zeroed in on Krista's chair. Festooned with a rainbow of helium-filled balloons, it had been the focus of the bachelorette games that had been concocted by Jenny, Shelby, and their waitress, Mariella, who was also the head wrangler of talking taxidermy at the Steak Shack.

"Well, there, little lady," the buffalo intoned in a mellow, masculine voice, "what do you and these other fillies say to a game of I Never?"

Krista raised her arms over her head and hollered, "Bring it on, Buffalo! Woo!" Bright, beautiful, and flushed with fun, she slung an arm around Jenny's neck as the others joined in with a cheer. Then, raising her Bachelorette Breeze—a fruity, frothy drink that was decorated with tiny spurs and a miniature pink cowboy hat, virgin for the nursing mom but rum-laced for most of the rest of them—she announced, "I've never done the so-called walk of shame!"

Then, grinning, she held up her index finger and drank deeply. As did most of the fifteen pink-hatted women at the table, including Shelby and Ashley.

Danny leaned in and whispered to Ash, "Clue me in?"

"We go around the circle and each make a statement like that. If the *I've never* part is true, you sit there and look innocent. If it's a lie, you hold up a finger and drink. The first person to ten fingers loses. Or wins, depending on your definition." She wiggled an eyebrow in Danny's direction. "No walk of shame for you? What, you didn't go to college?"

"I did, but we mostly played quarters and darts."

"Ah. You hung out with the boys."

"I guess maybe I did." That and girls whose idea of gossip was talking trash about their latest race time and bragging on their new bikes or whatever. Now, though, she was grateful for the silliness, which was helping keep her mind off Sam.

Sort of.

Jenny stood, raised her glass, and said, "I never cheated on a test or a boyfriend."

There was an awkward shuffle, and a few of the girls held up a second finger and drank.

They went around the table—*I never sang karaoke, I never served my family something the cat licked, I never kissed two or more guys in the same day*—while Mariella and two other waitresses whisked away the plates from their shared appetizers, delivered their entrées, and freshened the drink pitchers in the middle of the table. By the time the game got to Danny, most of the easy ones were gone and her head was spinning from the rum.

That was the only reason she stumbled over the "I never . . ." and then blurted, "let a guy break my heart."

Then, to her horror, her eyes filled and her throat locked down. *Damn, damn, damn.* She should have said she'd never eaten sushi or lost her bikini top while bodysurfing, then sucked down half her drink. She shouldn't have brought up the guy thing when it was guaranteed to make her think of The Guy.

Except Sam wasn't that guy. At least not for her.

Ashley nudged her. "Bottoms up, babe."

Flushing, Danny sniffed back the tears and reached for the tall glass. She had sucked down half of it before she realized someone had refilled it. Then, deciding it couldn't hurt, she finished the rest.

When she plonked the empty glass down, she looked up at the others. "Sorry. I didn't mean to ruin—"

"Don't say it." Krista was around the table before she could get the words out, pulling her into a big hug. "Don't even think it. Sam's an idiot, you're a rock star, and in case you missed it there's not a full glass left on the table."

"But—"

"No buts." Shelby put her arms around them both. "We love you. And don't think for a second we're letting you sneak off, thinking you're doing Krista a favor. We'll hunt you down and drag you back to the party, whether you like it or not."

Since that was exactly what Danny had just been thinking, she could only sniffle in her friends' embrace.

"Ladies!" Bootsy—resplendent in a tight, glittery blue dress and silver boots—stood up and raised her refilled glass as Ashley and one of the other girls hurried to top up all the drinks. "I'd like to propose a toast." She paused, and when she had their attention, she intoned, "To kissing frogs, playing the field, and falling for Mr. Wrong on the way to getting it right—whatever that turns out to be for each and every one of us."

Danny wasn't sure any of that applied to her and Sam—he wasn't a frog or the wrong guy, and she wasn't interested in playing the field—but she was grateful to the other woman for taking center stage. So she joined in with the "Hear, hear!" and took a shallow sip from her replenished glass.

Krista looped an arm around her neck and added, "Girl power!"

The resulting cheer shook the windows.

As it died down, Mariella stepped into the doorway. "Excuse me. Jenny? Can I have a word?"

The party resumed as they stepped outside for a quick consult, with Ashley claiming, "I never broke up with a guy by text."

The girl on Danny's other side gave an exaggerated, "Phew!" and said, "I really never have, thank goodness. I don't need any more of a buzz this early!"

Nodding, Danny reached for her water and took a long drink, hoping to lose the prickle of tears but keep the glow of knowing that her friends wanted her there, whether she was at her best or not.

"Danny?" Jenny said from the doorway. "There's someone out front asking for you."

"Who is it?"

"Just come on. Don't worry. It's nothing bad."

Hesitating, Danny glanced over at Krista. "I'm sorry. I don't mean to keep interrupting your day."

"Girlfriend, you're not interrupting anything. You're part of the whole."

It was really that simple, Danny realized. And, feeling her smile turn real for the first time in days, she paused by the balloon-decorated chair and kissed Krista's cheek. "You're the best."

"Back atcha!" Krista squeezed her hand, then said in mock warning, "And you'd better get back in here pronto, you hear? Or we're coming after you."

"Aye aye." Danny sketched a salute, then followed the waitress out through the main restaurant, where most of the tables were occupied and the trout trio was singing "Home on the Range" in high-pitched warbles that carried over a rumbling noise coming from outside. And, oddly, a whole lot of the diners and waitstaff were gathered at the front windows.

"This way," Mariella said over her shoulder. "He's waiting out front for you. And he brought company."

"He . . . company?" Her throat closed on the word as she got it—or thought she did. Though that was probably beyond wishful thinking. Because what were the chances? Even if Sam came for her, which he wouldn't, he'd never do it in public, and not in a million years would he do it with a whole lot of . . .

"Bikers!" Mariella swung the door open. "Look!"

Sure enough, the parking lot was jammed with several dozen black-and-chrome monsters straddled by denim-and-leather-wearing bikers, mostly men, older and with a whole lot of beards going on. Except for the guy in front, who stood at the bottom of the restaurant stairs. Wearing jeans, boots, and an unfamiliar leather jacket over a familiar ROCKHOUNDS DO IT IN THE DIRT T-shirt, he stood with his hands clasped behind him, handsome and very, very guarded.

*Sam.* She must have said it aloud, because she heard her own voice, saw a flash in his eyes that might have been determination.

"Danny." He held out a hand, inviting her down the stairs.

Feeling like the Three Ridges version of Juliet on her balcony, with a Wyoming Romeo and their problems personal ones rather than a family feud, she linked her fingers in front of her to keep her hands from shaking, and held on to the high ground. "You're interrupting Krista's bachelorette party."

"I know." His eyes went beyond her. "Sorry about that."

Danny didn't look. She knew that Krista and the others had come out behind her, while the diners and staff watched through the windows.

"I'll forgive you," Krista said, "but only if you get it right this time. Danny deserves the fairy tale, dang it. Don't disappoint me."

"I know. I won't. I hope." He came up a step, his eyes

locking on Danny. "I'm sorry I let you down, and I'm sorry I hurt you. But you were right when you said it wasn't about the two of us, and it wasn't about me wanting to play bachelor forever. You never asked me to stop playing or grow up. You just asked me to make you some promises that you have every right to. But to do that, I had to fix some things first." He stepped aside and gestured to the crowd. "I want to make those promises to you, Danny. I want to fix what needs fixing."

Axyl and a couple of the other bikers rolled their motorcycles back, parting the mob to reveal a riderless bike propped up on its stand. Black, low-slung, and futuristic, it wore a layer of scrapes along one side, showing where it had skidded and fallen.

Hand going to her mouth, Danny drew in a soft breath. "You did it. You fixed your father's bike."

He nodded, eyes intent on hers. "I did. It gave me some time to think, and figure things out. And I realized that you were right. Partly, I was pushing you away because I was trying to protect myself from losing you down the road. More, though, it had to do with luck and hard work."

"I'm not sure I follow." She wasn't even sure her feet were still on the ground.

"All through my life, the good things that have happened to me have been lucky breaks, lightning-striking kinds of things. But the stuff I've worked hardest at hasn't gone so well. I busted my ass for a baseball scholarship, got scouted, and blew up my shoulder. I nearly killed myself in college to pull average grades, and couldn't find a good job after. So I lost faith in myself, and I stopped believing in dreams. Which meant I stopped believing that I could work at something important—like a relationship—and have it succeed." He came up another step, so he was just one below where she was standing. "But where you were right about most of what you said to me yesterday, you were wrong about one thing."

Danny's breath thinned as she realized this was it—he got it, he meant it, he had come for her, and oh, holy cripes, this was really happening—she whispered, "What's that?"

"You said there aren't any guarantees in life except that it's going to end sooner or later. I've got three more for you: I guarantee that I love you as much as a man can love, that I'm going to learn how to dream again, and that I'll do everything in my power to prove that to you on a daily basis, for as long as you can stand me."

Tears prickled as her heart turned over in her chest. "That long?"

He came up that last step, so they were face-to-face when he said, soft and low, and meant just for the two of them, "Forever, if you'll let me."

It wasn't a proposal, she knew—that would come later. This was a promise. And it was exactly the one she needed. A future. An opportunity. A beautiful horizon that would require a long and wonderful journey to get there.

Drawing a shaky breath, she said, "I almost can't believe you're here. And that you said it."

"Said what? That I love you?" He tipped back his head and hollered, "I love you, Danny Traveler!" Then, as the bikers, bachelorette partygoers, diners, and restaurant staff all whooped and cheered, he pressed his forehead to hers and whispered, "I love you so much. Let me prove it to you."

"You've already proven it," she said at the same soft volume. "You're here. You came for me."

"Always," he said with the force of a vow. "I'll always come for you, from now on. Because I love you."

"And I love you." She said it softly, testing the words and feeling the lovely ache they left behind, the building stir of excitement as the rest of her caught up with the fact that this was really happening. Sam Babcock really loved her.

Better yet, he was ready to admit it. Ready to own it and work for it.

Looking beyond him to the grinning bikers, then back to where Krista, Jenny, and Shelby had their arms linked and huge smiles on their faces, she said, "You know, I've never been in love."

In synchrony, the partiers hooted and shouted, "Drink!"

Catching on immediately—no doubt the veteran of many a drinking game—Sam grinned. "Playing games, are we, ladies?"

"You betcha," Krista hollered back. "Haven't you heard? We're having a bachelorette party here, and you're interrupting!"

"Well, then. We'll just be on our way." He caught Danny's hand and tugged her down a step.

"Hey!" Shelby exclaimed. "Give her back!"

"We're just borrowing her for an hour. She'll meet you at the Rope Burn." To Danny, he said, "Is that okay? There's something I really want to show you."

"Go with him, girl," Bootsy called. "But you know

we're going to want to hear everything when you get back. And I mean *everything*." The others hollered and clapped agreement. And then, when Danny went up on her tiptoes to kiss him, the applause turned to a chorus of "Awwwww."

Drawing away, she grinned up at him. "Do you have a spare helmet?" When he nodded, she kissed his cheek. "Then let's ride, cowboy!"

When they reached a set of wrought-iron gates off in the middle of nowhere, well beyond the suburbs of Three Ridges, where age-stained headstones were scattered on the hillside like flowers after a spring rain, Sam eased up on the throttle and pulled over. With Danny pressed up behind him, her hands linked around his waist and the memory of her happy, excited laughter as he had gunned the V-Rod up into the foothills, he knew he could do this. Knew it was time.

Past time, really. But his parents would understand.

Axyl revved his engine and raised a hand in salute as he rolled past, and the others followed suit, forming an honor guard of black-and-chrome, returning him to the Prospect Hill Cemetery for the first time since he buried his father beside his mother, on a hillside overlooking the great wide-open.

As the last of the grizzled bikers passed them, shooting him a thumbs-up instead of a salute, he propped the bike and swung off, then turned back to Danny. "So," he said. "Here we are."

She looked up at the wrought iron. "Prospect Hill. I'm betting there's a story to the name."

"There is. I'll tell you later, if that's okay. There's

something I need to do first." He saw the understanding in her eyes, but he held out a hand in formal invitation. "I'd like to introduce you to my parents. If you're willing. I know it's a little weird—"

"It's perfect." She took his hand, eased off the bike, and then stretched up on her toes to brush her lips across his. "I'm glad you brought me here."

*Us, too.*

Sam heard the whisper deep inside himself, imagined he saw a pair of silhouettes in the purple clouds above them—a man and a woman, with their arms around each other as they looked down on their son and the woman he loved, walking hand in hand through the wrought-iron archway, toward the perfect sunset beyond. And the future.

## 24

The next afternoon, after a busy day of helping with last-minute wedding details, Danny slipped away to the apartment over the barn. She skimmed a hand over the rumpled sheets and smiled.

"Thinking of me?" Sam said, stepping into the bedroom doorway.

"Oh!" She jumped, then grinned. "You startled me."

"In a good way?"

He was already wearing his wedding getup—a lightweight navy suit, a striped shirt open at the throat, and a sparkly pink boutonniere that had made Wyatt's day. Thinking that he looked good enough to eat in big, greedy bites, she crossed to him and went up on her toes to kiss him, feeling a pang at how close they had come to losing moments like this. "In a very good way," she said, her voice husky with emotion. "I haven't seen nearly enough of you today."

He eyed the bed. "I don't suppose we have time—"

"No, we really don't, especially the way we do it. I have ten minutes to get dressed and get to my seat. And you, mister, need to go play groomsman!"

"I'll get there. Foster and Nick have everything under control." He wiggled an eyebrow. "Need help with your zipper?"

She blew him a kiss. "Maybe I will." Then, snagging the garment bag holding her pretty green dress, she danced into the neat little bathroom and shut the door. It added an extra buzz, knowing he was in the bedroom, waiting for her. Loving her. As she slipped into the dress, the smooth slide of fabric across her skin reminded her of his touch, his kisses. And when she turned to the mirror and got a look at herself, she pursed her lips in a soundless whistle. "Well, hello there."

Back when she had bought the dress, seeing herself in it had shown her just how far she had come. Now, with her hair and makeup done and a new softness in her eyes, with the green dress draping off one shoulder and leaving a whole lot of her tanned-gold skin bare, she didn't just look good, she looked *happy*.

Toeing her feet into the turquoise-blinged shoes that the others had found for her, she gave a little shimmy that swirled the long dress and played peekaboo with her legs. Then, throwing open the door, she swept out into the bedroom and did a twirl. "So? You like?"

He caught her hand and continued the twirl up against his body, so his voice rumbled approvingly through her when he growled, "Like it? I love it. And I love you." He kissed her to seal the deal.

The kiss was deep and thorough, his body solid against her, anchoring them both as their tongues touched and their fingers twined together. In one of his hands, he held something hard and bumpy, with a dangling chain.

She broke the kiss and looked down. "What . . ." The

air left her lungs as she opened her fingers and stared down at what he had given her: a perfectly faceted aquamarine, cut in a teardrop shape and hung on a delicate wisp of a chain. "Oh!" She held it up to the window, marveling as the facets caught the light. "It's beautiful. Is this the stone I found our first time out at Hyrule?"

"Yeah. I cut it myself." He hesitated, looking almost sheepish when he admitted, "This is a first for me."

Warm pleasure suffused her. "Giving a girl a gemstone you faceted yourself, you mean?"

"Giving a gemstone period." His teeth flashed. "Then again, being in love is a first, too."

Loving the gift, and the man, Danny turned to Sam and stepped into his arms. "It's beautiful. Thank you."

"It was yours from the first moment." He brushed his lips across hers. "Just like me."

For all the back-and-forth between Krista and her mom, Danny thought that everything came together in a perfect blend of Rose's traditional taste and Krista's casual cowgirl flair. The gazebo was wreathed in local foliage and beaded decorations made of braided horsehair, looking rustic and lovely. Vines and cornstalks had been woven into the lattice, offering shade and adding a soft rustle to the music that came from a lone guitarist standing off to the side.

From her spot a few rows behind Krista's family, tucked between Bootsy and Della, Danny had a good view of the wedding party assembled beneath the gazebo. Ashley, Shelby, and Jenny stood on one side of Mayor Tepitt, who—go figure—was also a justice of the peace. The three bridesmaids were wearing very different summer-colored dresses that matched their personalities—flirty green for Ashley, vivid red for Shelby, and a trim blue sheath for Jenny, a couple of shades darker than the accents on Krista's dress. Jenny had little Abby—adorable in a frilly white dress and tiny blue cowboy boots—in the crook of her arm, and the baby was making faces at the crowd.

Della gave a happy sigh. "The girls look amazing, don't they?"

"You know it," Bootsy confirmed. "And, hello, is there anything better than a man in a suit?" She wiggled her fingers toward where Wyatt stood in a cowboy-style tux and spit-shined boots, with Foster, Nick, and Sam beside him, all three of them wearing suits and matching pink boutonnieres.

Danny, whose eyes kept coming back to Sam, said, "The same guy peeling out of his suit?" As if he had heard her, he locked eyes and winked.

"Hoo!" Della fanned herself. "I think the temperature just went up ten degrees."

"Do you blame her?" Bootsy asked. "Our Sam is a total hottie."

*My Sam*, Danny thought with a smile. But he belonged to Three Ridges, too, just like she would soon. Maybe, in a way, she already did.

She didn't see the cue, but all of a sudden the music paused and the wedding party came all the way to attention. Then, as the guitarist started strumming the traditional march with a twang that turned it uniquely country, Krista and her father appeared at the end of the aisle, perfectly framed by an archway of flowers and vines. A hushed murmur rose from the audience as they made their way to the gazebo. "Oh." Della dabbed her eyes with a Kleenex. "She's so lovely."

Blue flowers were worked into Krista's upswept hair, echoing the pops of blue on the floaty white dress, which swished around her boots as her father kissed her cheek and she stepped up onto the raised platform to join Wyatt. He looked thunderstruck, as if he had never seen her before. And as if he had just been handed everything he'd ever wished for as he took her hands and the mayor began, "Dearly beloved . . ."

The words washed over Danny, who focused on the faces of the eight people standing beneath the gazebo, seeing their love, and the deep friendship that bound them together, and to her. Sam turned and met her gaze as Wyatt recited his vows, then Krista. He didn't wink or try to telegraph any message, just stood there, looking at her as if to say, *Here I am.*

And, yes, there he was.

"I do." Krista said the words loud and clear, her face shining as she looked up at Wyatt, their hands linked and their eyes blind to anything but each other as the mayor prompted him with the same question.

"I do," he said, the words coming out rough with emotion, but no less loud and clear.

From her spot, Danny fought a sniffle, thinking, *I never cry at weddings.*

Drink.

Della pressed a Kleenex into her hand. "You're leaking."

"Just a little," she whispered back, dabbing at her eyes and trying not to wreck her makeup.

"Do you have the rings?" the mayor asked.

"Here." Jenny stepped forward and held out Abby, who had them pinned to her dress for safekeeping.

"Repeat after me: With this ring, I thee wed." The mayor guided the bride and groom through the exchange. Then, with a broad smile, she announced, "I now pronounce you man and wife. You may kiss the bride."

Wyatt moved in before she had even finished speaking. Sweeping Krista up in his arms, he kissed her long and deep, the both of them grinning through laughter, tears, and wonderful love.

Danny sniffed again, not even minding the tears. It was perfect. Krista and Wyatt were perfect together, and this was the perfect wedding for them. And sooner or later, she would have a wedding of her own. In the meantime, she was darn well going to enjoy the next few stages in her and Sam's new journey—moving into the mansion, opening up a couple more rooms, starting her new business.

Wyoming Walkabouts. *Because we dare you.*

The mayor gave a grand flourish and intoned, "I now present Mr. Wyatt Webb and Mrs. Krista Skye Webb!"

Surging to her feet along with the others as the cheers and applause drowned out the cornstalk rustle and triumphant guitar riff, Danny added her whoops to the din. As the applause swelled, Wyatt and Krista dashed up the aisle hand in hand, with the bride calling out, "Let's get this party started! Last one to the tent is a rotten egg!"

"Come on!" Bootsy grabbed Danny's arm and urged her out into the aisle. "It's time to dance!"

"We will," said a deep, powerful voice from behind them. "In a minute."

"Sam!" Danny turned, whooping anew as he swung her out of the traffic flow and into his embrace. "There you are." Wrapping her arms around his neck, she went up on her tiptoes and pressed her lips to his, letting him know that she had missed him, even though he'd been standing right there under the gazebo.

Hidden speakers came to life with lively music, and a familiar voice said, "Hello, wedding guests! This is Fiddler, and I'm here to invite you to share Krista and Wyatt's first dance, country style. So every gent should grab his favorite girl and meet the newlyweds under the tent."

Sam swung Danny in a do-si-do. "What do you say? Can I have the first dance? And the last? And every one in between?"

She beamed up at him, heart so full that she thought it might burst. It seemed impossible that he was there, that they were together, that this wonderful new life was suddenly unfolding before her. "Yes," she said as the music kicked up a notch. "Absolutely yes!"

He caught her lips in an ardent kiss that made her head spin and her body sway against his. Against her mouth he whispered, "I love you."

Closing her eyes, she absorbed the words, and the joy they brought. "I love you, too. So much."

Up on the hill, Fiddler called, "And now for the newlyweds . . ." His voice went to a singsong. "Bow to your partner; bow to your miss. Mustang Ridge is a place of bliss. Grab that filly and give her a spin; there's nothing better than a fine weddin'!"

And as Krista and Wyatt followed his instructions and other dancers started forming new squares under the big, flower-studded tent, Sam grabbed Danny's hand. "Come on!"

Laughing, loving him, she joined him in a mad race up the hill, and into their future.

"All join hands and circle wide—now it's time for a doozy of a ride!"

Continue reading for a special
preview of the upcoming

# COMING HOME
# TO MUSTANG RIDGE

Available in August from Signet Eclipse
wherever books and ebooks are sold

"You did *what*?" Wyatt loomed over Ashley, seeming
to momentarily forget that he was holding his
eleven-month-old daughter in the crook of his arm. "Are
you out of your *mind*?"

Little Abby let out a startled "Awoooo!" that reverberated off the rough-hewn log walls and overstuffed couches
of the sitting room–slash–reception area in the main
house at Mustang Ridge—aka the gorgeous dude ranch
Ashley's brother had married into last fall, and where
Ashley had lasted six weeks as an employee before deciding that working there wasn't nearly as fun as being a
guest.

Thank God there had been a Help Wanted sign in the
window of Another Fyne Thing. Though Wyatt probably
didn't see it that way now.

He gave the baby a bounce, rearranged his face to a
fatuous smile, and sweetened his tone to say, "Sorry,
sweetie. Auntie Ashley started it." With his hat off and his
dark, russet-streaked hair standing up in agitated spikes,
he looked like an irate porcupine.

A very large irate porcupine.

Ashley just folded her arms. "You're the one doing
the yelling." Though she was pretty sure she was the only
one capable of hitting her big brother's bellow button.

"What did you expect?" he demanded, halfway losing

hold of his baby-soothing voice, so he sounded like an irritated cartoon character. "Of all the harebrained, irresponsible—"

"*Annd* that's my cue." Krista stepped in and scooped Abby out of Wyatt's arms. "Come on, kiddo. We're going to go find somewhere else to be." Propping the baby on her hip, the pretty, fresh-faced blonde kissed Wyatt's cheek, shot Ashley an encouraging finger wiggle, and whisked down the hallway leading to the kitchen.

"But—" Wyatt took a half step after them, then stopped himself with a muttered curse and took a couple of deep breaths. By the time he turned back to Ashley, he looked less like a furious porcupine and more like a concerned patriarch of a porcupine.

Which was worse, really. She could deal with his bluster, but his disappointment always got to her. There was too much history there.

"I can do this," she insisted. "It's a fantastic opportunity. And aren't you the one who was always telling me I needed to find something I love, something I'm good at? Well, this is it." From the first moment she had stepped through the shop door into the bright, chaotic interior and heard the jingle of the little bell overhead, she had been in love.

"I was talking about you going back to school and getting a degree," he grated. "You know, giving yourself a shot at a real future. Sound familiar?"

As usual, he didn't even try to understand where she was coming from. "Seems to me you went right back to cowboying after college." Sure, he was famous now—in a few high-dollar art circles, anyway—for the Wild West–themed sculptures he made from recycled farm equipment. But those successes hadn't come out of any classroom.

"We're talking about you, not me. And I've gotten plenty of use out of my degree. You would, too, if you'd just give it a try."

"Too late. I've already signed on the dotted lines. All of 'em."

Besides, she was allergic to school. Her brain was too quick, too flighty. Too ready to get distracted when things stopped being fun and started feeling like work. That was why Another Fyne Thing was perfect for her—the stock was always changing and the customers were a fascinating blend of locals and tourists. And as of today she could mix things up even more—the advertising, the sales, the window displays, all of it. Nothing at Another Fyne Thing would ever be boring again now that she owned it.

Ohmigosh. She owned it.

Even though she and Hen had thrown an impromptu celebration after they finished the paperwork, inviting everyone up and down Main Street to stop by for cookies, coffee, and ten percent off, there was still a frisson of shock at the thought.

She. Owned. The. Store.

It was impossible. Incredible. Wonderful. Terrifying.

"Are you even listening to me?"

She blinked at Wyatt. "What?"

"You can't afford this," he said between gritted teeth. "What if you miss one of the payments? You'll lose what you've already put into it and destroy what little credit you've managed to scrape together since you left the Douche-Bag Drummer."

Her chin went up. "I'll make the payments." She didn't want to talk about Kenny. She could only say *You were right and I was wrong* so many times.

Yes, her ex had been a douche bag, and yes, she had followed the family tradition—the female half's, anyway—by staying way too long in a relationship that was going nowhere but downhill. That was over and done with, though, and just because she had made a whopper of a mistake in her choice of men didn't mean that buying the store was a terrible idea, too.

That was her story and she was sticking to it.

*Scrub,* went Wyatt's hand through his hair. "You're getting in way over your head. You don't have the first clue how to run a business."

"Della is going to help me. Not to mention Krista,

Jenny, and the others." The friends she had fallen into—married into, really—when she'd crossed the line into Wyoming with zero to her name but Bugsy, some clothes, and her boxes of art supplies.

He scowled. "What happened to starting small? I thought you were going to stay at the shop until Della sold it, then come back to work here while you got an online storefront up and running."

That had been his plan, not hers. "I changed my mind."

"Change it back."

"No." It was a single word, a complete sentence. But it was one of the hardest things she had ever said to him. Unable to leave it like that, she added, "Please, Wyatt. Try to understand where I'm coming from. I can do this without your support—I will if I have to. But it won't be the same. I know I've let you down before, but this time it's going to be different. You'll see."

"Ashley." He sighed as some of the fight drained out of him. "Be—"

"Happy for myself?" she interrupted before he could say "reasonable" or "logical" or any of those other words he was so fond of. "I am. And I hope you will be, too, eventually. In the meantime, what would you say to making me a few mannequins? It'd be killer to have some F. Wyatt Webb originals in my window."

"I'd say you're pushing it." But his scowl lacked the punch it had carried before. "Have you told Mom what you're up to?"

"I'll call her in a day or so. I wanted to tell you first." And when it came to talking to their mother on the phone, she needed a dark, quiet room. Wine and chocolate were good, too. She stepped in, gave him a hug, and said, "Love you, Bro. Even when you treat me like I'm still ten years old."

"Back then, I could take away your allowance."

"Now the bank can do it for you."

He winced. "Don't say that. Don't even think it." A pause. "On second thought, do think it. Maybe knowing that you're just a couple of missed payments away from having it all yanked away will help keep you on track."

"I'll keep myself on track, thank you very much." And, yeah, the whole bank thing gave her a definite twinge. Hiding that behind a saucy smile—flirting was one thing that had always come naturally, even with Wyatt—she patted his cheek, near where she had kissed. "I'm leaving before you decide to scare more babies."

"Going back to the store?"

"That's the idea." It was closed to customers, but there was plenty to do. And it was all hers! Well, hers and the bank's.

"Change of plans," Krista announced, appearing in the doorway, carrying Abby, who was armed with a fat chocolate-chip cookie and was back to her usual smiling self. Popping the baby in Wyatt's arms, she said, "You're on kidlet duty, because Ashley and I are going out. I already called the others, and they're going to meet us at the Rope Burn. We're going to celebrate Ashley's big news!"

"I'll have a Let's Get This Party Started Cosmo," Ashley said as she and the other four members of the Girl Zone settled around their usual high-top bar table.

"Sure thing." The waitress poised a pen that had a miniature cowboy boot dangling off the end. "Do you want it in a light-up glass?"

"Absolutely." Why not? They were celebrating.

"White wine for me," Shelby said, then shot Ashley a wink.

Danny wrinkled her nose at them. "You two are such girls. I'll have a Corona."

"That's not exactly a manly-man's beer," Shelby pointed out.

"Better than a cosmo. In a blinky glass, no less."

"Tomboy," Ashley said.

"Priss," Danny fired back, and they grinned at each other.

The two were a study in opposites. Where Ashley

flirted, Danny was no-nonsense. Where Ashley flitted, Danny kept her hiking boots firmly planted. And where Ashley rushed headlong, Danny planned everything out to the last detail. But despite their differences, they totally clicked.

"Here are your drinks!" their waitress announced, arriving with a spur jingle that somehow carried over the crowd noise. She offloaded the wine and beer, and then set Ashley's tall glass in front of her and pushed the button on the bottom to activate the LED embedded in the stem, making red, white, and blue stripes move up and down.

Shelby raised her wine, which looked classy and grown-up in its traditional housing. "To Ashley. Congratulations on being the new owner of Another Fyne Thing!"

Danny held up her beer. "To being your own boss!"

Jenny added her glass to the group salute. "To loving what you do."

Krista raised hers. "To taking a leap of faith!"

"Hear, hear!" The four of them clinked, then looked expectantly at Ashley.

Who sat there, holding her blinky glass as she fought back a sudden wave of emotion. "I . . . You guys . . . Wow. I can't breathe."

Sometimes when she was out with her friends, it was hard not to feel like the little sister, even when Wyatt was miles away. The others were so educated, so accomplished, each of them a business owner in her own right. Now, suddenly, they were looking at her like she had done something important. Something they understood, even admired.

"So don't breathe," Jenny advised. "Drink." That got another round of "Hear, hear!" and the five of them clinked and drank.

The first slug of cosmo tingled going down; the second spread a warm glow that eased the pressure in Ashley's lungs and let the air back in. With it came some of the positive vibes she had been practicing. *Della believes in you. The customers love you. The window displays rock. You can totally do this.*

And she could. She would. Starting now.

"Speaking of the store," she said, setting down her blinky glass, "I could use some brainstorming help." Considering how many times she had helped the others spitball ideas for their businesses—everything from new theme weeks for Krista's dude ranch or Danny's adventure trekking business, to slogans and photo-shoot locations for Shelby and Jenny—she got a buzz out of it being her turn.

Eyes lighting, Shelby beckoned. "Bring it on."

"The second payment is due in forty-five days, and it's going to be tight." She had already filled them in on the financing. "The window display contest that Mayor Tepitt is running during the Midsummer Parade has a big cash prize, but it's right before the money is due, and there's no guarantee I'll win. So, here's the deal. I want to run a couple of special events at the store as a way to get customers through the door, and hopefully put product in their hands while they're there. Which is where I could use some help. I was thinking of holding a sale and letting people spin a roulette wheel right at checkout to 'win' an extra discount. Or maybe having a fashion show. Or what about a handyman auction? Highest bidder gets stuff fixed around their house. I figure there aren't enough eligible bachelors in Three Ridges for a sexier sort of auction, though that would tie in better with vintage clothing."

Shelby whipped out her phone. "Hang on. Let me jot down a few notes."

"What about a costume contest?" Krista suggested. "You know, sixties and seventies, that sort of thing. You could charge twenty bucks per entry, less if they buy everything from the store."

But Shelby shook her head. "You don't want the store to become a Halloween go-to, especially after Della did all that work for the drama club and helped out with the haunted house. Branding-wise, you need to focus on how you can make hip, trendy combinations with vintage clothes. That's the message you're trying to get out to your customers, right?"

"That's exactly what I'm going for!" Ashley grinned, feeling suddenly like she was surrounded by a warm glow of friendship. Or was that that the cosmo? Probably a little of both.

"So no costumes." Shelby hummed, tapping her lower lip. "But a contest isn't a bad idea. Or the fashion show."

They bounced ideas back and forth for the next twenty minutes, through another round of drinks, and pretty soon Ashley had decided she should totally claim the night as a business expense, because they were getting more planning done over drinks than she had in the past three weeks of sitting up late at night.

It was crazy, really, how much things had changed in the past year and a half.

Her lips curved. "Thanks, guys. I mean it. Thanks for the ideas, for coming out tonight, for being happy for me, even though some people—cough-cough, Wyatt, cough-cough—think I'm completely nuts for jumping in like this . . . for all of it."

"Well, we kind of think you're nuts, too, but that's why we love you." Danny lifted her glass. "To Ashley!"

"To Ashley!" the others chorused, then clinked and drank, with Shelby giving Ashley's glass an extra tap and adding, "We're here for you, girlfriend."

"Hello?" The hail came from the stage, where Jolly Roger—the bar owner's name was actually Roger Jolly, but he lived up to the nickname with his long dark hair, grizzled beard, and the patch-and-peg-leg routine he pulled out for special occasions—stood at the mic and did a *tap-tap*. "Is this thing on? Testing, testing. Are we ready for some live music?"

The crowd buzz dimmed for a second; then applause burst out.

"Awesome." Ashley turned in her chair. "I could dance."

"I'd like to introduce tonight's performers, who are guar-an-teed"—Jolly drew it out like the three-syllable word had a dozen—"to get your boots tapping and your booties shaking. Let's put them together, folks—your hands, I mean, not your booties—for Chasen Tail!"

The door behind him opened up and a guy came out, giving a big wave to the crowd. "Howdy, folks!" In his mid-twenties, with handsome features and sandy hair that brushed the collar of his shirt, he looked like someone had taken one of the cowboys from the crowd and turned the volume up a couple of notches.

"Oh!" Danny said, "I've seen him before. I like him."

"Meh." Shelby shrugged. "If a guy's going to pop the buttons on his shirt halfway through the show, his abs should be required to be seriously ripped. And his stage name sucks. I mean, really? Chasen Tail? Ew."

"I like his music," Danny clarified. "I agree that the name is dumb. And the shirt thing doesn't do much for a girl who's got a better set of muscles waiting for her back home."

"Now, that's just mean." Ashley turned her back on the stage to complain across the table: "Some of us are living vicariously, you know."

"I can already see this is going to be a killer crowd," Chasen said behind her. "How about we give a round of applause to my boys?"

As the crowd whooped and hollered, Krista's eyes went beyond Ashley, and lit. "That's no boy. And speak of the devil. There's my new head wrangler in his very fine flesh!" She waved. "Yoo-hoo, Tyler! Hey, Ty. Over here!"

Ashley froze, the name going through her like a bolt of hot lightning—searing and paralytic.

Wait.

What?

No. It couldn't be.

Setting down the blinky glass with calm precision, she turned in her seat. Looked up at the stage. And stopped breathing as her brain sproinged back and forth between *Oh, hell* and *Oh, my*, with a bit of *Wow* thrown in.

Then back to *Oh, hell*.

A drummer and a guitarist had set up behind the lead singer. The drummer was a cutie—young, flushed, and nervous-looking, as if playing at the Rope Burn was the high point of his life to date. The guitarist was his exact opposite—thirtysomething, solid, and totally chilled out as he bent his head and strummed a couple of chords that should have gotten lost in the crowd noise, but, thanks to some acoustic quirk of the room, carried straight to Ashley.

She didn't need to see the face beneath the shag of sun-streaked brown hair—she knew him by the mellow undertone and upper twang of the old Martin, and by the way his hands moved on the strings: slow and steady, but with an underlying strength that said here was a man that always hit the note he was going for.

Tyler Reed.

His head came up and his eyes locked on hers, as if she had said his name out loud. His gaze pierced her, brown eyes so dark they were almost black, putting a hot-cold-hot shiver in her belly.

Behind her, the others were talking about how he had come back to Mustang Ridge after spending the past few years touring with a country band, their voices sounding normal, as if the world hadn't just shifted on its axis. As if it hadn't shifted again when she got a good look at his face, with its high Viking cheekbones and the strong slash of a nose, bumped across the bridge, where it had been broken by what he had called "a short dive off a long bucking bull."

Last fall, at Krista and Wyatt's wedding. Where they had totally hooked up.